I0584220

THE THESEUS CONSPIRACY

A CID AGENT JACQUELINE SINCLAIR NOVEL

Victor M. Alvarez

Black Rose Writing | Texas

©2021 by Victor M. Alvarez
All rights reserved. No part of this book may be reproduced, stored in a retrieval system or transmitted in any form or by any means without the prior written permission of the publishers, except by a reviewer who may quote brief passages in a review to be printed in a newspaper, magazine or journal.

The author grants the final approval for this literary material.

First printing

This is a work of fiction. Names, characters, businesses, places, events, and incidents are either the products of the author's imagination or used in a fictitious manner. Any resemblance to actual persons, living or dead, or actual events is purely coincidental.

ISBN: 978-1-68433-746-0
PUBLISHED BY BLACK ROSE WRITING
www.blackrosewriting.com

Printed in the United States of America
Suggested Retail Price (SRP) $21.95

The Theseus Conspiracy is printed in Sabon

*As a planet-friendly publisher, Black Rose Writing does its best to eliminate unnecessary waste to reduce paper usage and energy costs, while never compromising the reading experience. As a result, the final word count vs. page count may not meet common expectations.

To Pamela-Jean, my wife,
My right hand, I could never do without

— ACKNOWLEDGMENTS —

I would like to take this time and express my greatest appreciation to the following people for their insight and their invaluable help: Daniel Russell, Pamela-Jean Murphy, Jack Adler of Writers Digest, and Michael Valentino.

I would also like to express my thanks to Mr. Reagan Rothe the creator, of Black Rose Writing Publication, and to others of his staff, that made this possible, and to Carrie Higgins, my publicist and marketing person, who offered her valuable help.

Thank you again to everyone who offered their help and their time. To my fans, I truly hope you enjoy reading *The Theseus Conspiracy*, as much as I enjoyed writing it.

This book contains an excerpt from the forthcoming book *The Price on her Head* by Victor Alvarez. This excerpt has been set for this edition only and may not reflect the final content of the forthcoming edition.

THE
THESEUS
CONSPIRACY

"Vengeance is in my heart,
Death in my hand,
Blood and revenge are
Hammering in my head."

The Titus Andronicus Act 2, Scene 3 – 35 Aaron
By William Shakespeare 1564/1616

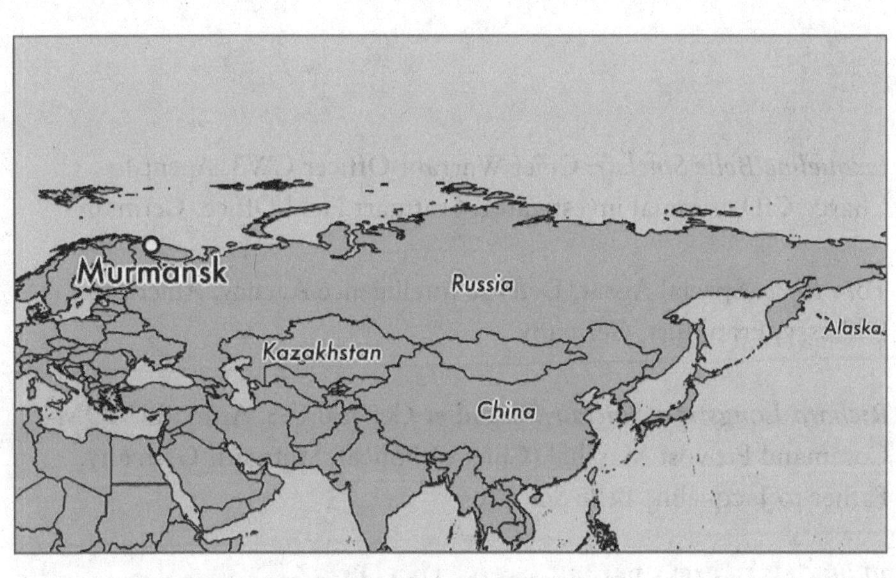

Murmansk
Russia
Kazakhstan
China
Alaska

—MAIN CHARACTERS—

Jacqueline Belle Sinclair: Chief Warrant Officer CW3, Agent-In-Charge CID criminal investigator, Stuttgart Field Office, Germany

Tom Price: Special Agent, Defense Intelligence Agency, American Embassy, Frankfurt, Germany

Richard Longstreet Sinclair: Brigadier General U.S. Army, EUCOM Command Provost Marshal (Chief of Police), Stuttgart, Germany, Father to Jacqueline Belle Sinclair

Phillip Anders: The President of the United States

Ilya Gadjiyev: The President of the Russian Federation

Jonathan Fakes: The Director of the Central Intelligence Agency, (CIA) Washington, D.C.

Earl Fleming: General, the Chairman of the Joint Chiefs of Staff, Washington, D.C.

Steven Summerset: The Director of the National Security Agency, NSA, Washington, D.C.

Daniel Russell: Special Agent of the Federal Bureau of Investigation, (FBI) U.S. Embassy, Frankfurt, Germany

Patricia Courtney: Special Agent of the Central Intelligence Agency, (CIA), U.S. Embassy, Frankfurt Germany

Jessica Alice Wayne: Major, U.S. Army U.S. Intelligence Security Command, Wiesbaden Airfield, Germany

Matthew Banks: (aka Anisi Sverchinsky) code-name Theseus, CIA American/Russian double agent

Pyotr Ivanovich: General, Russian Army Chief of Staff, Moscow, Russia

Viktor Mordvinov: Russian Ministry of Defense, Moscow, Russia

Sergei Vannovsky: Director Russian Federal Security Service (FSB), Moscow, Russia

Elizaveta Borovkov: Lieutenant Colonel, The Russian Federal Security Service (FSB) Chief of station, Russian Embassy, Frankfurt, Germany

—PROLOGUE—

Operation Code Name:
Theseus

*Port City of Murmansk, Russia, off the coast of the Barents Sea,
Sunday, September 8, 12:30 A.M.*

All five of them questioned the validity and dangers of operating in Russian waters. A Russian submarine could well attack them, get blown up by mines, and even be considered a provocation that could lead to war with the U.S. But they kept their reservations to themselves.

During their mission briefing they were told, and in no uncertain terms, that just as in any mission, failure was not an option. So, now the only question was—when would they start?

Much was riding on them, bringing their mission to a successful conclusion. They'd been practicing for two weeks, almost twelve-hour days, fine-tuning every little detail down to its core. There were failures, which they confronted and overcame. It's what they do well, as warrior elites called upon to perform this vital mission. They were a five-man team-SEAL Team 3: Code Name, Bravo from the Naval Special Warfare, Group One, stationed in Coronado, California.

Handpicked because of the area they would work in and where they'd launch from; plus, their success rate was immensely important; tops among three other teams considered for the mission.

The mission code name was—Theseus!

The Team leader was Bravo One, Master Chief Petty Officer Mark Hawthorne, a 12-year member of SEAL teams, and a highly decorated, career-oriented naval man. He was a six-foot-tall, stocky, and muscled warrior from Fort Worth, Texas, with a slow Southern drawl. His nickname was Tex to his team.

Bravo Two, the second in command, was Senior Chief Petty Officer William P. Grey. He was a 10-year veteran with an impeccable military record that included three Purple Hearts and two Silver Stars. From Boston, Massachusetts, he had been a newscaster for the local TV network before joining the Navy. At five-feet-nine-inches, he had a build described as resembling that of Arnold Schwarzenegger. The team lovingly had nicknamed him, Arnie.

Chief Petty Officer Dañiel Acosta was Bravo Three. According to him, the meaning of his Spanish surname was, *"God is My Judge."* A six-year naval man, his medium height and slender build was a perfect fit for the team. A Mexican by birth, his family entered the U.S. legally when he was six, and thirteen years later, he became a citizen. He'd served tours in Afghanistan and Iraq before joining the SEAL teams. His specialty was in demolitions and as a sniper.

Bravo Four, Chief Petty Officer Jessie M. Stevens, was just as tall and stocky as his team leader Hawthorne. A graduate of Harvard with a Ph.D. in Philosophy, he sought adventure and set a course to his life other than what his family wanted. He joined the Naval SEAL teams, much to the disappointment of his family. His specialty was as a combat medic.

Chief Petty Officer Thomas J. Alekseev, Bravo Five, was the fifth member of the team and was a seven-year Naval SEAL team member. He was a short, tough, stocky man and a last-minute replacement to the team. A Russian of Jewish descent, he was born and raised in New York City. His thorough knowledge of the Russian language was the reason they added him to the team. However, his specialty was that of a sniper.

Bravo team would launch from a *Hunter Killer* attack submarine and given free rein the moment they were within swimming distance of their first target. Their mission was to infiltrate the Russian Federal Prison at Murmansk and extract a prisoner code name Theseus, whose Russian name was Anisi Sverchinsky. The prisoner's ultimate destination was Stuttgart, Germany. It's what the SEAL teams called a "Snatch and Grab" operation.

The 377-foot long SSN-790, US advanced stealth attack submarine, the USS *South Dakota* was a Virginia-class-submarine that patrolled the seas with deadly silence, while built to dominate the world's coastal and deep waters while conducting antisubmarine warfare. However, taken from its normal operations, today it would transport SEAL team members on their mission.

The orders to Captain John Summers were to drop the operators off without a hitch and retrieve them with their target, regardless of hostile fire! The rules of engagement: if fired upon, they would engage return fire and elude capture by all means!

Submerged for well over nine-hours, the boat arrived at their assigned drop-off point (DOP). Captain Summerfield ordered his Executive Officer (XO), Steve Helms, "Bring her up to photonics-mast depth. Steady as she goes."

The photonics-mast, the replacement for the old periscopes, with a variety of electro-optical visible and shortwave infrared sensors feed imagery through strands of optical and low-light cameras directly to the mast operator's high-resolution display as well to the captain's viewer screen in front of him.

"Aye, aye, sir, mast depth, steady as she goes," Helms shouted to the helmsman and the mast's operator. Helms was a tall and slender man of thirty-two, blond and blue-eyed, who grew up in a naval family and aspired to become a submarine commander. Being the XO to one of the most renowned and capable submarine commanders, Captain Summerfield, was a stepping stone to that position.

Captain Summerfield, with the XO standing alongside him, set their eyes onto the screen. "Give me a 360-degree sweep," he ordered the mast operator.

Within seconds, once it completed a total sweep, the camera stopped. What they observed was almost total darkness, heavy snow-fall, with a few portlights and no movements in or around the port of Murmansk. No visible ships were sailing behind them. They gauged the distance to the port at twelve miles.

Yet it wasn't what he could see, but what he didn't which made him uneasy; they could've armed the port with mines and listening devices. The only recourse left involved the mini-sub.

"All engines stop," Summerfield commanded. Turning to his XO, he said, "Ready the surveillance drone for launch, and have the SEAL Team leader report to me as soon as possible."

"Aye, aye, sir," Helms acknowledged.

The drone, shaped like a torpedo, contained sensors and video-capable equipment able to see through the dark murky seas and relay its progress to the sub as it recorded every inch of obstacles in its path.

Still standing beside the viewer screen, Captain Summerfield turned and faced his XO. "Steve," he said, speaking low with a palpable excitement to his voice, "pull up the charts for this area. I need a clear picture of the entrance and anything else that could make me believe mines are waiting for us."

Summerfield's gaze fell on Chief Hawthorne who stepped into the CIC and approached the Con-center.

Impressed with the *Hunter Killer* boat, Chief Hawthorne, not having been aboard any like it, kept his observations to himself.

"Chief," Summerfield said, "we're at your DOP and about twelve-miles to the entrance of the harbor's inlet and additional two-miles to the harbor landing. What lies in between is an unknown. I wanted you to see what may await you and your men out there. I'm sending out a drone and we'll be able to confirm or deny the existence of any mines."

Hawthorne frowned, and giving the Captain an uneasy smile, said, "Mines! We weren't told that we go through a possible minefield."

"Well, we'll know soon enough."

"Can your sonar detect the mines?" Hawthorne asked.

"Yes, they can," Summerfield responded. "But if we ping the entrance to the harbor, whoever might have ears on, will surely know we're here."

Folding his arms about his chest, Hawthorne nodded.

Summerfield, once back on his Captain's chair, placed an elbow on the armrest and held his chin in his hand in contemplation of the chart's disclosure as Helms examined the charts on the touch screen monitor laying flat on the chart table.

A brief silence ensued.

As he scrolled through the charts on the touch screen monitor, Helms halted on a well-defined chart showing the Murmansk inlet harbor. He checked and double-checked, but it showed no signs of mines. Could they have placed the mines since then? He wondered.

"Sir, the chart doesn't show any mines positioned through the area however, these charts are not up to date."

"Right," Summerfield acknowledged.

Both Hawthorne and Helms gazed at Summerfield and waited for his orders.

The next few minutes could confirm what he suspected, and if that was the case, he probably knew his boat wouldn't be able to navigate through the minefield. *Would Chief Hawthorne suspend his mission, or find another way through?*

The thought raced through his mind. He wasn't sure.

However, he knew better than that, having worked with other SEAL teams in the past, and knew of their steadfast commitment to their mission. If that was the case, Summerfield had an ace up his sleeve—the mini-sub attached to the boat—if the mines distance to each other didn't impact on the width of the mini-sub.

Nodding absently, the Captain turned his attention back to the job at hand, and not wasting any more time, palmed his microphone. "Torpedo room, is the drone ready?"

"Aye, sir." was the quick confirmation from the torpedo room. "Drone is ready and waiting on your orders."

"Very well, launch drone," Captain Summerfield commanded.

"Aye, sir, drone away."

Seconds later, from the left front side of the submarine, a muzzle door opened followed by a torpedo-shaped underwater surveillance drone. As it shot through the water, its rear motor engaged. Its propellers activated, sending the drone through the murky waters as its beam of light plowed through as well.

Captain Summerfield, Chief Hawthorne, and the XO clustered around two monitors providing feed through the video cameras aboard the stealth drone. Traveling through the water, it had taken five minutes to reach the opening of the harbor.

"Okay," Captain Summerfield said, "Now we know the harbor's mined. XO, give me distance, depth and placement of the mines, and type."

"Aye, sir," Helms replied. Going to a separate computer, he transferred a feed from the drone, and as his fingers flashed through the keyboard, he started calculating distance, depth, and type of mines placed. Once finished, he said, "Sir, the distance between the mines read as 15 meters. The depth is 18 meters. The sea-mines are the Italian-made MN-103 Manta."

Shaking his head, Captain Summerfield said, "Those Manta mines are one of the most lethal weapons in the Russian arsenal. Damn! And the distance between them isn't enough room for the sub." Running his hand through his hair, he stared at Helms. "XO, retrieve the drone."

"Aye, sir."

"Sir, drone retrieved," XO confirmed several moments later.

"Looks like we might have to swim in," Hawthorne ventured.

"There is another alternative," Captain Summerfield said. "We have a mini-sub large enough to accommodate your men. Will that work?"

Grinning, Chief Hawthorne nodded, saying. "You just saved us a long swim, Captain."

<hr>

The mini-sub cut through the waters as it narrowly slipped through the minefield. Once the sub was safely away, the pilot surfaced about a half a mile from the harbor's landing. With Bravo team ready at the sub's hatchway opening, the co-pilot left his seat and headed to the sub's hatchway, climbed the short steps to the hatch, opened it, and dropped back down.

Facing Chief Hawthorne, the co-pilot said, "Ready when you are."

"Roger," Hawthorne acknowledged.

The teams armed with the compact suppressed Heckler and Koch MP5N 9mm submachine guns made specifically for the SEALs, with the attached mounted optical sights and an 800 (rpm) round-per-minute, the MP5 was an extremely accurate weapon. Each operator also carried the HK Mk23 SOCOM handgun chambered in the 45 ACP rounds, except for Bravo Four. Stevens also carried a Knight's armament HK 11 SWS chambered for the 7.62 mm NATO round. The weapon with its unique semi-auto-only sniper rifle could deliver effective precision beyond 1,000 yards. Everyone on the team wore night-vision goggles (NVG) and their comms system. Included was the SEAL Team-Kit backpack with extraneous equipment.

Bravo Two Grey led the way. He climbed the ladder, and once at the top, dragged himself through.

As he set foot atop the mini-sub, a heavy snow-fall and limited visibility greeted him, as an icy wind sliced through his face and his wetsuit like small bladed knives cutting through the skin with cold precision.

Stepping off to the side, he allowed the rest of the team through as he flipped down his NVG and gazed out toward the landing. Through the darkness and the snow, he could just make out a faint light from a building, but other than that, it was virtually pitch dark.

Slowly, each team member slipped on their fins, bit down on the mouth-piece to their regulators, and breathed the air from their tanks.

Once Bravo One was standing alongside the rest of his team, he set his GPS, slipped on his fins, and slowly they slid into the freezing waters and began their half-mile swim.

The co-pilot closed the hatch, walked back to his seat, and seconds later, was diving towards the bottom to await the operator's return. They were to wait for a set time frame. If they didn't return, the mini-sub was to leave without them.

At twenty-feet to the edge of the landing dock, one right after another, their heads popped out of the frigid waters. Immediately they flipped down their NVGs, and it produced instantly a monochrome shade of green light.

Making land, they stopped, flipped up their NVGs, and walked a few feet through the falling snow. They found a dark spot facing away from the dock, removed their fins, hid their backpacks and extra equipment, checked their weapons, and waited for Bravo One.

Hawthorne, on bent knee and with his team around him, pulled out a plastic-covered map and his compass, just as Bravo Two, Grey, turned on his flashlight and beamed it on the map. Hawthorne checked his destination and plotted a direct route for it. Factoring in the snow and wind, he believed it would take about fifteen minutes to reach the prison walls.

Flipping down his NVG, Hawthorne said, "Time to go."

With about half-a-mile remaining to the prison walls, Bravo One spoke through his comms. "Bravo Four, you're over-watch in case we're chased. Set up your position and be ready for our return."

"Roger that," Bravo-Four replied.

Without mishap, the rest of the team made good time, halting about forty-yards to the prison's main entrance in as little as eight minutes. Positioned in total darkness to any eyes from the prison, the snow-fall provided them an extra layer of protection.

Crouching down on the hard-packed snow, Hawthorne surveyed the perimeter. He made out several spot-lights shining down on the wooded mountainous terrain, with a few that shone into the prison itself. Luck was with them, he thought, as only one low incandescent light shone inside the guard-shack, and to either side of it, was darkness for several yards.

A Russian guard was posted in the wooden shack, while two other guards patrolled the interior on foot. They couldn't see any guards on the two guard-towers on top of the corner walls. The prison walls were two layers of chain-linked fencing. Between the fences was a four-foot walk path covered in snow. It was a small, one-story prison, made to accommodate maybe 50 to 70 inmates. According to Intel, it housed some of the worst dissidents opposing the Russian government.

Hawthorne signaled for his team to start. Bravo Two and Bravo Three set about cutting through the fence with a small set of cutters. It took them three minutes to create a big enough hole for a man to go through. They did the same to the second layer of fencing.

Bravo Two slowly walked toward the gate-shack with his rifle aimed solidly at the guard's head seen through the side glass window. The man appeared to be asleep. Bravo Three followed close behind. The rest of the team waited for Bravo Two to clear the way.

Silently stepping through a half-foot of snow, with the wind blowing hard against his back, Bravo Two halted about ten-feet from the shack and released the hold of his rifle. He drew his handgun when he heard a muffled conversation from the other end of the shack. It became apparent to him that the guards were making their return rounds.

Still undetected, Bravo Two knelt and waited. Tense seconds slowly elapsed when, finally, the two guards appeared through the darkness. The heavy snow-fall and winds shrouded them in a ghost-like appearance as they slowly materialized into two dark shapes.

Bravo One saw them, and speaking through his comms, he directed Bravo Five, who was closer, to take them out.

Seconds later, with two low muffled sounds, both guards shot through their heads as their dead bodies plunged back into the snow.

Hawthorne through his comms asked, "Bravo Two, all clear?"

Bravo Two quietly whispered, "Roger that."

Grey stood and continued on his way to the shack. Reaching it, he finally stood at the closed door. Grabbing the doorknob and slowly turning it, he gradually pushed it open with a harsh grating noise of the hinges.

Just then the guard awoke!

Grey squeezed off two rapid shots, one that impacted the guard's chest and the other which entered through his mouth, before the guard could utter a sound. His body hit a chair and came to rest in a sitting position.

Grey said through his comms, "Bravo One, all clear."

"Copy that. Coming to your position," Hawthorne replied.

Grey rummaged through the shack and found a key-ring with nine cast iron keys on the floor by the corpse, he believed would open the gate's lock. Picking them up, he made his way to the gate. He inserted the first key into the heavy-looking padlock, but the door didn't open. It took several attempts, but finally, the lock yielded, with the second to last key just as the rest of the team came up behind him.

Letting out a sigh of relief, Grey turned toward Hawthorne and grinning, said, "That's good timing, Tex."

Smiling, Hawthorne joked, saying, "Took you long enough."

Grey smiling shook his head. "Complain, complain."

Hawthorne, with his weapon at the ready, said, "On me, single file, watch your pace and distance. Let's go. We ain't here to play in the snow."

With the harsh strong northern winds, freezing snow, and dark clouds overhead, the darkness shielded their slow approach to an iron door on their right side. The four SEAL team operators on bent knees, weapons pointing, leading the way, moved as one. They made the edge of the building, and leaning up against it, they knelt and waited for Grey to once again use his set of keys. Seconds later, they were inside.

They'd expected guards stationed at the front desk, but there were none.

So far, so good, Hawthorne thought.

Two hallways branching left and right were dark and cold. Bravo One and Bravo Three branched off to the right. Bravo Two and Five moved toward the left side hallway. Both sides of the hallway had six cells; all unoccupied.

All this Intel, and we still don't know which cell houses the target, Hawthorne reflected. He could see there were six cells on each side of the dark hallway.

Just as they entered the hallway, Alekseev made out lights and two armed guards on the left side of the hallway. One guard was standing with his Kalashnikov rifle slung across his shoulder, and the other was sitting down on the other side of the hallway as he cradled his AK-74 rifle on his lap, while drinking from a bottle.

Grey and Alekseev soundlessly dropped to their knees. Then Grey held up three fingers. As they squared off and took aim, Grey's index finger went up for the first count, followed by the second a second later, and on the third, they both fired almost as one. In the closed confinement of the hallway, the sound suppressors were slightly louder than usual.

Back on their feet, they ran toward the guards. Alekseev found one still breathing.

"This one is still alive," he whispered, "but not for long." He pulled his knife and held it against the guard's throat.

Chief Grey, coming up to Alekseev, placed a hand on his shoulder, and said, "Wait, ask him where Anisi Sverchinsky's cell is."

Kneeling next to the wounded guard's side, and with the point of his knife held to the guard's throat, Alekseev in Russian asked, "Tell me in which cell is Sverchinsky held, and maybe I'll let you live."

With blood seeping through his open mouth, the guard stared at Alekseev with vacant eyes. "Last cell ... on the left," he mumbled before his head lolled off to the side, Alekseev knew the guard was dead.

"Come on, we ain't got too much time," Grey said.

Running through the darkened hallway, Grey heard yelling, shouting, and crying from men and women held prisoner. It became apparent to him that the cells weren't empty. Grey caught glimpses of those inside, who'd thrust their arms through the iron bar doors, yelling and pleading as they moved forward.

Glancing at Alekseev, Grey reached out and pulled on his arm, trying to slow him down. "What are they yelling?" he asked.

"Help us," Thomas replied.

Reaching the last cell on the left, both SEAL operatives came to a halt. Alekseev pulled out his flashlight and shone the light through the cell. In a corner, a man with long shoulder-length dark hair and a heavily bearded face, sat on the floor and glanced up at the light.

"Are you Anisi Sverchinsky?" Alekseev asked in Russian.

Through the beam of his flashlight, Alekseev saw the prisoner snap his head back and tried to stand, but fell back down; the mere attempt dizzying him for a moment, with only a gasp coming from his parched lips.

Glancing at the shadow on the other side of the door, the prisoner finally asked. "Who ... are ... you?" he asked in Russian.

"We're Americans, come to get you out of here!" Alekseev replied. "Don't stand, close your eyes, and cover your face."

Grey came up behind Alekseev, pulled a charge of plastic explosives from his backpack, set in on the locking device, slipped in a detonator, spooled out two wires, and hooked them to the hand-held switch. Standing back a few feet, he turned the switch, and a sudden blinding flash of explosion occurred, followed by a small cloud of dust.

With Grey standing guard at the cell door, Alekseev entered the foul-smelling cell. Standing in front of Sverchinsky, Grey held his breath, helped him to his feet, and trudged to the cell door. Standing outside the darkened hallway, Grey and Alekseev listened and suddenly heard loud weapons fire.

"We're under fire here," Bravo One said, "but we're okay. Any luck on your end?"

Hawthorne, on the left side of the hallway and Acosta on the right, while kneeling, laid down a sustained rate of fire to a bend in the hallway where seven heavily armed guards were being held off. Suddenly, they heard the harsh sounds of an alarm.

"Bravo One," Grey said. "We got our target and heading toward the front."

"Roger that," Hawthorne replied, "Right behind you."

Suddenly, Acosta spied a guard who had stuck his body halfway while holding an RPG-7 anti-tank launcher pull the trigger!

Madre de Dios! Acosta heard himself say. Then out-loud he yelled, "RPG!"

Both of them swiftly stood and started running, just as the RPG struck with a resounding *Bang!* A loud explosion of the wall followed it as it blew shrapnel and fire behind them. Acosta, closest to the impact, was immediately cut down as hot metal shrapnel entered through his backpack and sliced through into his back.

Hawthorne in one swift-motion turned back and dragged Acosta, who was semi-conscious, forward. Then he lay down a barrage of fire on the guards to cover their retreat.

Almost half-way to the front, Grey, who also covered their retreat by raining down a sustained fire, met him. They watched three guards run to their position, firing their weapons, but then sink to the concrete.

With Acosta in the firefighter's carry position, Hawthorne received covering fire from Grey. Alekseev, with their target in tow, slowly made it to the front door just as guards came running up from the other side of the hallways.

Loading an 'HE' (high explosive) round in his M-203 over-and-under rifle grenade launcher, Grey yelled, "Fire in the hole!" With a muffled *thump!* He sent it flying down the hallway, just as several guards busted through. He loaded a second grenade and let it loose toward the other hallway with several guards just stepping into view.

They went into the darkened forest with at least eight guards right behind them. Grey was walking backward, continuing to fire his weapon. One and then two guards went down to his gunfire as the guards sought cover from his deadly aim.

Pulling away from the guards, they were just about half-way toward Bravo Four's position, when Hawthorne and his men heard the sounds of one or two trucks heading their way. Grey, jogging alongside Hawthorne, said, "Tex, we got more company heading our way."

Hawthorne slowed down just long enough to face Grey. "As long as one of us is still alive," he said, "we have to get our target aboard that sub."

"Let's go then!"

Hawthorne broke squelch. "Bravo Four, Bravo One, you have your ears on?"

"Roger, Bravo One, please standby one," Bravo Four, Jesse Stevens said.

Just then, a running guard made out the SEAL team operators just ahead of him, stopped, knelt, and took aim. However, before he could pull the trigger, his head blew apart when Stevens fired one round from his sniper's weapon.

Suddenly, four more Russian prison guards broke through the forest. As quickly as he could pull the trigger, Stevens cut them down one at a time before they sought cover.

"Bravo One," Stevens said, "got you covered, sir."

But two more truck-loads of Russian soldiers now stopped at the fringes of the forest line, dismounted, and ran toward the SEAL team.

Once at Stevens' position, the group stopped and waited for Stevens to drop from his overhead perch atop a tree. Hawthorne gently slid Acosta off his shoulder onto the ground and tried to shake Acosta awake, but he was unresponsive. Checking his pulse, Hawthorne couldn't find one.

"He's dead," he whispered to the others.

With the snow still falling and the winds still blowing, they set off once again. Hawthorne's operators arrived first at the pickup location. They all donned their equipment as they waited for the sub to appear.

Hawthorne broke squelch and said through his comms, "Bravo One to Small-fry, ready for pickup, over."

"Small-fry here," came back the response, "Thought you would not make it on time, Bravo One."

Ignoring a reply, and shaking his head, Hawthorne stared at his men and said, "Let's go for a swim, guys."

A small rolled rubber raft extracted from their equipment backpack and inflated was used to place Acosta's body, which Hawthorne pulled behind him.

Arriving at their rendezvous point minutes later, they saw the mini-sub breakwater to their left. With Russian soldiers standing on the edge of the water-line, they fired at the SEAL team and the sub. Standing by the side of the sub, Grey and Hawthorne returned fire. Two minutes later, the sub with all onboard and one corpse were well on their way back to the mother submarine.

This leg of the mission had been a successful one. However, they still needed to deliver the target to a safe house in Stuttgart, Germany.

PART ONE

Anisi Sverchinsky

—1—

The seas were rough, Hawthorne thought as he stood on the bridge of the submarine at Saint Peter Port in France.

The splashing waves were loud with strong southern winds blowing against the tide, striking the front and sides of the submarine as it made its slow way into the port, leaving a white wake in its path.

A few minutes later, Captain Summerfield and his XO stood on the bridge next to him.

Hawthorne felt blessed to watch the sunrise, marveling at the natural beauty as the sky grew into an enormous ball of fire, changing from dark orange to dark yellow as it shimmered into the waters, and moved across the sky with grace all its own. It was beautiful, he thought and gave thanks for being alive.

With the dangerous part of the mission over, they now became glorified babysitters until the prisoner was out of their hands, he thought. And that would be soon.

As the submarine came to a stop a mile from the Havelet Bay, a small boat made its way to the sub. The SEAL Team's ride to Castle Pier lasted a few minutes before coming to three waiting Black SUVs. The drive was an uneventful four-mile trip.

Their destination was the Guernsey Airport, from where they would board a waiting Beech 390 twin-engine jet, and then onto Stuttgart Airport, in Southern Germany.

Their mission wouldn't end until they'd delivered the prisoner to a CIA safe-house, somewhere in the City of Stuttgart.

* — ·—— · —— ·—

"This Safe-House is one of the most secured that we have in town," Dwight Elders, the housekeeper said. He was an old case officer with several months left before retirement. Hawthorne knew German beer must agree with him, as he had a substantial beer gut.

"Make yourselves at home. There are two rooms in the back, and the fridge is full of goodies. Get your team some rest; you'll be going out later this afternoon."

Hawthorne nodded. They were in Safe-House #3 on Reutlinger Strasse, #136, Stuttgart. The house had five rooms; one bedroom for visitors and one for the housekeeper. There was an office with surveillance video CCTV equipment and state-of-the-art communications array with listening devices. Two cell rooms, located left of the office, padlocked and soundproofed were primarily used to conduct interrogations with no disturbances or distractions.

One of those rooms housed their prisoner, guarded by an armed CIA operative. Treated by the sub's doctor, Sverchinsky received a change of clothing, and notwithstanding the harsh psychological treatment he received while in captivity was very lucid and highly responsive.

The blocked windows were bulletproof, and the back and front doors were of solid wood and fortified with half-inch steel plates. A long narrow hallway led from the front to the rear of the house.

"Is anyone else here?" Hawthorne asked.

Before entering the safe-house, he had noticed three black SUVs parked in the back. It could be nothing, but he had to ask, anyway.

"Yes, a four-man CIA team," Elders replied, "sent to protect the house and our quest. They arrived about an hour ago and positioned at both the front and the back of the house."

"Y'all expect trouble?"

"Always; we try to run a tight ship."

With a brisk nod, Hawthorne said, "We'll get out of your hair then."

⁌ ⁍

The Russian unit approached from the north and south of the safe-house which was situated back on the edge of a forest line, several blocks from the outskirts of the city. Safe enough, that any loud gunfire might seem natural in a forest area. Two four-man teams clad in black clothing with hoods, all carrying Sig Sauer 516 assault rifles, made their slow advance through the early morning dawn using what little of the darkness there was for cover.

They were from the elite Russian Federal Security Service (FSB) who succeeded the old KGB agents assigned to the Russian Embassy in Frankfurt. Their mission was to retrieve the Russian Agent named Anisi Sverchinsky from the Americans, alive, and at all cost.

Staying hidden from possible surveillance cameras, the two teams radioed in their positions the moment they were thirty-feet from the unsecured back and front doors of the safe-house.

Two of the agents counted to ten and then pulled the triggers of their rocket-propelled grenades with high explosive warheads. A low rumbling sound followed by a thunderous roar as the rockets traveled for two seconds before impact and detonations.

They blasted the back door open, while the front door exploded with a plume of red, yellow, and orange-colored flames scant seconds later, leaving dark pale white and black smoke in its wake.

Instantly killed were the two-man CIA team guarding the inside front and back doors as the explosions of the RPG grenades sent chucks of red hot metal shrapnel flying that penetrated their exposed bodies.

Back on their feet, the two Russian teams donned gas-masks and ran forward. At the gaping holes, where the doors were seconds ago, they advanced into a semi-dark hallway and a barrage of gunfire.

One commando lobbed a flash-bang grenade. But by that time Bravo Team operatives had all taken positions by the cell guarding their prisoner. With no cover for his men, Hawthorne and his team, plus the two remaining CIA agent's met the intruder's head-on in a free-for-all gunfight.

Elders, with a gun in hand, had crawled to his office to radio in the attack to CIA headquarters in Langley, Virginia. But as he came to the office door, a bullet entered the side of his head, killing him instantly.

Seconds later, after furious hand-to-hand combat, the gunfire stopped. Dead were Hawthorne and the entire SEAL Team. Left standing was an injured Russian agent. With a bullet hole in his left arm, and one to his right leg, he sauntered into a room. Sitting on a bed, he bandaged his wounds. Minutes later, he pulled out his cell-phone and called his handler, reporting the outcome, not surprised when she directed him to determine the whereabouts of Sverchinsky.

In his padlocked room, Sverchinsky was in motion the moment he heard the explosions which broke the padlock. He surprised his guard, knocking him unconscious. Removing a set of cuffs, he secured the agent's hands behind him and took his weapon. Searching the guard, he found car keys.

In the hallway, he saw the bodies, but no one standing. Kneeling beside a fallen Russian agent, he took his cell-phone, wallet, weapon, and extra ammunition. Then he briskly walked to the front of the house, through the gaping hole, and disappeared into the thick forest.

Moments later, as Sverchinsky made his way through the woods; the remaining FSB Agent calmly walked into the hallway, removed a photograph of Agent Sverchinsky, and searched the entire house without finding who he was looking for.

She will not like my report; he thought with dread.

—2—

Deep beneath the north side of the Pentagon, in a highly secured and spacious room built as a reinforced concrete structure, The Chairman of the Joint Chiefs of Staff, General Earl Fleming, was in a high-level briefing with the Director of the CIA, Jonathan Fakes, and the NSA Director, Steven Summerset. Although the room kept at a modestly cool temperature, Fakes and Summerset were sweating.

The prevailing mood of the two men was tense and apparently nervous as they sat waiting for Fleming to begin. This was their first such briefing on the ongoing operation.

General Fleming, a tall, broad-shouldered man, with short-cut brown hair parted on the left, opened a black leather briefcase, and removed a folder. Pushing his briefcase aside, he shuffled through the folder and stopped at a particular two-page document. "Gentlemen," he said, "it's been several weeks since we decided on this course of action. And so far, without the president's knowledge of the operation, we've been successful in securing the agent known as Theseus."

Fleming paused for a moment as he made eye contact with both of them and saw relief wash over their faces at the news. "As you both know, he was being held incommunicado in prison suspected of being a double agent, for us and the Russians."

Fakes took this all in with a sigh of relief. Staring at Fleming, he said, "You should advise the President of this now, Earl. You can't lose any more time."

Fleming, not prone to panic or precipitous action raised a hand. "All in good time, Jonathan," he said. "We still have much to do."

Summerset was shaking his head and leaned back in his chair. "I have to agree with Jonathan, Earl," he said. "It makes little sense not to inform the President."

Fakes shrugged and nodded.

A silence settled over the table.

Fleming leaned forward in his chair, stood, and walked around it. He placed his hands on the back-rest and leaned in as he stared at Summerset and Fakes.

"On the contrary," Fleming asserted, "it makes perfect sense. But when I realized the potential danger the U.S. would be in if all this were true, I knew I couldn't do this alone."

After a brief silence, he continued. "We knew the possible ramifications of not alerting the President. But we needed confirmation before he was told of this likely attack. Let's wait until we extract the information from Theseus first. Once we have it, by all means, I'll report to the President what we've found. Then he can make a fair assessment of the situation and take action. And if it doesn't pan out, the President would have plausible deniability to fall back on. But until then, let's just wait."

"Pissed he'll be on not taking this to him beforehand," Fakes said, once again shaking his head. "And the use of Navy SEALs without his authorization, well—"

"Let me handle the President," Fleming responded. "It's going to be up to you two in making sure the rest of the plan goes off as smooth as it has been."

Both Fakes and Summerset nodded.

"One more thing," Fleming said rather reluctantly. "Already we lost a SEAL operative. We need this kept under wraps until we have all the facts and the information from Theseus."

Knowing that collateral damage would be slightly high, Fakes said, "So, it's started then."

"Hell, Jonathan, it started with the SEAL team and their extraction," Fleming said. "It was going to happen regardless of how finely tuned our plan was going in."

Fakes frowned as he licked his lips. "I don't like it."

Summerset avoided the back and forth and, staring at Fleming, asked, "Is the safe-house well secured?"

"Yes, I have seven well-trained CIA agents covering it. The SEAL Team and two interrogators will work on Theseus once they arrive."

"What's our time-line for all this?" Summerset asked.

Fleming stared at one, then at the other. "Forty-eight hours," Fleming said.

While the high-level conference was taking place at the Pentagon, two U.S. Air Force captains in the CIA's Drone Control Room were carefully eyeing eight sets of monitors as they controlled two unarmed General Atomics MQ-1 Predator Drones.

Observing two overhead large screen monitors, the pilots flew on station above Safe-House #3 in Stuttgart. Their job entailed the monitoring and recording of all activities in and around their target of observation—the safe-house and surrounding area.

Twenty minutes into the vigil, Captain Leroy Harris watched as the cameras and other sensors picked up several unknown black-clad figures approaching the left and right sides of the house. Pressing his microphone button, he said, "Sir, I'm observing an unauthorized approach of several armed intruders at Safe-House # 3."

"Stand by," Colonel Ed Burns replied.

"Sir," Harris quickly chimed in again, "two almost simultaneous explosions just happened at the left and right side of the house. Holy shit, sir, they're under attack!"

"I'm in contact with the project manager for the operation, CIA Director Fakes," Colonel Burns said. "They can take further action. It's out of our hands for now."

Not ten minutes had elapsed when Captain William Ryan, the second pilot, said, "I'm seeing a man exiting the safe-house, sir, heading into the woods."

Colonel Burns replied. "Try to stay with him."

"Yes, sir."

"Sir, a second man just exited the back of the house, working his slow way back to the main road."

"Keep visual on that man, Captain."

"I'm on it, sir."

A few minutes later, both pilots reported having lost sight of both men after entering the thick part of the woods.

"What do you mean, lost sight?"

"I mean, sir, we haven't been able to reacquire them."

"Huh?" he snorted, "What the hell."

Inside the basement's highly secured room, Fakes, General Fleming, and NSA director Summerset were contemplating their next course of action when they heard one of their cell phones ringing. They cast their eyes at Fakes, who was reaching and pulling out his phone. On the small screen, he read the name of Colonel Burns. Fakes knew it was from the drone room. On his orders, his people were keeping a close watch on the safe-house.

"This is Fakes," he said as a matter of identification. "Has anything happened at the safe-house, Colonel?"

A brief pause before Colonel Burns replied, "Yes, sir. I'm reporting the safe-house compromised. We observed two explosions. Then after several minutes, two men exited the house, one from either end."

Fakes nearly fell from his chair. He stared at the two men in the room, as he wiped a thin sheen of sweat from his brow with his other hand. He couldn't believe what he had just heard. The safest house was the most secure in the area, and no one, except those in the room, was privy to its present use or who was being kept there.

"Colonel Burns, have you identified the two men?"

"Yes, sir, one of those was the guest, and the other is an unknown."

"Thank you."

Slowly he pocketed the cell phone and stared at the other two men. "We have a serious problem."

—3—

Sverchinsky knelt inside a forest of tall trees alongside a gravel road. Ahead and to his left were two Ford Explorers. He didn't see anyone keeping watch and hoped the key he had in hand would start one. Overhead, he still heard the faint sounds of the two drones as they crisscrossed high above. They were already looking for him!

He waited to see if anyone came out to investigate. After a minute or two, he arrived beside the driver's side of the first vehicle, and did not see anyone about. He knew he had only one opportunity to start the vehicle until someone came to investigate.

He tried the key on the first car. With a slight roar, the car started at the first turn of the key! He just had time to speed away when a barrage of bullets suddenly crashed through the rear window! Then someone had started a second vehicle and was soon after him. He could only guess that someone an American or Russian agent were in pursuit. Not caring who it might be, he raced away down the gravel road. Glancing at his rear-view mirror, he noticed his pursuer was easily closing the gap.

The chase sped down the dark road, as the headlights behind him grew larger by the second. When he reached the end of the gravel road, he braked lightly without slowing his speed. Just as the front tires caught the asphalt road, he turned the wheel over to the left and steered into a power slide. With tires squealing, he turned down a two-lane road.

Seconds later, glancing at the outside mirror, he watched as his pursuer also pulled into a power slide but wasn't as fortunate. The car crashed into the trunk of a large tree. The groans of metal being twisted came to his ears. An eerie silence followed, except for the sounds of the radiator hissing.

An American or Russian driver must be dead or unconscious, but there isn't time to check, Sverchinsky thought. Then drifting forward, he heard a loud explosion and saw flames shooting up into the sky.

Behind the wheel, Sverchinsky drove away. He was somewhere in Europe, but where?

Reaching into the glove compartment, he found the registration and immediately knew where he was: Stuttgart, Germany. Grabbing the wallet he'd confiscated earlier, he opened it. It only revealed the identity of a Russian agent, and it might not even be his correct name.

Alone, he couldn't set his plans in motion. He needed to contact his people. They needed to know that he was alive and free. But to do that, he needed to contact his friend Carl Benz in Frankfurt. And to do that, he needed a place to stay. He also knew his top priority was quickly rid himself of the vehicle and gain another before he did anything else.

As he entered a suburb of Stuttgart, he spotted a parked and sporty looking Toyota Land Cruiser. Parking his vehicle two blocks from the Toyota, he walked back, smashed the driver's side window, slid behind the wheel, and hot-wired it. He pulled away from the curb and slowly drove away.

Driving through downtown Stuttgart, in the early morning traffic, took him to a one-way street and where several mid-size cars parked along a narrow street, were ripe for the picking. With no pedestrians out and about, he finally pulled in behind an old black two-door BMW.

Rummaging through the glove compartment of the Toyota, he found what he'd hoped for; a screwdriver. It took him five minutes to switch over the plates, and with no one aware of what he'd done, he was once more back on the road.

Driving for the better part of an hour, around the outskirts of the city, he caught sight of exactly the house he was looking for. Pulling over to the side of the road, he made out a secluded red-painted two-story home set back in the woods, which would be perfect. Parking on the opposite side of the street, he waited to see if anyone came or went into the house.

The only person he'd seen, in the better part of fifteen minutes, was a middle-aged woman who dumped a heavy bag into a trashcan and went back inside. It looked right so far. Not seeing anyone else enter or leave, he turned off his car, walked to the front door, and knocked. Pulling his weapon, he cocked back the hammer and waited for the woman. Seconds later, with the door opened, Sverchinsky shot the woman and closed the door behind him.

In the house, he found a door leading to a basement. Dragging the body of the woman, he dropped it down the stairs and closed the door. Next, he searched for the master bedroom. In the closets, he found men's clothing that would fit him well enough. After a shower, a hurried haircut, and shave, he went down to the kitchen and made himself a meal and chased it down with a couple of beers.

Next, he placed three phone calls. He hoped his plan was still intact and that no one knew exactly what date his plan would start. If all went according to his time-table, he would have his revenge soon enough. The matter of his family, well, they'd taken them out of his hands. It's what he would have done if the shoe was on the other foot.

As he sat to wait, he remembered back to how all this began.

—4—

Sverchinsky was his Russian name, but his true name was Matthew Banks, an American recruited eight years ago by the CIA straight out of a college ROTC program. His CIA handler, William Phillips, told Matthew they had captured a high-valued Russian spy named Anisi Sverchinsky, but he died under their interrogation.

And now here he was, slated to become a true "Russian!"

Two reasons they picked him out of several, he was told, was his uncanny resemblance to the dead spy, and his fluency in Russian. However, he felt the CIA was holding back information from him. What that could be, he didn't know. They asked him to impersonate the spy and take over his life with the goal of securing Russian war plans for the U.S. It would be his patriotic duty as an American to serve his country in its hour of need. Or so he was told.

A month later, with minor plastic surgery, he became Sverchinsky.

For six long years, now a highly placed Russian FSB Agent assigned to the Kremlin, he photocopied several Russian First Strike War Plans and other sensitive documents and forwarded them through highly encrypted messages directly to Phillips at CIA headquarters.

However, his role became much more difficult. Two years ago, the Russian FSB implicated him in a plot to steal seven nuclear suitcase bombs, the Russian W54 warhead with a critical mass of plutonium— the U-233. One dirty-nuke was enough to destroy a fair-sized city.

High-ups orchestrated and planned the theft of the bombs in the FSB chain of command. The head of the FSB, Sergei Vannovsky, after an intensive investigation of Banks showed he was highly receptive to a change in the Russian government; he was to steal the seven bombs.

The plan, according to Vannovsky, was top-secret, but they entrusted Banks with several aspects of it. It involved the nukes being used in a coup d'état attempt by the military to take control of the government. His job was to place the nukes throughout Russia in seven specific strategic locations and set them off once given the command. There were other elements of the plan Vannovsky kept to himself, which he later learned.

But he never placed the bombs, though he reported to Vannovsky that he had. His deception, suspected by a colleague jealous of his advancement in FSB ranks, set off his downfall. Why he failed to comply and lied about it was simple; something had gone wrong!

It was through his contacts, and close friends he'd made in the FSB that he learned there was an arrest warrant implicating him in the theft of the bombs, and that his arrest would be imminent. Now suspected of being made a patsy, he well knew once locked up in prison he would die in captivity, so he ran for his life.

Too late, it was shortly thereafter that the chains of events to further his downfall were in motion.

Banks, the double agent that he was, was no fool. In the back of his mind, he harbored the day they would discover his true identity, and feared for his life and that of his family. Later, learning the identity of the ex-Russian dissident responsible for turning him in, he had him killed.

However, his one insurance policy was the nukes, which he kept hidden in the event things didn't go well.

And worst, they accused him of diverting secrets to an undercover, ex-KGB agent. This was untrue. So now they had two crimes against him, both leading to his execution.

Before his arrest, he got word to the American Embassy using his code name–Theseus. But he never received a reply from his handler or anyone else in Washington. Ultimately, he knew he was a spy caught out in the cold—the Americans had disavowed him and left him to die or rot in prison, and the Russians wanted him as a domestic terrorist, or worse, a spy.

For several months before his arrest, Banks put together a plot involving three known ex-Russian agents whom he trusted completely. They did the planning stages in the seclusion of one of the dissident's *dacha* or country home.

There he hatched out his revenge against the CIA and the Russian FSB. Having completed the plan, he set the date for its initiation and kept most of the details locked in his computer. If all went well, his goal of World War Three would surely begin.

Several weeks later, one of Banks loyal ex-Russian agents, trying to get back into the good graces of the Kremlin, reported his knowledge of what Banks planned and offered detailed files of the plot to the Kremlin. But only two knew the whereabouts of the nukes, Banks and a Russian Jew named Nikolai Bobrov, his closest ally, and friend.

Later, finding out about the ex-agent, Banks shot and killed the man as he exited a jazz club on a darkened street, but not before it compromised his computer and files. He knew the man he'd killed somehow had hacked into most of his files. But several pieces of information weren't in the computer—the names of the conspirators, the hiding place of the nukes, and the exact date of execution. Those he kept safely tucked in the corner of his mind.

Not knowing the extent of knowledge the Russians had of the plot, the night of his arrest, he had Nikolai and the rest of his group leave Russia. He gave them burner phones with instructions that once Banks was ready, he'd get them back together, and told not to go back to their homes.

Finding where Banks and his family were hiding wasn't difficult for the searchers. They came for him that night, gagged and tied his wife of two years and his two-year-old step-daughter, who did not know of his double life, and killed them execution-style; gunshots to the back of their heads.

He remembered the torture he'd been under to extract the whereabouts of the nukes. But time, and time again, they failed to get the information out of him. He gave up hope of ever getting out alive.

—5—

Outskirts of Southern Uruzgan Province, Afghanistan,
Monday, September 8, 7:15 A.M.

Defense Intelligence Agency, Special Agent Tom Price, knew he would not get embedded with U.S. Service Members during an actual infiltration mission. His role instead, was the liaison, or go-between, to the U.S. Special Operating Forces (SOF), U.S. Army Green Berets, with Echo Team-One tagged to perform the mission.

Price's primary job was to track, identify, and determine the whereabouts of a high-value terrorist with a two-million-dollar bounty, known to be the head of a Taliban force operating in the region. That would have been the extent of his work. However, DIA higher brass and those in SOF command had other plans. Now ordered to accompany and assist Team-One in the identification of one Mullah Abdul Ahmed Urabi. Once done, it was up to the Team to eliminate Urabi's command presence, eliminate all of his higher personnel, and take no prisoners.

Accomplishing his part of the operation, which had taken him over three months of steady hard work to achieve, wasn't easy. When the opportunity presented itself, he, along with three DIA Agents, identified two of Urabi's operatives during the surveillance of a known Taliban meeting place and had taken them as prisoners.

The captives, in a Black-Ops safe-house, went through tough if not brutal interrogation.

Within two days, the prisoners gave up the information he was looking for. After a short drone period of surveillance, Mullah Urabi once identified, photographed, videotaped, they had his base of operations revealed.

Price voicing his objections to higher command was told to assist in the mission. Now, clad in battle dress gear and armed with an M4 Assault rifle with an M203 grenade launcher attached, the Team leader, Captain Gerald Bradley, placed Price behind him in the group. Sitting in the back of the Sikorsky UH-60 A/L Blackhawk helicopter alongside the seven Special Forces operatives led by Captain Bradley, he seemed to fit in well with the team of hard-looking men.

A second UH-60 bird flew alongside the first to offer covering fire once the first helo touched ground with its personnel.

The plan was to land about seven miles on the southern fringes of a rugged mountainous region and trek to the Taliban stronghold and pray they didn't encounter enemy forces along the way. The two helos, call sign Rub1 and Rub 2, would wait for extraction from the team at the landing zone.

But Price's main thoughts centered on Belle Sinclair, his fiancé, and a CID Agent stationed in Stuttgart, Germany. He looked forward to being with her once this mission ended.

Not one to shy away from any action, he needed to present himself to her in one piece. He remembered he had failed to contact Sinclair the past week because of the mission, and now she'd have to wait a few more days before he could communicate with her again.

Twenty minutes later Captain Bradley, through his comms, gave the two-minute warning.

Toward the front of the helo, Sergeant Wilson Miller, with his four men squad, would be the first out of the helicopter. They would provide security for the personnel and the bird, while above, the second bird would hover and provide additional fire cover.

At the LZ, as if on cue, Sergeant Wilson threw open the sliding doors and he and his squad jumped from the helo while keeping their weapons trained toward the surrounding desolate desert landscape.

The rest of the operatives disembarked from both sides of the chopper and knelt on the ground. Pulling out his map and compass, Bradley shot an azimuth to the nearest point of reference.

"It's going to take about an hour-and-twenty minutes to reach our target," he said. "Price, you're on me. Wilson, take the lead. NVG's down. Let's go."

As the choppers powered down, the team disappeared into the dark, cold desert.

The Team moved forward slowly in a column, spaced a few yards apart. They traveled through a stream of mountainous terrain. Urozgan Province bordered Zabul and Kandahar to the south, Helmand to the southwest, Daykundi to the north, and Ghazni Providence to the east. Seized in 2016 by the Taliban, they still held it today.

They were about five miles to their target when suddenly, the point man, Staff Sergeant (SSG) Eddie Cavalla, dropped to a knee and gave the go-to ground hand signal–a fist pump. All members immediately went to ground, waiting on SSG Cavalla.

"Do you see anything, Eddie?" Bradley asked through his comms.

"I'm not picking up anything through my NVG," Cavalla replied. "But I got a feeling we're not alone."

When the attack came, it was swift, accurate, and deadly!

SSG Cavalla had a nose for trouble, and according to team leader Bradley, Cavalla could smell an ambush before they sprang it. However, he was a little too late this time.

He was the first to die.

Bringing up the rear, Sergeant Mike Douglas was the second man to die. Then, all hell broke loose as the team returned fire. But it was too late. Caught in the middle of the ambush, and cut off from the front and rear, and their left and right flanks, Bradley and his men sustained heavy casualties!

Bradley knew they would not make it unless he radioed the choppers. "Rub1, Echo Team-One, we're under attack, request immediate extraction, over!"

"Echo-One, roger, on our way, tracking your GPS signals."

"Can anyone see an opening anywhere?" Bradley shouted out.

No answer.

"Damn!" Bradley muttered.

Within seconds, Captain Bradley, Price, and another operative were the only ones standing. Caught out in an open area, the surrounding darkness played against them, making their NVGs useless. With movement all around, the three delivered a continuous sustained fire, as Price loaded a 'HE' round into his grenade launcher.

It was at that moment Price, out of the corner of his eyes, saw Captain Bradley being flung to the ground from multiple gunshots. Without a moment to lose, he quickly unloaded the 'HE' round, killing two attackers. Suddenly, a quick glance around him showed he was all alone!

Price suddenly dropped to his knees, and prepared to load another 'HE' round, when a bullet plowed into his right hip and another caught his right shoulder, spinning him flat to the ground. Another bullet struck his back as his rifle flew out of his hands. With a steady loss of blood, he knew, if he was to remain alive, he needed to crawl away from the field of battle.

Slowly, he moved across the ground. Just when he thought he was clear, he heard them running and firing at his previous position. Two RPG rockets struck the ground where he was last standing. Feeling his life slowly being drained, and his life blood pumping out of his body, he kept crawling away, finding himself gradually going uphill. Although, minutes later, he was rolling down a hill, just as he lost consciousness.

—6—

Major Jessica Alice Wayne—better known as Jessie to her friends and subordinates at the 64th Military Intelligence Brigade subordinate to the U.S. Army Intelligence and Security Command (INSCOM) Joint Military Base at Wiesbaden Army Airfield, Germany, was sitting in the comfort of her second-story office of the 64th Military Intelligence Brigade Headquarters. Staring out of her window, she could just make out the airfield through a grey and cloudy morning.

She always loved the German mornings. The early softness of the day was always magical. However, in the mornings when the fog hung low and pregnant, she felt depressed while remembering the death of her late husband, John; killed two years ago at an early age while serving as an U.S. Air Force pilot, his F-35 fighter plane suffered destruction from a surface-to-air missile in Afghanistan.

Jessie, a tall brown-eye brunette in her mid-thirties, envisioned the warmth of John's soft kiss on her lips. Opening them, she shook her head and glanced at the wall clock over on the opposite wall: 10 a.m. and she hadn't even logged onto her computer.

Taking a deep breath, she glanced outside her office, through the glass windows and door, as work proceeded in step with military precision, as twelve of her staff sat at work. And here she was an hour into work and her computer was still off.

Jessie slowly released the breath. *Damn, I better get to work.*

Her position at the 64th was the section leader for multi-discipline intelligence operations in support Army, Europe. It also involved her in the cyber interception of any digital content through the use of electronic or other digital devices. Two of her staff, First Lieutenant Alvin Winchester and Sergeant Leroy Brown, were the two most responsible for the interception, identification, and reporting of such intercepts to her for further action.

Her responsibilities also included the operational control of missions in Afghanistan and Iraq.

Almost two hours later, as she prepared for her lunch break, First Lieutenant Alvin Winchester knocked on her pane-glass door leading into her office with a folder clutched in his hand.

Occasionally, Winchester would knock and then enter. However, this time he waited and watched her through the glass. But what struck Jessie was his apprehensiveness and almost tense, demeanor. Not like him, she thought, for a person who had a joyful outlook on life—a joker with a quick smile.

Winchester turned away, looking behind him. Returning his gaze to his chief, and arching his brows, he saw her waving him in. Major Wayne frowned with concern. "Lieutenant, you seem perturbed. Is there a problem?"

"I need to get into your computer. You need to see this, right now, Major!"

She squinted. "What's the problem, Alvin?"

He shook his head. His face was tight with unaccustomed strain as he said in a low, tight voice, "Please, Major ... please!"

Nodding, and sensing the urgency in his voice, she backed her chair away from her desk and waved him around.

At her side, Winchester pulled a small thumb drive from his pocket, slid her laptop in front of him, and inserted the drive into a USB port. He hurried his fingers over the keyboard and the mouse pad opened the contents of the file and transferred it onto her computer. Removing the drive, he placed it on her desk. Stepping away from her desk, he said, "There, I've uploaded it onto your drive, and ready for you to read."

Pulling back to the edge of her desk, she retrieved her laptop and swiveled it where she could read the screen. Using the mouse pad, she saw two files, both labeled "Confidential." One was marked Russian text and the other English translation of the Russian text. She clicked on the file marked English translation on her desktop, and it opened onto two plans or phases and a typed detailed plan or manifesto. She then clicked on the second file. It had several photographs.

She read the plans first, frowning throughout as shock, anger, and rage scrolled across her face. Then she clicked on the photos. She wanted to scream but thought better of it.

"This," she breathed through clenched teeth, "this … can't be true!"

Shaking his head, Winchester postulated, "But what if it is, Major?"

"Then, we … the world will be in grave danger."

A minute passed as she tried to wrap her mind around the contents to the files. The first thing she had to do, she thought, was destroy the copies in Winchester's file folder and the thumb drive. Second, she had to wait until after everyone had left for the day, to call her command, and outline the contents of what she'd just received. The only person she trusted was Colonel Alex Simmons; her commander. He would take this out of her hands.

"Lieutenant, have the drive and folder destroyed in the usual manner, and forget we ever had this conversation. I'll take care of this. Once you've completed the task, text me."

"I will, ma'am."

Watching him leave, Jessie pulled out an empty thumb drive from her desk and inserted it into a USB port. Then clicking onto her own personal security key using her own algorithm, she loaded it onto the thumb drive. Once done, she transferred the files onto the drive and removed them from her computer. Then she deleted the file on her laptop and emptied the electronic wastebasket on her computer.

———— • ———— • ————

At precisely twelve-forty-two that same day, in a secure three-story building outside Frankfurt, Germany, a communications person with earphones on, having finished transmitting an encoded message, heard his computer program beeping an alert. As he clicked onto the program, it showed that someone had intercepted the message in its encoded content. His fingers danced across the keyboard, and within a matter of minutes, he knew where the intercept occurred from; his/her computer and his/her IP address. After two hours of painstaking backtracking, he discovered it was a Lieutenant Alvin Winchester of the 64th MI group.

Picking up the cell phone, he placed a call to his handler.

Speaking in Russian, he informed her of the breach, and after receiving a tensed reply, he severed the line.

At 5:15 p.m., two average height, stocky men, wearing grey two-piece business suits, slid out of their black two-door sedan and closed their doors behind them. The early afternoon was crisp, a perfect time for what they had planned. They'd parked next to the 64th MI officers in BOQ barracks, in the Lucius Clay Kaserne, in Wiesbaden. They knew which room their target was located. Walking around towards the back of the barracks, they found the backdoor ajar and entered a stairwell that would lead them to the third floor.

Once at the third story landing, they opened the fire-door, looked left and right, and then turned left looking for room 316. They found it halfway down the hall. To their luck, as one of the two tried the doorknob, he found it unlocked.

Unhurriedly, they entered the room, lit only by a small table lamp off to one corner that gave off a subdued soft golden glow of lighting that came off a cabinet filled with wine glasses. Just then Lieutenant Winchester strolled out of the bathroom half-naked, drying his hair, and halted mid-step, and stared stupidly at the two men.

With surprise and shock written on his face, he opened his mouth to say something. However, they only heard the sharp intake of his breath.

One of the two asked, "Are you, Lieutenant Alvin Winchester?"

"Yeah, that's me. What the hell are you two doing in—?"

The man closest to the door closed the door behind him as his partner pulled out a silenced handgun. Without a wasted motion, he slammed the gun against Winchester's forehead. The lieutenant sank to the floor, unconscious.

Winchester woke and found himself naked with tied down legs and hands to a chair as the two intruders came into focus. One intruder pulled out a cigarette and lit it. While standing close to Winchester's stereo, he turned it on. With the music playing, he raised the volume, turned, and nodded at his partner.

"Welcome back," the dark-skinned man with a dark eye patch over his left eye, said with a Slavic accent, "I'm going to ask you some questions. Cooperate with your answers, and I will not need to use this."

He raised a hand-held stun-gun and pressed a button as a bluish spark of high voltage traveled through the prongs.

Winchester felt a deep pounding fear. He realized it was unlikely anyone was coming to his rescue. But he wasn't a coward.

"Fuck you," he yelled.

"Okay, if that's what you want, American."

Winchester, with eyes wide open, saw the man place the prongs to his bare chest and held it there for four seconds. He cried out in pain from the smell of his burning flesh.

Yelling, his body spasmed, and with an intense shaking of his body, he felt himself losing consciousness. Just at the point of passing out, his torturer pulled Stun-gun away from his body.

With a brief chuckle, his torturer said, "You speak now?"

Winchester's eyes rolled up to his head, but he was silent.

The man inched the stun-gun closer to Winchester's chest, "I must have names of all involved in the intercepted message."

Winchester was still silent as he stared at both intruders. "No!"

"Have it your way."

As soon as the prongs on the stun-gun touched his chest, he relented. Within minutes, he gave up the names of his supervisor, and command, with their phone numbers, and other valuable information.

"Good," the man said, nodding to his partner.

The man with the eye patch moved behind Winchester and shot him once in the middle of his skull.

Major Wayne glanced at her watch: five-forty-two. It was time to place the call. She knew her Commander, Colonel Simmons, never left his office early, always waiting until seven when his secretary had left for the day. She was hesitant, though, not sure if this was the right thing to do, or if there was someone higher to whom she could pass on the information. It was too volatile to let unknown hands come into contact with the files. Then, breathing in and breathing out, she picked up the phone's receiver; made sure the secure-link was on and dialed the Colonel's number.

After the second ring, she heard his voice on the other end. "Colonel Simmons."

"Sir, it's Major Jessica Wayne. Is your line secure, sir?"

"Wait one," he replied as he clicked on the secure-link to his phone. "Go ahead, Major."

In a concise, direct tone, she outlined the contents of the encoded message—stopping every so often to catch her breath. She spoke without interruption for several more minutes. Then, she heard a quick intake of breath over the line. Once she'd finished, she waited for his response and direction.

"Dear God, this is very dangerous information," he said, and in a low voice added, "if it's true, major!"

In a dry whisper she said, "Yes, sir, I believe it is."

"Who else knows about this?"

"Lieutenant Alvin Winchester," she replied, "who originally intercepted the message."

"So, besides me, you have told no one else?" Simmons asked.

"No sir, no one else."

"Let's keep it that way for now," Colonel Simmons said, "Until we can corroborate its implications."

She could see the logic behind his words and nodded, "Yes, sir."

"Major, meet me in my quarters and bring your drive with you. I'll expect you around nine tonight."

"I'll be there, sir."

"Good. Call your lieutenant and have him meet up with us as well. Something tells me, we're in danger if this gets out. I need to appraise higher command of this; the sooner the better!"

"Yes sir," she said, lowering her head. "That's why I came to you."

Ending her call, she heard a buzzing on the line, with two almost simultaneous clicks and an echo, as if someone had been listening to the conversation. But how could that be? Seconds later, she shook her head and tried calling Winchester. But after several tries, she gave up.

Knowing the young lieutenant, she reasoned, he was off on a date. She remembered telling him to text her once he'd disposed of the drive and folder. Damn, no text. *Did he do as I asked?* She wondered, afraid of the answer.

She hoped he had.

— 7 —

Having changed into a short-sleeve white dress and sweater with high-heels, Major Wayne arrived at the quarters of Colonel Simmons fifteen minutes before her appointed time.

Parking her vehicle in front of his quarters in Clay Kaserne, she grabbed her purse, pulled out the thumb drive, and placed it in her pocket, slid out of her car, and closed the door. Forgetting the car keys in the ignition, she started walking up the path to his door. Approaching it, she noticed it was ajar. A dim light source from inside spilled out through the crack in the door.

Wayne stood for a moment, glancing at the open door. *That's strange, why would he have left the door open and unattended?*

Calling out his name, she pushed in the door and walked into a small hallway. She hesitated, waited for any sounds, and when she heard none, she continued on into the semi-dark house. She came to an abrupt stop, for sprawled out on the living room carpet, was Colonel Simmons face down in a pool of blood.

"Oh my God!" she exclaimed as a hand flew to her mouth in shock.

Trembling, she ran and knelt by the body, pressed two fingers to his carotid artery, and didn't feel a pulse. Dead! She wanted to yell out, but there wasn't anyone to hear her.

Or was there?

From around the living room corner, two men dressed in grey business suits walked in and didn't stop until they were a foot more or less from the corpse and her, holding guns by their sides. Still clutching her purse, she knew what they wanted, but she wasn't about to give it to them.

"You must be Major Wayne," one with a dark eye patch in broken English said. "You have something that belongs to us. Please hand it over and you can leave here the same way you came in."

She picked up on the Russian accent and shrugged. "I don't know what you're talking about," shocked they knew her name. "How do you know me and did you do—?"

"No, that's not how this works," the other man said. "We ask, you answer. Understand?"

Nodding, she asked, "Your Russians aren't you?"

"That's not your concern," he said. "If you ask another question, I'll shoot one of your legs. Now, stand up and keep your hands out in front of you where I can see them."

Standing, keeping her hands out in front, just as they asked, she kept a hold of her purse. They terrified her! Not having experienced anything like this, she felt a ball of ice deep down in her stomach. Somehow she had to remain calm and not show fear. Her only hope of getting out alive from all this was to have one of them come very close to her, she thought. Then she could act! She had one chance at it.

Wayne soon realized she'd be dead, the moment she handed over what they came for.

As the gunman stopped in front of her, he said, "Raise your arms chest level, so I can search you."

Taking advantage of the semi-dark room, Wayne took a half-step back with her left leg, planted her right foot to the floor, and, as she let her purse drop, she clenched her right fist and delivered an elbow strike to the man's temple. He could have collapsed if she hadn't wrapped her arms around his chest and started dragging him to the living room entrance, using the gunman's body as a shield.

The second gunman froze for a split second. She took quick advantage. Releasing the body, she ran as fast as she could out the opened main door. The gunman ran after her. He fired three shots, not to kill, but to stop her. One bullet plowed through her left shoulder, eliciting a loud yell of pain. She blanched, stumbled, almost falling, but she was close to her car. She opened her car door. Sliding in as two bullets hit the open car door, she noticed the key still in the ignition, and starting it, peeled rubber.

Steering with her left hand, and with blood dripping down her right arm, she drove away. She had to get to *her*. The one person who could help her and take possession of the thumb drive, *she* would know what to do with it, her best friend, CID Agent Jacqueline Sinclair.

But the Russians had a car, too, and they were pursuing her. She had to lose them. Meanwhile, her wound throbbed, but the bleeding had stopped.

The dark skies thundered and lightning cracked in the heavens as rain fell with no signs of stopping. A torrential downpour came next, which left driving through the rain almost impossible and caused flooding in the streets.

It was one-forty-five in the early morning; the skies were still dark, the ground wet as the rain kept falling. Wayne had the car's windshield wipers on full speed, and it was becoming difficult to see through the rain.

She wore only a white short-sleeve dress and no shoes; her hair matted and dirty. It was cold with temperatures at forty-eight degrees and holding.

Earlier, she called another friend, but they seemed to have second-guessed her whereabouts and shot and killed the friend, wounding Jessie again in the process as she once again fled for her life.

Then, after a grueling long drive to the outskirts of Stuttgart, she spied their car still behind her. Then they shot out her front tires. She lost control and careened into a tree. Unhurt, she scrambled from the car and fled before the Russians could get to her.

On foot, Wayne began the trek through the streets of Stuttgart. Thunder and lightning scrawled across the sky, illuminating the otherwise darkened streets as the rain fell. Stumbling, Jesse fell to her hands and knees. Staying alive long enough to reach Jacqueline was her top priority; hoping and praying the Russians didn't know about this friendship. Regaining her feet, and taking one step at a time, she kept going, clutching the small computer thumb drive that held the fate of the world.

Uncertain if she was at or near Jacqueline's apartment for a minute, everything went black. Was she lost? Then she read the street signs and guessed she may have just a block or two further to go. She willed herself to go on.

Then, as the rain settled to a drizzle, she recognized the right house. And, to her relief, she saw *her* apartment from around the corner. Just then, a black two-door sedan speeding around the corner, and with tires screeching, came to a stop in front of the building. Ducking out of sight, she saw two men who looked different from those that followed her exit the car. *My God, how could they have known about my friend? What now?*

Wayne stood in the dark, waiting to decide what to do next. She was all out of options. Jacqueline was her only hope. The police were nowhere in sight, and she'd never make it to a hospital even if she knew where to go.

Jesse willed herself to go on.

Then, from inside the apartment, she heard gunshots. Then silence. After a few minutes she heard more gunshots, this time muffled. Jesse stopped breathing for about twenty seconds as she closed her eyes, and opening them, she saw her friend's silhouette back-lit against a streetlight, standing on the sidewalk with a gun in her hand.

Forcing the last ounce of strength in her body, Wayne crawled on all fours straight to her friend. Bathed in the soft glow of the streetlights, she reached the end of the sidewalk and heard running footsteps.

Reaching Wayne, the friend knelt beside her and cradled her head in her arms. "Jessie, it's me, Sinclair. Don't talk; I'll have an ambulance here in a few minutes. Hang on."

Wayne tried to get up and failed. She pulled Sinclair's face down to her and whispered, "Not ... going ... to make it. Take this ... it will explain everything."

As Wayne opened her hand, the thumb drive slid to the ground beside them. Eyes wide, she drew one last shallow breath, smiling up at Sinclair with content resignation. As her head lolled off to the side,

Sinclair swore she could sense the release of her friend's soul. With a tender caress of Wayne's face, and with tears flowing, Sinclair felt engulfed by sorrow as she closed her best friend's eyes. Sinclair placed two fingers on Wayne's neck, but couldn't find a pulse.

Reaching over and pocketing the thumb drive, Sinclair reached into her pocket and pulled out her cell phone and dialed the Military Police Desk Sergeant, ordering an ambulance and German police to her apartment, along with the duty CID Agent.

Fifteen minutes later, an ambulance arrived with several German police and Military Police vehicles. Sinclair watched with sorrow as they placed Jessie's body in the coroner's vehicle and drive away.

* * *

The military police along with the German police and the duty CID Agent, Ricardo Stubbs, combed her apartment, Sinclair noted. They also accepted her story of getting the drop on the two Russian agents, which was why the apartment resembled a battlefield. They found two dead bodies, shot center mass.

A few minutes later, a red 1969 Chevy Camaro came to a stop alongside the yellow tape markings. From the driver's side emerged her father, Colonel Richard Longstreet Sinclair, the Provost Marshal. He was a tall, broad-shouldered man, with a six-foot-three frame in his mid-fifties.

Meeting her father half-way, she fell into his arms exhausted. He took off his jacket, placed it around his daughter's shoulders, and nudged her toward his car. He held his hand out and she took it. "It was Jessie, Dad," she said in a low measured tone, "she's dead."

Turning his gaze on his daughter, the PM, stunned by her revelation, said, "My *God*, Belle, she was over for dinner just last week." And as he lowered his gaze, he asked, "Do you know how it happened?"

"No, but two goons kicked in my door and tried to kill me. I got the better of them. After that, I went outside thinking there could be more of them and found Jessie. She died in my arms, Dad, but not until she gave me a thumb drive and said it would explain everything."

He nodded in reply.

Catching her breath, she said, "She was my best friend, Dad."

"I know, Belle," her father said, using her nickname. "Let's get you in the car and drive you home to my place, where we can see what's in the drive."

<h1 style="text-align:center">—8—</h1>

Stuttgart, Germany,
Monday, September 9, 7:00 A.M.

It was the breaking news of the morning on German TV.

The rain continued unabated, as dark clouds formed, blocking out the first brightening flush of morning. The U.S. Army military police along with German police maintained their vigil as the crime scene investigators conducted their search for any further physical evidence.

A young blond female newscaster, standing under an umbrella in front of Sinclair's apartment with a microphone in hand, felt the heavy rain pelt her umbrella. She waited until the camera operator focused on her. As the cameraman finished panning the crime scene, he signaled to her, counted down to five with his fingers, and pointed his index finger at her as her cue to start.

With the camera on her, the newscaster raised the microphone to her chin, and waived her arm, taking in the entire outside crime scene. *"We are at the scene of a triple killing,"* she started, *"and with the death of an American female. Late this morning, two armed men attacked an American female identified as a US Army military CID Agent in her apartment. The agent was unhurt in the gunfight when she shot and killed her two assailants."*

With her last statement sinking into her audience, the newscaster fell silent and stared behind her toward the crime scene. A few seconds elapsed when she once again made eye contact with the camera and continued her report...

"The motive is unclear at the moment. The German police, along with the U.S. Army military police at the scene, have yet to identify the two assailants. However, according to the German police, they're assumed to be of Russian descent. A second woman, identified as an American, also died on the street next to the apartment complex. The identity of the second deceased female is unknown. Their investigation is ongoing. U.S. Army military police and the CID are cooperating with German authorities in their investigation. Stay tuned for further developments as we get them. Reporting for the Deutsche Presse–Agentur, from Stuttgart, this is Andre Bauer."

Leaning forward on her leather chair, CID Agent Jacqueline Belle Sinclair was wearing a pair of her father's athletic shorts and a white T-shirt which were too large for her. She grabbed the TV remote, lying on the coffee table in front of her, and shut the TV off. And with her merest understanding of the German language, it was enough to understand the newscast.

It was a mild September morning, as dark clouds turned to blue skies. The early morning sun threw shadows onto the window panes brightening the otherwise darkened living room of her father's on-post military quarters.

She'd only slept two hours. Her throat was dry and somewhat tight. Taking a sip of the warm coffee from the mug she held in her hand, it gave her some relief.

Earlier, after waking, she couldn't stay in bed, and sat in the living room and watched television, while her father, the European Command Provost Marshal, prepared himself for work. Soon it would be her turn to dress and report for duty as the Agent-In-Charge (AIC) of the CID (Criminal Investigation Division) Field office.

When she and her father arrived at his quarters from the crime scene, the first thing Sinclair did was sit in front of her father's computer. Pulling out the thumb drive from her pocket, she inserted it into a USB port and waited for it to populate. Once the computer recognized the drive, she clicked on the folder. With it open, she clicked on one of two files. It opened to a complete gibberish, unrecognized encompassing set of words and figures at random. The second file was also in an encoded mode.

With her father standing behind her, staring at the computer monitor, he said, "Honey, it's an encoded file."

Staring at the obvious, she replied, "I know. And without the proper key, it's useless."

Her father walked around his desk, sat in his leather chair, and leaning forward gazed at his daughter. "First thing this morning," he said, "you must open an investigation and get someone to break the code."

"What are you going to do, Dad?"

"First, I need to brief the commander on all that has transpired last night. And second, the direction you're to take on your investigation. We need to identify those two men that tried to kill you; who wanted Jessie killed, and what the hell is on that drive."

Sinclair nodded her agreement. "It won't be easy. But I'll see what I can come up with."

Bright and early that morning, Sinclair arrived at her office. Canceling her usual morning meeting with her staff, and not reading through the day's MP crime blotter entries, she had the newest agent, Ricardo Stubbs, a Sergeant-first-class, recently assigned to her CID vehicle out front and ready. Stubbs, not more than a week in-country from his last assignment at Fort Bragg, North Carolina, had fifteen years of service, and ten of those as a CID Agent before being assigned for duties at the Stuttgart field office.

Parking the white four-door Chevy Malibu around the back of the CID building, Stubbs walked into his AIC's office and reported that he was ready whenever she was.

Sinclair finished writing her initial report of the last night's affair and looked up at Stubbs. "Sergeant, have a seat," she said. "Since you were the duty agent last night, you and I will handle the investigation on the incident that took place at my apartment."

Stubbs took a seat in one of the three chairs closest to her desk.

"Yes, ma'am."

"Our first stop will be the 64th MI group in Wiesbaden," she said, "Then from there wherever our leads take us. We should be back late tonight. You have any further questions?"

"No, ma'am."

Standing, she opened a drawer and pulled out her Beretta M9 handgun. Releasing the magazine, and making sure a round was chambered, she slapped in the mag and grabbing her purse from the same drawer, opened it, and placed the gun inside.

"Are we expecting trouble, ma'am?"

Sinclair deflected his question with her own "Are you packing, Agent Stubbs?"

He rose, smiling, and opened his two-piece suit jacket, flipped it aside to reveal a shoulder rig with his M9 Berretta snug in the holster.

She walked around her desk and said, "I'm driving; keys, please."

Without a word, Stubbs nodded, handed her the keys, stood aside, and followed her out of the office.

<hr>

As Sinclair drove north on the A5 autobahn, she knew the first thing she had to do was try to retrace the steps taken by her late friend, Major Wayne.

The major had traveled from Wiesbaden to get to her. That, while injured and with Russian assassins chasing her, was quite an accomplishment. Sinclair couldn't imagine what Jessica must've felt, knowing she was her only hope. That took courage.

The nightmare Jessica had gone through was almost staggering to contemplate. She drove on, wondering what she'd find at her office and apartment. Something told her Jessica had some secrets tucked away; maybe the key to the thumb drive?

Christ, she could only hope.

Halfway through the long drive—it would take her almost two-and-a-half hours to reach Wiesbaden driving at top speeds—she would glance every so often at the silent agent sitting next to her. Stubbs had a dark olive tan, with fine features quite striking for a Hispanic. It reminded her of the actor *Antonio Banderas* in his younger years. His hair, that reached down to his shoulders, was almost jet-black with a sprinkle of grey showing and combed straight back as if you were staring at a gangster in the 1930s movies.

"Ma'am, since I presumed we're going to be partners, at least for the duration of the investigation, should I address you by your first name?"

"Chief would do just fine," she replied without missing a beat.

Agent Stubbs nodded, turned his head away from her, and smiled.

Her thoughts turned to Price. *Where was he? Was he alive? And okay?*

Why now? She couldn't put a finger on why. That he was in Afghanistan and wasn't due for several months, left an empty hole in her heart.

It had disappointed her when he mentioned he was being shipped overseas. Their parting was bittersweet. They'd made plans for an engagement party. However, their plans were on hold, just like her life. The last time he called was the previous week, and nothing since then.

Now the murder of her friend kept her going. Finding the murderer and anyone else involved was her job, but more than that, she owed it to her friend.

—9—

They sped north, heading to Wiesbaden and the 64th MI Group Headquarters. Sinclair always made it a point to check her outside and inside rear-view mirrors, scanning for anyone that might be following. Ever since the year before, in her deadly encounters with rogue elements of Special Forces operatives that wanted her dead, she'd kept an eagle eye out for any potential danger. An hour later, with Stubbs fast asleep and confident they weren't being followed, she left the A5 and approached the main gate to the Wiesbaden Army airfield.

Stopped behind two military vehicles, she waited her turn through the gate. The entrance into the Kaserne was the same as several others she'd seen throughout central Germany. On either side of the entrance stood two red and white twenty-five foot long wooden poles, with a brick-stone guardhouse in the center and two MPs, one on either side, directing traffic.

Once waved through, Stubbs woke, glanced to his left and right and stared at Sinclair. "Guess I slept through," he said, yawning and stretching his arms out in front of him.

"That you did, considering, you've been up half the night."

Through the Kaserne she drove, her destination was straight ahead, about a third of a mile. It was Bldg #5, the 64th MI Group Headquarters, and her friend Major Jessica Wayne's place of duty.

Rounding the parade field with the American flag flying full-staff, she found a parking space, pulled in and turned off the engine. Earlier, she'd phoned ahead to the local CID office and command staff as to her arrival. CID Agent Charles Munford would soon meet up with her.

Building 5 was an old Nazi era command center. With a high pitched black roof, four-stories high, with two entrances on either side of the building, it held an elegant, regal pose. In 1933, when the Nazis began a program to build and modernize their military posts throughout Germany, Bldg. 5 was the last one built. As was the norm, they saw several uniformed and civilian attired personnel entering and leaving the building.

On a pleasant September morning with sunny skies, she and Stubbs sat in the car without speaking for several moments. She knew the winter months were almost upon them, and soon the temperatures would drop to the low 30s with heavy snowfalls.

Glancing out the windshield, she saw a flock of birds in the sky flying with the winds. She enjoyed and loved the German summers, but hated its winter's cold. The German winters were often unpredictable; one never knew when a snowstorm was due, or how high the snow would pile.

With a silent sigh, she glanced at Agent Stubbs, and said, "Call the local CID office and have Agent Munford meet us here."

But just then, her cell phone rang.

Without hesitation, she lifted her cell phone from the center console, and pressed the talk button and said, "Agent Sinclair."

The person on the other end said, *"Good morning, ma'am, it's Charles Munford. Just wanting to know what time you'll be arriving."*

Smiling, she said, "I'm here now."

Munford replied. *"Huh, okay. I'll be there in ten minutes."*

"Thank you," she said, ending the call.

It took Munford seven of those ten minutes to arrive in front of the 64th MI Headquarters. He was driving an old white VW bug. Finding a free space, he parked, killed the engine and slid out. Looked around he saw who he believed were Agent Sinclair and her partner standing in back of their vehicle.

Closing the car door behind him, Agent Munford strolled up to her and introduced himself. "Agent Sinclair, I've heard so many stories about you, and here I am face to face with you."

Munford was a lean middle-aged individual, dressed in a two piece black business suit and with grey hair cut short, in the military style. He had an East Coast accent, heavy on the Bostonian side. He was a Chief Warrant Officer, and the AIC of the local office, with 20 year's service, fifteen of those as an agent.

She took the hand as a half-smile played across her lips. "I hope what you've heard is all good, Agent Munford."

"Please, call me Charlie. And yes, if all the stories about you are true."

"Charlie then," Sinclair said, glancing at Stubbs. "This is Agent Ricardo Stubbs."

Agent Munford glanced at Stubbs and after shaking hands, gazed back at Sinclair and said, "The 64th MI Commanding General left for Frankfurt yesterday, I'll get with his adjutant. But I see no problems if you want to start at Major Wayne's office. They cleared this for us."

"I've already cleared it with the adjutant over the phone," Sinclair said. "Let's get to it. I'd like for you and Stubbs to interview Major Wayne's staff, and anyone that has any information relative to our case. I'll take care of Wayne's office."

Munford hesitated.

Sensing his slight hesitation, Sinclair cocked an eyebrow and said, "Is there a problem, Charlie?" She wondered if there was a misunderstanding and whether Munford expected to be in charge of the investigation.

Munford stammered and shook his head. "No, no, ma'am, not at all."

"Let's go then," Sinclair said. "We're wasting time here. We still have her off-post quarters, and those killed who came in contact with her."

Munford remained silent for a moment. When he spoke, it was slow and hesitant. "I left … the reports of those killed back in my office. I … eh, could go back and get them."

As she listened, she felt as if Munford did not care to conduct the interviews. "No need. There's plenty of time for that later."

Instead of answering, he turned his head away from her and gazed at the entrance to MI Headquarters building.

After checking with the adjutant, Stubbs and Munford walked into the office where several of Major Wayne's staff personnel were working. Stubbs counted sixteen individuals, so they divided the workload. One by one, they got written statements from all the witnesses.

One hopeful witness was Sergeant Leroy Brown, the seventh person Stubbs interviewed. His information intrigued the agent, but he waited until the Sergeant signed his statement before divulging his observations to Sinclair.

In Jessie's office, she could sense her presence. Call it a women's thing or a sixth sense, but something happened here. She could almost feel it; something that may have triggered the events that may have led to her violent death.

Walking the circumference of the entire office, Agent Sinclair saw nothing remotely out of place. Coming back around, she stopped behind Wayne's desk, pulled out a chair and sat with her palms on the desk, and glanced left and right, up and down. She was looking ... for what? She didn't know.

Not yet.

Major Wayne's computer was off.

She noticed they had not changed this computer for the new ones that needed a (CAC) card or common access card, which provides rapid authentication and enhanced security for the military. Pressing the power button, she had it on within a few seconds. A logon icon appeared on the monitor. A password and username were necessary to log on, which she didn't have.

Shit, just fucking great. What now?

Sinclair frowned. Leaning forward on the desk, she rested her elbows on the chair's armrest, laced her fingers, and rested her chin on her hands. Knowing the military were stringent on passwords, and the policy of changing them almost twice a month, the CID Agent believed Jessica may have written them down and kept them safe in the event she'd needed them.

Pulling out each drawer from the desk, Sinclair turned them upside down. During physical security surveys, which she conducted at random for all military units in her area of responsibilities, she'd come across this violation of protocols often.

Here it bore fruit!

In the last drawer, the center drawer, she found a taped, small white envelope. Removing it, she opened it, and written on a sheet of paper were Wayne's username and password.

What a stroke of luck!

On a whim, the agent grasped the keyboard, turned it over and noticed a tape script of paper with what resembled an algorithm of some sort and other gibberish typed on it, which she couldn't understand or make heads or tails of.

Now we're getting somewhere!

However, she wasn't sure if she had the key or source of the algorithm Jessica used on the thumb drive. The only way she'd know was to have her computer guys look into it. She pocketed the strip of paper and went back to the computer. She typed in the login information and waited.

As she waited for the computer to populate on the screen, her eyes took in a day-planner on the far left corner of the desk. Sliding it towards her, she noticed a hand-written note to meet Colonel Simmons at his quarters along with Winchester that evening.

Who the hell were Simmons and Winchester? And why was she meeting them so late in the evening? These were burning questions which needed answers.

As soon as the computer showed the main window, Sinclair conducted a complete search of Wayne's main files, her electronic wastebasket, and other miscellaneous files that she could open. But she couldn't find anything incriminating that would reveal why Jessie died. Unless Jessica wiped the information, she reasoned, she'd have to have the hard-drive pulled and sent to the CID lab for examination.

As Stubbs opened the glass door and entered the office, he had a slight smile on his lips. Closing the door behind him, he approached her and placed a handwritten statement on the desk.

"I've interviewed several of the personnel," Stubbs began. "No one could tell me anything of value, except a Sergeant Leroy Brown. He worked with Lieutenant Winchester—"

"Wait," Sinclair said, cutting him off. For the moment, she looked surprised. "You mentioned Winchester. Who is he?"

"That would be Lieutenant Alvin Winchester. He works with a Sergeant Leroy Brown. And these two men's responsibilities are the cyber interceptions of possible classified messages that could be harmful to national security."

This could be it!

But she kept her emotions in check.

"Sergeant Brown, stated," Stubbs continued, "that, on Monday morning, the 9th, he and Winchester were working together, when the warning beeper on his L.T.'s computer went off. The beeper warns of any suspected coded messages. Brown stood behind Winchester as the L.T. scowled through the alert."

Stubbs paused for an instant.

"According to Brown," Stubbs went on. "It was Winchester who intercepted the message, a long string of code that took the L.T. about twenty minutes to break. Brown watched as his L.T. read through the message and heard him shout and exclaim, 'Oh my God. This can't be true.' Brown asked what was wrong, Winchester just shook his head. Brown, a few minutes later, saw the L.T. walk into Major Wayne's office. That was the last he'd seen of the L.T."

Sinclair may have found an answer to the question of what happened in the office, she reasoned, but the coded message was still a mystery.

"Stubbs, have someone go through Winchester's computer and find me that coded message, and anything else that we could use. And find me Lieutenant Winchester, I have questions for him."

"Will do, ma'am," Stubbs replied, walking out of the office.

They'd been in the office for the better part of an hour, and she may have found what she needed, but somehow she still wanted to search Wayne's off-post quarters. Things were looking up, though.

After turning off the computer, she was contemplating her next moves, when unexpectedly Agent Stubbs returned. "Ma'am, we have a problem. According to Agent Munford, Lieutenant Winchester died from a gunshot wound in his on-post quarters."

Sinclair went still and waited a moment to let that sink in. Then she stared at Stubbs for several seconds. "Jesus! What the hell!"

"Guess they killed him for knowing too much."

"You think."

"I tried to gain access to Winchester's computer," he said, "but it was password protected."

"*Shit!*"

—10—

Sinclair nodded to Agent Stubbs after learning of Lieutenant Winchester's death and puzzled over this recent development. Having stepped away from the picture window, she strode over to Wayne's desk.

Pulling back the chair, she sat and gazed out through the glass door toward the outer office where Agent Munford was busy interviewing and getting witness statements when her eyes centered on and locked on the Agent. She thought, remembering what he'd said earlier, about having left the list of those killed back in his office.

Sinclair shifted to one side on her chair and stared straight ahead. *Damn, I could use that list right about now.*

Glancing over at Stubbs, she said, "Stubbs, call Munford and have him come into the office."

"Right away," he replied, adding, "Chief."

Her gaze dropped for a second. As Stubbs was turning to leave, she looked up. "Wait, hang on a moment. Do we have any leads as to the identity of his killer?"

"Not at the moment. But I believe there's a high probability that the killers could have been the two you killed at your apartment."

Sinclair nodded, remembering the gunfight. The killers were professional in every sense of the word in their approach. However, she'd gotten lucky. If not, the outcome would have been different. Yes, she was thinking along those same lines.

Still gazing at Stubbs, she waved her hand and dismissed him.

Once Agent Stubbs strode out of the office, Sinclair leaned back on her chair, as with arms crossed she waited for the agent to make his appearance. Just then, her cell phone buzzed.

Not wanting to answer any calls at the moment, she plucked it out of her purse, and stared at the number displayed on the small screen—the caller was her father, the Provost Marshal. "Shit, what now?" she said before answering it.

"Hello, Dad."

"Hello, Belle," he said, with no further pleasantries, the PM continued. "I have somewhere you need to be before you do anything else."

"I'm all ears, Dad, but I hope this is important, I have a lot going on here that will last a few hours."

"Well, you need to go and soon." Colonel Sinclair's voice intoned toward the dramatic. "You're to make your way over to Reutlinger Strasse, #136, in Stuttgart."

Agent Sinclair frowned, not knowing what to make of this, and in a quiet voice asked, "Why? What's at that address?"

"It's a CIA safe-house. There's been an incident there that could impact your investigation."

Suddenly, her eyebrows shot up. "What type of incident?"

"The deadly type, Belle," he replied. "You're to meet a CIA agent and also, our friend FBI Agent Dan Russell. They'll be waiting for your arrival."

Frowning once again, she asked, "What's a CIA safe-house have to do with my investigation?"

"That's what you're going to determine."

"Is there anything else?"

"Yes, one last thing, you're to have the lead in the investigation at the safe-house. This is coming from high-up, Belle."

"Will I be trampling over someone's backyard, Dad?"

"You could very well be, so stay frosty and don't take any lip from those two."

"You know me, Dad."

Sinclair delayed her departure for Stuttgart long enough for Agent Munford to retrieve the death list. Now with the list in hand, she read through it, surprised by how many had died for what Major Wayne possessed and how many more could yet die to get it.

First to die, according to Munford's investigation and the list, was Lieutenant Alvin Winchester, 64th MI. Second, was Colonel Alex Simmons, Major Wayne's Brigade Commander; the blood trail led to Claire Allen, a close friend of Major Wayne.

There was no telling how many more had died who'd come in contact with Jessica during her flight for life from two suspected FSB agents. However, that was on hold for now.

Unquestionably, someone had to stay back, she thought, and sweep the crime scenes for evidence. The crime scenes were her secondary purpose of being there. So, she had Agent Stubbs stay and coordinate with Agent Munford in conducting the investigation, and do follow-up on any potential leads he may develop.

"But, Agent Stubbs," Sinclair said, "Keep me informed of any developments."

"I understand, ma'am."

Sinclair preferred to stay and do her own investigation, but what her father asked her seemed to have far-reaching implications which may or may not tie-in with what she was investigating—the death of her friend Jessica, the thumb drive and whatever was on it—mattered more than her friend's life.

Alone now, she'd have time on the two-plus hour drive to Stuttgart to piece together reasons she was meeting with a CIA agent and her old friend, Daniel Russell.

Scenario after scenario played out in her mind. However, she couldn't make any sense out of them.

—11—

Headquarters, Russian Defense Ministry,
Arbatskaya Square, Moscow

On a sunny but wintery afternoon for September, with a high predicted to be in the mid-60s, the sixty-five-year-old Chief of the General Staff, General Pyotr Ivanovich stepped out of his car and nodded to his chauffeur. Setting his military hat on, he turned up the collar of his thick woolen military coat. Placing his sunglasses on, he jammed his hands into the coat's pockets, and strode toward the guarded entrance of the vast complex that was the Russian Defense Ministry building.

As he reached the two guards at the entrance, he presented his credentials and removed his sunglasses. After a few minutes, once they made a complete identification, they allowed him to proceed.

He proceeded through the eight-story building, the walls of which were of marble, Ural stones, serpentine and granite, and stopped at the banks of elevators. He stepped into an empty one and rode it to the fifth-floor housing a secured conference room.

General Ivanovich thought, with a hint of a smile, he may have beaten his two comrades, but waiting in the conference room were the Ministry of Defense, Viktor Mordvinov, and the head of the FSB, Sergei Vannovsky. Both men were in their mid to late sixties, and both appeared pale with haggard expressions of worry written on their faces.

He knew what they were feeling. He felt the same way when things weren't going according to plan.

Having entered the conference room without a word, General Ivanovich gave them a curt nod as he made his approach. As the two others in the room watched, the general stopped and stood by the conference desk, removed his coat and draped it over an empty chair, pulled out another chair, and sat facing them from across the desk.

The general sat back in his chair and set his gaze on the two across from him. "I've received a communiqué from our embassy in Frankfurt, with some very disturbing news. It would seem the Americans have rescued Anisi Sverchinsky ... right from under our noses—"

"Hold on, sir," Mordvinov interrupted. "Please excuse me, but the prison at Murmansk ... wasn't that supposed to be impregnable? What could have gone wrong?"

The general shifted his gaze from one to another. "According to our intelligence report and satellite imaging, it's believed an American SEAL team extracted our prisoner."

"So you're saying the Americans have him now," Mordvinov said. "That is terrible news, but what about our plans, Comrade General?"

Ivanovich sat forward, placed his hands on the desk, and laced his fingers together. "Let's discuss those questions later," he replied. "Right now we have more pressing matters to deal with."

"I have more disturbing news, comrade," Vannovsky cut in. "They took Sverchinsky to a CIA safe-house in Germany. Our embassy sent a team of FSB commandos to extract him. They killed several of our commandos in the attempted rescue. However, Sverchinsky escaped and his whereabouts are unknown."

Vannovsky paused. "Also, Comrade General, as we well know the American military intelligence in Germany intercepted the encoded message we received through channels from one of our retired KGB operatives. The message outlined Sverchinsky's plans to use our seven bombs which, indirectly, we, eh, gained for him, and betrayed us, general."

There was another pause, after which Vannovsky continued. "Our agents at our embassy in Germany tracked down all those knowledgeable of the message and eliminated them. We know the last person who came in contact with it was a CID American agent named Jacqueline Sinclair, whom we believe still has possession of it. She alone killed two of our best agents. We also know that the Americans have placed a CIA operative and an FBI agent to investigate along with the CID agent and they might decode the message if they haven't done so already."

General Ivanovich slowly withdrew his hands and nodded. "Just a few days after Sverchinsky's arrest," he said, "We found evidence to suggest he may have been a double agent for the Americans."

Vannovsky and Mordvinov glanced toward General Ivanovich for a moment. Both knew well, they realized, this could be the end of their plans to take over the government. They feared for their lives if the Kremlin got wind of it. But if they worked together, there were ways to still achieve victory. They would stay and continue planning.

"Don't distress yourself, comrades," General Ivanovich said, "We'll get around this minor setback soon. Which leads us to what we can do in stopping the American agents, Sverchinsky, and his plans?"

There was a brief, awkward silence.

Vannovsky cleared his throat, nodding. "There is a solution, Comrade General. The FSB has two teams of commandos in training at the Tartus base in Syria's northern seaport. They're a twelve-man team. I can have a team of five of the best ready to go within a few hours that could do the job. Just need your okay, sir."

Without hesitation, General Ivanovich glanced at Vannovsky and nodded his agreement.

"We have a female Field Grade FSB officer," General Ivanovich said, "A Lieutenant Colonel Elizaveta Borovkov, at the Frankfurt Embassy, who has been monitoring the activities of her FSB agents. I want her to be in command of the team from Syria."

"It shall be as you say, sir," Vannovsky replied.

General Ivanovich nodded, leaned forward, and said, "One other thing Comrade, before they engage the Americans, I must have the Sverchinsky plans secured beforehand."

General Vannovsky nodded.

"Now to our further plans," Ivanovich said.

—12—

Three Hours Later

Pulling in behind a black converted Ford E-450 truck marked FBI *Command Vehicle* at the CIA safe-house in Stuttgart, with another truck parked closer to the house, marked *Evidence Response Team*, Sinclair turned off the engine, and slid out of the car. Slipping on her short brown leather coat and her sunglasses, she closed the driver's door and made her way toward the side of the command vehicle.

At the doorway, Agent Sinclair met FBI Agent Daniel Russell, the head of the US Embassy FBI Special Strike Unit, out of Frankfurt. Shutting the door behind her, once she entered the truck and after a friendly hug, Russell said, "Damn, Sinclair, it's sure, pleasant setting eyes on you again."

Agent Sinclair blushed as she gazed at Russell. "Since the last time we met, I never thought I'd see you again."

"Hell neither did I."

Taking in at a glance the interior of the truck, she saw a desk set into a sidewall with four laptop computers, along with two large-screen televisions mounted on the wall, and four captain chairs set off to the front of the cab. To one corner was a sink, a small refrigerator, and a pot of coffee brewing. Lighting was subdued with pockets of dark areas. It took her a minute or two for her eyes to adjust.

She then noticed a woman standing off to one side she took to be an agent. With the practiced eyes of a seasoned criminal investigator that she was, Sinclair sized her up; she was young, thirty-ish, attractive, and of medium height, wearing a black, tight-fitting leather V-neck long-sleeve jumpsuit, and black round toe-pumps; a brunette with a tight donut style hair bun, with a small two-inch scar under her left eye. She appeared to have had her nose broken at one time as it appeared bent.

"Agent Sinclair, let me introduce CIA Agent Patricia Courtney. She'll be joining the team for a few days."

Agent Courtney stepped forward out of the semi-darkness of her corner and stopped a few feet from Sinclair, who noticed Courtney's grey eyes kept staring at her.

Fair enough, Sinclair thought, as she returned Courtney's stare.

"I've heard so much about you," Courtney said with a ghost of a smile on her lips, and her right hand extended. "So glad you could make it."

Sinclair took notice of a Southern California accent from the agent. Much like one of her friends once observed: *They make the sound as if someone put a numbing agent on their tongues.*

Jacqueline Sinclair inclined her head and shook the proffered hand

The CID agent sighed but didn't say a word, as she heard faint disapproval in the agent's voice, which rather irritated her. She appeared not thrilled with working with a criminal investigator; and a female.

Russell took in a deep breath, glanced at the two women, and sensed a slight tension between them. "Ladies, please take a seat so we can get this party started."

Sinclair waited until she sat, then asked. "So, agent Courtney, tell me what happened in your safe-house."

The CIA agent, still standing, wore a smile, and replied. "Please, since we're going to be working together, you can call me, Pat."

Sinclair cleared her throat. "Pat, then."

Courtney hesitated. "Well, most of what I'm about to say, I briefed Russell on. However, for your benefit, I'll start from the beginning."

Courtney reached for a pack of cigarettes from the table, pulled one from the box, lit it with a book of matches, and took a deep drag.

"As Russell is well aware, the house behind us is one of our more secure safe-houses. That being said, yesterday, a SEAL team extracted a Russian agent, code name Theseus, out of a Russian prison, and transported him here for questioning. What that questioning is, my instructions were to give you both a brief rundown of the facts. But first, this morning a team of Russian FSB agents, assaulted the house, killed all those in it, with our prisoner vanishing. Whether the FSB had taken him or escaped is still uncertain. Although, it's suspected Theseus escaped. That being the case, my orders are to get him back and into our control at all costs. This is a National Security affair. I'm to render any means at my disposal in recapturing him and releasing him over to the CIA."

They fell into silence.

Sinclair took a few shallow breaths. She wasn't buying it. Something wasn't right here. But she waited until Courtney expounded on those *Brief rundown facts*. And so far, she still didn't know what part she played in this, a CIA case, and how they fucked it up.

Sinclair shifted in her chair. "Tell me about those brief facts you mentioned."

For a moment Courtney didn't answer. Then she cleared her throat. "Very well: Fact, Theseus is a double agent. He was working for us as an undercover Russian FSB agent. Fact, someone may have stolen the plans, described as the start of World War Three."

Sinclair and Russell both stared at each other. Then back at Courtney, who was still speaking.

"Fact, the 64th MI group intercepted those plans. Who may have them is unknown. Those are some facts in a nutshell. Other than that, for the time being, I'm not at liberty to divulge any further information."

At last, there it was, Sinclair thought. It was the intercepted plans on the thumb drive everyone was after, and it was the reason her friend Jessica Wayne, and those that came in contact with her, met their deaths. However, she wasn't about to confess her possession of it, not just yet. It was her ace in the hole, and she wasn't about to fold. Plus, she needed to know what the plans entailed.

Only one other person knew she had the drive; her father; so safe for the time being.

Sinclair sighed. "*Bullshit!* You can do better than that."

Russell shifted in his seat. He gazed at one, and then at the other woman, but didn't say a word.

Courtney dropped her cigarette on the floor and stepped on it. Then she nodded and gazed at Sinclair, and then at Russell. "In the folder in front of me is the complete dossier on Theseus. It's in the spirit of cooperation that it's being given to you, hoping it can lead us to him."

Courtney took in a deep breath and slid the file over to Sinclair. "But, that's as far as I can go with any more information. The rest lies in your hands."

For several seconds they remained in silence, as Sinclair reached for the dossier, flipped it open, and gazed at a photograph of the man they called Theseus. She stared at a man in his late thirties, rugged appearance, with a short fade black hair-style and blue-grayish eyes that sparked intelligence behind them. The dossier was three pages long, amid contacts, friends, and other relevant information she may well have to fall back on. But it contained just enough for her to launch the manhunt.

—13—

The Tartus, Russian Military Naval base,
Syria's Northern Seaport

Captain Alexei N. Kuznetsov finished the last day of a two-week training session with his team and now was looking forward to some much-needed rest; some drinking, the soft caress of a woman, and a two-week vacation promised for his team and their families.

The forty-five-year-old, a divorced former member of an elite military police unit, and the captain of his Alpha Unit FSB Special Forces team was walking away from his team preparing to head to his barracks. Removing his grey fur military *Ushanka* hat with its pull-down ear-muffs, he wiped the sweat off his brow with the back of his hand.

He still was sweating after finishing the grueling training with his men. Replacing the hat, he kept walking through the base's sand-blown ground, windswept from miles inland. He'd hoped to meet again the woman he'd been keeping company with for the last week. He planned to spend his remaining few days at the base, locked up at her home.

The H&K-416 assault rifle he carried was getting a little heavy in his hand, so he slung it over his back, and shoved his hands in his coat pockets. The walk, about half-a-mile, always invigorated him, and the solitude it brought was bliss to his senses. From the age of eighteen, he had seen more than of his share of blood and death. He could recall the faces of every kill he'd made, and his nightmares guaranteed endless sleepless nights.

He was the team leader of one of the most elite counterterrorism units in Russia. It comprised a twelve-man team, with the best of ex-Russian soldiers and military police officers ever assembled. Special Forces Operational Detachment Alpha A (SFOD-A), had taken part in several operations in various parts of the world and involved in the 1993 constitutional crisis, the Nord-Ost theatre, and the Beslan hostage crisis.

His solitude and lascivious thoughts brought a smile to his lips with his anticipation of being with *her* ... only, it didn't last.

"Comrade, Captain," a shrill voice called out from behind him. "Please wait, sir."

Coming to a halt, Kuznetsov turned and saw the FSB Group administration clerk running almost at a dead run straight at him.

Dressed in his winter outdoor gear with his heavy thick woolen coat, Kuznetsov felt warm, and although it was a mild winter, the chilly winds made it feel much colder than the current 47 degrees.

Coming to a stop an arm's length from the captain, the admin clerk, Private Anna Tatiana, came to attention and rendered a hand salute.

"Comrade Captain, sir," she said, "The general's staff wants you in their office, sir."

"What's this about, Tatiana?"

"I don't know, sir," Tatiana replied, and lowering her gaze from his grey steady eyes, added, "But ... I believe it may be a mission, Comrade Captain."

Nodding, and offering a smile, it had impressed him she knew that much. She was intelligent, and rather pretty, too, with soft auburn hair and delicate blue eyes.

"Tell them I'll be there."

"Yes, sir."

The conference room was like a small fortress, he thought. It had white cinderblock walls and a seven-foot-long wide table with six chairs. Mounted along three of the walls were several television screens. There were also various computers, and he saw two video cameras mounted high on either side of the back wall.

Kuznetsov glanced at the video cameras. They weren't in recording mode, not seeing any red indicator lights on them. So he figured the meeting was being kept secret.

"May I ask what this is about, Comrades?" he asked as he took his seat, glancing at the two men seated in front of him. One of whom he recognized as General Valery Zaitsev, the current FSB Assistant Commander, and the other a colonel he'd not seen before.

"Captain," General Zaitsev said, "We have ordered you and your team to Germany, on a classified mission, on orders from the Ministry of Defense and the head of the FSB. I shouldn't need to tell you, but you are of course not to speak of this to anyone."

There was a moment of silence after the general spoke.

Kuznetsov's gaze rested on the general for a moment and then shifted over toward the colonel sitting on the general's left. The man's countenance was impassive. He had an oval face, prominent forehead, a pencil-thin mustache, and wore wire-framed glasses, which he kept pushing up on his nose. From the moment he set eyes on the colonel, he took offense. Not for whom he was, but what he represented—old KGB.

Holding a steady gaze on him, Kuznetsov said, "I understand, Comrade General."

There was a slight pause.

"Colonel Yuri Agrapov, from the office of the Ministry of Defense, and I just arrived from Moscow for this briefing," the general said at last. "Colonel Agrapov will brief you on the mission."

Agrapov stood, pushed his glasses up on his nose, and walked around one side of the table, and stopped in front of the captain. "We handpicked you, Captain ... and your team, for this vital mission. I am of the understanding that your unit operates as a twelve-man team. Is this correct?"

"Yes, Comrade Colonel."

"So, it's safe to say that a five-man team would not be ... shall we say ... unusual?"

"No, Comrade, but a twelve-man team is necessary for the successful completion of any mission. There are specific talents that go into a team, and without the full resources of those talents in the unit, I would consider it unfavorable to have less."

The colonel glanced at General Zaitsev and nodded. Then he stared at Captain Kuznetsov, raised his brow, and pushed up his glasses once again. "For this mission, Comrade Captain, you will pick only five, including yourself. The mission will be short and requires only a small fraction of your team to be successful."

There was no use arguing the point any further, Kuznetsov told himself. At least until he heard what the mission entailed. "I see, Comrade Colonel, but I must protest."

"And you are in your right, however, it will do you no good," Colonel Agrapov said, in a tone suggesting it wasn't a request. "Your mission will be an armed excursion into Germany. You will arrive by air transport, and once on the ground, you'll meet your transportation, and taken to our embassy. There you will contact Lieutenant Colonel Elizaveta Borovkov, the head of the local FSB unit."

There was a momentary silence.

Kuznetsov couldn't believe he and a short-handed team were being sent out on what was another *wet-job*. On one hand, he didn't speculate on why they picked his team, only which it was his duty as a soldier of the *Rodina-mat* or *mother-land*. But on the other hand, it got him away from Russia and Moscow, which he considered the most dreadful place in Russia.

Turning away from the captain, the colonel started walking back around to his chair. "She will take command of your Alpha Unit ... with you as its second in command. Captain, your mission involves the elimination of certain American agents and the capture of a Russian spy. Comrade Colonel Borovkov will brief you and your team and offer you all the help to carry out your orders."

Son of a *bitch!* Captain Kuznetsov wanted to shout. For one, they wanted only a five-man team that he could understand; then they took his command and gave it to a woman. He'd trained and fought with his men on countless missions. They were a cohesive and productive team.

But a woman!

Shit!

As Colonel Agrapov stopped at his chair, Agrapov sat with his arms crossed; his face a deadpan expression. "Are there questions, Comrade Captain?"

Kuznetsov nodded, glancing at them both. His face not showing the contempt he felt for the colonel and their mission. "When do we leave?" he asked.

"Tonight," General Zaitsev said.

There goes our vacation, Captain Kuznetsov mused.

Within the team's barracks, all was silent, as they waited for their captain to brief them on their next mission.

With the twelve-man team gathered around him, he'd already decided whom he was taking with him into Germany. Those that he'd picked would be jealous they would not be going on vacation and would wonder why he'd picked them. And the grateful were those staying who at last would be with their families back in Russia. However, these were his men, his team, and they would understand.

They always did.

"Ok, so here's the story, I can only take four of you on this mission," he said while holding a clipboard and a pencil. "When you hear your name, gather your things and get set; we leave within two hours."

Staring around at his men, he felt proud to work with every single one of them. He didn't know the whole mission parameters, nor did he know the targets that needed eliminating. The danger appeared minimal. The five of them should be enough, he thought, in accomplishing the mission.

"My second in command is Anatoly Sokolov." As he called out to each man, they stood and moved off to the side, preparing their gear. "Next is Bogdan Volkov, sniper. The explosive man is Damir Semenov. And last my communications man will be Svetozar Belyaev."

Dropping his clipboard to his side, he fell silent for a few seconds as he stared at those who would not be going. He couldn't tell if it was joy or disappointment on their faces. They were professionals with strong moral character.

With a sigh and a smile, he said, "The rest of you, get out of here and have a great vacation."

<h1 style="text-align:center">—14—</h1>

Agent Stubbs was ecstatic to be working alone again. Although he respected the company of Chief Sinclair, it just wasn't the same. She'd given him the responsibility to conduct the crime scene investigation, and he would not let her down, or himself. Homicide and suicide were his specialized skills or expertise. He was no Sherlock Holmes, but after nine years of honing his skills, his arrest and prosecution rate were on a par with other more experienced agents.

According to Agent Munford, as Stubbs prepared to leave the CID office, pressing office business and unfinished investigations would keep him and his two agents busy. He was to work alone. If Stubbs needed help, Munford would see what he could do to help.

Somehow, Stubbs felt he was being given the brush-off. Though not concerned about it, it suited him just fine.

With the case file in his possession, and with supporting witness statements, Stubbs was now behind the wheel of a government car provided by Munford. He decided he'd head over to Clay Kaserne, to the quarters of Colonel Simmons, and then onto Lieutenant Winchester's BOQ. What did he expect to find at the crime scene that the investigators didn't? He couldn't answer. But his investigation will be more thorough instead of the cursory efforts they gave it.

Experience had taught him that, in most homicide investigations, it's the undiscovered pieces of evidence not found which could have a tremendous impact on the identification of suspects or subjects, and establishing guilt or innocence. A crime scene can take days or weeks to process, and more often than not, evidence may not present itself to those looking for it during the first or maybe the second go around. The adage, of having an extra pair of eyes, seemed quite fitting.

Arriving at the Simmons' quarters, it didn't take him but fifteen minutes to determine he could learn nothing further than what the reports in the file reflected.

Getting back to his car, the next stop was Winchester's BOQ. Pulling away from the quarters, Stubbs failed to take notice of an SUV, with two male occupants pulling out from the opposite side of the street and began following him.

Several minutes later, he arrived at the BOQ. Concerned more with his investigation than what was going on around him, he once again failed to take notice of the same SUV pulling up to his car and stopping directly behind it. As the two men watched the agent enter the building, they exited their car, and not in any sort of hurry, they both walked up to the entrance. Wearing dark two-piece suits and dark sunglasses, one entered the lobby and took a seat next to the entrance, while the other stood outside the entrance and waited, as several soldiers entered or exited the quarters.

———— · ———— · ————

Once on the third-floor landing, Stubbs found room 316. The door leading into the room had yellow police tape in an X with the door locked. He pulled a key from his pocket, provided to him by Agent Munford, inserted it into the lock, and turned the key. Grasping the doorknob and turning it once, he pulled away some police tape and nudged the door open.

He stopped, struck by a strong lingering smell that assailed his nostrils—the stench of death. The putrid odor of decay was something he'd rather forget, although it would never leave him after countless homicide cases he'd investigated.

Entering the room, he controlled the urge to gag. Instead, he put on his blue plastic gloves. The room was in shambles. They'd overturned every piece of furniture and threw the closet clothing on the floor. He first concentrated on the living room. They tied the body down to that chair.

Removing several photographs from the file which showed the body's position still in the chair, he noticed they took the photographs from several angles. One by one, he scanned the photographs, but there wasn't anything that he could learn from them. Taking several steps toward the chair, he noticed a large pool of congealed blood surrounded the spot where they tied, tortured, and killed Winchester.

Not sure as to the cause of death, Stubbs pulled the English translation of the German coroner's report and read: '*There were several burn marks found on the chest and neck of the deceased. These are indicators that some type of Taser-type weapon used left several prong marks that caused multiple, erratic burn marks which showed the deceased twitched and thrashed during the result of the weapon's shock effect.*'

But the Taser wasn't the cause of death.

That was a bullet to the head.

They tortured him for information. That was clear enough. The specifics remained unknown. Taking a wild guess, he thought it may have something to do with the information Winchester provided to his superiors. That would be his logical conclusion. Once they had what they wanted, they killed him.

Did Winchester hold up to the torture and give up the information, or did he take it with him to the grave? Stubbs wondered.

These were questions, for which he had no answers. Questions he knew Chief Sinclair would ask as well.

Placing the photographs back in the folder, he laid it on a chair and prepared to walk the crime scene. On the floor by the overturned dining table, Winchester's laptop was lying on its side. From the crime scene report, the computer was missing its hard-drive. There was no mention of it being recovered by the investigators. So, it would appear, the perps may have possession of it.

Scanning through the apartment, he glanced over at the refrigerator, which was still standing. On its door were four photographs pinned with plastic fridge magnet holders. He approached it and studied the photographs.

Two of the photographs showed the back wall and window of the living room, with whom he assumed was Winchester with his arm around a lady friend sitting on the sofa smiling, and staring up at whoever snapped the photo. They seemed a happy couple. But what caught his eye was toward the left side of the photograph.

He did a double-take, for in the photo there wasn't a framed picture on either side of the wall. However, when he scanned the room, an oil painting depicting a large vase of flowers was hanging to the left of the window.

Turning his head to the side, and raising his brow, several questions came to mind.

Stubbs glanced again at the photograph. Did Winchester purchase the painting after he took the photo, or before?

He mused in silence for a few seconds. *When did he hang the painting?* He kept asking himself. *Or am I reading more into this than I should?*

With light steps, and shaking his head, he strode forward to the painting. Taking it down, he turned it over on its back. At a glance, he saw nothing unusual, until he noticed a small two-by-two inch slit in the form of an L which appeared toward the bottom left-hand corner of the brown backing paper. A piece of clear scotch tape covered the slit.

Getting the dining table back upright, he set the painting on the tabletop. Removing the tape, he pulled a corner of the paper, and there taped to the painting's canvas was a small Micro-SD Card.

What was on the card that made the lieutenant conceal it in that manner, and who was he hiding it from? He mused.

Too many questions, not enough answers.

Pulling out his cell phone, he dialed Sinclair's number. After the third ring, her voicemail came on. "Found an SD card taped on the backside of a painting in Winchester's BOQ. Not sure what's on it. All finished here. I'll leave right away for Stuttgart. See you in a few hours."

Clicking off his phone, he jammed it into his pocket, picked up the file folder, and made his way out of the room. Locking it, he turned and made his way down the stairs. A few minutes later, and once in the lobby, he headed for the main entrance door, just as a man dressed in a business suit rose from his chair and followed him.

The late afternoon winds brought a chill to the air, which Stubbs welcomed after the foul stench of the room. Buttoning his two-piece suit jacket, and tucking a hand in his pocket while holding onto the file folder with the other, he headed towards his car. It wasn't a busy sidewalk, and the street he was on had one or two passing motorists.

The other man, the partner to the first and standing alongside the entrance, drew a Sig Sauer P-365 9mm suppressed handgun and held it by his side, and stepped in front of Stubbs about two arms length ahead, as the other man followed right behind, and he also drew a suppressed handgun.

Not in any hurry, Stubbs strolled toward his car. From behind him, suddenly, he felt the poke of something metallic jammed into the small of his back, and his left arm grabbed from behind.

Before he could jerk his arm from the grasp, he heard someone speak with what sounded like a Russian accent, "Don't make any sudden moves, or I'll kill you!"

Then he heard a distinct clicking sound of a gun's hammer being drawn back and knew it wasn't a piece of pipe in his back! From behind he heard the man say, "Walk faster toward the man by the car."

Stubbs knew he couldn't draw his weapon or try anything that could free himself without getting killed. He just has to wait for a better scenario to present itself. And he did not know what they wanted.

But he'll know soon enough.

The man behind him seemed to be the leader of the two. The man by the car was about medium height, short blond hair, muscular looking. "In the car," the man said.

It was a black Ford SUV. The guy motioned with his gun, letting Stubbs know they were both armed. Once Stubbs was sitting in the back seat, the man who stood behind him sat with him and kept his gun trained on him.

The other man came around and sat behind the wheel. The man next to Stubbs reached over and pulled Stubbs jacket flap, revealing his handgun. Removing it, he tucked it in his belt. Next, he reached into Stubbs front jacket pocket, where he kept his credentials and pulled that out as well.

This is so surreal! Stubbs thought.

Both of his captors started talking in what the agent now knew was Russian.

The man sitting next to him, muscles attesting to the large bulge in the tight suit he wore, stocky chest, blond-haired, and taller than his friend, said, "We have an American military police officer with us."

The driver replied, "So much better."

Stubbs wished he knew what they were saying. So, staring at one and turning his stare at the back of the driver's head, he said, "Hey, assholes, speak English."

Then his instincts kicked in, but the agent was a little slow to react. With clenched teeth, the Russian next to him struck Stubbs on the side of his head; a hard felt elbow strike.

Shaking off the blow, Stubbs felt groggy. Regaining his composure, he raised his hand to the spot where they struck him and pulled away a trickle of blood. With a shrug, he blinked, trying to shake off the effect of the blow, and held his head down.

The driver turned back around and glanced at Stubbs, "Soon, policeman ... soon."

He was motionless, tied down to a chair in a semi-darkened shed, illuminated by light from strings of bare hanging bulbs. The floor covered with straw. All his senses were alert. There were various smells: Animal smells, and he knew where he was being held—a barn. He was aware of his captors standing in front of him; one holding a long-bladed knife, and the other pointing a gun at his chest.

Stubbs knew what was to come—torture—unless he gave up what they wanted. Even if he did, he knew they would kill him. He started breathing deeply. With Lieutenant Winchester's image burned into this consciousness from the crime scene photographs, he knew they would subject him to the same fate. His heart started beating faster. There was no way he could pull himself out of his predicament. Death would be his only release.

Strange, he thought, that it didn't shock him as much as it should. He stared at the two Russians with a stoic expression.

The taller of the two Russians said, "You were in Winchester's room, policeman. We have what you found. What does it say?"

Stubbs didn't say a word and just stared at the Russian.

"You will talk soon," the second Russian promised while holding a knife. Then he plunged the knife into Stubbs's left thigh, about an inch or a little more.

He felt the knife going into his leg. Keeping his eyes closed, he felt like yelling but didn't. Stubbs felt the sensation of warmth, with a tinge of ice like coldness, and an intense pain that surged throughout his body.

"Tell us what you found, policeman," the Russian with the knife kept repeating.

"Fuck you, asshole," Stubbs said, as blood dripped down his leg and he felt the wetness down his pants. He knew he was losing a sizable amount of blood, and there wasn't anything he could do to stop it.

Down went the knife again, this time it was twisted left and right, up and down. He yelled and yelled, but the Russian twisted the knife and again and again. His ears were ringing with excruciating pain, and he was at the point of losing consciousness, when the Russian pulled out the knife. Then he passed out.

They threw water at his face and the coldness of it shocked him awake. How long he'd been unconscious, he didn't know.

"Tell us, policeman," the Russian with the gun asked, "and you'll not die."

Pulling his shirt open, the Russian with the knife carved an X on Stubbs's naked chest. Soaked in his blood, he howled and thrashed in the chair. Then yelling like a banshee, he asked them to stop. It was too much. He couldn't take the torture any longer, and as his eyes rolled up, he told them what they wanted to know.

The taller Russian nodded in satisfaction. He told his partner, "Kill him."

—15—

"So, tell us, how should we proceed?" Courtney asked, leaning forward, extinguishing her cigarette in the ashtray, and resting her arms on the desk.

Glancing over at Russell, she noticed him sitting back in his chair next to her, nodding and staring over across the desk at the CID agent. Courtney wondered if he too was thinking along the same lines as her.

In the FBI *Command Vehicle*, they'd been back and forth on the Theseus dossier for the better part of two hours. Concentrating on the photo of Theseus lying in front of her, Sinclair suspected the double agent could very well have gone to ground or was doing so.

If that was the case, he would be difficult, if not impossible, to track. Did he have friends in Germany, and would he try to contact them, or stay out of areas he knew could get him caught? Staring at the man's eyes, Sinclair knew he wasn't stupid; so, finding a safe, unknown place from which to live and work was his only hope.

Maybe somewhere not recognizable to anyone; before that, he would need transportation. He wouldn't stay with the vehicle he'd stolen from the safe-house, which was an easy bet. There were ample places where he could steal a vehicle.

Christ, this is going to be difficult. I must play this by ear, Sinclair thought.

Agent Sinclair would need help, though. Help from her agents and the FBI. However, her dissatisfaction lay with the dossier itself and Agent Courtney. She had a strong feeling the file was incomplete. Things were missing from it. Or was it just shoddy work on their part? Her conclusion, intentionally, done. The agent also believed Courtney knew more than what she let on.

Ok, but why? She asked herself.

For a time, Jacqueline Sinclair thought no more of it, as she closed her eyes. Then, her eyes snapped open when her cell phone vibrated in her pocket. Reaching for it, she pulled it out. The call was from Stubbs. He'd left a voicemail. Clicking it on, she raised the phone to her ear: *"Found an SD card taped on the backside of a painting in Winchester's BOQ. Not sure what's on it. All finished here. I'll leave right away for Stuttgart. See you in a few hours."*

Pocketing the phone, Sinclair wondered if Stubbs may have found a copy of the message he'd intercepted. But why would he be hiding it, and what was he going to do with it?

These were questions that would have to wait until Agent Stubbs return. She'd keep the information to herself for the time being.

She flipped through page after page, checking again, making sure she hadn't missed a thing. The interior of the vehicle was silent. Courtney and Russell stared at Sinclair as she read through the dossier, remaining still.

Sinclair's head bobbed up and down. "All right," she finally said, as she stared at the CIA Agent. "Courtney, I'll need a complete background on your man. I need to know if he has any Russian friends that may live here in Europe, anywhere he could find refuge with, to include phone numbers, addresses. These are things I didn't see in your dossier. The sooner I have them, the sooner I can set about to capture the asshole."

"I'll see what I can do," Courtney said, tensely.

Agent Sinclair reacted instantly, "Not good enough. Try harder."

Courtney pouted, swallowed a sharp reply, and instead stared right at Sinclair.

Sinclair thought that maybe the CIA agent was becoming annoyed with her. And judging by her slight facial grimaces, she believed the Agent wasn't all that thrilled being on the case.

Sinclair didn't care; she had a job to do.

The two women locked eyes on each other for a few seconds.

Dropping her gaze from Sinclair, and without another word, Courtney pulled her cell phone from her pocket, stood, walked away from the desk, and dialed the CIA personnel operations section chief in Langley, Virginia. Courtney spoke in hushed tones, which Sinclair couldn't make out.

Turning to Russell, she said, "Dan, I would like you to coordinate with the German Federal Police, and the local police, and get an APB out on him. Plaster his face on German television. Tell them he's a suspected murderer, armed and dangerous. Then set up a command center to answer calls from the police. Get the description of the vehicle he stole from the safe-house to the local German police. I'll have all MP entrances into all local military installations covered with his photo. There's something else, Daniel. See if you can get the German police to search within, say, a twenty-mile radius from his last known location. Maybe go door-to-door. It's worth a try."

"I'll get right on it."

Courtney fell silent for a moment, cupped her phone, and turned her gaze on Russell. "You have a fax machine in the vehicle?"

"Yes," Russell replied.

Relaying the fax information to Langley, Courtney a moment later jammed her phone back in her pocket and turned toward Sinclair. "The information you requested on the Theseus file will come through shortly."

It was an hour later when the CIA file on Theseus came through; all four pages of it. Standing by the fax machine, Courtney retrieved the file, turned around, and gave it to Sinclair without leafing through it.

With file in hand, the Top Secret designation marked on the cover wasn't loss on Sinclair, which suggested maybe prominent players were at work here and wondered how high up the chain it went. Once the three sat around the table, she flipped over the covering sheet and read over all the pages. Not once, but twice.

Knowing how the CIA wasn't that forthcoming with their information, Sinclair shook her head, not surprised to see a thin file. Hell, she half expected it.

With coffee and donuts brought in earlier on the table between them, Courtney and Russell ate and drank their coffee in silence as they waited.

Several minutes passed.

Russell and Courtney leaned back in their chairs. Courtney lit another cigarette.

Then ninety seconds.

With arms about his chest, Russell frowned and gazed at Sinclair. "Well, Sinclair, what's in the file?" he asked.

Courtney's curiosity also piqued, she asked. "What's wrong?"

"I'm afraid, we're going to rethink this through," Sinclair said, gazing up at the two agents. "From what I've finished reading, things aren't what they presume to be."

"Oh ... and in what way?" Russell asked.

Sinclair sighed and glanced over at both Russell and Courtney, then spoke in measured tones. "Well, listen to this. The man we're after is an American of Russian descent. The families were members of the dominant Slavic-speaking ethnic group of Russia. At age two, his family immigrated to the U.S. later becoming citizens. His family changed their surname before applying for citizenship. His given name was Matthew, Matthew Banks."

The news shocked Agent Russell. He thought he was dealing with a Russian agent, not an American agent. He made a face. "Well, I'll be!"

A moment later, Courtney inclined her head and said nothing.

The act not lost on Sinclair.

The CID agent continued. As she spoke, she kept a watchful eye on the CIA agent to see if she displayed any reaction to this information. Sinclair's nagging suspicion revolved around the agent knowing more than what she was telling.

Much to her chagrin, Sinclair felt mildly disappointed. This seemed news to Courtney, too.

Continuing, Sinclair said, "Several years later and after entering college, Banks joined an ROTC program. The CIA became interested in Banks and offered him employment."

Here Sinclair paused. "Banks had a strong resemblance to a captured Russian FSB Agent, but unfortunately for the Russians, but luckily for the U.S. the agent died while being questioned. They chose banks to replace the agent and take up the name of Anisi Sverchinsky. And with vocal transformation training, he would sound just like him."

"He must've been a twin," Russell said, "if convinced he could impersonate the FSB agent. Turning him loose among them would've been a great gamble."

"No, minor plastic surgery," Sinclair replied, "completed the transformation."

"For six years," Sinclair continued. "Banks, now a double agent, provided the agency with secretive and valued documents. Later, CIA headquarters received a communiqué from Banks stating that he was in grave danger, but what that entailed and its outcome, the CIA could not find out. Banks went missing. The Information substantiated that the FSB killed Banks's Russian family. Later on, information confirmed the worst; they had thrown banks into prison."

Sitting back in her chair, Sinclair gazed at Russell. "The file lists some of his friends in the U.S. Dan, I'd like for you to see if the FBI can get phone taps on them."

"That's a stretch, Sinclair, don't know if I can, but I'll make the calls."

Sinclair nodded.

Then her cell phone rang. Reaching into her pocket, she plucked it out. The screen registered her father's number.

"What's up, Dad?"

"*Are you sitting down, Belle?*" asked the soft, almost breathless voice of her father.

"Yes, as a matter of fact. What is it?"

"*I have some bad news. Munford called me from Wiesbaden. It's … it's about one of your agents, honey. They found Ricardo Stubbs, dead—*"

"Wait what, Stubbs dead, how?"

"*They're still piecing that together. But, they tortured him for information.*"

Then she told her father of Stubbs' call and of finding an SD card hidden away behind a painting.

"*You think it's the message?*"

"I believe so, sir."

"*Now they have it.*"

"It would appear so."

"*I'm so sorry about your agent.*"

"He was an excellent agent. Too bad I didn't get to know him better."

A brief silence passed between them.

"*I have more bad news, honey. It's about Tom. They have him listed as missing in action and presumed dead.*"

"Tom ...? *Oh, my, God!*"

Standing, Sinclair walked out of the truck, gasping and choking back tears.

—16—

Floating on the surface of the Sistan Basin, an 800-square-mile oasis fed by the Helmand River, in southern Afghanistan, and while bobbing in the water, Price heard Jacqueline Sinclair whispering in his ear: *"I'm right behind you, Tom."*

Rising above and sinking below the icy surface of the fast-moving river, with her smiling face, urging him to wake: *"You need to wake now, Tom. Please."*

"I'm ... not going to make it, honey," Tom Price says, falling in and out of consciousness...

Price's eyes opened and closed, awakening in a semi-darkened room, with Sinclair's beautiful smile and violet eyes, watching him as she floated high above him. With a lurch, he forced himself to keep staring at her face, but somehow her image shimmered and then disappeared in a haze.

"Sinclair!" he yelled out, uncertain if what he was seeing was real or not.

Squinting, he lifted his head from his pillow and felt a sharp pain emanating from the side of his head. Grimacing, he rested his head back onto the pillow as he lifted a hand to his forehead and touched a bandage wrapped around his head. He felt tired. His skin color was very pale.

His head was pounding as he closed his eyes. Then blinking, trying to clear the cobwebs from his mind, Price looked about the room. Not knowing where he was or how he came to be there, he blinked again, trying to remember, but it was no use. His mind was still too groggy. He tried hard to remember what may have happened to him before he awoke. Once again, closing his eyes with a fierce determination, he forced himself to remember. After a moment, prying open his eyes, the events became crystal clear in his mind.

Then he saw, in his mind's eyes, dragging himself from the field of battle.

The SOF members! All dead!

My God, why wasn't I dead too?

Realizing he was alone, Price's gaze turned toward his left side to a bank of monitoring machines they attached him to; an IV in his right arm, with a nasal cannula fitted to his nostrils. The first thing that came to mind was a hospital of some sort.

He felt the crisp, frosty night air as it blew through an open window.

How long have I been sleeping?

He ached with a pain that shot through the upper part of his body, and try as he could, he didn't know why he felt no pain below his hips nor could he feel his legs.

Then a slight commotion coming from a corner of the room caught his attention. Turning his head, he stared at a grey plastic curtain as someone pulled it back. A rather tall individual wearing a military uniform, and holding a hospital chart in one hand, entered.

With a wince, Price attempted to lift his head once again. He swayed as the pain of the effort subsided some.

"I see you're awake," the physician said, his demeanor and voice Price thought, sympathetic, as he approached the bed. "Just relax. You're in safe hands here."

Price hesitated, realizing maybe he wasn't being held as a captive by the enemy.

"How long have I been out?" Price asked.

"Two days," the doctor replied.

"Where am I?"

"You're in a triage medical tent," the doctor replied, stopping at the foot of the bed, "of the Royal Netherlands Air Force, Forward Operating Base or FOB here in Uruzgan. Or what's left of it. You're very lucky to be alive, young man."

"English, with a funny accent," Price said, squinting, turning and gazing up at the man.

The doctor shook his head, smiling. "You Americans are hilarious. I'm Dutch, Mr. Price."

"That explains it," Price said with a smile.

"I am Doctor Gerard Addens, of this facility, or what's left of it. We are standing down our operations here and heading home."

"How did I get here?" Price asked, "And how do you know my name?"

"Three Pashtun Afghan tribesmen brought you here in a cart. They found you beside a river; dying. I pulled your ID from your effects."

Price just closed his eyes and gently shook his head. Although he was thankful for being rescued and for the treatment he'd received in the hands of the Dutch, he was aching to get back home.

Price glanced up at the doctor. "When will I be able to walk out of here, Doc?"

"Mr. Price—"

"Please call me Tom."

Doctor Addens nodded. "Tom ... you sustained spinal trauma from a bullet. Besides that, you sustained gunshot wounds to your right hip, right shoulder, left leg, and a minor head wound to your temple. I removed those bullets and closed your wounds. You'll recover from them in time. Sorry to say, I couldn't touch or otherwise remove the bullet from your back. And you're still in shock from your gunshots."

Price heard what the doctor said. He was trying to concentrate on the first words he'd spoken. "What do you mean by spinal trauma?"

"As I mentioned Tom, you suffered a gunshot to your back," the doctor replied. "The bullet entered your spinal cord, and the penetration caused your spinal cord to be severed, or otherwise damaged. Result of this is the loss of function below the point of injury. Extent of the injury will determine whether your condition is complete or incomplete."

Price blinked. He did not like the sound of that. "What do you mean by complete or incomplete, doctor?"

"In order words, Tom, complete injuries result in total loss of function; while incomplete offer some functional loss."

"Wait! ... What you're saying is ... I may not walk again?"

"That's a possibility. But, you will need further specialized medical attention."

"Anyway, you could ... you know, remove the bullet?"

"No, there's no way I can. We're not equipped for those procedures. It takes specialized equipment which we don't have."

Grimacing with pain and with the possibility of not being able to walk again, he closed his eyes and with a deep sigh asked, "So, what now, doctor?"

Before replying, Doctor Addens removed a filled syringe from the medicine cart standing by the side of the bed and prepared to administer an injection. "I'm giving you something for the pain and to help you sleep. Tomorrow, a copter from an American Army unit will arrive and transport you to a hospital."

Price took this without replying. With a single brusque shake of his head, his thoughts turned toward Belle.

—17—

Each evening, like clockwork, as he checked his watch, Summerset, the NSA Director, drove home from the Pentagon. Most nights, the one thing he had in mind was to get home, shower, and be ready for dinner with the family. However, his singular thought tonight was about the botched operation executed at the safe-house two days ago.

Christ! He thought, not quite grasping the incompetence of those picked to accomplish the damn task. With the SEAL team and a handful of operatives, one would think there were enough personnel to handle the job and interrogation. But hell no! And just about now, if it had gone according to *his* plan, he'd be a rich man. He wanted to yell out his anger and frustration.

"For the love of *God*!" he shouted at the top of his lungs, striking the steering wheel with his fist, still not comprehending how it had all gone so wrong.

With over thirty years in the spy business, Summerset had accumulated a wealth of information; valuable data on friends and enemies, which made it much easier to bring his plan to a satisfactory conclusion.

He had seen some of his closest friends grow rich selling classified top secret Intel. And he wanted in. However, he was no rat. These were secrets that, if he was so inclined, could send his friends to prison for a long time.

But they were his friends, and as friends go, they each had damaging knowledge on one another. That alone pissed him off. He'd rather keep his secrets in the dark; secrets that could destroy his reputation, and land him in prison for life. Secrets his soon-to-be ex-wife couldn't or wouldn't understand, let alone support.

Now with everything happening around him—strapped for cash, a divorce on the way, and four of his six older children entering college—he needed cash. His plan; sell nuclear bombs to the highest bidder ... a bidder that would pay millions for one weapon and millions more for six.

Several months ago, two Russians approached Summerset, one of which was Catia, and told of the bombs' location and how to get to them. They planned to set off nuclear explosions in several key government locations and force the Russian government to their knees.

The goal was the surrender of the government to certain loyal military heads. But Summerset had another plan, one that would make him rich beyond his wildest dreams. It was his knowledge of Banks double agent status which gave him the idea to persuade Banks to steal the bombs and for Banks to hold on to them until he had a buyer all lined up.

However, with Theseus/Banks on the loose, and the unknown whereabouts of the seven nuclear suitcase bombs, well, his plan just went all to hell in a handbasket. The whole affair left him fuming.

He had one person to blame for his misgivings, and she'd get a piece of his mind. If he didn't get satisfactory results from her going forward, he would need to kill her as she was the only person who could implicate him in the conspiracy.

Summerset frowned. It had taken hard work and planning to pull it off. Good men had died. Not his fault. He had enough sense to back off from the deal once he realized it could backfire in his face. Now he needed to see it through. Too much invested already just to back away from it all.

Life wasn't fair, he reminded himself over and over.

But whoever said life is fair, he thought.

Summerset leaned into the backrest as he stopped at a red light on the corner of Royal and Wolfe Streets. Damn, he thought, he was going to be late for dinner. He shook his head, remembering what his wife had said a few days ago:

"Late again, and you get none from me ... and you'll sleep in the guest room." Her words echoed in his mind. And to think, he couldn't remember the last time he had sex.

What a fucking life ... everything seemed to go wrong around him. And he won't get laid tonight either, he mused.

Glancing over to his right, he saw a familiar face; the face of all his troubles.

She was driving a red late-model Mercedes-Benz coupe, and as soon as the light turned green, Summerset drove through the intersection. The coupe pulled right behind his vehicle, keeping to a safe distance, as traffic flowed left and right of his car on either side of the street.

With cloudy skies and about 65 degrees, with a light stiff wind blowing, Summerset drove on to his predetermined rendezvous location, *Lillian's* Mexican restaurant and bar off of Mount Vernon Ave. He'd set up the meeting for this afternoon, the earliest possible time available, according to her.

Fifteen minutes later, he sat face to face with her in a quiet corner booth. He sipped on a glass of bourbon on the rocks, and she on a glass of Pahlmeyer Napa Valley chardonnay, as he stared past her to the crowded restaurant.

Every so often he glanced back at her. Her beauty was alluring. A military attaché for the Russian Embassy in Washington, he knew her as Ekaterina or Catia as she preferred being called. He didn't know if it was her actual name, but at this stage, he did not want to know.

Catia had the features any man would consider attractive and enthralling. At five-foot-ten, with an hour-glass figure, a 23-inch waistline, or less, long light-brown hair flowing to her lower back, long runner's legs, and a beautiful round face.

The one thing, besides her 32D breasts, that impressed Summerset was her eyes. She had deep green eyes, sparkling with life, and once she sets them on any man, she had them in her grips.

If he was to guess, he pinned her age about twenty-seven to thirty. Catia, enigmatic as a spy and dangerous, was even more so as a woman. He always wondered why she'd become a spy. He once put that question to her, but only got a blank look in return.

She wore an expensive red-colored shiny fly-a-way jacket and knee-length suit dress, clear stockings with silver-colored high heel stiletto shoes.

Summerset, in his two-piece black business suit, picked up his glass as did Catia. Clinking glasses and he said as he toasted with a crooked brief smile, "N*a Zharovje*, to your health," then downed his drink, staring at her.

"*Za Vstrechu*, to our meeting," she responded.

Catia took a sip of her wine. "Well, you wanted this meeting," Catia said in a slight Russian accent, much like listening to Maria Sharapova. "What do you have, Steven?"

A brief silence settled between them.

From the other side of the restaurant, two men wearing two-piece black suits, both bald and sporting short trimmed beards and mustaches, watched the two seated at the booth with careful eyes. They sat sipping on cups of coffee behind the NSA Director and in clear sight of the woman.

"Damn woman!" Summerset said, cocking his head. "You know why I'm here. It didn't go well for your people, or us, in Germany."

"Steven, *Your* SEAL team," Catia said, "needed to be out of the safe-house that morning."

Summerset cleared his throat. "There was no alternative. They couldn't get out until later that afternoon."

Catia wanted to grin. "That was your problem; not mine. You failed to notify us of the change."

Summerset sat in his chair staring out across the restaurant's floor, and said, "Yeah well ... I couldn't get a message out to you."

"So, the screw-up, as you Americans would say," Catia said with a smile on her beautiful lips, "was on you."

As she spoke, the NSA Director stared. It could have been her eyes, or how she stared straight at him, or something else. He wasn't all that sure what gave it away. But it was there, in her manner, gesture, and in not so many words, that told him she did not like what she was hearing.

And that was dangerous for him.

The Director looked at her and remained motionless. Or was he reading too much into this? He asked himself. Although in the last few minutes, she'd changed from a soft-spoken friend to a jungle cat on the prowl.

Summerset's mouth tightened. "Shit," he said.

Catia raised her wineglass to her lips and, closing her eyes, sipped on the white wine. Then, with eyes wide open, she placed the glass back on the table and stared at him.

"We chose you, Steven, for our plan, with your dealings in the black market, to help us take over the Russian Government. And with your knowledge of disposing of sensitive materials, you were the correct person for it."

He cocked his head. "So, my plan is still intact, correct?"

The woman blinked at the question, while shaking her head in the negative, and narrowing her eyes on him.

"No, it's not," she responded, "Your plan to have your double agent steal the nuclear bombs from our arsenal and have them distributed for placement was a brilliant plan. We told Banks when and where the bombs would be. The plan to have Banks place them around Russia was sound too. If we have Theseus back in our hands and the bombs in our possession, the plan to take over the government would continue."

Summerset shook his head. "But Banks foiled that plan," he countered. "He failed to place the bombs, and he kept them for his use, seeking his revenge on America and Russia. Now they have the U.S. Army CID, the FBI, and a CIA operative, looking for Banks and those bombs. So, what are you going to do to rectify our predicament?"

"That's being done as we speak," Catia said, playing with her glass of wine. "A special forces group has arrived."

"Oh, what are they going to do?"

Catia stared at the two bald men on the other side of the restaurant and gave a slight nod. The two men rose. Staring back at Summerset, she said, "They're tasked to eliminate them and others at all costs."

A few minutes later, once the two FSB agents followed Summerset from the restaurant, Catia lifted her cell phone and dialed through to the Russian Embassy in Frankfurt, Germany, and to the head of the Russian FSB operations, Colonel Elizaveta Borovkov.

On the third ring, and hearing the voice on the other end, Catia said, "Comrade Colonel, we have carried out your orders." Without waiting for an answer, Catia disconnected the call, rose, and walked out of the restaurant.

Unhurriedly, Summerset exited the restaurant—hell, he mused, he was already late for dinner, what's a few more minutes—to his parked car in a darkened corner next to one side of the restaurant. Turning the corner, a little out of breath, he shoved his hand into his trouser pocket and pulled out his car keys, just as two black-suited bald men exited the restaurant.

Summerset felt no panic or even concern going forward; even after the strange look Catia had given him after the meeting. He was holding on to information; information that would incriminate the Russians in his affair, if they even thought of double-crossing him.

He felt rather composed knowing it could have gone wrong back there for him. He didn't think the Russian woman knew of his plan to sell the nukes. To think, this all started with a phone call, hooking up Catia and his knowledge of Russia's plans and that of Banks.

It was the Russians that named Banks as the fall guy. Yet, it was the Russians who tipped off the CIA of Banks arrest and where he was being held.

Reaching his car, and whistling a tune he heard in the restaurant, he unlocked the driver's door and paused with his hand on the door handle as small beads of sweat flowed from his temples. He stopped whistling as he felt someone walking up behind him.

Hearing footsteps approaching, and with a deep quick breath, he turned around. Too late, they pushed Summerset hard against his vehicle, knocking the wind out of him. He felt a prick on his neck as if someone jabbed a needle into him. He struggled with his assailant, but to no avail, as seconds later he stopped, losing consciousness while falling limp into the arms of his assailant, who caught him before it could hit the ground.

One of the two assailants shoved the body away from the car's door, while the other pulled it open, placing the body on the driver's seat. Grasping an open bottle of whiskey, given to him by the other man, he forced some contents into Summerset's mouth, and then splashed the rest on his body.

Pushing the body to one side, the killer pulled out Summerset's wallet, emptied the contents on the ground, and pocketed the money. Then he removed the wristwatch and cell phone. Once done, they walked away.

An hour later, a teenage couple, out for a walk, found the body. Curious as to the open car door, they approached the car, and once seeing the body, they notified the police.

Later, the police detectives would open and close their investigation, labeling it as a robbery of a drunk who died of a heart attack. But one unanswered question bugged the detectives: Why wasn't the car stolen too?

Much later, the detectives would reopen the investigation once identification of the body became known.

—18—

Sinclair heard his shrill screams resonating loudly in her head!

Shaking her head back and forth, she tried to wake. It was no use. In her dream state, she repeatedly kept hearing Tom's anguished tortured yells and loud screaming pounding in her head. Her inability to come to his rescue from his pain and suffering drove her furious.

She felt tied down to her bed, hand and foot, as her panicked efforts only brought on strangled sporadic body shakes as if she was trying to break free of her bonds and her nightmare. Was it just a horrifying nightmare she was experiencing, or was she somehow envisioning Tom's pain coming alive in her mind?

Her feelings were like a kaleidoscope with the continuous flashing of her eyes rapidly opening and closing. She couldn't concentrate on anything, except the yelling and screaming as she saw Tom's suffering.

Suddenly, as she finally shook herself awake, her eyes opening wide in terror, she could see a thin veil of light from her nightstand warmly lighting the small bedroom. Gingerly, sitting up in bed, she ran a hand over her brow and came away with cold sweat, as she finally realized where she was.

In her father's guest bedroom in his on-post quarters, Jacqueline Sinclair drove all other thoughts from her mind. Once her father had told her of Tom being reported missing in action, and not able to visualize life without him, everything else became inconsequential. Was he captured and being tortured? The thought raced through her mind.

She was a combat survivor who came away almost unscratched from many deadly and horrific encounters. But she'd experienced nothing like this. Tom, her *Tom*, was still missing and presumed dead. She had never once imagined him dead and expected to see him walk through her door and into her arms once again.

Slowly getting out of bed, she stood barefooted on the cold wooden floor and glanced around her bedroom, her heart beating fast. In the bathroom, she splashed cold water on her face, hoping it would wake her up completely.

A pulsing, pounding headache made her feel as if her head was about to explode. From the medicine cabinet, she grabbed a bottle of ibuprofen, twisted the cap off, shook four tablets into her hand, and swallowed them.

She wondered what would happen if she just went back to sleep and tried to forget everything around her. Would she again continue with her nightmares, or maybe find solace in the thought she couldn't do a damn thing to relieve her pain?—the pain of not knowing if Tom was alive or dead.

However, she couldn't forget about her job, and the peril the world could be in if she just gave up and stayed locked up in her room. Taking a deep breath, she left the bathroom, and stopped upon hearing a knock at her door. Instantly, she knew it could only be one person—her father.

"Hang on, Dad," she yelled.

The knocking stopped as Colonel Sinclair anxiously waited outside the door for his daughter.

Sinclair turned her back to the door. Through the curtains of the large picture window, she saw the sun rising on another day and watched the golden rays appear in the sky, growing into an enormous ball of fire. It gave her a sense of a new beginning and a new ending to her nightmare.

The clock on the nightstand read a quarter to eight. With a frown, she reached the edge of her bed, grasped her night robe, and slipped it on over her nightgown. Tying the belt, she slowly tiptoed her way to the door.

Another knock came just as she reached for the doorknob.

With a bright smile on her face and a twinkle to her eyes, Sinclair opened the door. "Good morning, Dad."

He stood at the threshold; tall, lean and handsome with piercing grey eyes, wearing his military uniform as he glanced at his daughter. "Ah, may I come in, Belle?"

"Of course, Dad," Belle replied as she opened the door further.

He entered and stopped at the room's threshold. "Can't stay long, have to go to work. I wanted to talk before you got back to work."

With a questioning look and a small tilt to her head, she asked, "What is it?"

"I know how distraught you've been ever since I told you about Tom." He paused again. "So, I called in a few markers, honey."

Suddenly she stiffened, and for a moment she just stood there. "I see," she said rather calmly. "When ... when, will you know?"

"I'm hoping to have some information for you today, but I can't guarantee it."

Sinclair inclined her head. There was a silence between them for a few seconds—and then she spoke the only words that came to mind. "Thank you, Dad."

Colonel Sinclair nodded. "I better get going. I'll call the moment I hear anything."

She looked straight into her father's eyes and smiled.

At nine-thirty-five that same morning, two silver and green 4-door BMW German police cruisers were parallel parked on a side street, in an upscale Stuttgart community. Their emergency blue lights atop their roofs flashing their caution to passing motorist and parked behind a black Ford Explorer SUV with American armed service's plates earlier reported stolen.

The two officers, once the Sergeant-in-charge called it into the dispatcher, canvassed the surrounding neighborhood for witnesses, and for the possibility of any vehicle stolen by the suspect when he'd abandoned the SUV. It was worth a try, and who knows, the Sergeant thought, they could get lucky and find the suspect. Glancing at one another, they both unbuttoned their gun holsters, just in case.

Each officer took one side of the street and began knocking on doors.

Even though the Sergeant was about to finish his tour of duty, the SUV he came upon was significant, because the driver of it was a suspected murderer wanted by the American FBI and German authorities, and presumed armed and highly dangerous.

Walking up to the door of the first house, he knocked, stood to one side, and with his hand on his weapon, waited.

A minute passed when an elderly woman slowly opened the door a crack. "Officer, are you here about my stolen car?"

The Sergeant frowned and asked, "When did you report your car stolen?"

"Two days ago."

"I see. What type of car do you have?"

"It's a blue, 1990 4-door Toyota Land-Cruiser. Wait a minute and I'll get the registration for you."

Fifteen minutes later, the Sergeant confirmed the report of the stolen Toyota. Then, the dispatcher gave the Sergeant a report of stolen license plates from an old black BMW, stolen about the same time as the Toyota.

In front of his partner, the Sergeant relayed the information about the stolen car and the stolen plates. "Shit, this could be the work of our suspect," he said to his partner.

The partner nodded.

Then they waited for the wrecker to arrive.

An hour later, Agent Sinclair parked her Chevy around the back of the CID building parking lot. With her window rolled down halfway, she felt the cool morning breeze blowing on her face as she closed her eyes, willing herself to concentrate on the job at hand, instead of focusing her mind on Price. Sliding out of the Chevy, she locked it and walked into the building.

Before leaving her father's residence, she'd called Russell and Courtney for a meet at her office and to coordinate on any recent developments. They were sitting in the secretary's inner office on the second floor, waiting for her. The moment she walked in, they stood.

Sinclair stifled a smile. "Good morning, you two."

"That remains uncertain," Courtney replied in a low voice.

"Step into my office," Sinclair said without further ado, "and see what we have and what we need to do. But first I need coffee."

With the office secretary out on vacation, Sinclair only guessed it was her on-call duty investigator who had made a fresh pot of coffee and placed a box of donuts on the table off to one side of the wall by the entrance to her office.

Removing her thin leather jacket and draping it over her chair, she ambled over to the coffee table, grabbed the coffeepot and filled her mug, and asked, "Anyone else for a cup?" Then, grabbing a cherry-filled donut, she went back to her desk and pulled back the chair and sat. Both Russell and Courtney grabbed a mug each and pulled chairs over toward Sinclair's desk and also sat.

"So, does anyone of you have any updates since we last met?" Sinclair asked as she watched both of the agents.

Sipping on her coffee, Courtney replied, "I don't."

"Listen, Sinclair. I know what you're feeling; I lost a good friend last year too. But Price will be back. I got a strong feeling he's in bed somewhere waiting to get back home."

"Thanks for that, Dan. How did you know, wait, my father ... right?"

Russell just nodded.

With a slightly confused look, Courtney asked, "Who is Price? Is he someone—?"

"No one you need to worry about," Sinclair cut in. "He's my fiancé."

"Oh, I'm so sorry."

They fell silent for a moment.

"I have some information," Russell broke in and said. "I got a call from the German police. They found the SUV Theseus stole from the safe-house abandoned on a street in an upscale neighborhood. When the police did a canvas of the area, they found another vehicle stolen."

At this, Russell paused. "But, that's not all. Sometime later, someone stole a set of German license plates. This may be just a coincidence, but don't bet on it. I believe Theseus stole them and placed them on his new car. Hell, he may still be around the area."

"Do we have a description of the stolen vehicle and the plates?" Sinclair asked.

"Sure do," Russell replied.

Sipping on her coffee, Sinclair kept her gaze on Russell and gave thought to this fresh development. "This could be a big break. Dan, you and Pat check it out. It could very well have been Theseus who stole a new car and also may have broken into a home. It's worth a look."

Russell rose from his chair and gazed at Courtney. "I'm ready," he said with a smile.

"What are you going to do, Sinclair?" Russell asked.

Sinclair knew exactly what she was going to do. She needed to get into the thumb-drive and finally see what this was all about.

"Paperwork," Sinclair replied.

The cool morning air blew softly through the partially opened window on the 2010 Mercedes-Benz GLA 250, 4-door silver sedan, as he sat smoking a cigarette after pulling surveillance for the better part of an hour. With several butts already on the ground just outside the driver's door, Bogdan Volkov, the sniper of the group, felt bored. He'd rather be out hunting wild-boar in the Ural Mountains of his Russian homeland, then sitting here being bored to death.

In Germany for less than a few hours, the rest of the group was comfortable in their room at the Embassy awaiting further orders. So his commander, Captain Kuznetsov, ordered him for this job. Being the youngest, less experienced of the five, he needed more training and opportunities to make important decisions of his own, Captain Kuznetsov reasoned.

Sporting a full dark beard and mustache, and only twenty-nine years of age with a tall six-feet-two slender build, Volkov had several kills under his belt. He didn't think he needed more training, at least in killing. However, he welcomed the respite of being alone for a few hours, away from the rest of the unit.

The information given to him from his captain was of their target, the Russian double agent known as Anisi Sverchinsky and known to be in Germany. He held a small photo of Sverchinsky, which he studied. Also, the photos of three other targets; an American FBI agent named Daniel Russell, a female CIA Operative named Patricia Courtney, and U.S. Army CID Agent Jacqueline Sinclair, that laid on the passenger seat next to him. Already setting to memory all four of them, he still kept them handy, just in case.

However, his primary aim was Sverchinsky.

He'd parked the Mercedes on the street corner next to the house from where a Toyota Land-Cruiser was reported stolen; maybe by Sverchinsky. His job was to wait and see if the Russian double agent reappeared, or if anyone else did, to follow and not engage, and report his observations. Although their orders, as he was led to believe, were to kill on sight the three agents, Lieutenant Colonel Borovkov, who was the commander of the overall mission, decided just to wait, observe, follow and report. Maybe it was his understanding that whoever showed would lead them to Sverchinsky, which he considered a sound tactic.

He had instructions to call in every half-hour.

It was at that moment when he was about to pick up his cell phone and make his call, that a black Chevy 4-door sedan bearing American license plates with two occupants, a man, and a woman, came from the other side of the street.

Grabbing his binoculars from the console, he trained them on the car, and once he'd focused them, he recognized the FBI agent and the CIA operative in the front seat. Dropping the binoculars back on the console, he picked up his favorite handgun, the Russian PL-14, 9x19mm Parabellum automatic handgun with a 5-inch long suppressor, clicked off the safety, and placed it on his lap. Next, he picked up his cell phone and made his report, all the while maintaining eye contact with the Americans.

Slowly the black Chevy made its way down the street, as the two occupants watched several people walking to and from their cars, probably on their way to work, or arriving home, Russell thought.

With Russell behind the wheel, Courtney kept a sharp eye for the house with the stolen Toyota, but she failed to see it on their first run. "Ah, go back around, Dan. I didn't see the house."

"No problem."

Speeding up some, Russell drove to the end of the street and made a U-turn. Just as he came off the turn, Courtney spied a silver car, parked on the corner street, with exhaust coming out the back of the car. And something else, which immediately caught her eyes, countless cigarette butts lying just outside the driver's door.

"Dan, did you see that silver car we just passed?" she asked.

"Yeah, I did. What of it?"

"I think it's been sitting there a while. It could mean trouble."

"Nah, don't think so," Russell said, "Maybe just waiting on someone. But, let's keep an eye out just in case. Let's see what we can find out. We'll drive around the area."

"There's the house on the left side, Dan," she said, a minute later.

"Yeah, I see it. I'll drive down a few blocks and come around the street."

With Russell pulling away, the Mercedes followed.

Seconds later, with Courtney staring out her outside mirror and Russell out of his inside mirror, he asked. "You see that?"

"Yeah, I think we got us a tail."

"I was thinking the same thing. Let's see what he does."

Courtney turned to stare at Russell. "What are you thinking?"

"Let's go for a ride and see if he is following us."

"Okay, then what?"

"We'll just have to wait and find out."

—19—

One of the greatest attributes Richard E. Crenshaw possessed was his analytical skills, along with an aptitude for problem-solving in the creation and cracking of encrypted algorithms and key generators, and he was a top-notch computer science major. They were the primary reasons Agent Sinclair sought his help in cracking and exposing the files on her late friend's thumb-drive.

These files were crucial to her investigation. She believed she had the algorithm and the key to the drive in her possession, and hoped it would be enough for Crenshaw.

Lacking the knowledge to use the key and algorithm herself to crack the encrypted drive, she had no alternative but to seek outside help.

Crenshaw, an ex-CIA Intelligence Collection analyst, was a friend of DIA Agent Tom Price, whom Sinclair met twice before while in the company of her fiancé at Crenshaw's ranch.

Crenshaw, a Wyoming native, was a sixty-five-year-old, narrow build, balding man, with a pair of too-small round eyeglasses he perched on his nose. He lived on a ten-acre ranch, in a residential neighborhood six miles from the city of Stuttgart, in a five-bedroom, two-story equestrian property with a family of four.

He was an American, married to a German national. The family lived in Germany after he'd retired from the CIA. He'd done odd jobs for the agency, and others, since being on his own; and frequently for Price, and once in a while, for certain other three-letter agencies as well.

According to Price, his friend Richard, or Rick, was a highly reliable and confidential person, and entrusted in all matters—a man of brilliant political and military abilities and quite fastidious. It was another reason Sinclair asked to see him.

She knew she couldn't go to the CIA or the CID crime labs, or any other agency associated with the U.S. or the German Government with her information—at least not until she knew what was on the drive.

Crenshaw and Sinclair stood in a brightly lit basement room, the walls of which were wood-paneled and had recessed glass-encased cabinets, with a large oak desk on one side of a wall.

As she entered the room, an area she had not seen before, during her last visits, she noticed books upon books dealing with computers and other assorted subjects, arranged side-by-side in the cabinets.

Two large monitors, and two tabletop computers, occupied the desk with several chairs set off to one side. And on a small roll-up desk, which sat next to the oak desk, there was an open laptop computer with an active computer chess game on its screen.

They went to the desk and Crenshaw, wearing a black T-shirt and shorts, took a seat facing his monitors and turned on his computers. Then he swiveled his office chair around to face her and watched as she made herself as comfortable as possible on one of the other straight-backed chairs behind him.

He sat forward, and pushed his glasses back to the bridge of his nose, elbows on the armrest, rubbing his palms together, and gazed at her for a few seconds, slightly bowing his head.

A few more seconds of silence ensued.

Then, leaning back in his chair, Crenshaw sighed and felt a little uneasy with what he was about to tell her.

Raising his eyes level with hers, Richard saw a faraway look come into her eyes. Taking a deep breath, he said, "Listen, when you called and told me about Tom, I got curious and made a few inquiries. Here's what I could find out," he explained in a low-level voice. "There was an operation involving Special Forces operatives. Tom's tasked was to provide a visual with an enemy, their target."

Crenshaw paused and noticed Sinclair had dropped her eyes from him, but didn't look annoyed with him. He hoped he'd done the right thing. After another brief pause, he asked, "If you'd rather not hear this, please tell me?"

"Please go on, Richard."

"Hey, please, call me Rick."

Sinclair smiled and nodded.

"Caught in an ambush, not one survived. Tom's body was the only one not recovered. Sinclair, I ... I, ah, couldn't dig deeper without getting people in hot water. I'm sorry."

She took several deep breaths and felt a little light-headed. Hearing it for a second time didn't help, while finding out about Tom saddened her even more.

The agent fingered her diamond engagement ring nervously, and her thoughts turned to Tom and the ring... *It was during a night of heavy lovemaking. Tom had afterward rolled over on the bed onto his side and reaching under his pillow he came away with a small cherry colored polished jewelry box. Opening it, he said in a hushed tone of voice, "Honey, turn around and see what I have for you."*

As she turned over on the bed and faced him, Tom Price extended the box to her, and asked, "Will you marry me?"

In the box was a diamond engagement ring with the biggest rock she'd ever seen. A small LED light from the inside lid of the box lit up the diamond as it sparkled and danced in the light. Sinclair was speechless.

Sinclair remembered the fact she had no idea he was going to propose, and almost fainted, caught herself and lunged over and embraced him. She whispered in his ear the answer he'd so wanted to hear...

Her reverie was momentarily cut short, when she heard as if from far away Richard's voice speaking to her. Then she nodded, closed her eyes, and took a deep breath. One day, she was going to find out what happened to Tom; she promised herself. It may take a while, though. In the meantime, she'd hope her father came up with more information.

Crenshaw considered Sinclair to be quite a remarkable woman. Price related stories about her—stories of their adventures together, which was the stuff of Hollywood. He admired her grit and her sand. She was a good fit for Tom.

"So," Richard said, smiling at her, "what's this about an encrypted hard drive you have for me?"

Sinclair sat back in her chair, as her pulse quickened upon remembering her best friend dying in her arms. She took a deep breath and thought for a moment. Then gazing at Richard, she related how she came to possess the hard drive in the first place: That those who came in contact with it subsequently died, and involved in a deadly attack in her apartment for it. And how her friend traveled a long and dangerous road to get the drive to her and died in her arms delivering it to her.

Crenshaw listened as Sinclair told the story of her friend Major Jessica Alice Wayne. Once Sinclair had finished, his curiosity piqued, and he wondered what the drive contained which cost her life and those that came in contact with it.

But more so, what if something should happen to him and his family now that he'd come in contact with the drive? It was a shaky dilemma, he thought, shaking his head. And a tough decision to make. Finally, deciding, he shook his head once again.

"So, Sinclair," Crenshaw asked as he again pushed his glasses to the bridge of his nose. "Does anyone else know you came to me?"

She leaned forward. "Not a soul, Rick."

"Okay then, show me what you got," Richard said, throwing caution to the wind for the sake of a friend. However, he suspected, he'd soon have to move the family to another location just to be on the safe side.

Sinclair rose, reached into her pocket, pulled out the thumb-drive and handed it over to Richard, along with two sheets of paper, and sat back down.

"The sheets have what I believe is the algorithm and her key," she said.

He shook his head as he glanced through the sheets with a critical eye. "Where did you find these?"

"She taped it under a drawer of her desk, and the other under her keyboard."

"Not a very smart move in hiding it there, I'd say."

"It's a common practice we found the military using when they couldn't remember their login protocols."

After reading through the sheets, he said, "Well, to begin with, reading what she'd written here, she used Bcrypt encryption with a sophisticated multiplication algorithm for the key."

"What's a Bcrypt?"

"It's a cross-platform file encryption utility and an adaptive password hashing algorithm which uses the Blowfish keying schedule, not an asymmetric encryption algorithm."

She held up her hand and rolled her eyes. "Rick, English please."

"Oh, yeah right, okay. It's a password hashing algorithm, and it's not the same as just any encryption and used specifically to encrypt and secure passwords. It's primarily used when a user enters a password and that password needs to be stored in a database in a way that the original password couldn't be guessed even if the system was attacked and the database became compromised."

"So, she was smart?"

"Yeah, but it's an old system. The Blowfish system dates back to 1999."

"Can you work with it?"

"Easy-peasy, Sinclair. It shouldn't take me more than a couple of minutes to open. Sit back and let me work this out."

*   *   *

Russell drove slowly for five minutes through several intersections while Courtney kept the vehicle following them framed against her outside rear-view mirror. Once or twice she turned on her seat and hazarded a glance behind her, trying to catch sight of their tail.

"They're keeping a low profile, Dan, staying back a three or four car distance."

"Can you tell how many in the car?"

"No, I can't. They're too far back and traffic is heavy."

"Yeah, tell me about it."

Twenty feet ahead, they came to another intersection.

Russell pulled into his turning lane, waited for the light to change, and made the turn. A moment later, driving through another intersection, he kept his speed below 30 mph. He noticed the tail just stayed back, lying low and not showing his hand. A glance at his inside mirror showed the tail had also made the turn and had also slowed.

Traffic was becoming heavier through the four-lane street as Courtney kept watch on the tailing sedan.

Slowing and maintaining a speed of less than 25 mph, Russell watched as vehicle after vehicle sped by him; but not the tail. It stayed about a two-car distance from his bumper.

At the next intersection, the FBI agent made another right turn.

"Check to see if they make the turn," he asked.

"They just did."

"Shit, okay, so now we know they're following us. Which begs the question; why and are they the Russians?"

"You think they know who we are?"

Russell shrugged, not startled by her question. He too was thinking about it himself. He didn't see any point in lying. "Yeah, that's my guess. They think by tailing us, we're lead them to Theseus."

Courtney raised her eyebrows. "What now? You have a plan?"

Glancing out the windshield, he replied, "No, but give me a minute."

Courtney's eyes opened wider. She kept noticing their tail gaining some distance. "You better think fast then because I don't think we're going to lose our tail soon enough."

It was mid-morning as Bogdan Volkov morosely stared out the windshield of his Mercedes-Benz as he kept track of the two agents' vehicle up ahead. Left and right of him, traffic swirled and herds of pedestrians and cyclists surrounded his car. There was bumper-to-bumper traffic on the left lane. If that kept up, he'll lose them in traffic.

Volkov snorted. He'd already suspected they knew he was following them. With fast-moving traffic flowing through the four-lane street, he reasoned they would now try to lose him in the swirl of traffic.

It's what he would do.

Waiting for the light to change, he glanced over at a Starbucks and a doughnut shop next to it and realized he'd not eaten a thing since breakfast.

Pulling his cell phone from his inside breast pocket of his jacket, Volkov dialed the number given to him before leaving the Russian Embassy. She would not like his report. However, he knew he'd done his best.

Lieutenant Colonel Borovkov, the head of the FSB security at the Russian Embassy, picked up on the second ring. To his standards, the colonel was a beautiful woman, with the bite of a black widow spider—yeah, very dangerous, he thought.

There was a strange quality in her voice that gave him pause. "Da, Comrade Volkov."

Volkov took in a deep breath. "I believe the two agents know I am following them, Colonel. What do you—?"

Her voice sounded bitter as she broke in, "You're to keep following them, try not to lose them, and if given an opportunity, take them out. Understood?"

"Da."

"Your commander recommended you for the job; he said you were very good at what you do. Don't make him into a liar."

Volkov had no immediate answer and felt anger welling up inside him. He was a trained killer and knew his job forward and back. Death and destruction were commonplace with him. This was no different.

One word came to mind, *bitch!* But his reply came slow and deliberate, "Da!"

"This is going to take a little longer than I expected, Sinclair," Crenshaw said.

"How much longer, Rick?"

"Soon; Listen, I have some whiskey in the counter cabinet and a couple of glasses. Pour yourself one, and one for me, three fingers full, if you don't mind."

Sinclair rose and smoothed her hands down her sides, took two steps away, stopped, and turned to face Crenshaw, who had turned back around to his keyboard as she watched his fingers fly through key after key across the board.

Turning back, Sinclair walked over to the cabinet. She needed something to cut the edge with, and whiskey was better than ibuprofen.

The day was halfway through, and she hadn't heard from her fellow agents. She hoped nothing had gone wrong. She'd wait thirty minutes before making any calls.

***

He was behind a blue and white trolleybus as it rumbled through the heavy traffic that showed no signs of lessening. Carefully, Russell turned plan after plan over in his head. He discarded several until he hit on the most viable. Now, he knew what he needed to do and where to do it.

His plan was simple. He'd allow the tail to continue following them, then wait for the proper place he knew of and find out who they were and why they were being followed. Sounded simple enough, he thought. In his experiences, the more you put into a plan, the more it's bound to fail. The military adage of 'keep it simple stupid,' rang true.

Glancing over at her, he said out of the side of his mouth, "Ah, Courtney, I may have a plan."

Courtney turned her gaze on Russell and waited to hear what he'd propose. Once he finished detailing his plan, a shiver raced down her spine. For all her time in the field, she'd never once used her weapon on anyone. But now it may well come to that.

She shook her head, shocked. "What ...? Are you crazy? I don't even have a weapon!"

"Damn, I just assumed—"

"Well, what now?"

"Okay, okay, open the glove compartment."

Opening the compartment, she reached inside and pulled out a Sig Sauer P320 9mm automatic handgun and two extra magazines.

"Know how to use that?"

Courtney's face was impassive. "I wouldn't be an agent, if I didn't."

"So now we're ready to put my plan to work."

Courtney released the magazine from the Sig Sauer to make certain it was a full mag. She then replaced it, chambered a live round and gripped it tightly in her right hand and then placed it on her lap.

With the approach of another intersection, Russell made another right turn and drove east. Driving through the underpass of Highway 14, and three miles ahead, he'd get the tail to follow them out of the town, then onto a forest road.

So far, his plan was working.

Five minutes later, they made sure the tail car was still with them.

Eight minutes had passed when they finally drove through a green countryside, through which the road, now two lanes, ran precipitous in terms of the terrain. Normally, the winds and rain might affect the area, but not so on this bright sunny day. With high mountain ranges on either side, they followed the winding road with the tail, as yet unseen, way behind them.

On a steep turn, Russell, once they were out of sight of the sedan, reduced his speed, pulled off to the side of the road, and stopped alongside a two-foot-high concrete traffic barrier two feet thick by twelve feet long, and waited for them to appear. Shutting down the engine, they slid out of the car, drew their weapons, and shielded themselves behind their vehicle.

— • — • —

Minutes later, Volkov suspected the agents planned on an ambush for him up ahead. It's what he would've done.

Reducing his speed, Volkov slowed and killed the engine, letting the vehicle move forward on its own before he came to the start of the curve in the road. Pulling over to the opposite side, he braked to a stop, and waited a few seconds, determining which weapons he was going to use.

Once he was out of his car, he walked around to the trunk, opened it, and removed his coat, and threw it in the trunk. Several handguns and various boxes of ammo and other gear were visible. He decided on and grasped an H&K MP7 auto-machine pistol, chambering in the HK 5.6x30mm armor-piercing ammunition. Tightening its sling, he slung it over his left shoulder.

Next, he grasped an M79 grenade launcher, which earned the nickname by American soldiers as the "Thumper," for its distinctive report. Pushing the barrel-locking latch exposing the breach, he loaded a 40mm high explosive (HE) round and locked the breach in place.

Leading with the M79 in both hands, Volkov walked forward about a hundred-feet by the side of the road and stopped just before he came to the curve. The forest was thick on his side, so dropping to his knees he used the bushes for cover and saw through the thicket, the stopped car, and behind it, the two agents.

This is going to be like shooting fish in a barrel, he said to himself.

The lone Russian operative cautiously stood and once again, leading with the grenade launcher, ambled forward until he'd cleared the bushes and was in plain sight of the car and the agents. Stopping, he raised the M79 to his right shoulder and took aim.

Just then, Russell and Courtney peering over the roof of the car saw the armed Russian. Russell instantly recognized the weapon the Russian was holding and pointing in their direction.

"Jesus, Mary, and Joseph!" Russell exclaimed. "He's holding a fucking grenade launcher!"

Knowing the car couldn't provide sufficient cover, Russell grabbed Courtney's arm and yelled, "Jump over the concrete wall; it's our only chance!"

Then in a blink of an eye, just as they cleared the top of the concrete barrier and slumped down behind it, suddenly, they heard a loud *Thump* sound from the launcher...

... and then the high explosive round traveling at a muzzle velocity of 75 meters per second, arrived seconds later impacting dead center of Russell's sedan.

The round struck the side of the car and detonated. The impact drove the car forward and its momentum stopped by the barrier. Two enormous explosions shook the car, and they heard sounds of rending steel above the din, as the crackling of fire and smoke filled the area.

Volkov dropped the launcher, slung off the MP7 machine gun, and pulled the trigger, laying a steady burst of automatic fire. The wave of bullets strafed and struck every inch of the burning car, pinging off the metal chassis. He ejected the spent magazine and took his time reloading the MP7, knowing no one could have lived through the explosion and the armor-piercing bullets. Slowly, he strolled over to the car.

Russell heard what he suspected was the clicking sound of the machine gun going dry. With Courtney next to him, he instantly reacted, and said, "I'll take the right and you the left side of the barrier. We'll come up, target the Russian, and we both fire on the fucker, don't stop firing until he's down or you're out of ammo. Ready?"

Courtney frowned. "Shit! Do I have a fucking choice?"

A smile flitted across Agent Russell's face. "You can stay here, if that's what you want."

"Fuck you."

"Go, go!" Russell yelled.

Jumping up from behind the barrier, they took their positions left and right of the burning car. Coming around from the sides of the burning heap, they saw the Russian, just as Volkov, with eyes wide open, mouth agape, brought his weapon to bear on the two agents as he jacked in a live round.

Russell and Courtney kept walking forward, holding their weapons gripped tightly in both hands, as they laid a steady burst of rounds at the stationary figure. The onslaught of the 9mm bullets hammered the Russian as they impacted his body. Then both agents stopped firing and watched as the body collapsed to the ground.

Approaching the body, Courtney asked, "Is he dead?"

With his attacker's body laying on the asphalt, his chest a bloody pulp, his mouth wide open and his eyes staring at nothing, Russell, with a fresh magazine in his weapon, fired a round into the body. "He is now! Let's call it in."

Russell grabbed his cell phone and called Sinclair.

—20—

Frieda and Karl Meir, both in their mid-seventies, had just come down the stairs from their bedroom. Frieda, being the first to clear the bottom landing, turned into the kitchen to prepare a pot of tea, while Karl continued into a wide-open but semi-dark living room whose closed curtains blocked the morning sunshine. Once seated on the sofa, he snapped on the side table lamp, turned the TV on and switched it to their local news station, as they did each morning, and waited for his wife to join him.

The station was running their lead stories. They were the same newscast from the previous day advising of a murderer wanted by the local police and American military police. They reported the fugitive as armed and dangerous. Then, the news shifted over to a shooting involving two suspected Russian agents and an American female military police officer.

"Is there anything on the news, dear?" Frieda asked, reaching up to the open cabinet above the sink, grasping and pulling down her favorite tea-plate.

"So far it's the same news as of yesterday, honey," he replied. "They're still looking for that wanted man."

"Karl, please open the curtains and let some light into the living room."

"In a minute, dear, I'm still watching the news," he replied.

Frieda had just turned on the burner, and with the blinds up and curtains pulled, she looked up and stared at the same man she'd seen once or twice before, exiting Helga's house from across the street. Now, with her glasses on, she'd gotten a better set of eyes on him.

It was a half-past ten according to the clock on the wall; light enough for her to capture the man's appearance and glean a general physical description. *And for what?* She asked herself: Maybe to use in her next novel she had promised herself to write.

However, it was strange to see a man, not of the family, at Helga's.

She hadn't seen her neighbor attending to her flower bed this morning, nor the day before. It was her neighbor's daily routine ever since her husband passed away several years ago. She'd never missed a day to trim her flowers unless it was because of rain.

That was strange.

She watched the young man wearing jeans, a dark shirt, boots, and a mid-length leather jacket, step out from the two-story house, and close the door behind him. She saw him clear as day, as he slipped on a pair of dark shades, went down the steps and walked around the back, and disappeared behind the house.

Minutes later, Frieda saw a blue Toyota being driven by the stranger as it came from behind the house. The driver stopped, allowing traffic to pass on the street, and then he turned left and sped away. Knowing Helga did not own a vehicle, she assumed the car belonged to the unknown houseguest.

Frieda did not know the man, nor had Helga mentioned she was expecting guests the last time she'd spoken to her.

Yes, strange, she thought, shaking her head.

Stranger still, Frieda believed she'd seen the man before, but couldn't remember under what circumstances or where.

With the tea-plate of two cups, with a pot of boiling water in hand, Frieda joined her husband at the sofa, just as the newscaster once again gave warning of the wanted man. Before she sat, a photo of the fugitive flashed and stayed on the screen. She turned to face the TV, and her eyes opened wide, and with a loud gasp, Frieda dropped her tea-plate to the floor, as her hands flew to her face, covering her mouth.

"Oh my *God* ...!" she shouted, feeling her heart hammering in her chest. "It's him ... it's him!"

"Honey ... honey. What's wrong? What's gotten into you?"

Still staring at the TV screen, Frieda fell backward onto the sofa. "It's ... it's the fugitive," she uttered, pointing a shaking finger at the TV. "He's living in Helga's house; call the police!"

With hesitation, Karl stared over at his wife. As she turned to face him, her face was pale and her eyes appeared scared. "What? Are you—?"

Frieda attempted to control herself, and taking a deep breath belted, "*Scheisse! Shit*, call the police, *now*!"

For a moment, Karl Meir remained motionless. Then he picked up the phone.

Matthew Banks aka Sverchinsky stepped out from the two-story house, set back from the road about fifteen yards from the residential street, and walked around the back of the house to his car.

The engine running, he waited before setting the car in motion. He needed some time to think and plan; time, which was not on his side, for both the police and the Americans would be hot on his tail. With a photo of him on the television, he knew the house he was in wouldn't stay safe any longer and also his car. Already, he thought, they may have put two and two together, have a description of the vehicle he was driving, and put an APB out.

He may well have already overstayed his time in the house.

However, he still felt in total control. He was confident in his abilities to elude and deceive those that would pursue him. The Russians and also the Americans may in fact have some knowledge of his plans, considering it came from his computer, but they were still lacking the most important aspects: time, date and location of the suitcase bombs.

No way around it, he suspected; this had to be the work of the Americans. The German police weren't that competent. Probably this was the doing of the CID or FBI or both, he mused. An interesting development occurred as he watched the TV the other night. The news had reported an American CID officer, shooting and killing two Russians in her apartment along with the death of another American female; a soldier shot and killed.

This was no coincidence. He assumed they connected both occurrences to him. Also, he knew the Russians were on his tail too. Of course, there wasn't much he could do about them right now. Although the CID agent sounded like someone he would like to meet.

Banks couldn't help himself as a thought crossed his mind. Maybe, just maybe, a meet with the CID agent could prove beneficial to pick her brain and see how much she knew.

It was worth a try, Banks mused.

Now, he was taking a big chance by driving around. Yet, he had no alternative. His friend, Carl Benz from Frankfurt, was due in town very soon with much-needed equipment, supplies, money and he needed a permanent place from which to set up shop.

So for now, another place to stay and another car were hot on Banks' shopping list.

He felt relaxed for the first time since being rescued from his prison. Fumbling in his jacket pocket for a pack of German Dimitrino cigarettes, he extracted one and lit it with the car lighter. Exhaling the smoke, he set his mind on the task at hand.

Like the steady hand of an artist, he was painting his masterpiece and the city of Stuttgart was his canvas. Soon the world would know his name! With a smile, he shifted the vehicle into drive and pulled away from the house.

———————

Crenshaw and Sinclair sat facing Crenshaw's computer monitor. On the screen was the English translation of two Russian files; with one file marked as photographs, and the other, a text.

She glanced over at Richard, who was staring at her with eyes wide open after reading the first few passages of the translation.

Sinclair spoke uneasily. "Rick, for the sake of our friendship and deniability, please, pull away from the monitor, and let me read these on my own."

Crenshaw slowly nodded, but didn't balk.

As soon as Crenshaw pulled away from the desk, Sinclair saw the two files, both labeled "Confidential." One was marked Russian Text and the other English Translation of Russian Text. She kept reading from the file marked English Translation that exposed two separate plans or phases.

With Crenshaw going after some drinks his wife had left at the entrance, Sinclair rather slow read through the text, not once but twice, as she digested the information it contained:

I, Matthew Banks, with eight of my most trusted comrades, have followed direct orders from the FSB in a plot to overthrow the Russian Government.

The plan called for the theft of seven nuclear suitcase bombs and placed at specific locations in Moscow.

I informed and sent all information to my CIA Handler, William Phillips, but I heard nothing from him or an acknowledgment of these plans or any backup orders.

The Russians' execution was going according to plan until they betrayed me.

I did not place the bombs as planned, but hid them for my use later.

The FSB issued an order for my arrest, as a spy, and charged with the theft of the bombs.

The CIA left me alone in the dark.

I plan, with the help of my comrades, to seek revenge on those that had thrown me to the wolves in a two-phase attack:

PHASE ONE – IDENTIFICATION OF CITIES AFFECTED
Washington, D.C. – The Pentagon
Langley, Virginia – CIA Headquarters
Moscow, Russia – The Kremlin
Lubyanka Square, Moscow, Russia – FSB Headquarters

PHASE TWO – PLACEMENT & LOCATION OF BOMBS

Three two-man teams will have assigned a designated location with one or two suit-case nukes to each team.

Training in the handling and storage for shipment of the bombs will occur at the designated location.

I will assign eight individuals according to specific needs, at the time they receive the nukes.

Photographs (attached) will outline the placements of the nukes.

I have assign travel to their designated location and type of conveyance.

We will give assigned personnel cell-phones to use once, and then discarded, and then wait for further orders.

Sinclair froze as she stared at the color monitor still displaying the text on the screen.

She swallowed. "Good *God* Almighty!"

"It's that bad?" Crenshaw asked as he walked back to his computer desk with a can of Pepsi in each hand.

Turning away from the monitor, she shrugged. "It's not good."

"Something I should know?"

Quickly Sinclair replied, "No, please stay away from the computer!"

Crenshaw bowed his head. "No problem. I'll just set the can on the desk."

"Thank you, Rick."

"Yeah," Rick said, as he dragged another chair and sat far away from his computer desk.

Sinclair sat back in her chair and ignored the soda can by her right hand.

She remembered the policies in place that might prevent a nuclear attack, and development of game theory models that could lead to stable deterrence conditions from her Officer's Training Academy days. She learned of different nuclear weapons delivery, but not with a suitcase bomb.

Facing the monitor, and glancing through the text again, she noticed Banks' plan was a bold one, but short on specifics. The agent estimated that the lack of further substance in the plan could have been intentional on his part. Did Banks have the rest of his plan somewhere safe; maybe in his head? It could very well be the reason he was being hunted. If the Russians had a plan to take over the Government, the U.S. would not intervene in their domestic strife.

They would almost welcome it. And that alone could be the reason Banks did not receive an acknowledgment from his CIA handler.

Sinclair moved the mouse and clicked on the second file. It showed several photographs, most of them of cities in the U.S. and Russia, with a red circle around possible target locations. However, most troubling were the photos of several nuclear suit case bombs labeled the Russian W-54 warhead with a critical mass of plutonium-the U-233. Reading through the photo file, she noted one dirty-nuke was enough to destroy a fair-sized city-with a range of fatalities upwards of 20,000.

Sinclair counted seven of them!

All piled in some type of Conex container. One photograph depicted the inside of the case.

Sinclair identified the labeled parts by the English text, next to the Russian text, on them. There were two Neutron generators, a battery, a mass of Plutonium U-233 in a silver cylindrical canister, about nine inches long by three inches in diameter, arming switch and an antenna with a radio receiver.

All in a black case measuring 16 x 11 x 4 inches with locking latches, one on either side of the case and centered was a carrying grip handle. It was very deceiving in its look and quite impressive.

Leaning back in her chair, a troubled and fearful feeling overcame her. She was thinking of ways to stop this madman and what he'd planned. Were they enough? An FBI Agent, a CIA operative and her, a criminal investigator, and so far, they weren't any closer to Banks or anyone else associated with him. Further, she had no idea how to deal with the Russian agents she'd encountered and killed.

Were they sent out of the Russian Embassy? And if so, how would she handle it?

Sinclair hung her head and closed her eyes. *Too many questions*, she told herself, *and little or no answers*.

It would seem to Sinclair that her investigation had stalled, in her estimation; this was becoming a troublesome case. Then her cell phone started beeping. She glanced at the caller ID on the screen; it was Russell.

"Hi, Dan, what's up?"

"Well, we had a little excitement. We ran into an unfriendly Russian who didn't take kindly to us. Blew up my car, as it was, but we're heading back to your office in a few."

Sinclair sat up straighter, winced, and said. "Wait, what? Y'all okay?"

"Yeah, a little shaken, but all okay."

"So, tell me, what happened to the Russian?"

"He won't be following anyone anymore!"

"Okay, meet at my office," Sinclair said. "I'm almost finished here."

"No problem."

"Hey. So, ah ... no car then, how are you and Courtney—?"

"Oh, that. No need to worry. We, ah, borrowed the Russian's car."

—21—

When Nikolai Bobrov's cell phone rang, he'd prepared for it, well aware of what it meant.

He knew only one person had knowledge of its number—his best friend. The call was his ticket to set the plan in motion. This was the evacuation order he feared, yet he knew his involvement was of paramount importance and so was his assigned mission.

Prior to his friend getting arrested, Nicolai, a tall pale-skinned burly man with messy brown hair, had known his friend, Anisi Sverchinsky for the better part of four years, and did not believe in the wild rumors, that Anisi was a double agent. They'd worked together in the FSB, had dinner with his family almost every Friday at his house, and acted like an uncle to his child. So, no, it could never be. He just couldn't believe it. However, Anisi now a thief and a traitor to his country, and branded so by the corrupt political system for which they both worked.

He'd promised to do whatever for Anisi, regardless of the costs.

Bobrov's friendship with Anisi began as a mission to safeguard a visiting dignitary. But the mission went hot, and took a turn for the worse, when a sniper threatened the dignitary's life.

He remembered the two shots that rang out from an assassin's rifle. He was standing in the direct path of those bullets and froze. An instant later, Anisi, out of nowhere, ran and pushed him out of the way, getting hit once on his shoulder as the other bullet entered through his right side. Later, when he asked Anisi why he'd taken a bullet for him, Anisi answered: "It was the right thing to do."

So, when Anisi told him of his plan and asked if he could take care of the nukes, his answer was, "Most definitely."

The call came several months ago when he was living alone in his small cabin in the hills of Novaya, Russia. The order had been a complete evacuation of Russia, with the seven suit-case nukes already in crates and hidden in a cave in the hills above his cabin.

Once he had his truck loaded with the crate, and his household goods being used to hide it from prying eyes, Bobrov traveled alone, and only by night through the dark lonely side streets and dirt roads, skirting several military and police checkpoints along the way. During the day, he rested in two small towns as he filled up with gas and food for the long drive.

They'd completed their plans just before Anisi's arrest; now, all they needed was to carry it out. First, he was to transport the bombs out of Russia, and into the city of Voru in Estonia, there to await his next call.

Second, Anisi planned through intermediaries to purchase a plane from the Tartu Airport about thirty-four miles south of Voru and have Bobrov fly the crates to a location determined later. The plane, a Piper Seneca with twin-turbocharged engines, was being kept in a storage unit until Bobrov needed it. A seasoned pilot who had flown various military aircraft, including the piper, Bobrov knew it would represent no challenge.

Bobrov's flying abilities were one reason Anisi had picked him for the mission and by his unfaltering friendship and loyalty.

Living in a one-bedroom pension apartment just outside the city of Voru, he waited for the last call. Money was no object; Anisi had given him one hundred thousand rubles and one thousand American dollars for his use.

Bobrov, the commensurate spy, played it safe. The moment he'd arrived in Voru, he'd stored his truck, with its cargo, in a secured garage and rented a car.

It was two days ago, as he sat on a bench around a large crowded park filled with running and screaming children, as he watched a flock of pigeons flying overhead that resembled a chaotic cloud of birds, the call came through.

Hearing the beeping of his phone, and feeling its vibration in his jacket, he reached in and pulled it out. Once he pressed the green accept button, he heard the voice of his friend on the other end. *"Hello Nikolai, how goes it there for you?"*

In a low sheltered voice, Bobrov answered, "Are we a go, Anisi?"

"Yes, the destination is Stuttgart, Germany."

"Do you have a place picked out for me to land?"

"Of course I do, Nikolai. You should know better than to ask, knowing how I like to plan."

"I should not have asked, Anisi."

"It's in an old abandoned strip. I'll text you its coordinates in a few minutes."

"I'll start tomorrow evening."

"What time do you think you'll arrive?"

"Best guess, eleven or twelve that night," Bobrov replied.

"Good, call me when you're an hour out of Stuttgart and I'll be there to meet you."

"See you then, my friend."

"Have a safe flight. Got to go, take care, my old friend, and I'll see you soon."

After shutting down his phone, Bobrov started making preparations for his flight.

In the Russian Consulate General office in Frankfurt, Captain Kuznetsov, with a Crystal tumbler glass filled with vodka in one hand, and a Backwoods Russian cream cigarillo in the other, sat as he watched Lieutenant Colonel Borovkov pacing up and down her office floor.

Kuznetsov found himself in a huge, high-vaulted ceiling room. A round crystal chandelier hung center of the room. Light oak colored paneling surrounded all four walls. Two high ceiling windows, curtained in white, were situated to one side of the room. On the other side of the room was a small six-chair conference table. In the room's front, up against the far wall, was a twelve-foot light oak desk, and a smaller desk centered on it with two high-backed chairs. Two flag stands with Russian flags were situated left and right of the desk. To the left of the wall was a large screen television.

As he gazed at her, Kuznetsov measured her up and down. She appeared young, maybe thirty-six or thirty-eight. She wore a collarless open-front black jacket, bow-neck white blouse, and black straight-leg pants with a pair of black open pumps. Her long brown curly hair cascaded down and over her shoulders. In his estimation, she had one of the cutest faces he'd ever seen in a Russian woman, with knock-out blue eyes.

Stunning and dangerous, mused the captain as he discreetly gazed upon her.

He took a deep breath, then a deep sip of his vodka.

Not knowing why he was in her presence, Kuznetsov, however, believed it had something to do with his man Volkov who hadn't reported in. He knew Volkov had missed his second call-in. In his last check-in, Volkov mentioned he was following the two American agents. Something was amiss, he thought. It wasn't like Volkov.

Once he'd stepped into her office, she'd offered him a shot of vodka and asked for him to pull up a chair by her desk. At her desk, he saw an empty glass and an expensive bottle of Jewell of Russia Ultra Edition Vodka. *Besides beauty, her taste was on par with his,* he mused. Then he poured three fingers worth of the clear liquor and sat.

That's when she rose from her chair and began pacing.

Not saying a word, he drew a few puffs on his cigar, and then he swirled around the smoke before expelling it. He loved the sweet aroma it gave off, which took him back to his beautiful historic city of Samara on the banks of the Volga River; the place of his birth. He waited to hear what was on her mind.

She stopped pacing. "Things have not been going the way I like," she said, staring at the captain. "And, your man Volkov is dead. According to the German police, they found him on the side of the road with several bullet holes in his chest."

Captain Kuznetsov raised his eyebrows and cocked his head to one side. "Shit, I knew something was wrong!" *Someone's going to pay for it*, he told himself.

She nodded. "Ah, yes, something is wrong. We have underestimated the Americans."

Borovkov turned and walked back to her chair and sat forward, hands on her desk. "So the question is, what are we going to do?"

He glanced at her but remained silent. He knew it was a rhetorical question. She already had her answer, or he wouldn't be sitting in front of her.

She took in a deep breath. "Your orders, Captain, are to take the rest of your men to our consulate in Stuttgart. There you will report to the Consulate office and you'll conduct operations from there. All you need is in that folder in front of you. Your job will be to find our Russian spy, retrieve a set of plans and kill the American agents. Am I clear, Captain Kuznetsov?"

"It's quite clear, ma'am."

"Good."

"When do you want us to leave?"

"*That* captain would be immediately!"

—22—

Carl Benz had completed all the details requested by his friend Matthew Banks. It had only been two days since he received his call and now packed and ready; he was to drive the two-and-a-half hours to Stuttgart via the E41 highway, the quickest route, today.

Benz was a tall, dark, clean shaven-faced man, and for his age of seventy-two, he was athletic, five-feet-nine, with broad shoulders and narrow at the hip. His closely cropped black hair showed signs of graying along the temples. His eyes were a steel grey. Twice weekly, he spent his off-duty hours in the gym, keeping up his youthful appearances.

A retired member of the European Court of Justice, Benz had a small practice in Frankfurt. He'd been a friend of the Banks family for several years. Matthew's father, Jason Banks, had requested Benz's services years ago through mutual friends. These involved the transfers of sizable sums of money from America to Germany for disbursement throughout Europe and his large business holdings in Germany. Jason Banks had been a multi-billionaire.

His billions were old money that ran through his family since the early 1800s. With several property holdings around Europe, including Germany, his services involved also purchasing real-estate properties for development. Jason Banks holdings waxed and waned, but overall were very successful enterprises with huge shareholdings. And Jason Banks, like his son Matthew, paid him well.

However, Jason Banks and his wife died in a traffic accident in Germany, while Matthew was still in college in the USA. His father had made provisions for his son, his sole heir, to be the beneficiary of his estate. It also made several provisions for his holdings in America, although Jason Banks had his own set of lawyers from that side of the pond.

Benz had, from time to time, assisted Banks with his dealings whenever he was in Europe. Banks had requested money be transferred to an aircraft sales company in the city of Voru in Estonia for the sale of a two prop airplane made out in the name of Nikolai Bobrov. Who Bobrov was wasn't explained, nor did he care to know.

Banks requested other provisions; a supply of eight cell phones, two laptop computers along with inexpensive handguns, and ammunition which he'd paid for from the black market. Why he needed these, he didn't ask, and not even a perfunctory explanation was provided.

After he'd purchased some snacks for the drive, he slid behind the wheel of his blue 2019 BMW 6 Series Gran Coupe, turned over the engine, and set the gear in drive. Pulling out of his driveway, he entered the main road and sped off towards the E41 Autobahn.

—23—

Banks was working off a list he got from two local property rental agencies he found on the web. They listed five potential homes along with a ranch and emailed the information to his iPhone. It was the phone he'd confiscated from a fallen agent on his way out of the safe house. He changed a few of its settings before using it.

The instrument, to his luck, was not password protected, nor did it have facial recognition or thumb-print access. He considered the fact, which was staring him in the face, that he needed to dispose of it, and soon. But for the time being, he would continue using it. Yet, the possibility they may trace it back to him—sooner, rather than later—played upon his mind. He was hoping no one had reported it missing.

Although two days ago, he received several calls and a text which he hadn't bothered to answer. Then it stopped altogether. *Yeah*, he mused, *I'll just have to take the chance.*

The places on his list he'd agreed to visit seemed to fit his needs as a base of operations. Working with his smart phone's GPS app, along with Google Maps, he followed the driving directions and found the first three homes. But they were disappointing. Those three were inadequate for his needs; houses were too close together with an abundance of neighbors and loud children. He needed something more substantial and away from prying eyes and nosy neighbors.

The fourth was a rundown uninhabited shack; not worth a closer look.

Banks felt frustrated.

He was just about to call it quits; it was getting late, and he needed to get back to the house for a few things. However, he had a small suitcase packed with clothing in the car's trunk; his 'go-bag,' in the event he needed to move fast.

He set the address on GPS for the last house—the ranch. A moment later, he drove east for several miles into the country. Following a winding two-lane road, he passed three ranches then nothing for several miles. This, the main road, according to the GPS, was Gablenberger Weg, and he was on the lookout for Albert Strasse and his turnoff on the left side of the road.

After driving through an almost barren tract of land, he found his turnoff further ahead. Turning left onto Albert Strasse, he slowed after the turn, as he glimpsed the ranch from around the bend on the dirt road. He came to a stop as a gate barred his further progress.

Sliding out of his car, he stood straight up, did a 360-degree turn, liked what he saw, then walked a few feet and stopped in front of the rusted metal gate. Pushing it open, he took two steps, stopped again, and ripped off a for-rent sign on the gate and threw it into the surrounding woods.

Banks paused for a moment to think. So far, this could very well be the place he was seeking. Taking his time, he circled the path-way and approached the front of the farmhouse. According to the listing, it was an 1870s German Schulz farm, a one-story house with a barn. It was an old cow farm. Coming to the wood ranch style rail-fence, he hitched a foot and leaned his arms on the top of the fence.

Gazing out, he spotted a large front yard, a cow pasture, and a large pigsty. Wooden fencing surrounded the property. He also observed the power grid was intact as a light shown on the front porch. Toward the back of the house, a forest of tall oak trees spread out as far as the eye could see.

It was his intention on renting the place for two months, but no longer. His plan would take several days to complete. Enough time which would raise no suspicion from prying neighbors.

Back in his car, he drove back to the two-story house he had been staying in. He looked over to the car's clock: 2:23 p.m. It had taken him about forty-five minutes to get back, and now he was two blocks away. Yet, before he arrived at the house, what he saw up ahead brought a snarl to his otherwise serene face.

Banks frowned, for in front of him, there were six German police cruisers along with two MP Jeeps, with blue warning lights flashing, in front of his house. He saw a bevy of German and military police officers walking in and as if they owned the place.

As the color drained from his face, he pulled over to the curb behind a VW Bug. Keeping the engine running, he gazed over to the house. He watched as two men in white hospital garments, whom he took to be medics, carried a stretcher out of the house with a covered body on it. He knew it was the body of the woman he'd killed.

Banks felt a little edgy being so close to the police. And yet, he did not feel any anxiety creeping upon him, even though he'd come so close to being arrested, or killed.

Gripping the steering wheel hard, his knuckles started turning white. His dark eyes flashed with a mixed look of anger, for he knew he couldn't get back into that house again. Was it some nosy neighbor or something else which gave him away or did someone recognize him from the TV newscast? Banks realized his heartbeat had increased in the last few minutes as he looked around at all the police activity.

Keeping his gaze toward the front, he noticed barricades were going up on either side of the street. He could not drive past the house, for they had set up barricades blocking the passage in or out of their crime scene.

Taking a deep breath, and with a sigh, he had known they would find the house at some point It was just too bad it was so soon. *Could it have been the female CID Agent who found me?* He thought. That could have well been the possibility. There was only one way to find out, but not yet.

And then the rain fell.

A drizzle at first, getting harder as the seconds ticked away.

It pelted the windshield and beat against the roof of his car, and then it poured down in heavy sheets across the roadway as the pitter-patter came to his ears. It was becoming impossible to see the front of the house.

With his window rolled down about three inches, the only sounds were the rain, the random chatter from the police radios, and the muffled shouting the cops yelled to one another for attention.

It would appear to the untrained eye a chaotic scene, Banks thought. Yet in reality, to others, it was far from that. Most would say a normal police occurrence. But to Banks, it was his cue to leave.

He drove out of the area. Keeping an eye out through the inside mirror, he drove back to the ranch.

At three o'clock that afternoon, in the second-floor conference room of the Stuttgart CID field office in Patch Barracks, Agent Sinclair met again with Russell and Courtney. "I'm going to let you guys fill me in on what you have found so far, and about your near-death encounter, before I give up what I found."

Courtney and Russell stared at each other.

"You want I should go first?" Russell asked Courtney.

With a graceful nod, Courtney replied, "By all means. You can tell it better than I."

"Well, several things happened," Russell began. "The most interesting occurrence . . . we were tailed by the Russians. When that started is anyone's guess. That was very clear when we first caught sight of someone following our ass. We confirmed it when we tried to elude the Russian. Which begs the question ... do they know about us three, or just Courtney and me?"

As he spoke, Sinclair watched him, thinking they must know about her too. "My guess is all three of us. And if I'm not mistaken, this could have been their opening salvo."

Russell nodded. "I was thinking the same. The Russian wasn't just following us, he wanted to kill us. He fucking used an M79 grenade launcher on my car and blew it to bits."

Sinclair said, "We know now what we're dealing with. They want us out of the way so they can have free rein in their search for Banks. And they think we have what they're after."

"Which is?" Courtney asked, now more interested in what she may say.

"Banks' plans held in a thumb drive," Sinclair responded.

Courtney arched an eyebrow and nodded.

However, Russell had not finished speaking. "Another interesting tidbit, the MPs, along with the German police, found where Banks had been hiding out. He's still here in Stuttgart. He killed the owner of a house and set up shop there. Seems a neighbor recognized his photo from the newsfeed. But, instead of holding surveillance on the property, the German police screwed things up by raiding the place and then calling the MPs."

"It would stand to reason then," Courtney chimed in, "that Banks may have shown up, saw the police, and is out looking somewhere else for his next home."

"Yeah, I agree," said Sinclair. She glanced at Agent Courtney, believing she may yet keep some vital piece of information from the group.

Sinclair didn't trust her. She was an unpredictable element in the group. Hell, she thought, I prefer a reliable to an unpredictable friend. At the moment, Sinclair knows where Courtney stands with her.

Trust is a fragile thing, and Agent Courtney has not earned it from me, Sinclair mused.

After a second or two, Russell felt Sinclair's eyes on him. "What?"

Sinclair replied, "You have anything else?"

"Oh, yeah," Russell said, "I received the following information from D.C. Seems, our boy's parents were multi-billionaires. When his father passed away, the estate went to his son, Matthew. According to records, Banks owns several properties around Europe, but none that he would use as a base of operations. He has large companies and some large corporations his father gained, but they were businesses and tenement housing, which shows why he chose *that* house."

"By far, the man is not stupid," Sinclair said. "He wouldn't use his given name, knowing the FBI would flag him. So, he knows he has to keep off the grid to be successful in his plans."

Both agents nodded.

Courtney, in one lithe, graceful movement, crossed over a leg. The movement not lost on Russell, as his brow lifted, cocking his head in her direction.

Courtney asked. "Ah, do we know what those plans represent?"

"We do; World War Three!" Sinclair said.

A brief silence passed between them. Sinclair said nothing for a moment. Then she removed the thumb drive from her pocket and placed it on the desk. "Encrypted in this drive were his plans. They killed my best friend for what's in it. Along with several others, of which you both know of."

Courtney, with a hardened expression, rose and in a voice tightly mixed with anger said, "And you had that all along? What the fu—?"

Sinclair jumped off her seat and stared right at Courtney. "I, ah, just don't trust you, Courtney," Sinclair cut in. "You haven't earned the right for me to trust you. From the beginning, you've shown a lack of willingness to give up what you know concerning Banks until I made a fuss about it. So, yeah, trust goes both ways."

Without a word, Courtney sat back down and dropped her gaze from Sinclair. "My orders were that I couldn't divulge specific information. With just enough, though, so you and Russell could chase after Banks for us. *'They are the detectives,'* my superiors said, *'let them find him for us.'* Those were the exact words they used."

Russell just sat there, shaking his head and shrugging. "Gee," he said, as he crossed his muscled arms and leaned back on his chair, "for a moment there, I swore you ladies were coming to blows."

With a grin, Sinclair shrugged and eased back down on her chair. "I wouldn't say that, Dan."

Sinclair pulled her chair closer to the desk and opened the folder. "What I'm going to say, I know you're not just going to keep to yourselves. It's okay though. Please notify your superiors. I have. The Provost Marshal will receive a copy of this tonight when I go to see him. There's a lot to learn from the file. I've made copies for the both of you."

"Tell us what you have, Sinclair," Russell said.

Agent Sinclair shifted focus, working backward to the intercept of the original message, how it came to fall into the hands of U.S. Army Intelligence in Stuttgart, who intercepted it, and how her best friend, Major Jessica Wayne, had possession of it.

Agent Sinclair said. "To preserve the integrity of the file, she used her algorithm and encoded the thumb drive that you see here in front of you. This has been what, four days now, since that occurred. With her death, and of others, I decided that someone would pay for her murder."

For the following few minutes, Sinclair explained placement of the seven nuclear suitcase bombs were in four well-defined places, and his plan called for a two-phase operation. Phase one, she went on, identified the cities targeted; two, the placement and location of the bombs. And the message also showed photographs of the devices.

Once she'd finished, Sinclair pulled out the copies of the plan from her folder and passed them on to the two agents, along with the photos of the bombs.

There was an unusual silence.

"God, *Almighty!*" Russell said, after reading through the file.

Courtney shook her head. "Sweet mother of ... this is the work of a madman."

"A very smart and dangerous madman," Sinclair acknowledged.

Russell asked. "Do we know how and when they'll place the bombs?"

"No, but they detail the target places in the report."

Sinclair turned to stare at Courtney. "Someone ... dropped the ball on Banks. And according to him, his CIA handler; a man named William Phillips was the one."

"Sinclair, I have no information on that," Courtney said, "I didn't know. I was in the dark too."

Sinclair paused, thinking as she leaned back in her chair. "No use placing blame on anyone until we have facts to back them up."

Russell shook his head. "Um, well, what's your game plan, Sinclair?"

Sinclair inclined her head. She had earlier outlined what she needed them to do. She knew she could trust Russell, but Courtney was still an unknown.

"First, if those bombs are not already in Germany, here's what I would like done. Russell, alert the German coast guard for any unusual activity on dock and sea, along with German customs service. Second, the German police must conduct police patrols in a radius, of, say, 60 miles of Banks' last known location. If they need additional police patrols, the army MPs can help. I'll have my father see if that's workable. Third, I want to know of any report of stolen vehicles, and from where it happened."

"I'll see what I can do."

"How can I help?" Courtney asked, in a low tone.

Sinclair gazed at her. "You've been working in Germany, what, five years now?"

"How did... Never mind," Courtney said, "Closer to six."

"So, in your six years, you've made several contacts in your world since, correct?"

"I have a few CIs; my confidential informants I've used from time to time."

"Good, then get your CIs to work," Sinclair said. "Show them a photo of Banks and let's see what they can turn up for us."

"I'll get them on it."

Sinclair sighed. "Excellent."

Next, Sinclair glanced at her watch: 4:30. Then she reached over to her desk phone and dialed her father's office, knowing he would still be there. She then left a note with the secretary she was going up to meet with him shortly.

"If you two have anything else," Sinclair said, "let's get moving. We have a madman to stop."

Russell rose, thrust his hands into his pockets, and gave Sinclair a wink and walked toward the office door, with Courtney right behind him. At the threshold, they halted as Sinclair called out, "Good hunting, you two."

PART TWO

Complications

—24—

Colonel Richard Sinclair attentively eyed his daughter while clutching his glass of whiskey. He knew the emotional struggle of not being with the one person she loved was eating at her heart. He didn't say a word at first, as he gazed into her eyes, aware they were holding back tears. She was always a strong, prideful woman, but losing Price had made it that much difficult to cope with. Yet, he knew, she and her fellow investigators would bring this case to a satisfactory conclusion.

"So, honey, tell me what you've found so far."

With the curtains open on both windows, the light of the full moon streamed through and fell onto the huge office floor, bathing it in a soft expanse of silver light, as the overhead chandelier also gave off a soft radiance to the office.

Should I tell her now, the colonel wondered, *or wait until she finishes her report for me?*

He was feeling the stress of needing to tell her what he'd learned about Tom, and it was eating him up.

"Belle ... Belle, honey."

"I know, Dad, my report."

With a deep breath, she let it out and made direct eye contact with her father. "Dad, we found out several things." She then described all that had transpired in the last few days and hours. "And I had the thumb drive decrypted."

She detailed the contents of the drive: the suitcase nuke bombs and the plan's ultimate targets, the person responsible for the mad plan and those individuals involved.

A silence ensued, while Colonel Sinclair gawked in horror, and stared into space; his body still, his expression not betraying the terror of what he'd just learned.

He couldn't help feeling that this time it could be even worse if she couldn't stop this evil SOB's plans of destruction that would cause the death of millions. Then he reopened his eyes, as he composed himself, and taking in another deep breath, he wiped his brow with the palm of his hand. He needed to get her story out to the Pentagon, and soon.

"Dad ... you okay? You look pale."

We live amid a world gone mad, he thought.

Colonel Sinclair looked up at his daughter. "Yes, Belle, I'm okay. Go on, please."

"Dad, the crazy thing about all this, and mind you—this is just a theory of mine without hard facts—I believe the CIA knew about the bombs and who was behind it months before Wayne's office's interception of the plans. And further, there's no telling how high up the chain of command knew of it beforehand. And my gut is telling me, someone isn't being honest with me."

"Whom do you think it is, Belle?"

"I'm working with a CIA operative, who I don't trust. I've been getting bits and pieces from her ever since she teamed up with me and Dan Russell."

"Do you want me to send her back?"

"No, not just yet," she said, with a slight grin. "I may still have some use of her."

"Very well then," Colonel Sinclair said as he gulped down his whiskey. "This is interesting as a whole. On their own, I wouldn't even think of it. Nukes and murder, a terrible combination, but there has been a report concerning the murder of the NSA Director, Steven Summerset, in Virginia. What, if any connection to his murder the nukes might have, I'll leave that for you to determine. There's speculation that the director was working on a classified project. Hell, this could be it. The FBI is taking the lead in that investigation."

"You think there's a connection?"

"It's hard to tell," he said, filling his glass once again. "But until I get orders from higher up, I want you to follow up on it. Something stinks; just don't know what."

"No problem, Dad. I'll see if Russell can learn anything from FBI headquarters."

"So, now tell me, what your plans are moving forward?"

"I have the German police, along with the FBI, watching the ports for any suspicious persons entering the country carrying a suitcase described in the Banks plans. It's a long shot, but one worth playing. The German police found where Banks had been hiding out."

She paused for a moment. "However, they missed their chance of capturing him when they pulled a raid on the house way before attempting any surveillance. Banks never showed and may have known the police were at the house. Was he there in hiding, watching the police? He may have. So we spread a dragnet of about 60 miles to see if he found a new home. In the meantime, I'm having Courtney alert her CIs to see if they could find any information on Banks' whereabouts and any contacts he may have made."

Again, she paused a moment. Then she came around her chair to a coffee table, with an empty whiskey glass, and a half-full bottle of a whiskey decanter. She poured about three fingers of the liquid, returned to her chair, and sat. Taking a long pull of the whiskey, she said. "The FBI had in the 70s had what they called a suitcase nuclear detection kit. I'd like to see if we could get our hands on one or two for our use. It would make our search of the nukes more efficient in the possibility that they're now in Germany."

"I remember reading about those. They worked very well in the field. Read where it was used to stop several bomb threats. I don't know, Belle. They're antiquated kits. Don't know if they still have them, but I'll make a few phone calls and see what I can find out."

"Thanks, Dad."

"If you don't have anything else, Belle, I'll need a full written report in the morning."

"Yes, sir."

"Now honey, on a personal note."

"I'm all ears," she said, downing her drink.

Leaning forward in his chair, he placed his elbows on the armrest, rested his chin on his tight fists and gazed at his daughter. "Belle," he whispered. "They found Tom alive and—"

The agent stiffened as she tightened her grip on her empty glass.

She asked, ardently, "And what?"

"Villagers found him and they took him to a Royal Netherlands base hospital, near to where they found him. After being treated, and once in a stable condition, a U.S. Army helicopter transported him to an American hospital. He's on his way to Walter Reed hospital in Bethesda, Maryland as we speak."

"What ... happened to him, Dad?"

"Well, according to my information, Tom and his group fell into a hasty ambush. Tragically none survived, except for Tom. He was the only one that escaped. After being wounded several times, he sustained a gunshot wound that lodged in his spinal column."

Sinclair's face paled. She lurched forward in her chair as if she might fall.

"They won't be able to extract it until he arrives in the U.S. They think ... he may not walk again. Then, honey, he slipped into a coma."

Sinclair's gaze lingered on his last words for a moment. Thoughtfully, she asked, with a lump in her throat. "When did you hear about it, Dad?"

"Not more than a few hours ago."

"What now, Dad?" she whispered, almost on the verge of tears.

In response, he rose, approached her, and in a fatherly sense of urgency, scooped her up in his embrace, and whispered in her ear. "He's in excellent hands now, Belle. All we can do is pray. I'll make sure I get notified of his ongoing condition."

She felt joy and sadness envelop into one feeling. It was with a heavy heart she closed her tear-filled eyes and cradled her head on his shoulder.

Russell looked up as he and Courtney passed the dinner menus and wine list to the waiter. Across the table, she looked up at the waiter and said in perfect Italian, "*Avro il insalata con pollo, parmigiano e succhine a griglia. E una bottiglia di vino biano Vinsanto.*"

They were in the Perbacco Bar Restaurant just off Tuebinger Strasse, in a dimly lit atmosphere that catered to a higher class of customers. A bar set off to a corner and filled with men and women were enjoying their drinks. Rated the number one restaurant in Stuttgart, was the reason he'd chosen it. The other being, it wasn't the first time he'd eaten there, so he knew the menu.

"*Grazie, signora,*" the waiter said, thanking her and jotting down the order.

With a smile, Russell glanced over at Courtney. "The chicken salad with parmesan and grilled juice sounds like an excellent choice, Pat. The white wine sounds good too."

"Thank you, Dan."

Everything on the short menu sounded very delicious and all within his budget, Russell thought, so he decided on the Salmon, "*E avro, Salmone in crosta di mandorle.*"

"*Grazie, signor.*"

Across the table, Courtney nodded her approval. "The salmon in almond crust sounds rather good too. I'm impressed. Your Italian was perfect, Dan."

"Well, my mother was Italian. She grew up in Tuscany."

"You have any other tricks up your sleeves?"

"The night is still young. We'll see," he said, with a wink.

Russell felt rewarded by a broad, warm smile and eyes that held a certain promise. Could it be romance he saw in her eyes? Then he felt her foot under the table, as she was lovely rubbing on his leg, and he smiled back. Reaching out his hand across the table, her extended hand touched his, as their eyes met and a slow-burning desire gripped his loins.

After their meal, and while sipping on their wine, they looked across at one another with smiles. She said, catching his eyes on her, "Do you think Agent Sinclair likes me, Dan?"

Oh, shit, that was a loaded question. He was hoping for something more romantic out of her.

"Jacqueline is a complex person. To tell you the truth, it took her a long time to warm up to me. Don't worry, she'll come around. Just be honest with her. You shouldn't have any problems."

She nodded.

"On another note," she said, resting her hand on the table. "Did I ever thank you for saving my life?"

Russell eyed her as he slowly sipped the last of the wine. "You, know, come to think of it, no, you didn't."

"Let's go to my place," she said, "I'm looking forward to paying my debt, proper."

—25—

"Don't lose them!" Captain Kuznetsov yelled over the din of heavy traffic from both sides of the crowded streets. They lagged five cars behind, while the driver, Damir Semenov, maintained visual contact with the American agents. Yet the glare of oncoming traffic made it that more difficult in the almost bumper-to-bumper traffic.

With a casual glance to his left, Semenov saw traffic had thinned and took quick advantage. After shifting lanes, he could make out the target car, a vehicle ahead of them. "And damn it, Damir, don't let them see us!"

"Yes, comrade," Semenov replied, keeping his cool with his captain. "I'm trying. But this fucking traffic is heavy. It's worse than driving in Moscow."

Kuznetsov knew that Semenov, a Russian Circuit Racing Series touring racecar driver, had captured second place in 2017 and 2018, in the Moscow races, and knew how to handle fast cars. But the art of mobile surveillance was all too new to him.

Then Semenov saw the opening he was hoping for just ahead. Shifting lanes again, he pulled the steering wheel to the right, slid behind the car up ahead, and was now a car behind the agent's vehicle.

Kuznetsov glanced at his GPS on his iPhone. He needed to get a sense of where they were heading and record the address for potential future use. It was eight-thirty-five as he stole a glance at his watch. They'd started the surveillance two hours ago when they had pulled into a space just outside the U.S. Army installation. Unable to gain entry into the Kaserne, they had parked to the right, just enough to watch the vehicles that came in and out of the installation, and enough to remember the faces of the drivers.

Just as the two hours were ending, they established contact with the American agents as they drove out of the Kaserne. He had taken a chance on the assumption that the agents were still inside the Kaserne, and it had paid off as he recognized the driver, an FBI agent named Russell, and his passenger, CIA agent Courtney, from the photos in his file resting on his lap.

It wasn't his intention to kill the Americans. No, not yet. He planned to follow, observe and listen. Once the Americans determined the whereabouts of the traitor Anisi Sverchinsky, they would eliminate the agents on sight. Their goal lay with Sverchinsky.

He knew he was dealing with rather smart American agents. Somehow, they'd gotten the upper hand on one of his men. That never should've happened. He would not underestimate them again. But now he needed to know what they knew. The only way to gain the information would by interrogating the two agents. He also planned to attach a small round GPS magnetic tracker on their car to facilitate tracking and surveillance.

Earlier, he'd ordered his second in command, Anatoly Sokolov to pull surveillance on the agent named Sinclair and extract information from her as well, and if possible, to attach a tracker onto her car.

There were two ways of gaining entry into the house, he thought, before the Americans knew someone was inside. Which one he'd had not decided yet. Once he did, it boiled down to its execution.

———

With the night wind rushing through his half-open window, Russell increased his speed, wanting to get to Courtney's apartment and out of this traffic as soon as possible. An overcast sky was pressing down on traffic, leaving the skies a dull grey and promising rain.

"How much further?" he asked.

"Not far now, Dan," Courtney replied, as a smile spread across her lips.

Just then, Russell felt her hand messaging his leg, and he felt himself aroused by her touch: *Was she asking for something, or just being a tease?* So, ever so, he placed his free hand on her leg and rubbed it. Then she opened her legs for better access, and with her warm hand, she held his and directed it between her legs. Feeling her mound, he felt her wetness and noticed she wasn't wearing panties.

Taking his hand away and licking his lips, Russell said, "I can't concentrate on my driving, Pat."

They had been on a first-name basis ever since the Russian had tried to kill them.

"Oh, um, darn. And I was just getting a rise out of you."

They both broke out laughing.

"Hope that fire you have," Russell said, "doesn't get extinguished soon."

"No chance."

He took a glance her way and saw a different woman. There was a sincere longing in her eyes. The same longing that was running through his loin.

Agent Russell kept his emotions in check. Yet, he was nursing a strong feeling for her. She reminded him of his late wife, Irene. It was going on ten long years since her tragic death by a drunk driver, since he had felt such a powerful attraction to another woman. He considered himself an excellent judge of character, and he admired her grit and tenacity. She was damn good looking, too!

Should I tell her how I am feeling? He asked himself.

No, not yet. There was plenty of time afterward, he reasoned.

Courtney bit her lip. The attraction to Dan made her feel wanted and appreciated. He was rugged, handsome, and strong, confident of himself, and a good listener. Was she feeling something for him?

This was more than sex, she told herself.

Then she saw her turnoff. "Dan, hang a right here. My apartment is the second on the left."

Taking the turn, Russell saw her apartment building.

Cruising along, he found a parking space and pulled in. Sliding out of the car, he came around to her door. There he opened it, held out his hand for her, as she slid out of the car with his help. She moved in close to him, and they kissed as they explored each other with enthusiasm and a sense of urgency. Seconds later, they leisurely separated, and hand in hand, they walked to the front door and into her apartment.

As the Russian operatives rounded the corner, up ahead they observed the American agents disappear inside the building.

Finding a space under some broken street lights, Semenov turned into it and turned off the engine. They had just rolled down their windows partway when a light rain fell. A light wind brought a chill to the air.

"How long should we wait, Captain?" Semenov asked.

Captain Kuznetsov glanced at his watch. "Let's give it an hour. That should be sufficient time for them. And the rain, if it keeps up, is a welcoming sight. It will muffle our approach."

"Yes, sir," Semenov replied.

After several minutes, and not hearing plans of gaining entry into the apartment from his captain, Semenov coughed and through the semidarkness of the car's interior, he asked, "Sir, how do you want to approach the apartment?"

Kuznetsov didn't reply for a few seconds. "Do you have your phone?" Kuznetsov asked.

"I do, sir."

"Good, you will take the rear, and I, the front window, or the door. Once you gain entry, text me. That will be my cue to enter. We must both be inside before we make our move on them. Clear?"

Semenov nodded, "Yes, sir."

Once his captain advised him of his orders, his second in command, Anatoly Sokolov, driving a black four-door Jeep Cherokee with German plates he'd commandeered earlier, started his drive toward Patch Barracks, Army installation.

With the falling rain, and traveling east on the A8 Autobahn, he reached the exit which would lead him to the Stuttgart-Vaihingen, then onto Hauptstrasse, and his destination, Patch Barracks. Just about gaining sight of the main gate, he veered off to his right and followed the side streets around the installation's fenced area.

Twelve minutes later he stopped and pulled over to the side of the road and killed his engine. It was dark, and the rain fell in sheets. No living persons were about, and lights from homes were far away to his right.

Then he reached over to the backseat and grasped a pair of bolt cutters. Sliding out of the jeep, he ambled over to a thicket of tall grass, walked a few feet and stopped against an eight-foot-high chain-linked fence.

Working as fast as he could, he made enough room for the jeep to go through. Back in the jeep, he backed out a few feet, and then in drive, he jumped the curb, and rapidly drove through the sizeable gap he'd made in the fence. It was a tight fit, but eventually, he made his way inside. Shifting to all-wheel-drive, he drove through the wet muddy grass, and several minutes later, onto a paved road.

He knew where he needed to go, and working off a map of the Kaserne, he knew it would take him a few minutes to reach the Provost Marshal's office where he hoped to catch sight of CID Agent Sinclair.

Arriving at the building, Sokolov saw office lighting, and figured someone was home. Now he had to wait.

Agent Jacqueline Sinclair strode away from the Provost Marshal's office, heading to her car as the wind and rain whipped all around her; drenching her. She walked, oblivious of the rain, as she remembered what her father had said about Tom. It brought a smile and sorrow at the thought that he might not walk again. One thing kept alive in her heart and of seeing him once again, was—hope. Hope for them both.

Arriving at her car, she looked around, as was her nature, but only saw a jeep parked in a space away from her car. She didn't see anyone in it and didn't give it a passing thought.

Unlocking her car, she slid behind the wheel and drove toward her father's military quarters on the Kaserne. Her place was still a crime scene. So home for the present was with her father.

Pulling away from the parking lot, she drove away and failed to notice a pair of headlights coming on way behind her.

Driving below the posted speed of twenty-five mph, she arrived at the quarters and pulled into the drive-way. Killing the engine, she started walking to the main door just as a passing jeep glided past. She did a double-take and bit her lip. Was there something to this? And was it the same jeep she'd seen before? But then her fears allayed as she watched the jeep pulling into a drive-way some houses further down the street.

<hr>

Watching the American agent, Sokolov placed the jeep in reverse and parked out on the street. He waited a whole twenty minutes, until he saw no lights in the house, to make his move.

Once out of his car, and as he made his way to her house, Sokolov stopped by the car's right front side. Kneeling beside the wheel, he placed a tracker device under the wheel-well, and then he made his slow way around the back. The back porch had a sliding French door and a window off to one side. He tried the door first, but found it locked. Then he moved off to the window. It was open, with at least a two-inch gap.

Without hurrying, he opened it just enough to squeeze his body into a dark living room. Removing his shoes, he proceeded at a slow pace to the open front glass doors leading into the room and stopped. He saw a flight of stairs leading up to what he assumed were the bedrooms. Reaching behind his back, he flipped his jacket's coattails back and pulled out an Israel made Masada-9 9mm, 19 shot automatic silenced pistol. Holding the weapon in both hands, he stepped onto the first landing and made his way up the stairs.

He quickened his pace as his stocking feet made no sound.

Reaching the top-landing, he heard someone in the shower on his left. He glided through the door of the bedroom and stopped. The bedroom only had a bedside table lamp on, giving the room a ghostly atmosphere. Then, he moved to the open bathroom door and stood behind it, waiting for her to make her appearance.

Seconds later, he heard the shower being turned off.

Sinclair, having finished showering, wrapped a towel around her head and another around her body and walked into the bedroom. Someone, or something, struck the side of her head and she went down on her hands and knees, still conscious and shaking her head.

Instinctively, Sinclair knew there was someone behind her; someone who wanted her alive, or otherwise, she'd have been dead by now.

Behind her, she heard someone speaking. "Get up slowly."

She heard an accent, what she thought was Russian.

Oh shit!

Sinclair did as she was told. She rose, but just at the point of standing straight up, she unraveled her body towel, and still on her knees, flung the towel at the gunman's arm. However, in reflexive action, his trigger finger squeezed off a shot that flew away from her, striking the far wall.

Before Sokolov could regain control of his weapon, Sinclair rose and ran the two feet to the side of her bed and the nightstand. She opened the drawer, reached in and pulled out her gun. As fast as she could, she wheeled around to face her attacker.

But before she could fire, he fired off a sustained burst in her direction.

Instinctively, she dropped to her knees, and with the cover of her bed, she heard the whiz of passing bullets as they sped just inches above her head. Still drawing a bead on the Russian, she topped her head over the bed and fired off a three-round burst of her own.

Before Sokolov could react, two of the bullets entered his left shoulder. Running backward and aiming his weapon, he fired on full automatic at the space where the agent was hiding. He ran out the door, and down the flight of steps, with Sinclair suddenly right behind him firing her weapon.

Sokolov, once on the ground floor, felt another bullet striking his right side, but it was not enough to stop his escape. He bolted through the living room, and without stopping, jumped through the open window.

Mere seconds later, reaching the window, Sinclair saw a running shadow off to her left and fired another three-round burst, but to no avail, she lost him in the darkness.

"*Shit*, God damn it!" she yelled.

Then she realized they had attacked her *here*! Were Russell and Courtney also next on their list? Running back upstairs to her bedroom, she found her cell phone on the bed and dialed Russell's cell phone, but got no answer.

Dressing as quick as she could, Sinclair called the MP Desk Sergeant to shut down the installation, informing him of the attempt on her life. Would she be too late to stop him from getting out? Minutes later, Sinclair was out the door running to her car, and on her way to Russell's apartment.

⸻ · ⸻ · ⸻ · ⸻

Once in bed, their lovemaking had been hot.

After twenty minutes and exhausted, Courtney fell asleep as he too closed his eyes. Yes, he mused, he was in heaven.

Sleep overtook him and his dreams were of Pat.

⸻ · ⸻ · ⸻ · ⸻

Moving smartly, Kuznetsov and Semenov made their way to the apartment. The two Russian operatives reached the drive-way, and Kuznetsov stopped by the car, while Semenov continued toward the rear of the house.

Kuznetsov reached into his jacket pocket and removed a small miniature tracking device and placed it on the front left wheel-well. The tracker's magnet would keep it from falling. Rising, he made his way to the door and tried the handle. To his surprise, it turned, and he opened it a crack and waited for Semenov's text advising him he was in.

After a few minutes, Simonov's text pinged on his phone.

He was in!

Calmly they met in a small dark living room with only the night's moonbeams lighting the room from an un-curtained window. Off to one side was a bedroom whose door was ajar. To this, they made their slow way.

Pulling their silenced handguns, they crept to the threshold and pushed open the door. Taking one side of the bed each, they moved to the front of the bed and held their weapons to the heads of the sleeping agents.

Kuznetsov shook the American FBI agent awake. And with Russell suddenly wide awake, he couldn't take his eyes away from a gun pointed at his head. From the corner of his eye, he saw another man pointing a gun at Courtney.

"What the fuck—!" Russell began.

"Shut up," Kuznetsov commanded, "Do what we say, or she dies."

"You're Russians," Russell said.

"And you're very smart for an American," Kuznetsov said. "Now on your feet and move over to that chair in the corner. No sudden moves. Nod your head if you understand."

Nodding, Russell slowly rose out of bed, completely naked, and did as instructed.

"What the hell do you want?"

"We'll be doing the questioning," the captain said, not impressed with the American, "and you'll be answering very soon."

Just then, with a burst of speed, Courtney rose straight up and tried to reach for the gun leveled at her head. It was a quick move, but Semenov was a bit faster. As she began reaching for the weapon, he struck her on the side of her jaw, snapping her head to one side. As blood gushed from her mouth, she slumped back on the bed.

"Jesus, Christ! You son-of-a-bitch, I'll kill you for that!" Russell yelled.

Before Russell took a step to her side, Captain Kuznetsov, with the barrel of his gun, struck him a hard blow to the back of his head. And as he fell, he lost all sense of consciousness falling hard on the wooden floor.

Russell woke with pain emitting from the back of his head. He gently lifted it and tried to move, but couldn't. They'd tied him hand and foot to a chair. Then moving his head around, he saw Patricia tied down as well, to another chair just to his right side. Sometime, he guessed, when he had gone to sleep, she'd slipped on a short silk nightgown.

"Good, you're both awake," Kuznetsov said. "So now we begin the asking."

"Fuck you, you'll get nothing from us," Russell swore.

"Oh, I believe we will," Kuznetsov said with a sneer.

Captain Kuznetsov came around and faced Russell. Smiling down on his upturned face, he struck Russell, not once, but three times in a row, hard across his jaw. With blood dripping from his mouth, and spitting out a tooth, Russell yelled out. "Kiss my ass, asswipe!"

Russell tried to breathe deeply, to calm himself. But all he took in was his blood. He winced, and knowing what was coming, he closed his eyes.

Bang! They hit him again and again. Yet, the result was the same.

"Where is Anisi Sverchinsky hiding?"

"I don't know," Russell replied, opening his eyes and choking back blood.

Repeating his question several times, Kuznetsov got the same answer.

Removing a three-inch knife from its sheath down his right leg, the captain asked again.

Russell said nothing.

"Let's see if this will jar your memory, Mr. FBI man. Tell me or I will drive my knife into your leg!" his torturer barked out his words.

"Fuck ... you!" was all he could reply.

Pulling back his knife hand, the Russian plunged it deep into Russell's thigh.

A loud yell of pain burst from his lips, as he almost passed out, but said, "Go ... to ... hell!" Feeling his warm blood rushing down his leg, his chin fell to his chest.

Realizing he was getting nowhere with the FBI man, Kuznetsov turned to his partner. "Semenov, it's your turn on the female."

Russell felt on edge as his head snapped back up. "Stop ... don't ... hurt her!"

Semenov, standing in front of her, grabbed the top of her nightgown, and with a violent yank, ripped it apart exposing her bare breasts.

Staring down at her bare chest, with pleasure in his eyes, Semenov licked his lips, fondled her breasts, and pinched her nipples. "Nice soft pair." For a second, he just stood there.

Then he struck a hard blow across her jaw, causing her head to snap to the side.

"Where is Sverchinsky?"

"Fuck you!" she muttered between her bloody lips.

With blood streaming down her face and over her breasts, Russell couldn't take it anymore. "Stop it! I'll tell you what you want to know."

"That wasn't so bad," Kuznetsov said with a grin.

For the next ten minutes, Captain Kuznetsov interrogated both Russell and Courtney as to the whereabouts of Sverchinsky. Yet, after the grueling torture of them both, they realized the American agents had no idea of the traitor's whereabouts.

They left the agents tied up as they made their way to their vehicle. They would live, and eventually, they would lead them to the traitor. But the longer it took, the more his mission was in jeopardy of failure.

———— · ———— · ———— · ————

Sinclair arrived at Russell's apartment and found it empty. Were Russell and Courtney together? Opening up her phone, she found Courtney's address and phone number. She phoned but got no answer. Moments later, she was back in her car en route to Courtney's apartment.

At the door, she found it ajar. Pulling out her weapon, she moved, ambling through and into the bedroom.

What she found just about choked her, for there tied to chairs and sitting in their blood were Russell and Courtney! Russell was sitting naked with blood running down his chest. Courtney had her nightgown ripped open and stained with blood. Blood had congealed on the floor, which spread out in concentric circles around their chairs.

They were both unconscious.

Running to their side, she checked their pulse and found that they were still breathing, although Russell's pulse sounded weak. Pulling out her cell phone, she called for an ambulance. Then she covered their bodies up with blankets. She sat, discouraged. The Russians must have done this, she thought. They were desperate to find Sverchinsky. But what could Russell or Courtney have told them? Did they know something she didn't?

—26—

At that same moment, as Sinclair burst into Courtney's apartment, twenty-five miles away, Carl Benz arrived in Stuttgart. According to his GPS, he would arrive in fifteen minutes at the address his friend Banks had texted earlier. Leaving the A8 Autobahn, he came to a two-lane road and followed it through some barren tract of land. To his right, in the distance, he saw lights which he assumed were from homes. There were no streetlights to guide his way; only the lights from his car's headlights set on high beam. He was alone on the road; he saw neither car's, in front, or his rear, for miles.

Now, his GPS showed he was to make a left turn just a kilometer ahead. Benz saw lights off to his left.

Was it the ranch Banks had spoken of? He'd find out soon enough, he thought.

As if from nowhere, suddenly, a deer materialized from the right side of the road and flitted across his windshield. Slamming on his brakes and jamming the horn, he swerved to avoid a collision. The deer leaped into the air, landing on the opposite side of the road. Fishtailing, almost to the point of losing control, and fighting with the steering wheel, he brought the car to a screeching stop.

Benz couldn't believe what had just happened. He looked to either side of the road and saw no more of wildlife.

Moments later, getting back on the road, Benz said a small prayer of thanks that he and his car were in one piece.

A few minutes later, Benz hung the left onto a dirt road and then onto a graveled extension. Up ahead, his headlights caught an open gate. Driving his 2019 silver BMW, he kept his speed below 10 mph, not wanting to get the car scratched or dented with loose pebbles.

Rounding a bend in the road, the first thing that caught his attention was someone standing on the porch, hands in his pockets—as a yellow porch light bathed him in its glow—of what he believed was the main house. He glanced sideways out his window, but couldn't see much of anything else but darkness.

The beams of his headlights highlighted Banks; a tall, powerfully built man much like Bank's father whom he'd known years ago.

Benz angled his BMW to a stop in front of the porch. Shutting it down, he turned off his headlights, opened his door and slid out, clicking his remote to lock the car. Then, with squinted eyes, he peered into the night, as nocturnal noises assaulted his ears such as the croaking of a bullfrog, crickets chirping and the soft, two-note hoot from an owl in a nearby tree.

The sounds were all new to him as a city dweller that would spend ninety-nine percent of his time inside of a building. It was disconcerting. He couldn't wait to get back home.

"Tell me you didn't just ... lock your car?" Banks asked, meeting Benz half-way.

"I, ah," he uttered, as he looked around him. "Oh, I see what you mean." He realized the futility of what he'd just done in their isolated setting.

"You're still the same person I met so many years ago, Carl," Banks said, smiling and extending his hand to his friend.

"A little older, perhaps," Benz replied as he shook his hand.

"How was your drive?"

"Besides the deer, I almost ran into back there on the road," he said, "uneventful."

"Well, come inside, we have a lot to talk about."

<hr>

The Piper Seneca lifted gracefully into the air.

Gaining flight speed and reaching his desired altitude—low enough to evade any ground radar detection—Nikolai Bobrov banked the yoke to the left as it came around for the cruise phase of the flight ahead of him. Then, setting the engine's cruising speed, he set the automatic pilot. At his current speed, he should reach Stuttgart, Germany, around midnight.

With the plane flying at top speed, a short time later, Bobrov—as the autopilot flew the plane—went to the cargo-hold and checked the tie-down straps on his cargo. There were two wooden crates. The medium-sized crate contained the seven nuclear suitcase bombs. A smaller crate contained several automatic assault weapons, handguns, with a large supply of ammunition, several two-way radios, and ten cell phones for use as burner-phones.

Getting back behind the flight controls of the cockpit, he reached between the two seats for a metal lunch pail. Opening it, he pulled out a large sandwich and chips. As he sat back and enjoyed his dinner, he opened a bottle of wine from an ice chest sitting on the co-pilot's chair.

The plane shot across the dark cloudless sky, and as he ate, Bobrov checked his instruments, speed, and altitude settings. Glancing at his watch, he calculated he had less than six hours of flight time until he reached Germany to call his friend, Anisi Sverchinsky.

According to the coordinates given to him by Anisi, the airstrip was located just east of Stuttgart. It was an old abandoned Luftwaffe airfield. According to Anisi, the airstrip's only structure, still standing, was the control tower.

It was pre-arranged that before Bobrov started his descent, Anisi would flash a signal with a large LED searchlight. In the event Bobrov failed to spot the light, he was told to ditch the plane, along with the cargo, into the ocean.

Let's hope I don't have to ditch; I can't swim that well.

Bobrov's flight path would take him over Latvia, and then Lithuania into Poland. Veering east, he would make the border of Germany. And then, at eleven-fifty-five, his plane crossed over the border into Germany.

"Hello, Anisi," Bobrov said when he pulled out his cell phone and dialed his friend's number.

"Hi, there, Nikolai," Anisi/Banks said, feeling relieved on hearing his friend's voice. "Your journey is drawing to a close, Nikolai. I worried something may have happened."

"Oh," Bobrov said, "well, I flew well under the radar for the duration of the flight, and I removed the plane's transponder to be on the safe side. With it, ground radar would've been able to pick me up on their radar."

"That was a smart move. How much longer before you arrive?"

"Give me about thirty minutes."

"I'll be waiting."

On hearing the good news from Nikolai, Banks had Carl Benz drive him to the airstrip.

Now all that Banks needed was to set the plan in motion. However, before that, he first had to have the nukes in his possession and that would be soon.

The moment he hung up the phone, Banks dialed seven cell phone numbers; all in Russia. His seven closest allies would then deliver a nuke to different parts of the world after coming to Stuttgart.

Banks conveyed the address of the ranch to all seven of his men. Most would arrive by boat and some by plane. They were to purchase or rent vehicles once in Germany. It would take those two days to arrive at the ranch, and then his plan of revenge would begin.

Thirty minutes later, they arrived at the short strip of tarmac. They slid out of the car as Benz shut down the engine. Then they heard, far in the distance, the drone of a plane.

"Could that be him, Matthew?" Benz asked.

"We won't know until it's nearer to the landing strip."

Then silence.

Opening the rear door to the BMW, Banks grasped the searchlight and turned it on, making sure it worked and closed the door.

"Carl, stay by the car," he instructed Benz. "I'm going to the tower."

In the middle of the night, the Piper touched down on the short tarmac, on the abandoned airfield and west of the city of Stuttgart. Bobrov taxied it to a halt in front of the BMW.

The two crates were unloaded, and the nukes placed in the car's trunk. They opened the smaller crate, revealing the contents, and loaded them into the car's trunk as well. They stored the rest in the back seat. Bobrov returned to the plane and grabbed two cans of gasoline from the cargo hold. He splashed the interior of the plane with the contents, struck a match and ran out of the plane.

With a loud *whoosh*, the plane caught on fire.

Turning his attention to the two men next to him, Bobrov observed that Banks had changed little since the last time they were together. Matthew stood tall and proud, wearing hiking boots, blue jeans and a tan sweater.

"Nikolai Bobrov, meet Carl Benz."

Shaking hands, Benz stared at Bobrov. "Ah, so you're the man I purchased the plane for?"

"That would be me, alright," Nikolai replied. "A great plane it was. Sorry to put the torch to it."

Banks said, "It needed to happen."

All three men slid into the BMW. Keeping within the posted limit of 72 km on the quiet streets, they arrived twenty minutes later at the ranch.

Good so far, Banks thought. *Now we have to go over the rest of the plans.*

—27—

Office of Special Plans (OSP) the Pentagon,
September 11, 8:45 A.M.

Angela Marie Cobbs was a stunning single young twenty-ish woman with sun-bleached blond hair and deep blue eyes. Single men in the office, and those married, couldn't keep their eyes off of her. Jealous were most of the other women workers of the attention and the attraction she had with the office males. Asked out on dates since the very first day she arrived, she declined the offers. She had been off and on with her college boyfriend for the last few months, and wasn't that interested in dating.

Known by her nickname of Angie, she sat in front of her computer screen in the Special Plans section of the Pentagon. Around her were eight men and women whose job was to supply senior presidential administration officials with raw, unvetted intelligence by intelligence analysts.

Clicking through several intelligence reports, Angie found the mention of a SEAL Team operation, and that of a classified investigation conducted by the Army Criminal Investigation Division, out of Stuttgart, Germany, which looked troubling.

The first thing she took notice of, were the president's signature on the document was missing. Instead, the signature authority was that of General Earl Fleming and countersigned by the Director of the CIA, Jonathan Fakes, and the NSA Director, Steven Summerset. The operation involved the use of a submarine and the rescue of a certain CIA asset from a prison in Russia with an approval date of August 28th.

If the President did not approve the operation, she thought, someone failed to submit it through the intelligence chain of command. Angie reasoned it involved invalid and unlawful activities, but that was not her concern. However, the reporting of it was.

She kept digging through several other classified materials and found a reference to a safe-house in Germany attacked by Russian FSB agents. Why and what were the Russians doing there? Again, that did not concern her; only the Intel was pertinent.

Then, after an hour of digging, she found a reference to a nuclear strike. *Where, by whom, and how?* She found no further reference to it.

Angie raised her head over her computer monitor, stood up slightly from her chair and looked around the office. She felt as if someone had been watching her, more so now than ever. But after a few seconds, she thought she was being paranoid and continued.

She spent a better part of an hour typing all the information she had dug up and made copies of the reports. The report was about three pages long with several attachments. Placing a TOP Secret cover on her report, she went to the head of the OSP, Richard Straight, and submitted her report to him.

It was half-past four in the afternoon when General Fleming, the Chairman of the Joint Chiefs of Staff, received the call from the White House. At sixty-two, with big lumberjack hands, he stood well over six feet, with short-cut brown hair and without an ounce of fat on his muscular physique.

His military career might be in jeopardy, he feared. He knew the reason he was being ordered by the President of the United States, for the meeting at Camp David was because of the actions he had taken without the President's consent. Meeting away from the Pentagon or Oval Office spoke volumes.

And he knew what could happen.

Acting as the head of the JCS, he had violated protocol and may have committed a crime for which he could lose his career and face a devastating court martial. His direct boss in his chain of command was the Secretary of the Army, and he didn't have operational control of U.S. military forces. That was damaging, construed as an act of treason!

How can I express and justify my actions?

Would other members of the president's cabinet also attend? He believed the answer was yes. Grabbing his briefcase, he placed all the information on the Theseus project in the case, closed it up and prepared for the chopper flight to Camp David.

Opening the left drawer of his desk, he pulled out a half-empty bottle of Old Crow Bourbon whiskey and a short shot glass. He poured two fingers of the liquid, downed it and poured another. Now he was ready. As he rose from his chair, his phone rang.

He stared at the instrument and let it ring several times. Whoever was calling it could wait until he returned, he thought. Or, it could be some very important news on a project he'd been working on in the last few weeks. He sighed and lifted the receiver.

"This is General Fleming," he said in a gruff voice.

"Earl, it's Jonathan, they want me at Camp David. The President wishes to speak to me on an urgent matter."

So the CIA would be there, too. Who else?

"I leave soon," Jonathan continued, "they're sending me a chopper in the next few minutes."

Standing still, General Fleming said nothing for a moment. Then he sat on the edge of his desk, with the receiver just off his ear, contemplating what they would say to the President, how the President was going to take the information, and why he acted without specific guidance and authority from him.

He had only one option.

"Earl, are you still there?"

Placing the receiver back on his ear, Fleming said, "I'm also heading to Camp David, Jonathan. I was just leaving when you called."

"Shit!" he muttered. "What do we say?"

Without hesitation, Fleming replied, "We tell the truth ... leaving nothing out. It's the only thing we can do."

"This ... may cost us our careers," Fakes said

General Fleming sighed in disgust. "I'm well aware of that, Jonathan."

He thought back to the rescue of Banks and the massacre at the safe-house. If the fuck-up at the safe-house hadn't happened, all this would be a moot point.

He sighed. It could get messy; we'll see what happens.

<hr>

Fleming and Fakes arrived within fifteen minutes of each other at Camp David.

Their helicopters, twin Sikorsky VH-60N "White Hawks," landed on the tarmac behind the huge retreat with General Fleming the last to arrive. As he disembarked, two Secret Service Agent personnel, dressed in black, carrying assault weapons clutched in front of them escorted him to the retreat's back door entrance, where another Secret Service agent escorted him to the living room.

As the agent opened the living room door, Fleming immediately observed three personnel sitting around a coffee table in the room's center. Fakes, seated on a rattan armchair, a folder on his lap, stared up at him. Sitting next to him was the President's new Chief of Staff, Brigadier General Alvin Meadows. Rear Admiral William Savage, the Deputy Director of the CIA, sat by a large picture window.

They diffused the living room with two table lamps set on either side of the room. Two large picture windows, with the curtains opened, showed a forest of green, with the view of the setting sun as the backdrop.

"Earl," Meadows said, "please have a seat over here, by William."

Fleming noticed the President wasn't present as he strolled over to the proffered chair and sat. Opening his briefcase, he removed a folder, closed the case and set it on the floor to the chair's left side. He kept the folder closed and on his lap.

A moment later, two staff personnel, in cook's uniforms, entered the room. Each was carrying a tray with two coffee decanters, cups, and ham and cheese sandwiches and placed them on the coffee table. Without a word, they turned around and departed the same way they'd entered.

Just then, through the living room's main entrance, the President entered.

Phillip Anders was at the end of his first term in office, and for the last few months, had been campaigning throughout the country for his reelection bid. Consensus showed it could very well be a landslide victory.

Anders, Fleming noticed, still had thick wavy blond hair, cut short, with deep-set pale grey eyes. With grey slacks and grey opened button-neck shirt, he eyed each person around the coffee table. The moment he entered, they all stood until he took his seat on one of the two cushioned chairs facing his security cabinet personnel.

Anders, grabbing a sandwich from the coffee table, took a big bite, and sat back. "Gentlemen," he began. "I brought you here to discuss a sensitive matter, which needs my direct involvement, and yours. Earlier today I received some information through the OSP office of a possible nuclear strike against our homeland and an attempt to overthrow Russia's government, by its military, through the use of nuclear weapons." They stared at one another, but no one said a word.

General Fleming rose and handed the president a folder. Glancing through it, the President said, "It would appear that we have a rogue American undercover agent to thank for this situation. From what I understand, several days ago, Army military intelligence officers found an intercepted message in Germany. They killed two of those officers for the knowledge of those plans, which detailed a madman's scheme to have suitcase bombs brought into the U.S. and have them set off. Do any of you know of this madman, Banks, who seems to have worked for us at some point?"

General Fleming said. "Sir, Banks tried to warn us, but we ignored him and when he asked for help, we ignored that too. The Russians arrested Banks for treason and jailed in a maximum-security prison.

They executed his Russian wife and daughter as he was being arrested and in his presence."

"Whom did Banks report to?" Anders asked, looking around at them. "And was he or she reprimanded or fired?"

"Sir," Savage chimed in. "We found his CIA handler, William Phillips. It was Phillips who recruited Banks. According to Phillips, Banks resembled a captured FSB agent, who died at the hands of his interrogators. After inserting him into Russia, Banks acted out his part for about eight years without mishap. According to Phillips, Banks secured important first strike information for us, until Phillips dropped the ball, and let Banks rot in prison. As to your second question, sir, I have placed Phillips on administrated leave without pay."

Anders nodded.

Then the President turned his attention on General Fleming. "The Army Criminal Investigation Division, in Stuttgart, Germany, General Fleming, was the ones that brought the follow up to our attention. When and how they plan to bring the nukes into the States is unknown. However, what concerns me the most—who failed to brief me of this beforehand?"

Clearing his throat, General Fleming replied as he locked eyes with the President. "It was I, sir. In answer to your question, Mr. President, I take full responsibilities for my actions and those of the two other personnel, one of which is sitting here and the other deceased."

"Go on, General," President Anders said.

"Thank you, sir," Fleming said, once again clearing his throat. "You're correct in saying that the Army's MI group in Germany intercepted a coded message sent from Russia bound for the Russian Embassy in Germany. The Russians planned to have our CIA undercover operative, Matthew Banks, posing as an FSB agent, recruited into their ranks to steal seven nuclear suitcase bombs, and plant them around Russia, in an attempted coup by its military. However, it didn't go as planned."

Fleming paused for an instant. "Banks kept the bombs for himself. His intention was revenge on the US for not helping when he asked to come home and left him high and dry. He also intends on bombing the Kremlin."

Here, General Fleming went into detail on all that transpired the day they killed Steven Summerset. "I, along with Summerset and Fakes, planned the entire operation, but it was I, and I alone, that set it in motion. I needed to have Banks rescued from his prison and extract the location of the nukes. But as we know now, it failed."

President Anders in a solemn voice asked, "Do we know how many got killed in the safe-house and how many did we lose in total?"

Fleming responded. "We lost the entire SEAL team, sir. With them, they killed twelve personnel along with a CID Agent."

Anders stared long and hard at Fleming. "It's one too many, General."

Fleming simply nodded.

"All those deaths are on your hands, General," Anders said, in a low voice. "Are we any closer in capturing or killing Banks and his people? And who the hell is running the show over there?"

Savage said, "Sir, I can answer your questions."

Anders turned his attention to his DCI's deputy. "Please go on, William."

"Yes, Mr. President, we have agents of the FBI, and the CIA, along with that group's leader, a CID Special Agent named Jacqueline Sinclair, a counterterrorism expert, sir."

The mention of the name Sinclair had Anders scratching his head. "Why does the name Sinclair sound familiar?"

Chief of Staff Meadows cleared his throat. "Sir, she was the agent that found information about General Thomas Randolph Scott's plans to nuke North Korea, sir."

"Oh, yes, right, and she did a bang-up job too. Give her all the help we can give her, gentlemen, and let her do her job. But if this escalates to where I have to take military action, I'll send them some boys to help."

"Sir," Fleming said, "if I may, the underlying reason I took action without your consent and knowledge was for plausible deniability on your part. That was the only reason."

"Thoughtful but unnecessary," the president said, "Very well. The important thing is what we do now. General Fleming, and Jonathan Fakes, you will continue in your present capacity. I need both of you to coordinate whatever the agents may need in bringing an end to Banks and his plan of massive destruction. Earl, I expect a full briefing on their progress, every day, COB."

General Fleming felt slightly relieved. However, he knew this wasn't over, not by a long shot, but he kept his mouth shut. "Yes, Mr. President."

Fakes just nodded, but also felt relieved.

"In the meantime," the President said, as he stood, "let's all head out to the dining room and have dinner. The First Lady is expecting us."

—28—

The doctor, a tall Major, pulled back the white privacy cubicle curtains and walked into the recovery room of the Clinic's ICU ward. He glanced at the female sleeping on a chair, and said in a low voice, "Agent, hello agent."

Not getting a response, the doctor proceeded into the room.

Several medical charts and X-rays lay on a corner roll-up desk by the entrance. The doctor ambled over to it, but not before taking another glance at the woman still sound asleep. He paused, for even in sleep, she looked stunning.

With a sigh, he glanced away. At the desk, he picked up the charts and started reading through them, making annotations, just as the sleeper awoke.

Sinclair, as if from a distance, heard a man's voice calling out to her. Then, she felt a presence in the room and sat straight up. Reaching for her holstered weapon, she realized where she was.

Not quite awake, she made out a doctor standing by a desk holding some X-rays.

"You must be CID Agent Sinclair."

"I am, sir." Her throat felt dry and tight. She stared at the doctor while wishing for coffee to wake her up.

"Doctor, how are Russell and Courtney?" she asked.

"Mr. Russell's knife wound has been closed and will require healing. He has lost a great deal of blood; not to mention the brutal assault to his face and jaw. The X-ray of his head showed minuscule broken bones to his nose, while they dislocated his jaw. Ms. Courtney's X-rays showed no broken bones, just cuts and bruises, but she also lost a considerable amount of blood."

The physician continued in a somber tone. "It's very fortunate they brought them here in time, or else, Russell may not have survived much longer because of his blood loss."

Sinclair nodded.

"Doctor, what's their prognosis?" she asked. "And how soon will they be able to get back to work?"

"Well, when they wake up, they'll be in severe pain for some time, and in need of close medical supervision," he said, glancing down at his notes. "As far as work, well, they need to stay in the hospital for several days."

Sinclair nodded, swallowed, and shook her head.

Damn, there goes my team for now.

"I suggest you go home and get some rest. We'll get in touch with you when they wake."

Sinclair rose, shook the doctor's hand, and turned toward the two agents. With a sigh, she turned back and walked out of the room. She wished she could rest, but there was no time. She had to stop the Russians and find this rogue agent before they did. Until Russell and Courtney were back in harness, she would use another agent under her supervision—Agent Richard Wesley Smith, who had combat experience. He was young, under thirty, but tough.

Now he needed to get tougher for what she had planned for him.

Captain Kuznetsov comforted Sokolov in the recovery room. His wounds weren't serious. And, according to the doctor, Sokolov would need to stay in the hospital overnight; the sooner the better, Kuznetsov thought.

Back in his cubicle, he took a phone call from Colonel Borovkov.

"So, what went wrong, Comrade Captain? Your report was vague."

"Nothing, it wasn't all a total loss."

She sighed. "Oh? Seems one of your men got involved in a gunfight with the female CID Agent who escaped getting killed by a woman. Besides that, we aren't any closer to learning where Sverchinsky is hiding."

Kuznetsov sat motionless for a moment, taking his time to reply. "We interrogated two of the agents. In my professional opinion, I believe they have no idea as to the whereabouts of the traitor; not yet, at least. And also we placed tracking devices on their vehicles and we're monitoring them as we speak. So yes, like I said, not a total loss."

"I don't require your opinion, captain, just results."

"Da, Comrade Colonel." *What a fucking bitch*, he thought.

"I will command your activities in person. Expect my arrival within three hours. And in the meantime, don't conduct any activities until I arrive. Is that understood, Comrade Captain!"

He sat straight up in his chair, taken by surprise, "It's quite clear, Colonel Borovkov. Is that all?"

"Yes!"

He hung up the phone with a suppressed sigh of anger and frustration. This was not good. He didn't need a woman breathing down his fucking neck! Nothing good is going to come out of this, he thought.

———————— · · ————————

There was a chill to the morning air, and it was a cloudless day. Notwithstanding the brief gust of wind heard from outside the window, snow flurries fell. It was a bright, snowy, quiet morning.

Earlier, Banks had sent Benz into a small town a few miles from the ranch for takeout breakfast meals. He'd had coffee already waiting as Benz arrived with three large paper bags filled with enough food for the three.

The furnished one-story three-bedroom ranch house had all the amenities one could ask for; food in the fridge, warm blankets, running hot and cold water, electricity and a fire blazing to keep them warm.

After breakfast, they sat around the fireplace with cups of hot steaming coffee. Banks had an open laptop computer on a table by his side.

"When will the rest of our team arrive?" Nikolai asked.

"They've taken different routes. Some will arrive by boat, one or two by commercial flights and one by train. They all have forged paperwork, identification and travel documents out of Russia."

"Think they'll have any problems," Benz asked, "I mean getting out of Russia?"

"I don't see how," Banks replied. "Unless the Russians and the Americans know who they are, which I doubt."

Glancing down at his laptop, Banks clicked on the Stuttgart U.S. Army Military Police information website on Patch Barracks. Scrolling through different numbers, he found the listing for the criminal investigation section. Grabbing his cell phone, he dialed the number and waited for someone to answer.

"CID, how can I help you," a woman's voice came on the other end.

"May I speak with Agent Sinclair?"

"Please wait a moment while I try her number."

Then Banks heard a sweet, sexy voice come on the line. "This is Agent Sinclair. How can I help you?"

Without introducing himself, Banks said, "I heard the FSB tried to kill you and your agents, I—"

"Who the hell is this?" Sinclair almost yelled into the phone.

"Easy, Agent Sinclair," Banks replied with a smile on his face. "Don't get your panties in an uproar."

Somehow, she knew who the caller might be. And if he was the person she thought it was, it was better to listen to what he had to say.

"I'm listening. But tell me who you are first."

Banks grinned. He said, "In due time. So, here's a little help with your investigation. The FSB gets their orders straight from the Russian Embassy in Frankfurt, and they have a consulate here in Stuttgart with FSB agents too. They could be the ones who tried to kill you."

Sinclair caught the reference *to here in Stuttgart* bit. So it would tell her he was still in the area if it was the same man.

Banks continued. "You'll get your answers from them, but they won't tell you a thing, as long as they are in the Embassy. Catch my drift, agent?"

"Why are you telling me this?"

"My reason is quite obvious. I'm giving you fair warning, Agent Sinclair, stay away from me, or the FSB won't be the only ones gunning for you."

Before she could reply, Banks hung up.

Banks closed the computer and smiled. So far everything was running as planned. In a few hours, his comrades would arrive and he would set in motion the catastrophic events which would mark his total revenge. And if Sinclair tried to impede that, he would put a bullet in her head!

—29—

Dispirited, Sinclair sat in her office after hanging up with the person who had to be Matthew Banks. The most wanted man under her radar and he had called *her*. She would've felt flattered if he wasn't so nefarious.

Banks had a soft-spoken Southern accent she couldn't place because of the German inflection in his voice, which changed the tone and pitch. But what was the real reason for his strange boldness in calling her? It had to be more than to just warn her about looking for him. Was he just trying to distract her into worrying about the Russians?

An unpleasant sense of déjà vu gripped Sinclair as she remembered a General Scott from last year with the same vindictive heart as Banks. Revenge had driven Scott to a point of self-destruction; spreading out to those around them.

Jesus Christ, for what? A perverted sense of duty!

She remembered a quote by Confucius that's always resonated with her: *Before you embark on a journey of revenge, dig two graves.* Banks made a hell of a lot of graves, and one that'll soon be waiting for him, Sinclair mused. She felt Banks had taken the darker side of revenge and now he's digging his own destruction. She'll prove that once she lodges a bullet in his brain!

Banks had seven nuclear suitcase bombs in his possession, each one enough to level a fair size city, leaving it uninhabitable for years or decades to come. And he planned on setting them off in the U.S. and

Russia; the ultimate revenge against those that wronged him and to those who senselessly murdered his wife and child.

Sinclair couldn't fathom the logic behind the depraved mind that would kill millions just to satisfy the death of a few.

Not logical, she thought.

Sinclair sat behind her desk studying the CIA file on Banks. The file contained a few pages. It was enough, in her belief, to determine that the man had his reasons for what he hoped to accomplish. And in his twisted mind, it was those reasons that more than justified a terrorist act and mass murder.

Agent Sinclair had already decided on the course she would undertake with her investigation. It seemed justifiably clear to her, that surveillance of the Russians was way overdue; now more than ever, she needed to know who she was up against, and their numbers. Once that's accomplished, she'll play it by ear. Maybe she'd get lucky. Hell, she knew the Russians were after Banks too. So, it was a game of who would get to him first.

The Russians had shed first blood, and she was going to shed the last with theirs. She had a score to settle, and she vowed that nothing, and no one, would keep her from it.

A firm knock on the door caught her attention. "Come in," she said, looking up from the file.

The door opened slowly and one of her CID agents stood at the doorway. "Ma'am, Agent Richard Smith, reporting as ordered."

"Come on in and take a seat, Smith," Sinclair said as she watched the well-dressed Smith enter her office. In the morning briefings, before starting the day, Smith was always one of the best-dressed agents. She told him to sit, to put him at ease.

Smith, she knew, was an enlisted man holding the rank of Sergeant First Class. He was of medium height, with curly black hair trimmed low almost in a buzz cut, with dark black pools for eyes. And by any fair measure, fit. A man that dressed in a light blue two-button plaid suit, light blue shirt, and white tie and tan shoes.

However, he would have to lose the suit for what Sinclair had planned.

He's a looker, I give him that.

Sinclair knew Smith was a married man, with two young children, and had come up through the ranks of the Military Police Corps. Before that, he spent two years of combat in the infantry serving in Iraq.

"How good are your stake-out skills, Smith?" she asked, locking eyes with his.

"My ... eh, stake out skills? Well, I haven't conducted surveillances in over a year, Chief, but I guess I haven't lost my touch. What type of surveillance do you have in mind, fixed, or mobile?"

"Lose the suit, bring your weapon and meet me here in half an hour. We'll play it by ear once we get there."

As an afterthought, Sinclair asked, "What type of vehicle do you own?"

His eyes widened. "I don't own a car, Chief. I have an electric 2019 Livewire Harley-Davidson bike."

"I see. Is it fast?"

A smile spread across his face. "It's a bolt of lightning, ma'am." He paused. "Chief, mind if I ask what the case is about?"

"You can ask."

Shrugging again, Smith, slow and steady, shook his head.

Flashing a smile, Sinclair rose. "Okay. Come where you can see the computer."

They studied a face profile on her laptop monitor, the glow of which reflected on their faces. "This," Sinclair said, placing a finger on the screen, "is a CIA spy. His name is Matthew Banks; our target. He's a double agent for us and the Russians. So far we have no leads to his whereabouts and both sides are killing each other in the effort."

"Understood," Smith said.

She revealed everything that happened, including two of her agents being hospitalized, the death of one other of her agents, Ricardo Stubbs, and her own near death. "The nukes are our biggest concern."

She waited for an instant and then continued. "Now we're on the clock to locate Banks, get the nukes and put this to rest."

"*Christ*, Chief. What a sick dude!"

"Yeah, tell me about."

"I'm sorry to hear about Agent Stubbs. I'd met him off and on in the office after being assigned to here."

Sinclair glanced at the computer screen as she remembered Stubbs. "I appreciate that. Thank you."

For a moment, Smith hesitated. "What do you want me to do?" he asked.

"I was coming to that," she said, leaning back in her chair. "We're going to pull surveillance on the Russian Consulate here in Stuttgart. I need you to grab the office binoculars, a parabolic mic and camera with long-distance lens, and radio communications gear, get them into my car; we'll leave in twenty minutes."

"I'm on it, ma'am."

However, Sinclair had another reason for wanting to be at the consulate.

With the snow falling on a lonely stretch of road, a silver BMW cruised along just below the posted speed limit, not wanting to attract attention of a police cruiser six or seven cars behind in the far lane. Banks kept glancing on and off to the rear-view mirrors in the event the officer followed.

With no other traffic on either side of the road, the police cruiser started gaining on the BMW. Then, two cars behind him, the cruiser pulled up behind the BMW and its flashing lights came on. The officer set the siren to one blast, wanting the BMW to pull over.

With an oath, Banks pulled over to the side of the road, came to a stop and waited for the officer to appear.

Stealing furtive glances through his side mirror, he watched a female German police officer step out of the cruiser, place her hand on the butt of her weapon and approach the driver's side door.

Banks pulled his Heckler & Koch HK VP9 9mm automatic handgun, held it by his right leg and rolled down his window. Within seconds of the officer appearing at the window, Banks leveled his gun to chest height and squeezed off a two-round burst.

Both of the bullets struck the officer's chest, and in a blink of the eye, Banks fired a third-round that plowed through her head as it exploded in a cloud of arterial spray. The impact was so violent the officer slammed back away from the BMW dead before her body hit the pavement!

With a sigh, Banks shook his head, returned the gun to its holster, raised the window, placed the gear in drive and pulled away from the scene before any vehicles drove past.

Banks earlier thought he should check out the Russian Consulate's office. It would be a daylight soft recon, or probe to check potential points of vulnerability, ingress, and egress from certain points. He was planning on a night penetration of the consulate. He'd made a Google map search of it, but not enough information was available.

His aim was to end all searches of him by the FSB. He knew it would only be temporary, maybe for a few days, which were all the time he needed; a bold plan, but one that needed to be done.

Back on the road, and checking the car's console clock, he should arrive at the consulate in about fifteen minutes.

At the Russian Consulate, and in the office of Captain Kuznetsov, preparations were underway for Colonel Borovkov. She would arrive any minute now. He, Anatoly Sokolov, and Damir Semenov, sat around an oaken desk planning their next move, with or without the Colonel's presence.

Sitting next to the Captain, Sokolov, with a sling over his right wounded arm, leaned back on his chair. "How can we—"

Just then a steady beeping sound came from one of several cell phones on the desk. Grabbing the phone, Kuznetsov saw a clear blue circle, and in its center, a blinking green dot showing a moving vehicle.

"It's an agent on the move," he said.

"Okay, which one?"

"It's the female. She's on the autobahn. The map shows she's heading into the city."

"You want one of us to catch up and follow her?" Sokolov suggested.

Kuznetsov shook his head. "That's alright, but no. Let's see where she goes. We'll make contact there."

The other two glanced at their Captain waiting to see which one would go with him.

"Semenov," he said, "Bring the car around and have it ready."

"Yes, comrade Captain."

Kuznetsov stood and pulled out his handgun holstered to his leg, a Ruger-57, chambered with a 20 magazine capacity. Sliding out the mag, he checked and made sure a round was down the tube, replaced the mag and holstered the handgun as he sat to wait for Semenov.

<hr />

With Sinclair behind the wheel of her government Chevy, Smith was following behind her on his Harley-Davidson.

She planned to use mobile surveillance on the consulate. Sinclair would stay toward the front and Smith would position himself either toward the back or side entrances.

Moments later, having arrived, they came to a stop just two blocks away from the consulate. Seen from their vantage point, the consulate was a three-story building surrounded by seven-foot-high wrought iron fencing. Pedestrian traffic was heavy around the consulate with some exiting or entering the compound. And there was a steady flow of vehicles on either side of the street.

With Smith in the car, she brought out her binoculars and surveyed the consulate. Smith did the same.

"Only one place for me, Chief, the side parking lot."

"Yeah, okay. Go on then, stay on the commo."

"Roger that."

A few minutes later, Smith straddled the motorbike, and with a burst of speed, he maneuvered the bike through tight traffic and disappeared from her sight of view around the consulate.

As Smith came around the structure, he found a corner, way in the back of the parking lot and away from a roving CCTV camera he had spied driving into the lot. He watched as the camera made an arc from left to right, but seemed to stop before it focused on his position. The parking lot was almost full.

Sinclair noticed that the front entrance had several steps that led to the top landing and the main doors. Although she didn't see any guards present, they could've been on the other side of the doors. In-between the right side of the consulate, she saw another tall building separated by at least six feet. The ground, around the outside of the consulate, had a small accumulation of snow.

Sinclair set the selector gear to drive and pulled away from the curb. She knew where she wanted to position the car. There were empty parking spaces across the street from the consulate. Once there, she backed into a space with an unobstructed view of the consulate's front entrance.

She reached toward the back seat and grabbed the parabolic microphone and headphones. Opening her window, she opened the Omni-directional microphone and hooked it on the edge of the window. Then she attached two leads from the microphone to the single-channel sound device, which had a knob for volume control, and set the headphones over her head.

With the binoculars in one hand and with the other, she used a finger and touched the throat mic, making a commo check with Smith. "Commo check, how do you read me, over?"

Smith came back. "Read you 5 by 5, over."

After that, they settled in for the wait.

• • • •

In Captain Kuznetsov's office, he stared at his phone, confused.

The blinking dot put the agent's car in their vicinity, just a few blocks from the consulate. What could be the reason she'd stopped there?

Standing on the other side of his captain, Sokolov coughed and asked. "What's happening?"

Captain Kuznetsov replied in a low voice. "It's the agent. She just stopped in front of the consulate."

"What would she be here for?"

"I asked myself the same thing."

At this, he paused. Then he realized why: it was surveillance. Could that be it, and was she setting up to see the coming and goings of the consulate? Then he remembered the Colonel was due at any minute.

"Shit!" he shouted as he strode away from the room, heading to a window out front.

Moving with the slow and steady moderate traffic flow on LeitzStrasse, the BMW made its way toward the Russian consulate just a few blocks away.

Banks kept his vehicle behind a trolley in the event he got spotted by the police or anyone else keeping watch—which he assumed someone was—it's what he would've done. Slowly he approached the consulate and turned his eyes onto the front door. No guards. Perfect.

They're inside.

So far it looked good. His next step, find a parking space away from the consulate and walk back.

Two blocks away he found it, the perfect parking space, and from where he could pull away in the event he needed a hasty getaway. Taking a deep breath, Banks tried to control his emotions. He was entering enemy territory and anything could happen. Yet, it was a gamble he had to take.

He reached into a paper bag lying on the passenger seat, removed a pair of dark shades and a stick-on mustache. Using the car's mirror, he applied the fake hairpiece underneath his nose, slipped on the shades, and slid out of his car, but didn't lock it.

With a pair of running shoes, jeans, leather jacket and a New York Yankees ball cap, he began walking back to the consulate. Halfway there, Banks felt, rather than saw, a feeling that he was being watched.

He slowed, almost coming to a complete stop. Looking around, he didn't see anyone, but his gaze caught sight of a Chevy parked deep inside a parking lot with its window rolled down. All the other cars had their windows up. Not giving it a second thought, he shook his head and continued forward.

Sinclair paused from gazing at the consulate to check her emails on her cell phone. Before she could click on a particular one, she looked back up and spied two pedestrians, a man and a woman walking in opposite directions. Forgetting the phone, her trained eyes caught something familiar with the man.

The stranger arguably fit the description she had of Banks. The mustache could be a ruse.

Sinclair fixed her gaze on him. When Banks came to a halt in front of the consulate's entrance, he turned his head and removed his shades for a moment.

Sinclair took a deep breath and kept her emotions in check. This was highly unexpected. What in the hell did Banks hope to accomplish by showing himself here? He had balls; she granted him that. But damn!

Then, with his shades back on, she saw him climbing the steps and walk inside.

Into her mic, she said, "Smith, come in Smith."

"I read you, Chief."

"Good. Listen. I've made eye contact with our target. He's entering the consulate. Standby, I may need you to follow him the moment he leaves and see what kind of vehicle he's driving. Then we'll follow."

"Roger that."

He was inside by the information desk and saw his mug shot plastered on an information board. Banks was correct in giving himself a different appearance. To the left of him was an armed guard, and to the right, which he assumed led inside the consulate.

The lobby, filled with customers seeking information or applying for visas, jammed two lines, as the murmurings of anguish souls went through the lines of those waiting their turn at the main information desk.

He needed to go past the guard, but the guard kept turning people away from the entrance. Not good; not good at all. He needed to find some way in.

Walking past the information desk, Banks looked past the crowd, to the far side of the lobby, at a rather tall man dressed in black with a sidearm strapped down his right leg, turning away from a window. FSB was Banks first impression. Now, he had no chance to see further into the consulate. But he had seen all he could.

Gazing around the crowded lobby, Captain Kuznetsov kept staring at the man wearing dark shades and a mustache which seemed to be lower on one side than the other; a disguise, maybe? Then something about the man gave him pause. Something he'd remembered about the traitor!

"Hey, you there stay where you are!" Kuznetsov shouted as he drew his weapon.

Banks hastened backward. He drew his weapon, but before he could get off a shot, one of the guards fired a warning shot, and then leveled the weapon at him. Banks, in a blink of an eye, fired two shots at the guard, dropping him dead just as Kuznetsov dropped to a knee and fired his weapon. But an innocent customer ran into the path of the bullet and dropped to the floor yelling for help.

Then pandemonium broke loose!

The sound of automatic weapons fire cut through the air inside the consulate, as the other guard cut loose with his AK74, as Banks flew out of the building. Hot lead whistled over the heads of those lying on the floor, and thudded into the walls by Banks, and shattered windows. The screams of the wounded echoed throughout the lobby!

Sinclair heard the gunshots loud and clear through her headphones that came from inside the building and caught sight of Banks running out of the consulate and up the street.

"Smith, our target just ran out into the street. Follow the asshole!" she shouted into her mic. Then, pulling on the parabolic mic, she closed the window.

"Roger that. Just saw him running past."

Sinclair, without further haste, turned the engine over and peeled rubber as she tried to catch up with Smith. With spinning tires on the wet pavement, she fishtailed and almost lost control. Straightening the wheel, she then stepped on the gas pedal and gave chase.

One second he was standing still, the next he shot through the parking lot entrance. Smith, shifting his weight to the left foot-peg for steering, and without turning the handlebars, hung a left, burning his tires. Gaining his balance, he sped after the running man, a block out in front of him.

From the side of the consulate, a black Chevrolet Suburban flew through the side entrance, tires slipping on the wet pavement, as they gave chase to the female's vehicle on the tracking monitor. Captain Kuznetsov knew that she was giving chase to the traitor. Seconds later, he caught sight of her vehicle.

And the chase was on!

—30—

Banks sprinted hard and fast, his legs pumping!

The rain had stopped and left the sidewalks slippery, as ominous clouds lingered overhead with the promise of snow. Coming to the end of the first block, his eyes lit up when he caught sight of his car a block ahead.

He turned on the speed and barreled through the intersection as cars honked their horns and came to a screeching stop just inches away from colliding with the fleeing man.

Up ahead, crowds of pedestrian traffic blocked the sidewalk. With his head down, Banks dashed and shoved pedestrians out of his way. Almost slipping, he elbow-crashed into a woman and scrambled to get away from her. He swiveled his head back and glimpsed a motorbike speeding his way.

Banks' eyes went wide. *What the fuck, FSB, or CID?* He thought. Either way, he had to get away!

Facing forward again, he made a mad dash the few feet remaining before reaching the car.

Throwing open his car door, Banks jumped behind the wheel. Slamming the door shut, he fired up the engine and rammed the shifter into drive. Then, driving forward, he maneuvered a car spin, engaging the emergency brake and stomping down on the accelerator. He spun the BMW into a 180-degree spin on the wet pavement just as two cars collided with each other, trying to avoid the BMW.

Both cars veered out of control with the drivers yelling out curses. One car spun to its left side as the second slammed into its left rear fender, spinning it around. They collided with a mighty crash of steel on steel and came to a halt up against several parked vehicles.

Both cars avoided colliding with the BMW.

Once Banks was facing forward, he released the brake from his spinning tires, caught traction on the wet pavement, and sped away, avoiding the wrecked autos in his path.

Seconds earlier, just up ahead of him, Smith caught sight of Banks getting into his car, complete a car spin, and spun away, traveling south at break-neck speed. Leaning into the Harley, Smith gunned the motorcycle, and with a burst of speed, he weaved in and out of stopped traffic caused by the accident.

Hazarding a glance in his rear-view mirror, Banks saw the same motorcycle coming up fast behind him.

Son-of-a–bitch! Who the fuck was that?

His only chance was to make the 295 Autobahn about two miles ahead and lose him in traffic.

Goddamn! *Was the biker after me?* Banks not sticking around to find out increased his speed to over 152km/h!

"Chief," Smith almost yelled into his vibration-mic strapped around his throat, "Banks driving a BMW silver colored; he's a couple of cars ahead of me. Careful, he may try for the Autobahn coming up."

Through her throat mic, she said, "Stay with him, I'm right behind you and we may have company."

"Roger that," he hissed into his mic.

A minute later, Agent Sinclair had to slow down to maneuver through the accident scene. It took her a minute longer as she threaded a path through the stalled traffic, but when she was beyond it, she stomped on the gas pedal, and with a hand on the horn, rocketed forward passing cars left and right as if they were standing still!

Up ahead, she caught sight of Smith's taillights growing smaller by the second. Keeping her foot down on the gas pedal, the car engaged its turbo-drive capabilities, pushing past the 145 km/h limit down straight away with any traffic barring her way. And behind her, she saw the same black Chevy Suburban that zoomed out of the consulate.

She knew they were FSB agents. If that were the case, she and Smith could very well be in for the fight of their lives.

<hr>

"Get us out of this Semenov," Captain Kuznetsov said as two German police cruisers made their appearance.

Semenov took a deep breath. "I'm trying, sir."

Kuznetsov eyed his comrade. "Try harder!"

Just then, he was clear of the heavy traffic. Semenov putting pedal to the metal, powered the big 355 horsepower V8 engine into overdrive and roared down the four-lane street.

They caught sight of Sinclair's Chevy in the distance. Rapidly increasing their speed, they started closing the gap.

Far ahead of Sinclair and the FSB, and still on LeitzStrasse, Banks made the intersection to the Autobahn, and decreasing his speed, hung a quick right, skidding on all four tires. The BMW fishtailed, almost out of control. Just when he thought he'd lose it, Banks turned the wheel a little to the left and regained control of the BMW and made the ramp onto the Autobahn.

With a burst of speed, Banks weaved the BMW in and out through oncoming traffic, almost colliding with cars that wouldn't move over or slow down for him. Now in open traffic, he sped up to over 180 km/h zipping along with traffic. Left and right, he weaved with expert control of the wheel.

Seconds later, Smith made the intersection, and on sliding tires, he made the right turn almost losing control of his Harley, as he extended his right leg hugging the pavement for balance and gripping the handlebars for dear life. Then with a roar of the dual mufflers, the Harley shot forward and made his turn onto the Autobahn.

"I'm on the Autobahn heading north," Smith shouted into the mic.

"Copy that," Sinclair replied. "I'm almost there myself."

Now at the intersection, Sinclair slowed and took a glance in her rear-view mirror and saw the Suburban coming closer. She made the turn onto the on-ramp of the Autobahn as she stomped on the gas pedal, putting distance between her and the FSB vehicle.

Roaring down the Autobahn, Smith inched closer to the BMW. Snow flurries fell, almost blurring the visor on his helmet and his vision. However, Smith pushed the Harley hard as he passed traffic on the left and right lanes. He saw the BMW weaving through traffic, keeping his distance.

Then the snow came down harder.

Up ahead, Banks gave thought to rid himself of the biker. His only option was to let the mysterious rider come abreast of the BMW, and then he could take care of it once and for all.

Reducing his speed, Banks kept glancing in his rear-view mirrors and waited for the biker to take the bait.

Minute by minute, Smith was gaining on the BMW who kept weaving through traffic. But he smelled a rat. Why the hell was Banks slowing? As if he's letting him catch up to him, but why?

Taking advantage, he reached behind him, pulled his handgun, and switched off the safety and kept it ready by his side as he drove one-handed. He wasn't taking any chances.

"I'm just about gaining on Banks. Gonna try to put a couple of rounds into his car and slow him down."

"Roger, be careful, Smith," Sinclair said with concern in her voice. "The man's dangerous."

So am I, he said to himself. "Copy that."

Yard by yard, Smith gained on the BMW. Then, with a burst of speed, Smith placed the Harley just about a car behind the BMW's right rear bumper. Bringing his gun across his chest, he aimed at the tire.

However, just before he squeezed the trigger, Banks tapped his brakes twice and ended up side by side with the Harley. In a blink of an eye, Banks ripped the steering wheel to the right.

Smith's eyes widened. Too late, he knew what was coming. He lost his weapon as he attempted to jerk away out of the BMW's attack. And then *BAM! The BMW* struck the bike's front tire, sending the Harley and Smith skidding down hard to the pavement. Then the BMW sped away.

The CID agent, once thrown away from the bike, saw a speeding car run over the Harley and dragged it along, missing his body.

Attempting to stand, Smith guessed he had a broken right leg as he tried crossing the road, when out of nowhere, a speeding car, unable to maneuver around him, struck Smith hard, spinning him back onto the ground.

Traffic came to a standstill in the far lane.

It was at that moment that Sinclair saw what had happened and pulled off to the side. Getting out of the car, she ran to Smith's side.

She helped Smith to his feet. "Come on, hang on to me."

"Chief," Smith said with a groan, "I think my leg's broken."

Agent Sinclair nodded. "We'll have a doctor look at it."

"Chief, I fucked up."

Sinclair shrugged and asked. "Oh, tell me, in what way?"

He inclined his head. "By letting the SOB get too close to me."

Shaking her head, she said, "Don't worry about it. His day will come."

Three miles up ahead, Banks pulled off the Autobahn. He drove off down a country road as the snow fell harder, making visibility and driving difficult. Pulling off to the side of the road, he waited until the snow subsided a bit before returning to the ranch.

Back on the Autobahn, the black Suburban, with the two FSB agents, slowed because of the heavy snowfall and failed to notice the turnoff Banks had taken.

Captain Kuznetsov said. "Let's return to the consulate. No use searching for him in this snow."

—31—

The Kremlin, in downtown Moscow, is a fortified complex in the center of the city overlooking the Moskva River to the south, Saint Basil's Cathedral and Red Square to the east, and the Alexander Garden to the west.

It is the best known of the Kremlins (Russian citadels) and includes five palaces, four cathedrals and the enclosing Kremlin Wall with its towers. Also, within this complex, is the Grand Kremlin Palace that was the Tsar's Moscow residence. The complex now serves as the official residence of the President of the Russian Federation.

With temperatures falling, the weather in September announces the approach of autumn, and despite the showers and overcast skies, they predicted to be a superb sunny day.

Ilya Gadjiyev, the President of Russia, and the Commander-In-Chief of the Armed Forces, was a tall, broad-shouldered man of fifty-two and into his first year as President. With dark thinning hair, solemn brows offset by a cruel appearing grin, his hazel eyes could bore through a person's soul, as they gleamed behind a pair of round-framed glasses.

Through his stained-glass windows, he could see the skies were clearing and the sun shining, yet he felt rather grim, as if a dark cloud had crossed his face. And he knew the cause. It happened after he hung up from taking a personal secured telephone call from the President of the United States.

It had been a chilling and gloomy conversation. And if what he just learned from President Phillip Anders was correct, then he couldn't trust the FSB, or his military generals, in what he needed to have done. Gadjiyev had to discover who was behind the conspirators trying to take over his government by force and in complete secrecy. For that, he knew of one person who could pull this off.

Picking up the phone's receiver, he dialed from memory.

"Yes?" came a strong-sounding male voice.

"Oleg," Gadjiyev said. "How fast can you come over?"

"I can be there in twenty minutes, Ilya."

"Good. We have much to discuss."

After replacing the receiver, Gadjiyev poured himself a full glass of Vodka.

———————————————

After hanging up with President Gadjiyev, Oleg Grin sat back in his chair. His apartment in Moscow was utilitarian. He kept a dark apartment, with closed curtains, and one lit table lamp.

At sixty-nine, unmarried, and the last son of three siblings, he was an old KGB operative who worked under the General Secretary of the Central Committee of the Communist Party of Russia, Leonid Brezhnev, and Ilya Gadjiyev's father, Andre Gadjiyev, was a deep undercover agent for fifteen years. He was the most trusted friend of Ilya. He still had an eye patch over his left eye, and walked with a noticeable limp, after he had taken a bullet aimed at Andre Gadjiyev.

I remember it well as if it was yesterday.

On a controversial assignment to Kosovo in late 1972, Gadjiyev and Oleg had come under extreme gunfire. Andre Gadjiyev lost his life attempting to save Oleg's life. For that event, Oleg kept a sacred vow to take care of Andre's young son, Ilya Gadjiyev, if he ever became involved in politics.

He shook his head at the memory.

Frowning, he thought of the phone call. This wasn't the first time he'd called Oleg to his side. Now Gadjiyev needed him once again.

Grabbing his Walther PPK handgun off the table, he strapped on his shoulder rig and holstered the gun. Over his dark suit, Grin slipped into a dark winter coat, grabbed his keys off the table and left his apartment.

It was twenty minutes later when Grin strode into the President's private office in the Kremlin. Then, after three security-check points, he walked through a brilliantly lit hallway with armed guards on every corner.

Easing the door closed, he leaned up against it and smiled at Gadjiyev sitting behind his desk, speaking on the phone as he took off his coat. As Grin moved into the room, the President motioned him to a chair. Grin stepped in front of it and draped his coat over the chair and sat. The President hung up the phone. There seemed to be a distinct look about his friend. Grin sensed something of great importance troubled him.

Staring over at his friend, Gadjiyev smiled one of his rare smiles. "Thank you for coming. Would you care for a glass of Vodka?"

"Mr. President, it's too early for me. Tea would be fine."

Speaking into the intercom to his secretary, he placed the order.

A severe look spread across Gadjiyev's face. "Let me start from the beginning, Oleg. I received a call from the U.S. President who is under the assumption that several members of our military, including members of the FSB, are planning a military takeover of the government."

There was an awkward silence, and Grin shook his head, not sure now to reply to this astonishing and yet deadly story.

Not hearing a reply, the President continued. "There have been several nuclear suitcase bombs stolen from our arsenals. When or how and by whom, are the reasons I called for you. They plan on using those bombs here in Russia and America. The other reason being is I want you to ferret out the responsible personnel in our military, no matter how high they go, and any other conspirators and report back to me."

For a moment, Grin considered his request. With the military, there were few he could turn to for information, but of those, he had considerable pull. No problem there. But with the FSB, it was a different story. Although he was ex-KGB, he knew of one or two that would help and that would entail the threat on their families if need be. Yes, he could pull it off. How much he could learn was another story and how long it would take.

"Is there a timeline here, Mr. President?"

"Complete reports back to me in, say two days."

Oleg Grin shifted some. "Yes, that should be sufficient, sir."

"I know you'll do your best, my friend."

After a long moment, Gadjiyev rose and said, "One other thing, the Americans planted a double agent in the FSB named Anisi Sverchinsky. Find out all you can about him. In particular, I need to know the damage this spy did to our government and who were his closest allies and friends. Get them to tell you how they helped him, if at all. I don't care how you get the information."

—32—

Eight hours earlier, over Russian skies

The Russian Utair airlines Boeing 737, a shorter, lower-cost twin-engine, derived from the 707 and 727 planes, shot through the sky at its cruising speed of 490 knots rushing toward its destination of Berlin; and on schedule.

For both Sergei Objedkov and Yuri Sergeev this would be their fourth commercial plane ride, considering most of their flight experiences had been on military aircraft. They had their tickets already purchased by their friend Anisi Sverchinsky.

The flight was brief, just two hours, but it wouldn't end there. They were to rent a car, make their way into Stuttgart, Germany, and meet up with Sverchinsky, with further travels to parts unknown.

Fifty-year-old Yuri, tall and powerfully built man with long straight black hair and deep piercing grey eyes was in street gangs since the age of nine. Abandoned as an infant and dumped in a trash can outside Moscow, a passing group of Bratva or "brotherhood" mafia hitmen out finishing a job, heard baby cries, and rescued the child. One of the group's members took in the child; his wife welcomed the baby as their own. When he became of age, he began a ruthless life with his adopted crime family.

Objedkov, at forty-eight, was a smaller version of his friend, and just as stocky. His unruly curly brown hair reached his shoulders. With no family to speak of, Sergei's family had died in a house fire. Killed along with his parents were his grandparents. Sergei was the sole survivor. Alone, with no other living relative, he became a ward of the state.

In their late teens, they enlisted in their country's armed forces. Within four years of service, they recommended them both for the Russian Federal Security Service or the FSB. There they became noble friends.

Objedkov and Sergeev were a team. They received their training as spies receiving instructions to carry out assassinations from FSB headquarters. Old KGB instructors trained the two men in advance espionage and killing techniques.

After several years of blind service, they quit the organization. Now, they both took arms with Sverchinsky. They would make on this mission more than what they would make in five years in the FSB and be a lot safer. Also, they had known Anisi for several years and both placed great trust in the man.

What Sverchinsky had planned was inconsequential to the two men. Only the pay mattered now. They would have more than enough to leave Russia and begin anew in freedom somewhere else.

They knew what the mission entailed, and the dangers associated with it. Sverchinsky had explained it to them. They had no allegiance to the motherland. All they wanted was to live well and not in fear.

Two hours later, their plane touched down in Berlin.

Unbeknownst to the Russians, a German customs agent dressed in civilian attire, with instructions of surreptitiously photographing all single male passengers coming in from Russia, had his reservations about two rather stocky men walking into the terminal from their plane. They didn't seem to be the tourist type, plus these two were hard-looking individuals.

To the agent, they moved with a military posture, their heads always moving left and right, as if someone were following them, or on the look-out for trouble. They fit the bill of those they had instructed him to keep watch for.

Snapping the images of the suspicious men with his Smartphone, he ambled over to the car rental clerk hoping to ID them.

As the customs agent approached the clerk, he presented his badge. After questioning, the clerk disclosed the two men were dropping off the vehicle upon their arrival in Stuttgart. After receiving the names of the two Russians, he sent the photos and information to his headquarters.

Having rented a car as instructed, Yuri set the vehicle's GPS with the address given to them, and forty minutes and a meal later, they were on the road to Stuttgart with an arrival time just under five hours.

Anton Zemitsov, Vadim Rybakov, and Peter Abakumov were traveling together. Ex-FSB agents, they would fly from Moscow into Frankfurt, Germany; a three-hour flight duration. Once there, one of them would rent a car for the ultimate destination of Stuttgart.

With tickets already purchased by Sverchinsky, they boarded their plane and sat down for the short flight.

Once they landed and were in the airport terminal, they separated. With their training and their suspicious attitude, they kept looking for potential danger from any corner. And they found one.

Zemitsov caught wind of a tall individual wearing blue jeans, winter jacket over a white shirt, and holding a Smartphone that had taken photos of his two comrades and was directing the camera over to him. Somehow, someone knew something.

Did they know of their arrival?

He didn't think so. Maybe a general order to be on the lookout for anything suspicious, he thought. They had to know something.

Damn it all to hell! I couldn't let them get our photo.

He made his slow way to the man with the phone. Just then, Abakumov suspected something was amiss, or his friend would keep walking behind and not in another direction. Glancing behind him,

Rybakov noticed his two friends heading to the men's room. Turning back around, Rybakov continued to the car-rental desk. It was his job to secure a vehicle.

Aloysius Schmitt had just turned twenty-two and had been on the job as a customs agent for the last six months. This was his second posting. His first was as a customs clearance clerk, which he had considered boring. When his supervisor suggested a cushy job of taking photos of passengers, he jumped at the chance. He wasn't the only one, though. They would detail two other agents for a nine-hour workday, which suited him just fine.

Now, on the job for the last two-and-a-half hours, he was about to end his tour of duty. Having already taken the photos from the three arriving passengers, and those from the last two flights, he needed a break. Pocketing his phone, Schmitt walked fast, hands stuffed into his pockets, whistling the low soft *Die Gedanken Sind Frei* tune as he walked toward the men's room.

Not having the advanced training in avoidance and recognition when being followed or targeted that most advanced agents possess, he failed to take notice of two men that were following him.

Crowds of people scurried about, some hurrying to their flights, some with small children in hand and others waiting for flights to arrive. And through it all, Zemitsov and Abakumov followed Schmitt.

Once the customs agent entered the men's room, Zemitsov walked in too, as Abakumov stood standing guard outside the door.

Closing the door behind him, Zemitsov leaned up against it and observed the agent up against a urinal. He couldn't yet put his plan in place until another man, who was washing his hands, departed. Stepping away from the door, he let the man pass out of the restroom. Quietly, he came up behind the agent.

With his head bowed and his eyes closed, the first sign Schmitt knew he was in danger, was a quick hard felt punch into his right kidney, by someone standing behind him. The savage blow caused the kidney to tear loose from his blood vessels and Schmidt went into shock as his head jerked backward; his mouth filled with blood.

A rough hand and forearm suddenly wrapped around his neck and tightened around his throat. Just then Schmitt blacked out, his mind refusing to grasp what or who had attacked him. Without a sound, Zemitsov grasped the head and with a strong twist and a snapping sound of his neck, he was dead.

He dropped the body onto the tiled bathroom floor, pushed it into a cubicle and closed the door.

Rifling through the dead man's pockets, he found a cell phone. Pocketing it, he strolled out of the restroom.

Staring over at this friend, Zemitsov shrugged, and said, "He was a customs agent. He took photos of us."

"And?"

"He won't be taking any more photos."

"Good. Let's go. We have a long trip ahead of us."

"Da."

The large fifty-eight foot *Katarina* fishing trawler, with a crew of ten men and two passengers, set sail from the St. Petersburg dock en route to Rostock, Germany.

Traveling from Moscow, Tokarev and Povarov teamed up for the voyage. Carrying forged identification papers, they boarded a train from Moscow to the port city of St. Petersburg. The train ride was lengthy, and it wasn't easy. Different customs agents frequently requested their identification. They would scrutinize the documents and leveled stares at the two as if they were fugitives. However, not finding anything improper with their documents, they continued their travels.

Aboard the trawler, and unable to travel by air, they paid the captain. Tokarev, through a friend of a friend, knew the captain used his boat as a cover for his smuggling operations.

Tokarev and Povarov had no passports. They hadn't had time to secure them. And time was of the essence, according to Sverchinsky. They left both men to seek travel arrangements on their own.

According to the boat captain, it would take about six hours to arrive at Rostock. Yet, their trip wouldn't end there. Once in Rostock, they would rent a car and drive seven hours to the city of Stuttgart.

—33—

It was four-thirty that evening when Sinclair walked into the main lobby of the Army Health Clinic at Patch Barracks when her cell phone rang.

"Belle" She heard her father ask.

Was there something troubling Dad?

She knew by the sound of his voice.

Agent Sinclair cleared her throat. "Yes, Dad, is there something wrong?"

"Yes. Can you tell me where you're at, honey?" he asked, sounding concerned.

Agent Sinclair took a deep breath. "I'm at the hospital, about to inquire about my team's condition."

"Belle, I need an update on what you've done so far on the case. The brass is all over my ass demanding an update."

Sinclair took a deep breath. "Of course, Dad, give me about two hours, and I'll meet up with you at your office."

"I'll be here."

Pocketing her cell phone, she proceeded to the emergency room to check on Smith. Once at the front information desk, they advised her that Agent Smith was already out of the hospital.

That was excellent news.

She ambled over to the clinic's recovery room to check on Russell and Courtney. The door was ajar, and from the inside, and she heard their voices.

"Damn, you two are awake," Sinclair said, surprised as she walked through the door. "The doc painted a gloomy picture of your recovery. You two should still sleep it off."

The moment she walked in, their conversation halted.

The two agents were sitting up in bed, holding containers of fruit juice. Sinclair noticed they removed their IV tubes. That was an excellent sign.

"Not likely," Russell said with a grunt. "Pat and I were discussing plans to leave here. We're ready to get back to work."

"I'm ready anytime he is," Courtney said with a smile.

Shaking her head, Sinclair said, "Hell, you won't. That's out of the question."

"Come on, Sinclair," Russell said, low, earnest and pleading. "You can get us out of here tonight."

Sinclair hesitated with a blank expression. Realizing she was without the team, and without support, with the possibility she wouldn't be able to continue alone. She needed them.

"You're putting me on the spot, Dan, but, I'll see what I can do. I'll check with your doctor."

Without another word, Sinclair stepped out of the room.

Russell gazed over at Courtney and gave her a wink. "We're out of here."

* * *

Captain Kuznetsov sat across from Colonel Borovkov, the head of the FSB operations in Germany, not sure what to expect.

"First, Comrade Captain," Colonel Borovkov began. "Let me state, I can have you stripped of your rank, send you back in disgrace to Moscow, and let them take further actions in your insubordination and lack of understanding orders. Second, I need a full written report of your actions and its unfortuitous outcome."

Captain Kuznetsov shifted disconsolately. He'd been waiting outside the office for the past thirty-minutes before being ushered into her presence, and now his ass was being chewed by the woman. Most times, he would relish the chewing in his lovemaking, but this harsh criticism was too much. However, he reminded himself, the woman in front of him was a high-ranking officer of the state.

"Third," Colonel Borovkov continued. "I need all the details of your operation, leaving nothing out. Fourth, tell me what other plans you have that I need to know about."

Staring her down, Captain Kuznetsov figured he should attempt to show his respect.

"So, to your first point, Comrade Colonel," he began. "I acted as I did because of the time frame and the circumstances. I didn't have the luxury of waiting for your arrival to act. Time was of the essence if I wanted to catch the traitor."

Then he started relating the circumstances of his subsequent actions, what transpired during the chase of the American agents, and his loss of the traitor.

"On your second point, Comrade," he continued, "the only recourse left to me and my people were to wait on the American agents to make their move. As I stated, I have tracking devices on their vehicles. The moment they move or I think they will leave the comfort of the military installation, I will know. Suffice to say, Comrade, it's now a waiting game."

She said rather straightforward. "Do you have any timetable when this would happen?"

Kuznetsov shook his head. "Maybe it will be soon ... how soon? I can't even guess."

"I've planned to have another group of agents assist us here. They should arrive in a few hours."

He took this without replying as he nodded, masking his feelings, though he was sure she understood.

— · — · — · —

Colonel Sinclair sat frowning behind his desk, arms resting on the chair's armrests as he glanced at the three agents sitting in front of him.

It was half-past six before Belle arrived. Gazing at one, then at the other and what he saw didn't give him a warm fuzzy feeling inside.

First, there was Russell dressed in a grey business suit, white shirt, no tie and leaning on a cane. His face filled with scars stitched and cuts and with an eye that still had some swelling to it.

Then Courtney, wearing tight blue jeans, black blouse, a leather jacket, and cowboy boots with her hair pulled up in a ponytail. Both of her eyes were puffy. Her face still had black and blue bruises, showing color back to her otherwise pale face, as he had seen her last at the hospital.

It became self-evident to him that these two may not be ready to get back on track with the investigation. However, he trusted his daughter in the matter.

Colonel Sinclair focused as his daughter reiterated past events and of those that happened of late. "We almost had Banks, Dad. If it hadn't been for my agent getting knocked off of his motorbike, I believe I could have caught him. As it was, he got away; where, is what I need to find out."

Russell gave a slight cough.

Colonel Sinclair gazed at Russell. "Yes, Russell, you have something to say?"

"Yes, sir, if we had been with Agent Sinclair, Banks would've been rotting away in jail by now. She needs our help, sir."

"I wouldn't go that far, Dan," Agent Sinclair said with a grin.

Colonel Sinclair gazed over to his daughter, locked eyes, and allowed the faintest of a smile. "Belle, tell me what you need," he asked.

"Right now, I don't know," she replied. "With the three of us together, though, we'll come up with a plan and work it out from there."

The Colonel leaned forward in his chair. "I have several pieces of information you three may not be privy to." He paused as he opened a folder he pulled out of a drawer and thumbed through a few sheets until he came to the one he was looking for.

"I received information from the German customs agents," he began, "of great interest. It seems the dragnet you three put out worked. At two separate airports, in the last few hours, suspicious Russian males have entered Germany. They took photographs of these individuals of whom I have copies. According to the German customs, two Russians came through Berlin. They rented a car, their destination next was Stuttgart."

At first, both Russell and Courtney didn't get the connection.

Russell felt a slight shiver. "Holy, *shit!* They've begun coming in."

"Yes, which tells us the bombs are here in Stuttgart somewhere," Agent Sinclair said.

"Quite so," Colonel Sinclair said. "Three others came through the Frankfurt airport. Somehow, the customs agent that took the photos got himself killed, but not before sending the photos along to his headquarters."

After a pause, the colonel continued. "You three are getting some help with your security. We have detailed a SEAL team to assist you in any way they can. They're coming out of Italy. SEAL TEAM 5 is their operational code name."

"Damn, a SEAL TEAM! How did we rate, sir?" Belle asked.

"Orders came from the Pentagon through the President," he replied.

Courtney blinked once, twice. "I see someone's got our backs."

"I know you both have to report back to your superiors, but they know you're been assigned to us for the duration."

Both Russell and Courtney nodded.

Sinclair knew what she intended to do in the next days to come. Now that she had the team together, it would make her job much easier. With the SEALs, they would provide ample security for her team. But how much time did she have before something tragic happens? Would Banks set off a nuclear explosion in the U.S. or Russia first? Did he intend to show the world what he could do?

Those questions were driving me crazy. And yet, I'm not even close to capturing Banks or his conspirators.

"I've also instructed the company commander of Company B, of the 385th MP Battalion to provide security for you and the team until the SEAL team arrives. They're waiting for you outside. Use them in any way you see fit."

"Thanks, Dad."

Colonel Sinclair peered at the group; more so at his daughter. He could now breathe a little easier knowing help for her and her colleagues were on the way.

The PM glanced at Agent Sinclair once again. "That bomb detection box you wanted, Belle, is waiting for you at your office."

"That's excellent news, Father," Belle said. "Thank you for that."

"When will you be able to pick up on the investigation, Belle?" the PM asked.

"First thing in the morning, Dad," she replied with a smile on her lips. "These two need a few more hours of rest."

"Hey, I am ready to go now," Russell said.

"No, you're not," Courtney chimed in.

The three laughed.

The Colonel smiled.

———— · —— · —— · ————

Several miles away, on the other side of the City of Stuttgart, in a secluded ranch, an ominous bank of dark clouds was forming as two cars, carrying five men, were making their slow way heading for the beginning to the end for Russia, the United States and the rest of the world!

—34—

The Ranch, Stuttgart, Germany
Wednesday, September 11

The ranch, in a combination of deep darkness and deafening silence, was lit by house lights streaming through the open window and the screened doorway. In the distance, breaking the stillness of the night, Banks could hear the singing of mockingbirds.

A pack of coyotes howled through the darkness as a breeze stirred the leaves of the cypresses, bringing the scent of honeysuckle. In times like these, it reminded him of a lifetime ago, back home in the United States; calm and peaceful.

With grey skies, snowfall ceased and a stiff icy wind now began to blow down from the mountains to the west.

Sounds of someone opening the door interrupted his free-flowing thoughts. He didn't turn in the noise's direction. A second later, he heard the soft steps of someone entering the porch and coming to a stop beside him. Without turning, he knew the person who stood beside him was Carl Benz.

"Yes, Carl?"

"Matthew," Benz replied, "I just received two phone calls. The first group should arrive within the hour."

They have been apart far too long, Banks thought. But they'll soon come together once again.

"How many are in the group?"

"They're five of the seven arriving in two separate vehicles."

"Is everything ready inside?"

"Yes, the two laptop computers are up and on Wi-Fi through the use of our smart phones. I have laid the information sheets on the bombs out on the desk. The one bomb is open and on the table too."

"Have you heard from Nikolai?"

Three hours ago, Nikolai Bobrov was to meet with the leader of an underground group of mercenaries, and enlist at least six good men to secure the ranch, and serve as back-up, if needed. So far they hadn't heard from Nikolai and that troubled Banks.

Christ, he had a headache just thinking about it. But Benz's next words seemed to dispel some of his pessimistic thoughts.

"Yes," Benz replied. "Sorry, Matthew, I meant three phone calls. Nikolai is on his way back. He was successful in gaining the six men you requested along with their leader. The price offered was sufficient. He should be back in two hours."

"Good, get some rest, Carl. We're going to be very busy soon. But before you do, I need you to find out through your contacts everything you can on a CID Agent named Jacqueline Sinclair. I need to know if she has anyone she loves here. And anything else you can find out about her."

Banks paused, setting up his thoughts for his next words. "Carl, I need to stop her before she gets any closer to me or my plans. So it's imperative you get a detailed accounting of her life."

"I'll see what I can do."

Once Benz reentered the house, Banks reflected on what he was about to accomplish. It was history in the making for him. He remembered how the First World War began. If memory served him right, it started with the assassination of Archduke Ferdinand. The Second World War began when Adolph Hitler's Nazi forces invaded Poland and of the entrance into the war by the United States when Japan attacked Pearl Harbor.

Now *his* war—the Third World War—would begin with the nuclear bombing of Russia and parts of the United States. And the world would know and remember his name and the treacherous acts committed against him and his family.

Under a bright starless sky at ten-forty-five that evening, the first of the two cars appeared at the ranch. Through the large plate-glass window and the night's darkness, Banks saw a set of headlights approaching in the distance.

Not taking any chances, Banks and Benz both grabbed from the desk full of weapons, the Russian PP-91 KEDR submachine guns and Makarov ammunition with sound suppressors. Pulling the charging lever, they made the weapons hot and thumbed off the safety. Taking one side of a window each, they waited for friend or foe.

The car came on, still slow and cautious. Then it came to a halt in front of the house. Peeking through the curtain, Banks couldn't make out if anyone had gotten out of the car because of the high-beams that made him squint as he turned his head away.

Seconds later, the car's interior light went on as someone exited the driver's side.

"Anisi, are you in there? It's Sergei and Yuri!" Objedkov cried out.

Banks dropped his weapon to his side and tried to look through the window, but only saw a blurred figure by the car. "Sergei, please turn off the headlights."

Once the car and headlights were off, Banks and Benz opened the front door and stepped out to greet their two friends.

———— · ———— · ———— · ————

Banks ate dinner across from Benz at a table occupied by the two ex-FSB agents. The large pinewood table, enough for them, and then some, had eight solid wood dining chairs around it. It was part of the furnishings that came along with the ranch.

With three large pepperoni pizzas on the table, and three more in the refrigerator, and a large order of chicken wings, they ate in silence while they kept warm from a large fire blazing in the fireplace.

A room for the team members contained eight portable sleeping cots. Their workplace and planning room was in the basement with sufficient room to accommodate them all.

Banks' two arriving friends seemed sharp-eyed, healthy and ready to do their part.

Sergeev, having finished his dinner first, and sipping on a cold beer, glanced over at the person he knew as Anisi. "When do we start?"

"Did you encounter any obstacles anywhere in your travel?"

Sergeev gazed back at Banks, "None."

"Good. Now here is what I must have you and Sergei do, at least until the rest of the group arrives. In an hour or fewer, six mercenaries and their leader will be arriving. I need a perimeter set up. Guards to stand post and a two-man roving patrol started."

"These six men are they any good and are they trustworthy?" Yuri asked, frowning.

"Not as good as you and Sergei," Banks replied. "And no, I don't trust anyone of them. They're being paid for their trouble. Once they exhausted the money, they'll ask for more or leave. However, I won't give them up until we're ready to vacate the ranch."

Banks paused. "Now, as soon as the rest of our men arrive, we'll get down to the essence of my plan and your part in it."

Both Sergei and Yuri nodded.

Staring at the two FSB men, Banks said. "Grab weapons from the table in the corner and keep a sharp eye on the road coming into the ranch. Peter, Anton, and Vadim should arrive soon."

The first to arrive was Nikolai Bobrov, along with the six mercenaries in a 2017 black Chevy Suburban. With Yuri Sergeev, the most experienced operator of the bunch, Banks placed him in charge of the Merc's.

The leader, Hermann Weber, was an ex-Kommando Spezialkrafte (KSK) Captain who had led one of the four German Commando Operational companies' combat-ready troops. He was tall, in his late forties, with thick grey hair flowing across his weathered face and wide-set eyes.

Behind him were the six Merc's. All were hard-looking men comprising prior members of KSK and the German Bundespolzei (GSG-9), either from the Border Protection Group or from the elite tactical unit of the German Federal Police, and two foreign nationals from the French Commandement Des Operations Speciales (COS) Special Forces units.

They were all dressed in varied military uniforms, equipment, and armaments and equipped with night-vision goggles. They designated one of the GSG as their medical corps-man.

Sergeev met Captain Weber by the front of the house.

"Captain Weber," he said in English. "It's my understanding that you speak both English and Russian. Which would you prefer?"

"English comes easy for me."

"Good, so you and your men will bunk in the empty room toward the back of the house. There are several cots in there for you and your men. I'll be your commander for the time being. You understand that you and your men are here for support, guard duty, and securing the ranch, plus combat, if it comes to that."

"That's my understanding, sir."

"Good, get your equipment unloaded, and men situated and then set up a perimeter with a two-man foot patrol. There's food inside for your men. You'll find communication radios inside on a table off to one side of the main house. I'll assume your men have their own communications setup?"

"Yes, they do."

"Excellent. Let me know once you've established perimeter security."

"Yes, of course, sir. It shouldn't take too long to set up."

Just as Sergeev turned away, Captain Weber asked, "Sir, besides you ... who's in charge of this operation and what's the goal here?"

Yuri turned back and remained motionless for a moment as he stared at the Captain. "You'll get to know him soon," he said, with a slight agitation in his voice. "As far as the goal here, he'll make it known in due course."

The two men looked at each other for a moment.

Sergeev turned and stopped, "One last thing, park your vehicle in the barn."

Without a word, Captain Weber cocked his head to the side and swallowed.

At eleven-forty, the second car, carrying three occupants, made the left turn onto the dirt road that led to the ranch proper. The driver kept visual with the house lights far ahead of him.

A guard, one of the four German KSK personnel squatting behind a dense growth of shrubs, shielded from the dirt road to anyone or any vehicle that passed safeguarded the road. Twenty minutes into his watch, a vehicle approached. Unseen by the occupants of the vehicle, he spoke through his comms and said, "Section one to base. I have a slow-moving car approaching the house. You want it stopped?"

Captain Weber quickly replied, "That's a negative, Section-one. Let them pass."

"Section one to base, copy that."

The driver, Vadim Rybakov, drove to the front of the house and stopped. Then Basil Povarov and Anton Zemitsov slid out of the car. All three saw Anisi Sverchinsky standing on the front porch staring down at his three friends.

"It's great to see you three again. Come into the house; I have food and drinks and you three can tell me how your travels went."

Zemitsov said."It's great to see you too, Anisi."

"Vadim, please park your car in the barn with the others," Banks said.

The group sat around a large table in the basement portion of the house. Missing from the group were Dmitry Tokarev and Basil Povarov. Banks had no clue as to their arrival time; as yet they've had no phone contact with the ranch. If they didn't, by late in the morning, then they may have run into problems. Were they captured? If so, what could they say? He knew that continuing with his plan was a calculated risk. But, come hell or high water, he could live with it for the time being.

They had sheets of documents pertaining to the bombs operation laid out on the table. A nuke case, showing the interior workings of the bombs, sat opened on the table. Two silver canisters, each with a yield of up to five kilotons—one at the front of the case and the other toward the back end—had two separate wires which led to two black 3x3 inch boxes, the neutron generators. Placed on top and centered of the canisters laid a red metal box 4x7 inch, the arming switch. Next to the switch box was a key-pad.

Fifteen open boxed cell phones sat to one side of the table along with several land maps, and various assault weapons and handguns. To one side of the basement were several boxes of ammunition. Three Russian RPG grenade launchers stood by the wall.

The looks the group gave Banks convinced him they were unhappy with the nukes operation. "Alright, I perceive your apprehensiveness. But, let me reassure you I'll train you in its operation. Your part is quite simple. The case has a key-pad," he said, pointing to the box. "On the key-pad, you'll key in the cell phone number from one of these phones in front of you. But only when you've placed the suitcase at the location I'll send you to. We have already recorded the cell phone numbers."

Banks paused for a moment and gazed at the group. Next was the crucial part they needed to understand before being sent out. "You all see the switch on the red box? That's the arming switch."

Banks gazed up at them once again, making sure they were all paying attention, and continued. "Having keyed in the cell phone number, you pull that switch. It will arm the bomb. Once that's finished, close the case, hide it as best as you can and call Benz to authenticate the phone number to the case. Then, and only then, you'll destroy the phone. Having completed the task, you'll be free to travel anywhere you wish. I've already wired your money to your accounts."

Without a word, the group of men gazed at each other and nodded. Two or three, as they shook their heads, appeared quite unsure they understood all of it. However, they would train until they had it all figured out.

Banks settled back against his chair. He was fully confident in their abilities—this wasn't that difficult—but, when you're dealing with a nuclear weapon, everything assiduously needed to be stressed to the limit. Despite all this, he knew he could count on them to deliver.

"Do you have questions so far?" he asked in a level voice.

One by one they shook their heads.

Banks glanced at his watch: 12:30. "Good. We'll go through this again in the morning. Let's all get some sleep."

Without another word, he rose, turned and left the basement.

35

At the ranch, Benz after he'd taken a shower and changed into a two-piece pajama, he ambled over to the kitchen. Pouring himself a hot cup of coffee, and feeling more relaxed, he approached the laptop computer on the table and logged on to the internet.

The room was empty. Everyone was asleep or walking guard duty. The large table in the center of the room provided ample space for what he needed to accomplish. Pulling up a chair, he sat at the far end facing the door; a habit he'd gained from years in the military. He felt a slight chill. He glanced over at the fireplace and saw the fire was dwindling to ashes. A slow sip of the hot Java warmed him somewhat as he set the mug down.

He'd combed back his black graying hair and ran his hands over it and then dried them on his pants leg. With another sip of his coffee, he settled back on the chair, closed his eyes and ruminated. He thought of calling his partner at his law office in Frankfurt, but didn't. He did not want to lie about the reasons for taking two weeks off. Before leaving, he'd canceled all his appointments.

Benz glanced at the computer's clock: 1:45 A.M. He needed to start his search and track information on CID Agent Jacqueline Sinclair and find out all he could about her. Pulling the computer closer to him, his fingers flew across the keyboard. Time and time again, from one website to another, he stayed glued to them for several hours.

Hacking into several American military websites, including the CID Command site, he'd gathered all the information he felt was sufficient for Matthew's use. It was a treasure trove of information and insights he'd accumulated.

What he'd learned of the agent was that she was quite an investigator. Her military awards were many, and her combat experiences were commendable. There were no brothers or sisters. She was an only child. Her mother had passed away. Joining the Army, the agent excelled in hand to hand combat. She was an expert with handguns and combat rifles and a black belt in karate; a formidable opponent. There was no mention of a husband, or boyfriend, that he could find.

Her file, Benz read, stated that Agent Sinclair had investigated an incident involving North Korea. The circumstances of her investigation were Top Secret. However, he noted Sinclair had been the agent that brought down those responsible.

Shaking his head, Benz concluded that the one item of vital interest was the agent's father. The father, of all things, was the command's Provost Marshal, with quarters at Patch Barracks. This should interest Matthew, and then some, he thought.

Sinclair's only connection, or Achilles' heel, was through her father!

* * *

Banks woke early, as he always did, and stepped outside the house. Overhead stretched a cloudless expanse of bright blue sky. He squinted as the sun shone down on his upturned face. The cool air was refreshing, just right for a quick jog.

In an Adidas tracksuit and a wind-breaker, he climbed down the steps of the front porch. A brisk jog helped to keep him in shape. It also gave him time to plan the day's agenda.

Glancing at his watch, it read: 7:00 a.m. Banks breathing in exhaled and started jogging at his usual pace. Halfway into his jog, he thought he heard, from the front of the house, the hum of an approaching car. Banks knew the last two of his friends were due at any minute. No matter, he thought, Yuri and the mercenaries will take care of it.

Banks had entrusted the gathering of information related to Sinclair to Benz. Not knowing whether Benz had already collected the information he'd requested, he had to wait and see just what it entailed and if any of it was of use. However, all he needed was slight leverage to use against her and make her stop meddling in his affairs and plans. If that didn't work, he would have to go with Plan B: Kill her outright!

Also, knowing the FBI and CIA agents were with Sinclair, they would have to be put-down as well. He had capable men to take care of it, or even himself.

Deciding to stop training those responsible for handling the nukes, Banks wanted to wait on the last two men to begin. And when accomplished, and satisfied they knew the exact operational parameters, he would send them out. However, first, he needed another plane. For that, he would task Bobrov with aid and backup from two of his FSB comrades. But this time they would steal the plane, instead of purchasing one, to avoid the unnecessary paper trail if they purchased through normal channels.

Everything needed to be planned with the utmost care and diligence, knowing a majority of his plan Sinclair and her friends are knowledgeable. It stood to reason that he would need to take care of her, and soon.

Coming around towards the end of his jog, he spied a car parked headfirst in front of the house with several men around it. In the distance, he recognized Dmitry Tokarev and Basil Povarov. Again, he had them all around him.

Jogging up to them, they turned in his direction and smiled. Stopping in their midst, and shaking hands all around, he said, "Comrades, welcome to the ranch."

———————— · ———— · ———— · ————————

The night before, they tasked five MPs to provide security for Sinclair and her team. This morning, two of those were on guard in the living room of her father's quarters where she was making her home for the time being.

Sinclair had known Agent's Russell and Courtney were seeing each other. Although they tried to hide it from her, she knew. So Sinclair positioned two MPs in their patrol car just outside their apartments. All three agents were due back at the CID office early this morning.

At a quarter to eight, she paused at the front door to her father's quarters. It was going to be a bright sunny day. The forecast called for no chance of showers or snow for the day; a grateful change from all the rain and snow of the past few days.

Sliding into her Chevy, she watched as an MP patrol car pulled up behind her just as she pulled away from the curb and followed. With a deep breath, she drove to her office. A few minutes later, she parked behind the CID office and the patrol car parked as well. The two MPs stepped out of their vehicle and kept their distance behind her as she entered the office complex. Then one MP stood at the front entrance as the other stood at the rear entrance. Improbable as it may sound; they weren't taking any chances in case of an attack in the office.

Climbing the short set of stairs to her office, Sinclair stepped through her open door, closed it behind her and ambled over to her desk. She had an interminable day of planning and sorting out information on Banks and of what she suspected was a sleeper cell of Russians that may have already have arrived in Stuttgart.

But what was their purpose?

Were they the ones to deliver the nukes? And how would they do that? Things needed to move faster now that she had faces put to them. It was just a matter of time before one or more would run the possibility of being recognized somewhere around the city.

Then she saw a communiqué on her desk next to the telephone. It was from her father. She read:

"Belle, the SEAL team we spoke about arrived early this morning. They're quartered at the MP Company and instructed to provide you with an emergency contact number in the event you require them. I listed the number in a separate note attached. Take care, honey, and keep me informed."

Dad

That was splendid news. Now she waited for Russell and Courtney to arrive.

Banks tasked certain personnel to enhance his plan forward.

Tasked first was for Bobrov, along with Objedkov and Abakumov, to gain entry to a mid-size hangar at the Stuttgart Airport about 15 miles south of the ranch. They were to leave for the airport after task assignments.

Parked there were two mid-sized personal jets. Although both offered the same requirements, the Gulfstream G600 jet offered almost 6,500 nautical miles before re-fueling, beating out the Cessna Citation with less than 1,440 nautical miles. The G600 was the faster of the two, with a top speed of Mach-0.90 or 666 mph.

The Intel on the planes suggested one owner had passed away, and no one had taken control of the Gulfstream, and the other owner was on vacation for the next few weeks. So, if anyone discovered the jet missing, they would assume the plane was on consignment to persons unknown.

His figures suggested that it was 3,520 nautical miles to the U.S. mainland from Stuttgart. The flight would take about seven to eight hours. And depending on the weather, they shouldn't have any problems.

He held another training session with a live nuke. It lasted twenty minutes. This time, they all understood the procedures and their responsibilities.

Banks, seated at the table, glanced at all the men seated with him and set the task at hand. "On top of the desk behind you are folders marked with the team's number. Inside the folder, you will find the exact placement location of the nukes. Make sure you study the file and then destroy it."

He paused for a moment.

"The tasks are straightforward and you're all ready for the assignments." Opening a folder laying on top of the table in front of him, he opened it and grasped several sheets and outlined their tasks. As he called out to the teams, he glanced at them.

"Team One, Sergei Objedkov and Yuri Sergeev, you'll have two nukes–Target, the U.S. Pentagon. Washington, D.C. Team Two, Anton Zemitsov and Vadim Rybakov, you will have two nukes–Target, the CIA Headquarters Langley, Virginia. Team Three, Peter Abakumov and Dmitry Tokarev you will also have two nukes–Target, the Kremlin, Moscow. And team Four, Basil Povarov, one nuke–Target, the FSB Headquarters, Lubyanka Square in Meshchansky District, Moscow."

Banks paused again. He made sure that they all knew ahead of time that he'd targeted their homeland. Yet, this didn't affect their mission. None had relatives that close to Moscow and had advised their closest family and friends to leave for the farmlands.

"First to depart will be teams three and four," Banks said, "Your plane should be here soon. It can't land on Russian soil, so you'll parachute in. I listed the landing zone in your folder. Once the plane returns, teams one and two will depart. Follow the instructions in your folder."

That completed, he sat back in his chair. He felt as if someone had lifted the world from his shoulders. The entire task was handed out and his people were all set. Now, for the information Benz had gathered on Sinclair, and if he could use it against her.

A few minutes later, those gathered rose and, one by one, made their way to the table behind them to pick up their assigned folders.

Objedkov stopped with his folder in hand and stared at Banks. "How soon will the plane arrive?"

"In about two hours."

———— · —— · ————

An hour later, Bobrov, Objedkov, and Abakumov arrived at Stuttgart airport.

Before departing the ranch, the four men loaded up two Russian Izhmash AN-95 assault rifles and magazines. The AN-95 is the preferred assault rifle of the FSB, as opposed to the Kalashnikov AK-74M rifle. Along with two MP-443 Semi-auto service pistols, chambered in the 9x19 Parabellum, they would be ready in the event things went south on them.

Once gaining entry into the hanger area, they searched for hanger number eight on the other side of the airfield.

Minutes later, they drove through the open hangar doors and stopped beside the white with blue striped colored Gulf Stream G600 twin-engine jet. Bobrov, once out of the car, walked toward the plane. Halting at the side door, he pulled it down and secured it open, as Abakumov stood off to one side acting as security.

At the cockpit controls, Bobrov went through the starting procedures. Turning on the generator's switches, he proceeded step by step through the start chart. Then pulling on the lever, he started engine one, then engine two. Keeping them on for a few seconds, he shut down the engines, having satisfied himself that the batteries and engines were in excellent shape.

Once out of the jet, Nikolai secured the door. With Abakumov and Objedkov staying to watch over the plane, Bobrov drove to the flight control building and submitted a bogus flight plan. Once approved, he was ready to fly.

Back at the plane, Bobrov sat once again in the cockpit, turned on the engines and was ready for takeoff. As he pulled away from the hangar, Peter, with Sergei in their car, waited until Bobrov was ready to taxi before starting the drive back to the ranch.

After getting takeoff clearance, Bobrov taxied the plane to his runway. Soon the jet shot across the clouds, heading for the ranch.

In the meantime, back at the ranch, Benz began briefing Banks on his findings related to Sinclair. Opening a mini iPad, he clicked on a page marked *Profile Sinclair*. Clicking to the first page, he read: "Name, Jacqueline Belle Sinclair, and Belle is her nickname, age 32, five-feet-nine, attractive, a very self-assured, confident woman. She's known for her sharp mind, her cool head under pressure, and held in high regard by the EUCOM commander and her fellow agents. She is a Chief Warrant Officer and the agent-in-charge of the local CID office in Stuttgart. Her exploits as a criminal investigator and an intelligence officer were the stuff of CID legend."

"Carl, are there any friends or relatives I should know about?"

"She had a friend, another female, and murdered last year. No other close friends. She was an only child. Her mother passed away several years ago. Her father is Colonel Richard Longstreet Sinclair, the EUCOM Provost Marshal. He's her only living relative."

"Anyone she's involved with or a husband?"

"She has a fiancé, a soldier in Iraq, presumed dead or missing in action. No current affairs."

"A most impressive woman," Banks acknowledged. "It's a pity she's not backing away from her investigation. We must see to that."

"What are you planning?"

"Get me Anton Zemitsov and Captain Weber. We're going hunting."

36

Bobrov's plane shot through the nearly clear blue skies. Flying the Gulf Stream G600 jet just below radar tracking, almost hugging the shape of the earth, he kept away from the flight-paths of any major city or town. With the course set, he'd be able to distinguish the landing lights he'd help set up behind the ranch in a matter of minutes.

Within the short time of flying the jet, Bobrov fell in love with it even more than the plane he'd set on fire. He liked it so much that he planned on keeping it. The jet's cruising speed of Mach8.5 made it fun to fly, and it literally flew itself. And with the aircraft's flight range of over seven thousand miles, it made it more desirable for long-distance flights.

Coming in from the south, and just ahead, he caught sight of the make-shift runway lights directly behind and to the east of the ranch. He banked over to the left of the landing strip, circled once around and then back once more than he set the jet's nose center of the field.

In the late morning light, Bobrov touched down. The plane bounced slightly, settled onto the short runway and seconds later taxied to a halt next to the rear of the ranch. There, he met with an armed crew of four guards.

Heinz, the co-manager of the Pizzeria da Primo in Stuttgart, was a little annoyed, but not with his job. The reason he felt irritated was that every time he'd deliver six or eight pizzas to the ranch, that once belonged to a close family and friends, they would never give him a fair tip.

The round trip delivery was about seven miles, and for that alone, he should've gotten a large tip. On his last delivery run, he met some guy at the front of the house, and for the life of him, he thought he'd seen him before. He would think that he would remember meeting up with a guy who looked so dangerous. His German appeared to have a Russian accent, he mused. Shitty was more representative of the accent, he thought with a smile.

Now he had eight pizzas to deliver, along with other goodies, and he was the only driver available to make the run. He loaded the food in the back of his yellow two-door Vesper 400 microcar, pulled out of the parking lot and headed toward the ranch swearing if he didn't get a large tip, he would ask why.

The eight-minute drive to the ranch found his Vesper entering the dirt road leading to the ranch proper. At three mph, he drove through the open gate, halted in front of the ranch house and turned off the engine. As he eased his six-foot frame from the compact car, two burly men came out of the house and stood by the entrance.

"I have eight boxes and three bags of food."

One of the two men stepped down, unloaded the rest of the food from the car and walked into the house.

With the rest of the pizza boxes and bags delivered, Heinz approached Banks for payment. As Banks reached into his pocket, Heinz kept staring at him.

Damn, but I've seen you before too, he said to himself. But for the life of him, he just couldn't place him.

Banks pulled out a wad of cash and gave Heinz a generous tip.

"Vielen dank!" Heinz said, smiling, thanking him for the tip.

But then he was astonished to spot out of the corner of his eye, something unusual behind the ranch house; the tail of a plane sitting on the grass!

Du Hurensohn! Son-of-a-bitch! It's a plane.

But he didn't stop. He didn't want to cause a stir. Yet something else was bothering him as he spied several armed men patrolling the ranch.

Something is just not right.

He decided he was going to have a word or two with his friend at the police station across the street from the pizzeria.

However, when he returned to the store, he took a break when he noticed his favorite soccer team was about to start its home games. With his eyes glued to the television mounted on the wall, the news came on and he saw photos of several wanted Russian nationals. Suddenly, he stopped eating and swiftly rose as he recognized two of the wanted men whose photographs were being displayed!

<hr>

Seated behind her desk in her brightly lit office, Sinclair leaned back in her chair and contemplated the upcoming day's work as she waited for Russell and Courtney to arrive. With Agent Smith back to work, she had left him to handle the cases that came in. This would leave her available to concentrate on the Banks investigation.

Resting her chin on her closed fists, elbows on the armrest, she closed her eyes and gave thought to where her investigation had so far lead her. She strongly believed the sleeper cell could very well be the ones to deliver the bombs. But it was still early, 10:30 a.m., according to her watch and the day still young. Anything could happen, but she wasn't waiting around for the other shoe to drop.

When she locates Banks base of operations, the use of the bomb detection box in her office would make it that much easier to help locate any or all of the bombs.

Now that the photographs of the suspected cell, and that of Banks, were on national television and the FBI's Most Wanted in the States, it was just a matter of time. However, if a break in the case didn't materialize soon, there would be hell to pay. She and her team could only do so much. She had ideas swirling around in her head, but she needed to get her team together to discuss the way forward.

Just before eleven, Russell, walking with the slight help of his cane, and Courtney, walked through the open door of Sinclair's office.

Sinclair gazed and smiled at the two. "You two have been ah ... having fun?"

Courtney shook her head. "What gave it away?"

"It was just a hunch, none of my business. You're both grownups."

Russell stared at Courtney, then at Sinclair with a slightly confused look. "What are you two ladies talking about?"

"Should we tell him, Sinclair?"

"Na, he's a detective," Sinclair replied with a grin on her beautiful lips. "Let him figure it out."

Then Russell's eyes lit up. "Oh, I get it now."

"Took you long enough, Dan," Courtney said, staring at him and offering him a wink.

The slight levity was good. Sinclair had a strong feeling that in the coming days they would be too busy to joke and laugh.

Turning off her computer, Sinclair rose and came around her desk and leaned back on it. Crossing her arms about her chest, she stared at the two seated. Squeezing her eyes, she had few options to work with. The ideas she had just made little sense to her. She just couldn't put together a scenario that would work. Then it hit her and she began. "The way I see this, there's only one option left open to us—the Russian FSB operatives."

Russell frowned. "What are you proposing?"

"We stake-out of the Russian Consulate."

"Didn't we try that once before?" Courtney asked.

"Yeah, and it didn't get us anywhere except getting one of my agents hurt," Sinclair replied.

Russell rubbed his head. "When do you want this done?"

"The sooner, the better, and I recommend using two cars with two separate surveillance points."

"Good idea," Russell said, agreeing to her recommendation. "But there's a minor problem."

"What?"

"I don't have a car here. Pat and I are sharing her car," Russell said, arching an eyebrow. "You wouldn't have an extra one handy?"

"See Agent Smith on your way out. He'll have one ready for you."

"Thanks."

"You two get going," Sinclair said, leaning back in her chair.

Just as she was preparing to call Agent Smith, her desk phone rang. Lifting the receiver, she pressed it to her ear.

"Yes," she said.

"Chief," Smith's soft voice said on the other line. "Your father is on line two."

Sinclair pressed the amber blinking button. "Hello, Dad."

"We have a situation, Belle."

"I'm listening."

"A little over an hour ago," her father said on the other end, "the MP desk Sergeant received information from the German police out at the small town of Baltmannsweiler, in Esslingen, of the sighting of two of our Russians. One of whom they have identified as Matthew Banks."

On hearing the name Banks, she sat up straight in her chair.

"It was a pizza delivery guy," Colonel Sinclair's voice went on, "that recognized them. There's something else. When questioned by the German police, two things stood out. There was a plane parked behind the house and walking armed guards patrolling the area."

"Damn, Dad! I think we just caught a break!"

"Yes, that's also my understanding."

"What do you want me to do?" Colonel Sinclair asked.

Sinclair drew a long audible breath. "Not a thing, Dad. I'll get a hold of the desk Sergeant," she said, feeling the excitement quickly overtaking her senses. "I don't want the German police near the place until I get there."

"All right then."

After hanging up with her father, Sinclair called the MP desk Sergeant, with certain guidelines and instruction to follow, and prepared for her drive.

This was the most promising lead yet and she would not let the German police screw this up, she thought. Sinclair needed to conduct her investigation and gather as much information as possible without arousing suspicion.

Then she called the SEAL team, had them prepare for action at a moment's notice.

But then again, she wasn't sure what she had until she conducted a soft probe first. Grabbing a parabolic mic, earphones and binoculars, she strapped on her Beretta M9 9mm handgun and extra magazines, and called off her MP bodyguards for the time being. After several minutes, she headed to her car.

————— · ——— · —————

Colonel Sinclair, sitting behind his desk in the Provost Marshal's building, was pondering his options. Should he advise the EUCOM commander of the possibilities of having knowledge of Banks' whereabouts or just sit back and wait for his daughter to call with her findings?

As he chose the latter, he stood, decided on an early lunch, grabbed his hat and left his office. His destination was a quaint little Italian restaurant just a mile from the Kaserne where he'd eaten frequently and the food was great. The service was slow, which gave him plenty of time to think things through, not just of Belle, but of other duties associated with his office. However, his mind always revolved back around to his daughter.

————— · ——— · —————

From a black SUV parked just outside the Kaserne, Banks watched Colonel Sinclair intently. He pulled out a photo of Sinclair, which he had downloaded from the CID website, and nodded. "That's him alright," he said to his driver, Anton Zemitsov and Captain Weber sitting in the back. "Let's go. Keep your distance, Anton."

"Yes sir," Anton said.

Driving his red Chevy Camaro, Colonel Sinclair was now several cars ahead and pulling away fast. Anton expertly drove in and around noonday traffic and slowly closed the gap between them.

Twelve minutes later, Zemitsov pulled in directly behind the Camaro and waited for Colonel Sinclair to exit his car. As Zemitsov and Weber exited the vehicle, Banks grabbed a cloth from the glove compartment, and a bottle of clear liquid and soaked the cloth with it. Then all three gathered to approach the Provost Marshal. With the parking lot fairly empty, this was the right moment to strike.

Zemitsov was the first out of the SUV, then Captain Weber, with Banks following. Zemitsov walked past Sinclair and slowed as Weber came up behind him. Banks, holding a piece of cloth in his hand, moved off to the right of the Colonel.

Before the colonel knew what was happening, suddenly, the three Russians stepped closer to their target. Oblivious to the trap and the danger facing him, his attackers grabbed him, holding him tight as he tried to wrestle free. Banks shoved the cloth full of chloroform, covering Sinclair's nose and mouth. Just as it took effect, they dragged the limp body to their SUV and shoved the unconscious Sinclair into the back seat.

As they pulled away from the parking lot, a petite young lady walking and talking on her Smartphone from across the street, turned at that moment and saw what was happening. Aiming the phone in their direction, she filmed it along with the license plate of the SUV.

At the Russian Consulate, Captain Kuznetsov and Colonel Borovkov ran to the parking lot after hearing the beeping of the tracker phone on Sinclair's car. Once there, with Kuznetsov driving, he wheeled around and took off at top speed out of the consulate and onto the main road. The American agent was on the move, and pulling away, traveling southeast on the B-10 autobahn!

With Colonel Borovkov navigating, they made the autobahn, then speeding up as they watched the speedometer reached a hundred and seventy kilometers per hour!

Colonel Borovkov's gaze didn't leave the small screen of the tracker as she watched the blue blinking light showing the agent's car and the yellow blinking light that showed their car. They were slowly closing the gap. Mile by mile, they were getting closer.

The agent's car pulled off the autobahn onto a side street. Then arriving ten minutes later, onto the side street taken by the agent, they followed.

A few seconds passed when Borovkov gazed at the man driving. "Do you think she's leading us to the traitor?"

"It's a possibility, Comrade."

"Or it could be a wild goose chase."

"We won't know until we get there."

———————•———————

At the ranch, teams three and four were making last preparations for their flight.

Bobrov had just finished the last-minute plane checks and all he needed was to start the engines. However, they needed at least an hour or more before taking off. This would give them enough time to get everything on board the plane. Twenty minutes later, having loaded two nuclear suitcases and their personal effects, they waited for Basil Povarov to load his parachute and his nuke case.

—37—

It was eleven-fifteen in the morning when Grin arrived at the President's office at the Kremlin. He had called the President for a face-to-face meeting to keep him informed of his progress and to request more time to continue with his investigation. It was something he couldn't afford to do over the phone.

The ex-KGB operative gained most of the information the President had asked him to put together, but it would be up to Gadjiyev to decide whether to act on it or wait. *I know the information is incomplete,* he thought. *Will he allow me to continue with it, or will he act on what I have? I just don't know. However, I'll wait for him to let me know what action to take. If I'm not allowed to act soon, I fear this will turn into something the President could not control.*

The waiting area had no windows as Grin stared at a large oil painting of Joseph Stalin on the far wall alongside photographs of other Russian leaders. With the Soviet national flag placed on either side of the painting, it was an impressive sight to behold. A halogen covered art-lamp shone down from the top of the painting, illuminating it and giving it a sense of depth. The waiting area was dim and somewhat cool. Something to do with energy conservation measures, he thought.

Toward the other side of the double doors, leading into the President's inner office, stood two burly guards, dressed in two-piece black business suits, white shirts, and black ties with their hands clasped in front of them. White curly wired earpieces hung from their ears. These were the private Kremlin Regiment guards, also called the Presidential Regiment, Grin mused. And he knew these were a unique military regiment and part of the Russian Federal Protective Services.

At the moment he was about to check his watch, one guard pulled open the two doors of the President's inner office. Grin looked up as a guard called out his name and said the President was ready to receive him.

Grin rose, adjusted his suit jacket and tie, and walked toward the guards. As he approached them, a guard held up his hand, in a signal to stop, while the other guard held a scanner. He instructed Grin to raise his arms as the guard waved it over his body. They found his weapon, removed it and told they would return it once he was done.

As the doors closed behind him, Grin approached the President's desk. The president looked downcast.

"Please have a seat," President Gadjiyev said, with a calm voice. "I hope you bring me good news, Oleg."

"Good news is something I strive for, my President," Grin cautioned. "Often I fail, but in moments like these, I'll let you decide."

"Fair enough," Gadjiyev said, leaning forward on his chair, resting his arms on his desk, and steepling his fingers. "Tell me what you've uncovered so far."

"Mr. President, my investigation, as you described the problem to me, was two-fold. First, as you and I suspected, there is the possibility of a coup d'état; the absolute control of the government by the military. Second, those responsible are several high ranking FSB officers ordered by the highest-ranking military generals in your staff."

"Aha! I suspected as much," President Gadjiyev said. "So, the American President was right."

Grin nodded. "Yes, sir, it would appear so."

"Have you identified by name those responsible?"

"Yes, sir," Grin replied. "The intelligence that I gathered so far points to two of those staff officers, along with the head of the FSB *and* the head of FSB in our Consulate in Germany. So far I'm compiling evidence, along with their connections, and will add names to those that I unmask."

"How did you gain this information, Oleg? Or should I ask?"

"I know you're familiar with my methods, Mr. President. So I'll leave it at that. With the methods at my disposal, I conducted an in-depth background on Anisi Sverchinsky. He is not who he claims to be. My investigation led me to the real Sverchinsky, captured by the Americans, interrogated and died while in their hands. The CIA recruited a look-a-like and planted him in place of the real Anisi."

The President raised a brow. "How could that be, Oleg? Are you sure?"

"Yes, without a doubt, sir," Grin replied. "The American CIA operative's name was Matthew Banks. He fooled everyone. Even marrying a Russian woman and adopting her child."

"He was that good?"

"Yes, sir, and he was very lucky. Within six-years, Banks unmasked several classified documents considered essential to our well-being. I've sifted through them, from his login at our classified vault when he pulled them. Those documents, Mr. President, were of our military posture in and around the world, our first strike options; just to name a few."

"Did he get to transmit them back to the CIA?"

"Of that, I am not sure," Grin replied. "It stands to reason, Mr. President, he may have done just that. It places our military in grave danger from a first-strike attack at the hands of the United States!"

A slight pause, as Oleg Grin saw the tightening of his jaw and anger rising in those piercing eyes. He didn't continue until the President had once again settled back in his chair.

"Sir, most of his comrades have fled the country, of that I am sure. I'm also sure Banks plans to use them to deliver and place the nukes. The only friend's Banks left behind in Russia were a husband and wife team and two old retired FSB agents."

"Is there a timetable for his attack?"

"There wasn't any I could find, sir."

"Who are these people?" President Gadjiyev asked.

"Dissidents, sir," Grin replied. "Some are from the FSB ranks and the military taken in by the imposter."

The President shook his head. "Please go on, Oleg."

"Sir, one of those FSB agents transmitted Banks' plans to nuke the U.S. and our homeland using our nukes. However, it didn't get to its desired location and routed it to our Embassy in Frankfurt. But U.S. Military Intelligence in Germany intercepted it. Sir, the plan, according to one of Banks' agents, was to have the nukes placed around certain targets in Russia to topple your hold on the government and to have the military seize control. It would come down to power. And the military would have full control."

Gadjiyev's head jerked at the mention of the use of the nukes. They would exterminate thousands, even millions of Russians, just to gain power and control! He felt a chill run down his spine and his face pulsed with rage. But now, all that didn't matter. The conspiracy was out in the open. The only thing that mattered was to stop the nukes from being set off.

"With the help of one or two of my agents," Grin continued, "we tracked down and arrested all that came in contact with the imposter. They're being held for interrogation. It was the husband and wife team who at first denied ever knowing the man they knew as Anisi. However, with the interrogation and threat of killing his wife, the husband gave up the names and the total workings of their plot. I eliminated the two FSB retired agents after extracting the information."

"I see," the President said, still seething with rage. "Do you have any idea how this imposter took control of the nukes?"

"Yes, sir, I do. And those responsible are being watched as we speak. However, Banks with the help of members of our military staff stole the nukes, seven of them. Banks' recommendation to perpetrate the crime came from FSB by way of the NSA Director of the United States; a Steven Summerset. My information is that Summerset tried to get the nukes so he could profit from their sale on the black market."

The President grunted. "Good. Do you know the imposter's current location?"

"Yes, sir, he's in Stuttgart, Germany."

"Outstanding work, as usual, Oleg."

Grin grunted and went on. "I must tell you, sir, the head of the FSB at the Frankfurt Embassy, ordered Summerset's elimination."

Gadjiyev nodded. "I would have given the same order."

"I would have done the same."

"What are the names of the Generals involved, Oleg?" the President asked.

Grin settled back in his chair. Reaching into his inside jacket pocket, he extracted a small leather-bound notebook, opened it, flipped through several pages, and came to a stop. Reading to himself, he memorized the written page, closed the notebook, and stuffed it back into his pocket. Staring at the President, he began... "They are, sir. Chief of Staff, Pyotr Ivanovich, Ministry of Defense, Viktor Mordvinov, the head of the FSB, Sergei Vannovsky, and Colonel Elizaveta Borovkov, assigned to the Frankfurt Embassy in Germany. The Colonel is attempting to locate Banks. She has an FSB team of operatives assisting her. There are others whose names I haven't yet uncovered. But in time, I will have them."

The President inclined his head to one side. "For now, until I give you the word, Colonel Borovkov can continue her assignment."

"Yes, sir, do you wish me to continue with my investigation?"

"Absolutely, I want all of them rounded up."

"What do you want me to do with my prisoners, and those I mentioned, sir?"

"I want them terminated with extreme prejudice! But with the others, keep them under surveillance. And when I call you, you can proceed. And, Oleg, make it seem like accidents!"

"I'll do that, sir."

Russell and Courtney drove to the American Consulate. Their first order of business, before setting up their surveillance on the Russian Consulate, they were to connect with their respective superiors. The only way of accomplishing this was through a classified official communiqué sent from the agent's office.

The information they needed to convey was their after-action and follow-up reports of the past few days. This was to include the names and photographs of the sleeper-cell they suspected of transporting the nukes into the United States. Most important was the threat assessment profile the nukes represented, including the agent's apotheosis as to the potential targets the terrorist intended to strike.

Once in his office, both Russell and Courtney set about writing their reports. They wrote the same thing; with their own assessment of the situation. Russell spelled out the doomsday effects while Courtney played it down some. Each of the directorate's differences was shockingly brought out.

However, the results were the same—they were coming! How and when were the unknown factors?

Sinclair, behind the wheel of her Chevy sedan, reached the western outskirts of the Esslingen district. Far ahead she could see the outlines of the small town of Baltmannsweiler. It had taken her half an hour of driving to reach it.

She drove through a densely wooded area full of what she could discern as spruce and oak trees and others she could not identify. Moments later, she made out some cows grazing on green open pastures on one side and horses running in pens on the other side. Rolling down the window, the air smelled clean.

Such was country life. Sinclair was uncharacteristically charmed.

Far behind her Chevy, unbeknownst to her, the black SUV followed the blinking light, identifying Sinclair's vehicle on the tracking device held by FSB Colonel Borovkov.

Minutes later, Sinclair entered Baltmannsweiler tucked within the sheer forest of the tiny town. Driving on the cobble-stone two-way street, she followed the signs to the police station. The quaint town was small. She passed several shops, a grocery store, a pizzeria, a hardware store and a blacksmith's shop. Without traffic on either side, she caught sight of the police station on the left side of the street two blocks away.

Arriving at the station, Sinclair brought her vehicle to a stop beneath an overhang in front of the primary entrance to the police station, as two German police officers stepped out of the building. They paid little attention to her or the vehicle.

As she stepped around the car, and toward the glass door's entrance, she felt a slight cool breeze which blew her short-cut hair about her face. It was a welcomed feeling after being inside the stuffy car.

The CID agent walked into the station. It was warm and brightly lit. Off to her left was the Desk Sergeant's counter. To her right were several wooden chairs, and to her immediate front, was a caged entrance, which she believed led into the station offices.

The station appeared deserted. There were no visitors or any activity that resembled any police station Sinclair was familiar with. It wasn't a typical station, and it smelled rather pleasant. It was a far cry from most American police stations.

Taking a step toward the desk, she pulled out her credentials. Once standing in front of him, the Sergeant took notice of her.

"Do you speak English?" Sinclair asked, holding up her badge.

In broken English, the Sergeant asked, "You are ... American CID?"

"Yes," Sinclair replied, tucking back her credentials.

"Please, eh? ... Einen moment," he said, picking up his phone. A second later, he rattled off in German. She could understand only *Beautiful CID woman*.

"Please ... a seat," the Sergeant said, pointing to the chairs.

How long would they keep her waiting, she didn't know? By her experiences with the German police, it could take minutes or hours. So, she resigned herself to wait.

A short while later, the FSB parked in the back lot of the police station. But, unlike Sinclair, both FSB agents remained in their vehicle, waiting on the American agent. One burning question came to mind: what was the agent doing this far away from Stuttgart?

It wasn't hours, but minutes later, when a patrol officer hurried over to her to escort her into the detective squad offices through the caged entrance. After an introduction, and checking her credentials, she followed the officer into the far corner of the squad room. Walking behind the officer, they reached the desk of a seated detective who had his back to them and was on the phone. They stopped and waited. She noted with impatience that she was about to wait yet again.

Four other police personnel dressed in civilian attire stopped what they were doing; Sinclair guessed they were detectives. Two on phones stopped whatever conversation they were into and stared at her with smiles spread across their faces. Their eyes looked her up and down and lingered just a little too long on her figure.

One detective came over and smiled.

"I'm CID Agent Sinclair from Stuttgart, here for ..." she began.

He interrupted her as he held up a hand and said in excellent English, "Agent Sinclair, I know why you're here. I just finished talking with my Captain about it. How can we help?"

Before Sinclair could utter another word, the detective held up his hand once more and said, "Excuse my rudeness; I am Detective Andreas Schneider."

"Thank you for seeing me, Detective," Sinclair began. "I would like to interview the pizza delivery man and visit the place in question."

The detective nodded. "There is no need." He pulled a folder from atop his desk, opened it, removed two sheets of paper and handed them to her. "This is his written statement. We had it translated into English. You'll have a copy furnished to you when you're ready to leave."

Taking the statement, Sinclair started reading. There was nothing she hadn't already known.

"When can you show me to the ranch?" she asked.

"We can leave now if you're ready."

"Yes, I'm ready, thank you."

A momentary silence followed as she returned the statement to the detective who placed it back in the file folder.

"I need to ask for your understanding on my next request," Sinclair said,

"Yes?" Detective Schneider replied as he arched a brow.

"Once we're in the vicinity," she began, "I need to this on my own, if that's okay with you?"

"Well, I don't know," he said, shaking his head. "From what I understand, these are dangerous men."

"I'm only doing a recon and nothing more."

He remained silent for a moment. When he responded, he rose, grabbed his jacket from the back of his chair and donned it. Pulling a handgun from a desk drawer, he tucked it behind his back.

"Okay, I understand. Follow me to the ranch. My car is around the back. I'll meet you out front in a few minutes."

"Sounds like a plan. Thank you."

Sinclair drove slow following the unmarked Volvo police cruiser ahead of her. They were driving into a darkened area of the woods. Left and right of her, dead leaves and branches littered the road. As they drove on, the forest all around her seemed to close out the daylight rays of the sun, almost giving it a ghostly environment. The density of the tall trees, with their overhanging branches, created a canopy of green becoming an almost dull, vast empty place swallowed up by the surrounding forest.

Glancing at the car's clock, it read: 11:35. She shook her head. Outside of the forest, it was still daylight. This is so surreal, she thought.

A few minutes later, she noticed the Volvo had reduced its speed. It pulled off and came to a stop on the side of the road. Sinclair stopped her Chevy behind the Volvo. Just before sliding out of her car, she saw Detective Schneider walking up to her car's window, and seconds later, he stopped and leaned in.

"The ranch is about half a mile further up on the right side of the road," Schneider said. "There's an entrance or a dirt road that leads to the principal ranch house. I would advise you to park your vehicle on the left side of the road and walk from here."

"Sound advice, thank you."

"Would you rather ... eh, I stay with you?"

"No thank you, I can manage."

"Well, if you need my help, just call."

"I will. Thank you again."

"Good hunting," he said.

The detective stood there staring down at her for a second, then turned and walked back to his car. Seconds later, he pulled a U-turn. He waved goodbye as he passed Sinclair's Chevy.

Shifting into drive, Sinclair pulled onto the road. She hung a U-turn and spied a small muddy dirt track. She stopped just at its entrance and backed the Chevy into it. Exiting the vehicle, she checked and made sure she hid it from either side of the road.

Walking behind the car, she popped the trunk and removed her knapsack full of equipment and extra magazines for her Beretta. One thing she failed to bring was night vision optics. But she didn't gamble on working in darkness. Reaching into her pocket, she pulled her Smartphone and set it to vibrate.

The surrounding forest smelled clean as the scent of resin with dead leaves hung in the air. Banks had chosen well for his base camp, she thought.

Turning, she started walking into the forest through what she thought was a small game trail, chock full of tiny hooves and animal tracks, that led straight toward where the detective had pointed. On she trudged. The wide trail gave her ample space in which to walk. Then it turned into a bend. Coming out of the bend, the trail became narrower.

Minutes passed when she heard people talking. Slowing down, she cautiously edged forward and pulled her Beretta.

"We've been waiting close to ten minutes, Comrade Colonel," Captain Kuznetsov said, as they waited in the vehicle for the agent to move once again. He'd parked the big SUV about a mile from where the agent's vehicle had stopped. "Something is not right."

Colonel Borovkov nodded. "I'm inclined to believe you, Captain."

"What do you want to do?"

"Drive up closer to her signal. Let's see what she's up to."

Setting the vehicle into drive, Kuznetsov drove forward. A half a mile went by when Borovkov slowed to a crawl and pulled over to the side of the road.

"Let's find someplace to hide the vehicle."

Minutes later, using the tracker's signal, they came upon Sinclair's car. With a penlight in hand, Captain Kuznetsov scanned the ground and observed fresh foot prints behind the Chevy. "She went this way, Colonel."

Turning off the penlight, they crept through the forest, following the same path Agent Sinclair had taken.

Moments later, Sinclair suddenly stopped and dropped to her knees. Up ahead she distinctively made out two armed men, guards, she thought, in a heated conversation. Then they stopped and started walking away from each other.

Unhurried, she made her way to the ridgeline of the ranch and stopped by some wooden fencing. There she removed her knapsack from around her back and dropped prone on the grass. Here, there was no canopy cover as daylight shone through, showing her the ranch and other buildings in the area.

Removing her binoculars, she scanned the area from left to right. She made out the main road leading into the ranch, the two guards patrolling the grounds and two men standing on the porch of what she guessed was the principal house.

The agent arranged herself in such a manner that she could make out the back of the house and the jet parked on the grass. *Have they already delivered the bombs? Is that how they're delivering them?* She asked herself. She didn't think they'd left yet or they would've all left the ranch, she reasoned. So the bombs were still somewhere on the ranch. She needed to find out exactly where. And to do that, she had to search the ranch grounds; but not in daylight. This was just a soft probe.

She had to wait.

In the meantime, she needed to make out what was being said on the porch. Pulling the parabolic mic, and putting on the earphones, she opened the reflector dish of the mic, hooked up the wiring to her recorder and pointed it at the two at the house while cranking up the volume.

Adjusting the mic, Agent Sinclair started picking up their conversation in German. "They should be here soon with our prisoner," the man on the left said.

"What are the first teams waiting on?" the other guy asked.

"They're waiting to load the plane," was the reply. "They should leave in a few minutes."

Then, three things happened within a matter of minutes. More men exited the ranch house. How many were there, she wondered? They all had suitcases in hand.

Picking up the binoculars, Sinclair watched as all three walked down the steps and proceeded behind the house to board the jet.

Not seeing any suitcase bombs, Sinclair reasoned they must have already loaded the bombs onto the plane. Now, taken aback by seeing them ready to leave, she felt hopeless and angered.

Damn it all to hell, there's nothing I can do to stop them!

Then, she heard the plane's engine start-up, saw it taxi out and then lift off. The plane flew higher until it became a mere speck in the sky.

Watching the plane disappearing over the horizon, her head cocked to the side as she suddenly heard a vehicle approaching from the main road and saw it pull up in front of the ranch house.

Sinclair watched as she identified Banks getting out from the back right passenger door as another individual also exited the vehicle on the other side with the driver. All three dressed in black.

Banks remained standing outside the door and then leaned in and seemed to help someone out of the vehicle. The other guy, with the driver, came around and stood next to Banks as they hauled out another man who appeared to have his hands tied behind his back and wearing a black hood over his head.

The prisoner, the one she had heard talked about, was taller than the three holding him up by his arms and shoulders. There was something vaguely familiar about the prisoner that kept Sinclair glued to the man. He appeared drunk and unable to stand. Maybe drugged, she thought.

Dropping the binoculars, she pointed the parabolic mic on them. Adjusting the volume a little, she heard Banks, clear as day and in perfect English: "Come on, we have a lot to talk about." Just then, Banks reached over and pulled the hood off the prisoner's head.

At first, she couldn't see the features, for the head hung down and turned away from her. The prisoner turned to face Banks. He was pale looking from the angle he posed to her and agitated, and still not able to see his face. He tried to untangle from their grasp, but Banks delivered a blow to the men's stomach, ending his struggles.

Then Agent Sinclair stiffened, now able to see the full contours of his face.

Shaking her head, she swallowed hard. Her eyes widened, taken by surprise. This can't be happening! She caught herself, as her body wanted to jump up, pull her gun, and run right into them, firing her weapon for all it was worth. She drew in a deep breath and watched helplessly as they dragged her father into the house.

PART THREE

Bloody Aftermath

—39—

The Russian Consulate in Stuttgart faced east and west along LeitzStrasse, bordering HeilbronnerStrasse. LeitzStrasse was a two-way street. Parked alongside the buildings were back-to-back vehicles, leaving barely room for any other cars trying to find parking.

Across from the Consulate was the intersection of JunghansStrasse with parked cars on either side of the road. The seven-story office building was a large sprawling complex shaped as an L.

Dan Russell parked his black Chevy behind two other vehicles on the east side of the complex. His surveillance point was the east-end entrance into the building. Courtney parked her vehicle on the west side behind several cars. Her point of observation was the back of the complex, and its side entrance, which led into an underground parking garage.

Just a little after noon, with a clear blue sky, the two agents began their surveillance. Having transmitted their reports earlier to their respective superiors, they set about to situate themselves and wait to see what transpired at the Consulate.

Russell knew this was a long shot. He'd tried to explain that to Sinclair, however, she wouldn't listen. Their aim, she outlined, surveil the FSB agents. Follow and report their destinations and obtain photos of them if possible.

But an hour into their surveillance, Russell received an urgent call from Sinclair to report post-haste to the CID office. "You two just get back *ASAP*. I'll explain once we meet up."

⎯⎯⎯ · ⎯⎯ · ⎯⎯ · ⎯⎯⎯

Once Sinclair finished the call with Russell, she pocketed her phone and stood rock-solid as a familiar tingle crept up and down her spine. She knew something was wrong. Intuitively, she crouched low.

As silently as she could, she rose to her knees, gathered her equipment and stored them back into her knapsack. Standing on bent knees, she was conscious of where she was stepping, avoiding the twigs and branches that she came upon.

As she slung the knapsack over her shoulder, and with her weapon drawn, she kept moving to her left. With no alternative but to leave through the left side of the forest, away from the way she entered, she would avoid whoever was out there with her.

Was I followed, or did someone find my car? The questions kept repeating through her mind as she inched forward.

⎯⎯⎯ · ⎯⎯ · ⎯⎯ · ⎯⎯⎯

They were kneeling shoulder to shoulder and leaning up against a wooden fence line, watching the activities and the men at the ranch. The next moment, they watched as a vehicle drove up and stopped in front of the house as two other men stood on the veranda watching the SUV drive up.

Colonel Borovkov and Captain Kuznetsov stared at one another. It was Colonel Borovkov who was first to ask in a hushed whisper. "What do you make of this, Comrade Captain?"

"Comrade Colonel," he replied, in a hushed tone, a smile on his lips, "I'm inclined to believe the American agent has just shown us the imposter's location."

"It's what I believe too."

Then the movements of those at the house gave them pause.

They watched as three men exited the SUV. They then saw another man, his hands tied behind him and wearing a hood over his head, being dragged out of the back seat of the vehicle.

Borovkov's squinted eyes centered on the one man and fully recognized the imposter from the photographs in her office computer; the man they sent her to capture!

She gripped her gun as if ready to rush forward.

"Colonel, what are you planning on doing?"

"That's our man, the imposter over there!" she said, "We're going to capture him and take him back to the Consulate."

Standing and facing her, Captain Kuznetsov admired her grit, although he thought it misplaced. "Comrade, don't be so hasty. I've seen armed guards around the property. It would be suicide to launch an attack right now with just us two."

"You have a better idea, Captain?"

"Yes, Colonel, I do. I recommend we return to the Consulate and return tonight with my men. If we play our cards right, we can take them without firing a shot."

"What of the American CID agent, what if she returns before we do?"

"We'll take care of that when the time comes."

After several minutes, Sinclair paused. As through the thin forest line, she made out the entire ranch. She unslung her knapsack, reached into the sack, grabbed her camera, and adjusted the telephoto lens to take rapid photographs of the entire front and sides of the ranch. The photographs will prove useful when planning the attack on the ranch, she reasoned.

The trail, if that's what it was, made a ninety-degree turn to the left, and she saw another fence line. As she came up to it, she climbed over, and once on the other side, continued her way through.

Not much time had passed before she walked out of the forest line and onto the dirt road, the same road where she'd left her vehicle. Turning right, she started walking in the direction she believed would lead to her car, when she came upon an SUV tucked in the forest line and almost invisible in the brush.

Could this be owned by whoever had come upon her?

It could very well be. Approaching the vehicle, she noticed it had Russian diplomatic plates.

Shit, the Russians. *FSB agents and she'd led them straight to the ranch.*

But Sinclair had other more important matters on her mind; her father!

Her safety wasn't even a concern anymore. The rescue of her father and capturing Banks and finding the bombs were foremost in her mind!

She believed she knew why Banks had kidnapped her father. It well could be a bargaining chip of sorts, as a potential concession in his favor. His goal, it would seem, was for her to stop her investigation: *Whatever*. This was emotional blackmail, and she vowed Banks would learn not to mess with the Sinclair's.

Back in her Chevy, she pulled a U-turn, and with dirt kicking up behind the vehicle, she sped away back to the CID office to plan her attack. Also, she was betting, eventually, she'd be receiving a call from Banks.

So now she had to contemplate, not just her father's safe rescue, but a likely attack by the Russians on the ranch.

Behind the wheel of the Chevy, she pounded the steering wheel, unable to stop the few tears that fell down her cheeks. And as a sob escaped her lips, she mouthed the words, *Dad, I'm coming.*

—40—

Sky above the Russian landscape, fifty-two miles west of Moscow City
September 12, 1:15 P.M.

Bobrov's Gulfstream jet streaked across the sky, and heading due east he would make Russian airspace in less than ten minutes. He flew the jet at NOE (Nap-Of-The-Earth) until the very moment he would enter Russian territory. Flying at a very low-altitude, he hoped to avoid radar detection.

The flight had taken an hour and a half; a little over forty minutes remained until the drop-point. Flying over the country of Belarus, and approaching the city of Mahilyow, he banked left, avoiding the city altogether; then banking right, he flew straight back on his course.

The terrain, teams three and four would jump into, was a large forested area just south of Landschaft, K.P. Russia. Comprising a few homes, it was well away from the LZ (Landing Zone) Banks planned for their drop.

Within five minutes of the LZ, Nikolai turned toward the copilot, Basil Povarov. "Five minutes out, get the rest of the group ready to jump."

Each of them had donned chutes and goggles, and with their suitcases and their suitcase bombs packed in a parachute placed by the door—the first out—they waited for the signal to jump.

Then increasing speed and gaining jump altitude, Bobrov flew into Russian airspace.

Several minutes later, through the plane's intercom system, he said, "Two minutes."

Hearing the two-minute warning, Povarov, the closest to the door, turned the door's handle and pulled it inside. The plane experienced a slight loss of altitude as the cabin's depressurizing occurred. Through the doorway, the fury of the wind, and the drone of the engine's, consumed their ears, making it difficult to hear.

Bobrov, within seconds, maneuvered the jet into the correct altitude for the drop-off. He knew at his present altitude the jet would be open to ground-radar detection within minutes and for the next few minutes, it didn't matter

Back in the cabin, all three knew jumping at these speeds and altitude could be dangerous. Although they had jumped frequently, they still experienced uneasiness and fear. They stared at each other without smiling, without uttering a single word, each wrapped up in their thoughts.

Then, through the cabin's loudspeaker once again, Bobrov gave the command to jump.

If everything went to plan, they would land about ten miles from the nearest highway into Moscow—the A-109 highway—which would take them straight into the heart of the city.

Povarov, with the cargo chute by his feet, had already hooked up the chute and was pushing it out the door. It opened as it floated down to earth. Standing by the door, he and the others also standing, hooked up to the static line they'd improvised on the jet, and casually approached the door. With his hands off the static line, Povarov, the first to jump, made a right face and leaped toward the speeding ground beneath him.

One, then the other, jumped.

Their chutes opened as they adjusted for their target. The roar of the jet engines gave way to the peaceful experience of descending to earth.

Directing their chutes, they all made landfall just a few feet from the cargo chute and about a yard apart from one another, well away from any substantial tree line that could have spelled trouble for their landing.

Removing their chute harness, they wrapped them up and tossed them into the nearby woods.

Five minutes later, all three knelt in a circle while Povarov consulted his map. "The first home is about five miles north of here," he said.

"Hope they have something good we can ride in," Tokarev said.

"Yeah, and with a heater," Abakumov added.

Gathering up their suitcases, they headed north for the short five-mile walk toward the first home depicted on Povarov's map. They intended to confiscate a vehicle and drive the rest of the twenty miles into Moscow, with maybe moderate traffic to contend with. They should reach their objective in fifteen minutes.

As they walked, Povarov reached for his satellite phone in his jacket pocket and keyed in the pre-arranged number. From the other end, he heard, *"What's your status?"*

Speaking into the phone, Povarov said, "At the LZ, all three heading north."

"Copy that," the voice from the ranch replied. Then he heard it click off. Pocketing the phone, he kept up with his two comrades.

High above them, Bobrov, having already accomplished his mission, banked the jet over to the left, and flew the NOE out of Russia.

Not taking any chances in the event they detected the Gulfstream, Bobrov, still too far from the Russian border, had already identified a small abandoned runway just after entering Russian airspace. To this, he set his course. And with the plane's transponder turned off, it would be difficult, if not impossible, to keep track of his plane.

In the meantime, a stealth fighter jet, a Sukhoi PAK FA, a single-seat, twin-engine aircraft sliced through the air at an altitude of 30,000 feet following the path of the unknown jet that had entered Russian airspace through its last ground radar detection marker. His mission was to determine the aircraft's identification, and if warranted, destroy it!

Two minutes later, in the early afternoon light, Bobrov aligned the jet with what remained of the runway. Within seconds, the Gulfstream touched down.

To his left, there was just one building, an old rundown decrepit hangar which seemed to sag under the weight of the rotting roof with its doors wide open. To this, he taxied the jet. Once inside, he shut down the engines.

Not a minute too soon as Bobrov froze on hearing the boom of a jet flying above the hangar.

Bobrov peered around the inside. The way he came in was the only way out. He would have to use a *power-back* procedure to reverse the engine's thrust and back the plane out of the hanger when the time came to leave. He planned to wait for two hours before taking to the skies again.

The three men didn't follow any roads, as none were in evidence; only indistinguishable paths cut through the forest. Several minutes later they came upon a creek. They made out the outlines of the home they had targeted first.

Crossing to the other side of the creek, they came to a halt. Here the grass seemed recently mowed. Clear tracks led toward the back of the property.

They gazed at a typical two-story thatched cottage surrounded by large oak trees. From the chimney smoke, it was clear someone was home.

Leaving their suitcases behind them, they unhurriedly approached, scrutinizing the building and the barn on its other side. The barn was open and they could see a vehicle inside.

Without making a sound, they walked on and halted on the back lawn. Povarov pointed to Tokarev, and then at the right side of the structure, showing he should move around that side. Getting a slight nod from Tokarev, Povarov then pointed at Abakumov, showing him to take the left side.

Turning away from Povarov, Tokarev, and Abakumov both drew their SR-1 Gyurza semi-auto handguns and began walking toward the cottage with their weapons pointing to the ground. As Povarov approached the slightly opened back door, he pulled his weapon, held down by his right leg.

The door, constructed of galvanized sheet metal and plywood, had enough room for him to walk through without pulling it open.

At that same moment, inside the cottage, an eighty-seven-year-old homeowner, wearing a thick set of warm clothing, saw an unknown visitor approach stealthily from the left side of the house. It caused him to drop the pipe he was smoking as fear gripped him the moment he saw the gun the stranger was carrying.

His first instinct was to yell out for help, but who would hear out here in the country, he thought. And he was alone. He hesitated for a moment. Then he did the next best thing he could think of.

As the elderly man rose from his couch, and as quick as his legs would carry him, he walked across the living room and stood in front of his weapons cabinet.

With hands wrinkled and blotched with sun-spots, he opened its two doors, grabbed a double-barrel shotgun, two slugs, and armed the weapon. He turned, walked halfway back into the living room, stopped, and leveled the heavy shotgun at the front door, and waited, without saying a word.

As Abakumov stepped around and faced the front door, Povarov entered the cottage gun-first. He moved inside and found himself in the kitchen. Stepping through the kitchen door, he rounded a corner and stopped just at the threshold of the living room. Povarov saw the back of a man standing facing away from him.

At the front door, Abakumov, standing to one side of the door, tried the door handle, felt it unlocked, and cracked the door opened.

Povarov suspected the old man of having a weapon and was waiting for someone to walk in. Suddenly, before Povarov could voice a warning to his comrade, the old man pulled the trigger.

BOOM!

The blast sounded like a thunderous explosion inside the living room. The old man, thrown two steps back by the shotgun's recoil didn't get to trigger another shot, as Povarov's weapon rang out. A two-round burst struck the old man in the back, dead before he slumped to the floor.

"Peter! You okay?" Povarov called out.

The shotgun blast went past Abakumov. "Yeah, didn't get a scratch."

Thirty seconds later, they were in the cottage and searching for the keys to the vehicle. It was Tokarev who found them hanging from a nail in the kitchen by the door.

Five minutes later, in an old, but well maintained Russian Gaz-M20 four-door Pobeda vehicle, and with Povarov driving, they struck out for the highway and Moscow. One outstanding thing about the car, Abakumov noted, was that the heater worked.

—41—

It was a mild afternoon in mid-September, and Sinclair's office was empty and chilly. The afternoon sun tried to shine through the closed, curtained window behind her, which kept her office in a semi-darkened atmosphere. But she relished the quietness and solitude of it all.

Shutting down her laptop, she leaned back in her chair. On her desk, on her right side, was a framed photograph of her father. She grabbed the frame and clutched it to her bosom. She felt a rising fury that her father was now in the hands of the enemy, a pawn in Banks' twisted scheme.

Would her father be in danger, knowing Banks' determination to commit mass murder? She asked herself. *Damn right he was.* The sooner she acted on his rescue, the sooner she could breathe again.

Would Banks use her father to have her stop her investigation of him? Sinclair was sure of it, although she had received no further phone calls. However, she felt it was coming soon. Her ultimate question was, would it come as she set her attack in motion on his ranch, or before?

Only time would tell.

Sinclair recalled her time with her father, those times since her mother passed away stricken with cancer. They were the best years of her life. He had been a strict father. From the very beginning, he raised her in the discipline that was the Army and she loved him for it. She remembered back to how loving he'd been with her and still was; so agreeable and an absolute saint.

Her throat was tight and dry. The memory of watching her father overwhelmed her. Thinking back on how they tied him up and shoved him into the house. For a moment she didn't think she could go on like this.

"God, please give me the strength," she whispered in a hushed tone, "For what I have to do." With her mother's passing, all she had left with was her father, and Tom, who may or may not come out of his coma. If he did, would he be the same person she'd known and grown to love? She just didn't know. And without his legs, his life could be a burden that he may not want to share with her. She'd seen that in other veterans who'd shut out those they loved and suffered for it.

No, she thought. *They can't take him, I won't let them. I'll do everything in my power to stop Banks from whatever he's going to do to my father.*

As for Tom Price, her fiancé, she could only pray.

She gazed around the office in solemnity and drew in a sharp breath.

Returning her father's photo on her desk, Sinclair wiped tears that flowed down her cheeks with the back of her hand. She swore that would be the last time she would weep; not until she had her father back with her.

She fortified herself with a shot of Jack Daniel's whiskey she kept in her desk drawer. *That was for you, Dad.*

Now she was ready for the meeting, which could determine her father's rescue amid an international disaster.

———————————

Waiting for her to appear in the conference room were Russell, Courtney, and five members of the elite SEAL team-5, led by Captain Kit Stone, a ten-year veteran. Also in attendance were three German police special warfare personnel along with the German Detective, Andreas Schneider. The office secretary had placed hot coffee and two trays full of sandwiches on a folding table.

It was a normal military conference room whose two pieces of furniture were a central long wide oak desk and twenty leather-back chairs. And seated in attendance were those involved in the attack planning.

Three sets of long LED lights hung from the ceiling over the desk, keeping the room well lighted. Two fifty-five inch televisions hung side-by-side on the far wall, displaying photographs of the ranch Sinclair had previously taken.

Two doors led in from a long hallway. One door, the main door led through from the stairwell, and the second into the principal agents' offices.

The room itself was of medium size. Russell found it smaller than what he'd remembered.

Sinclair turned first to Russell; the person she placed in charge of planning and coordinating the discussions. "Dan," she began, "this group has had time to study the ranch photos, along with my brief rundown and layout. Where are we with that?"

Russell's eyes narrowed. "The first thing that came to all of us was that we need more Intel; the size of the opposition, armaments, communications capabilities, and layout of any guards and escape routes, comes to mind. We just can't go in blind. You gathered great photos, but we need more."

Shit! A look of what may have passed as impatience spread across her face. She needed to get the show on the road, and the sooner the better. "How do you plan on acquiring that information?"

"I asked that same question to all here and all our plans were flawed," Russell replied. "However, it was SEAL team commander, Captain Kid Stone, who came up with a plan. I'll let him explain it, Captain?"

For a moment, Stone didn't reply. When he did, his voice was low, commanding, as if he was in charge of the operation. All eyes trained on him as he stood.

"As we all know, the best forms of intelligence gathering we have, besides digital photography, sketching, and physical surveillance is aerial. So I propose a drone flying very high with HD video recording that can pipe in the video right to my computer here. For that, we need an unmanned aerial vehicle (UAV) or eye-in-the-sky capable of getting us the footage. A PD-100 Nano unmanned aerial vehicle would do the job. It's shaped like a helicopter and flies like one, but it weighs only 18 grams. It's very silent and equipped with three HD cameras and has a range of 1.6 kilometers, just what we need."

"And how can we get our hands on one, Captain?" Sinclair asked.

"No need to look far, ma'am," Captain Stone replied with a smile. "The team has two in our equipment. We're always prepared for any eventuality, ma'am."

In her feeling of elation, she forgot her slight impatience. She thought fast. "Since it's your drone, Captain, we need the information before nightfall. How soon can you get it ready?"

"We can be ready in a matter of minutes."

"That's excellent. Thank you."

Then she turned to Detective Schneider. "Detective, can you provide a ride for the SEAL team members to the ranch?"

"I can do that," Schneider replied. "My men and I will provide the needed transportation."

Captain Stone gazed at Sinclair. "Ma'am, I have one request to make of you."

"Go ahead, Captain."

Clearing his throat, Stone began. "My team and I request that we lead the attack, giving us the first strike. My reason for asking is Banks and his mercenaries killed a brother, Master Chief Petty Officer Mark Hawthorne, and his SEAL team, and he was a good friend of mine."

Sinclair shrugged. "I have no objections, Captain. Your team is better suited to be first in, than the rest of us."

"I, and my team, thank you, ma'am."

There were murmurings and nods of agreements, disagreement passing between them. After an hour of planning, they were just about to end the conference. However, it would start again once they'd gathered the surveillance and the information to arrive at a clearer picture of the ranch defenses.

Abruptly, Sinclair's cell phone rang.

Answering it, Sinclair said, "Agent Sinclair."

"Well hello, agent."

"Who is this?"

"You should know my name by now, agent."

Her voice and one word boomed out clear in the room, "Banks!"

That one word stuck in her throat.

A freezing silence fell on the room as all eyes turned toward Sinclair.

<h1 style="text-align:center">—42—</h1>

A brief heated exchange passed between her and Banks, then clicking off her phone Sinclair sat back, absorbing the information Banks mentioned concerning her father and the demands placed on her. However, it didn't change anyway, shape, or form her decision to assault the ranch that night.

Agent Sinclair was in a state of shock from the moment she'd seen her father dragged away, but now her thinking became crystal clear and active. She focused briefly on how to get her father back rather than the problematic issues raised by Banks. There was no use in resentment or hatred of him, it was counterproductive. With the fate of the world hanging in the balance, she wasn't about to cave into his demands just because he had her father.

On the contrary, she mused, she'd plan on getting him back, one way or another.

But any signs of weakness on her part and the team would forego the assault. She needed strength and fortitude for the coming hours.

For the first time, she felt fear of losing her father. The same feelings she felt when just last year a sniper's bullet almost ended his life. And yet, here he was in the grips of another madman! Now her teams were waiting for her plan.

"I ... we have another situation at the ranch. As you know, that was Banks on the line." She paused. "He ... he's holding my father hostage!" Her voice was low, soft, almost detached.

A short silence ensued.

"My God," Russell cried out, shaking his head. "I'm so sorry."

Sinclair inclined her head. "No time for that, Dan. We have more pressing matters to attend to."

"Did he, eh? ... Say what he wanted in exchange for your father?"

Sinclair glanced around the room to one, then another. "Yes, for me to drop our investigation, and stop searching for him, or he would kill him!"

Murmurings went through those gathered as faces turned away from Sinclair.

"What now?" Captain Stone asked. "Do we continue or hold back for now?"

"We move forward with our plans, Captain, but with an added caveat ... that of rescuing my father."

Stone grunted as they stood in silence for a few moments. "With my team being the first in," he said, holding a fixed stare on her. "I'll make it our primary objective of getting your father to safety."

"Thank you, Captain Stone," she said. "Let's hope you can. Coordinate with Detective Schneider and have your men ready for transportation to the ranch."

"Yes, ma'am, we'll be ready to depart in fifteen minutes."

Sinclair looked over at the German detective. "Detective, when would you be ready to move out?"

"As soon as Captain Stone finishes up," Schneider replied as he started for the door.

"The rest of us, let's work on our plan of attack," Sinclair said.

Fifteen minutes later, with Detective Schneider driving and Captain Stone occupying the front passenger seat, they left with SEAL team member, Petty Officer Blake Andrews, who sat in the backseat. On his lap was a small black case that stored the micro drone.

In an unmarked black SUV, they made their way through the back roads where tall oak trees lined both sides of the unpaved dirt road. As they traveled through the forest, it had grown dark as the overhanging limbs, full of leaves, blocked out the sun.

A few minutes later, Stone looked over at Schneider. "Ah, Detective, how soon before we arrive?"

"Please call me Andreas, Captain Stone," Schneider replied. "In answer to your question, it's just around the next bend."

Stone nodded. The news didn't come fast enough for him. Pulling his M9 handgun, he made sure a round was chambered. Then he grabbed his cell phone and called in his position relative to the ranch to Sinclair back at the installation.

Rounding the bend in the road, Schneider slowed and pulled into a dense alcove of trees and tall grass and came to a stop. Killing the engine, he turned in his seat and faced Stone. "We're on the fringes of their ranch; it's to my right about a quarter-of-a-mile through the forest line."

"How close do you need to be with the drone?" Stone asked Andrews.

"As close as we can get," Andrews replied.

Turning to the detective, Stone said, "Andreas, this is your neck of the woods, please take the lead."

They slid out of the unmarked SUV, closed their doors, and crouched by the front of the vehicle. Andrews collected the drone and control unit and followed behind Captain Stone. Without a sound, they slipped through the tall grass and towering trees, following the detective on a narrow dirt path. Stone and Schneider both had their sidearms drawn and pointed at the ground as they walked forward.

"This is the boundary line to the ranch," Schneider said, once the two SEALs were by his side. "The ranch should appear in a few minutes' walk."

Stone nodded. "Lead the way."

Five minutes later, they came upon wooden fences, and still hidden in the forest line, they saw the ranch off to their right.

"Andrews on you," Stone said.

"Roger that, sir," Andrews replied.

With Andrews pulling alongside Stone, he gave the chopper drone to his captain. "Hold the drone by your thumb and index finger and raise it over your head, sir."

"Copy that," Stone acknowledged.

With the control unit in one hand, Andrews operated a few buttons and a dial. The rotary blades on the micro chopper began rotating, then faster, until it reached takeoff velocity.

"Sir, please release your hold on the chopper," Andrews said.

"Roger that."

Gradually, the chopper lifted skyward, with only a minute noise sounding like the humming of bees to break the quiet of the woods. On the control unit, Andrews watched as he flew the drone toward the ranch at a height of 400 feet.

Once the drone was airborne, Stone grabbed his cell phone and called Sinclair, advising her to turn on his computer in the conference room and watch the action.

Then, off somewhere in the distance, they heard the faint rumbling of a jet getting closer. Someone shone a spotlight on the back of the ranch out in the field, and what appeared to be a private jet came into view, making its approach for a landing.

<hr>

Colonel Sinclair was conscious but in severe pain as he spat out blood. They had his hands tied behind his back with a rope around his chest and under his armpits. From a rafter, they lifted him off his feet as he hung a few inches above the floor. His eyes swollen shut and severely beaten about his face, with scarred welts and cuts in several places, his blood quickly pooled under his feet.

Not giving up on any hope of rescue, Colonel Sinclair slowly and painfully tried opening an eye. However, all he could do was just squint. Gazing around him, he could only make out a semi-darkened interior. His first thought maybe he was in a cave or a basement, but he couldn't be sure. Struggling against his bounds, he stopped as the pain shot through his entire body.

Suddenly, they started in again.

There were two of them, his torturers, both Russians, one on either side of his dangling body. One held him steady while tilting his head. And the other, holding a one-liter plastic bottle filled with water, drained it into his mouth and nose. Colonel Sinclair started gagging and coughing.

From a far corner, another man crept toward Sinclair. "How are you feeling, Colonel?" the man asked.

Unable to fully open an eye, Colonel Sinclair guessed the identity behind the voice.

"Son of a bitch, Banks," Sinclair said with a slurred voice as blood seeped down from his lips and cuts above his brow that flowed down into his eyes. "You'll get nothing from me, you fucker!"

"That remains to be seen, Colonel," Banks replied. "We've only just begun."

"You're gonna have to kill me ... asswipe."

"You're correct on that. But not yet."

"My ... my daughter," Sinclair began, "will hunt you down. She won't rest until you fall under her gun."

"So, in the meantime, let's get down to my questions."

"Kiss my ass!"

"First, does your daughter know about my ranch?" Banks asked, ignoring the colonel's choice of expletives. "Are they planning an attack, and if so, when?"

"Fuck you!"

"Give him some more water," Banks said in Russian to the man holding the bottle.

"*No!*" Sinclair screamed, understanding what he'd said while trying to twist his body away from the Russians. But it was no use.

One jerked Sinclair's head back violently, holding it in place, while the other poured water down his throat until he couldn't breathe. He was drowning and unable to do anything to stop it.

Banks raised a hand to stop the Russian

"Shall we try again?" Banks asked in a low and conversational voice.

"There's nothing I have to say to you," Sinclair said, coughing and fighting to stay alive. "Except ... go ... to ... hell." His voice came out like a gasped whisper. Although he knew he wasn't long for this life, he had but one regret—that of not being able to see and kiss his little girl again.

With a nod from Banks to one torturer, he said in Russian, "The bat then, three times."

The Russian picked up a baseball bat from the floor next to the swinging prisoner. Grasping it with both hands, he swung hard once, then...

Bam!

The colonel felt a brutal blow against his abdomen that knocked all the air out of him as blood spattered on the floor in front of him. Twice more, they repeated the blow!

Just then, someone yelled down into the basement. "Matthew, the plane is coming back."

"I'll be right up," Banks' replied.

"Saved by the bell, Colonel," Banks said with a smile. "But I'll be back." And with a smile, as he stared at the swinging body, he walked to the stairwell.

———•———•———•———

"That's the same plane I saw take off with three men on board," Sinclair commented just before the plane touched the ground. The video feed was coming in clear and in color to the laptop.

Russell reached the computer, and in a few clicks, sent the image onto one of the two televisions on the wall. They watched as the drone circled to the front of the house.

Sinclair made written observations on the topography of the grounds and the number of guards walking the perimeter. Although they didn't see permanent guard stations, they knew they were there, hidden away.

Then the drone panned over to the jet. They watched as the plane dropped its nose and moments later the wheels touched the ground and taxied to the rear of the house.

Three men were there to greet the plane. Sinclair picked out Banks, standing with his hands clasped behind his back, between the other two next to him. The drone then circled to the back and hovered there.

As Sinclair watched the TV screen, she heard her phone ring.

"Sinclair, are you catching this?" Captain Stone asked.

"Yes, clear as day, Captain."

"What do you want me to do?"

"Captain, stay on station, at least for the next ten minutes. Let's see what they have planned."

Just then, three men carrying suitcases came from around the end of the house and approached Banks' group by the plane and began conversing with one another. Of what, she couldn't make it out.

With Stone still on the phone, Sinclair said, "Captain, can you pull closer to the group? I need an unobstructed view of the suitcases."

"Yes, ma'am, wait one."

On the television set, they watched as the drone dropped to about five feet above the ground and moved closer to the group. Coming to a halt seven feet behind the men, it held a hover position.

"Stone, please move around them and concentrate on the suitcases."

"Stand by, ma'am."

The drone moved again, but this time flying toward the left side, and then it stopped.

Stone said, "How's that?"

"Yes, perfect."

Sinclair kept a steady, fixed gaze on the suitcases, immediately recognizing what the cases represented. These didn't have clothing. They were the black cases she had been looking for. And one by one, they were being loaded onto the plane.

I'm too late! She thought.

She shifted in her chair and glanced around as she realized the implications. "They're carrying the nuclear bombs in those cases!" she alerted everyone.

—43—

"There's no way we can stop that plane from taking off with those bombs," Russell said, looking away from the television as the drone still hovered in place. "There's something else though, we don't know where they're heading—Russia or the U.S."

Shifting over to Russell, Sinclair sat back, folding her arms across her chest as his words echoed in her head. "No, we don't but there are other means we can use, and that will fall on you, Dan. However, I suspect these three are heading to the U.S. It stands to reason. From what I observed earlier, I believe they'd flown the first group into Russia with the plane returning the same day. It's the only logical conclusion. So, what we're seeing now is the last group."

Russell rubbed his chin, frowning. "So, okay, let's assume these are the second group. What do you want me to do?"

"I'll explain in a moment," she replied.

Watching the television screen, she noticed the drone was still hovering in the same location as before. Picking up her phone, she dialed Captain Stone's number.

"Stone, it's Sinclair. Bring it home. We have enough information to plan with."

"Copy that."

"Okay, Dan, your turn. Here is what I need from you. First, report to your superiors, let them know we have Banks' location, and will strategize an attack plan soon. Then have them inform DHS on what to expect. Send the photos once again of the three bomb carriers. Make sure you have that plane's tail number; DHS will want to have it. That part of the game is out of our hands now."

Russell grinned as he rose while pulling his phone from his hip pocket. "I'll get right on it."

Sinclair watched as the FBI man walked out of the conference room, phone to his ear, heading, she believed, to find a computer.

"For the rest of us," Sinclair said, "We must wait until we're all back together. But in the meantime, let's brainstorm a plan."

However, there was something that was causing her to step back slightly from the group. Something that may well throw a monkey wrench into any plan they could come up with—the Russians: *Would they get involved now that they also knew Banks' location?*

------·------

At the Russian Consulate, Colonel Borovkov and Captain Kuznetsov had already planned for their attack on the ranch.

Sitting across from Kuznetsov, Colonel Borovkov drained her glass of vodka, grabbed the bottle, refilled her shot glass, and watched Kuznetsov sip his drink.

Borovkov noted his silence. "You haven't said a word since we agreed on the plan, Comrade."

Kuznetsov leaned forward. "I was just thinking, Comrade Colonel, that we may not have enough firepower going in."

She frowned. "You're thinking of the American agents, no?"

"Yes. Our plan seems almost flawless, except for the Americans. What if they arrive first and start the attack before we get into position? By the same token, if we start early, they could come up behind us. Those are just several variables that could jeopardize our plan. Also, Comrade, I checked the weather. They're expecting a storm for later tonight. I just don't know. But my biggest concern is the number of men the traitor has at his disposal."

She shrugged. "Besides your five-man team, we have an additional seven FSB agents. That should be a sufficient force. The storm could play into our hands. We can use it for cover."

"Another thing, we haven't decided on when to attack."

"Right after darkness falls," Colonel Borovkov replied. "However, we'll set up a fix position before then."

"I agree."

It was late afternoon when they pulled off the E-30 highway just before entering the Mamonovo District City outskirts. With Povarov behind the wheel, Abakumov in the front passenger seat, and Tokarev in the back, Povarov pulled over to a gas station off the four-lane highway and parked.

Abakumov suggested that he should do a little recon up ahead to determine if any roadblocks were in place into the city proper. However, Abakumov decided first to seek that information from the station attendant.

They all knew it was a precaution they would have to make, knowing the security around the city could very well be tight. There were a few back roads, and those were just dirt tracks through the forest line that led into the city. If they watched the major roads, then they would have no alternative but to stick with the back roads.

Slipping out of the car, Abakumov steadily made his way into the gas station. At the counter, behind the cash register, was the attendant, an old man he guessed in his late sixties, short and gaunt, sat smoking a pipe.

"Hello, sir," he said. "Are there any security checkpoints ahead?"

The old man looked him up and down. Removing his pipe, he gazed at the stranger. "Why, yes, the city is in lockdown. Why do you ask?"

Abakumov cracked a brief smile. "Did they give a reason for it?"

Replacing his pipe between his teeth, the old man shrugged. "Since when did the government give any reason to do anything, young man?"

"True."

Abakumov pulled some money from his pocket and handed it over to the old man. "Thank you for the information."

Back in the car, Abakumov snorted. "It's the backcountry roads for us."

Pulling back onto the highway, they headed northwest into the forest.

An hour later, they saw two posted police officers and concrete barriers blocking the road—a checkpoint in the middle of nowhere! Was their luck running out? Reducing speed, almost coming to a stop, they pulled their handguns and kept them at the ready. If the officers insisted on searching the car, they'll act accordingly.

In the distance, they watched as the police officers separated from one another with one crossing the other side of the road. Approaching the checkpoint, Abakumov, slow and easy, raised his gun from his lap and the other two did the same.

Before coming to a stop, the driver, Povarov, had his window rolled down preparing for any eventuality, as Abakumov likewise rolled down his window.

Once Povarov brought the vehicle to stop, one officer approached the driver's door and the other, the front passenger door. On the driver's side, the officer, maybe six-feet-tall and skinny, kept his weapon pointed to the side. "Step out of the car. We need to search it."

Both officers took a step or two back from the car and waited.

One officer, from the driver's side, crouched down and peered at Povarov. He stared hard at the driver's face and demanded, "Out of the car!"

Povarov raised his weapon and pointed it through the window at the officer whose face lit up with terror. His eyes flicked side to side. Just as the officer swung his rifle at Povarov, his mouth worked as if shouting out a warning. Then, in a flash, he turned his head sideways as two shots rang out from Povarov's gun. Anyone hearing it would think they fired one shot. They were that close together.

The two bullets tore through the side of the man's face, forcing him back onto the ground. Then in quick succession, three shots rang out from the passenger side as the rounds fired from Abakumov's gun plowed through the man's chest, dropping him dead where he stood.

At that instant, from the woods, they heard the cough of an engine starting up. They turned in their seats and watched as an armored vehicle pulled out fast from its hiding place and swung out over onto the road.

Just as fast, Povarov placed his car in gear, and with gravel kicked up from their tires, he drove around the barriers. Clearing them, he stepped on the gas pedal and saw the armored vehicle give chase.

"Step on it, Povarov, they're gaining!" Abakumov yelled.

"I have it floored!" he yelled back. "This isn't a Porsche."

Moments later, having gained sufficient distance from the escaping vehicle, a hatch opened from atop of the armored vehicle. An officer's upper body appeared holding an RPG launcher. Placing it on his right shoulder, he aimed and pulled the trigger.

From the back of the car, Tokarev was watching the approach of the armored vehicle. His eyes lit up as he yelled, "Holy shit, RPG!"

Then Tokarev yelled again, "Evade left now, Basil, now!"

Povarov, without a second to lose, yanked the steering wheel hard left.

They heard the sudden howling of the high explosive round zooming overhead. The round crashed to earth a few feet from their car, in a billowing orange explosion, showering the car in rubble and dust. Shrapnel struck the vehicle on the right rear fender as they sped off.

Povarov, ashen-faced, said, "That was too close."

"We're not out of the woods yet," Tokarev commented as he watched the armored vehicle gaining ground. "They're still behind us."

With the police vehicle a car behind them, Povarov zinged left and right. The stutter of automatic small arms weapon's fire sliced through the air as round after round struck the side of the car, shattering the side back right window into hundreds of pieces.

Abakumov yelled to Tokarev, "Shoot the fucking driver!"

Povarov allowed the police vehicle to come abreast of the car, and when it did, Abakumov and Tokarev concentrated their fire on the driver. A few seconds later, the police vehicle veered off to the right and crashed into some trees erupting into flames.

—44—

Decreasing his speed down to 35 mph, Povarov drove through a forest of denuded oak and poplar trees. As darkness steadily approached, he crept along to just under a mile west of the E105 highway that rings Moscow.

Having encountered no more police checkpoints, they emerged from the forest line, as Povarov pulled over to the side of the road before coming to a stop. Killing the engine, he reached over, opened the glove compartment, and pulled out a street map of the city he'd purchased earlier. Laying it spread out on the steering wheel, he checked his position and then calculated the distance from his position to the center of the city.

"How much further do we have, Basil?" Abakumov asked.

"Not far, seven or eight more miles," Povarov replied. "We'll stay on this road for five miles and then hit a primary thoroughfare into the city."

"Good, let's get going then. The sooner we get this over with, the sooner we can leave Russia for good."

From the back seat, Tokarev said, "I'm all for that."

Refolding the map, Povarov stowed it and pulled away from the side of the road. He had a sense of calmness in him he couldn't explain. He'd left a life of death and destruction in his wake since he could remember. And now, he was at the final crossroads between life and death itself. Whichever came first, in the next few hours, he would welcome it with open arms. He believed his two good friends next to him shared the same feelings.

———————

For the past thirty-minutes, Sinclair sat listening to the ongoing preparations between the SEAL team leader Captain Stone, Detective Schneider, Russell, and Courtney.

It was the German police officers, and the rest of the SEAL team members, and Sinclair's bodyguards, the MPs, who did not voice any comments or opinions. They left that up to their leaders.

It went back and forth, each side with their ideas. At some point, the answers to questions posed were difficult to hear amid the babble of conservation. Sinclair, although not well versed in combat attack scenarios, seemed impressed with the option Captain Stone brought forward.

She said, "All right, let's settle down, please. Captain Stone, please repeat your plan."

A hush fell over the conference room.

"Yes, ma'am," Stone replied.

They nodded as all eyes turned toward the Captain.

Stone rose and stood over the desk. Tall, broad-shouldered, and stocky, with well- ripped muscles, full growth of beard, and wearing a T-shirt and dark pants, he was a most imposing individual. "This is what's termed in the SEALs as a short-term execution battle plan. First, we identify a specific objective."

"We've done that already," Russell was quick in his comment.

"Yes, yes, we have," Stone said, staring at the FBI man, not perturbed that he'd interrupted. "So our goal is that of capturing our primary target. Eliminating the opposing force and mitigate the risk as much as possible to our side."

"And how do we do that?" Schneider asked.

"By making a list of all the actions for execution," Stone replied. "So typically, the what, when, and who, although the next logical step would be team training, of which we just don't have the time for."

Captain Stone continued with his plan, assigning teams to specific locations and what their actions would entail. They put together teams. The specific placements of those teams and their points of initial attacks were also outlined following the ground photos.

First-in would be Captain Stone and his five-man team coming from the left flank, followed by Captain Schneider and his police officers from the right.

Sinclair's team, composed of Russell and Courtney, would advance from the center. They would be the backup. The signal to attack would come from Sinclair.

The SEAL team's primary aim was to penetrate the house. Second, find and rescue Colonel Sinclair and eliminate all opposing forces in the house.

"Detective Schneider and his team will engage outside guards. Once done, secure the back of the house for escapees through that quarter."

"Timing is important," Stone finished. "Once Sinclair gives the go-ahead, we should have sufficient time to attack."

Agent Sinclair liked the plan; she couldn't have done any better.

CIA Operative Courtney sat listening, head bowed, arms crossed, frowning.

"That's a bold plan, Captain," Courtney, said. "But, do you think it will work?"

Captain Stone looked at her, fell silent, and rolled his eyes. "Any plan has the potential for success or failure. It's up to every one of us to ensure the total successful mission outcome." And as an afterthought, "If you can come up with a better plan, Agent Courtney, I'm all ears."

"Yeah, well," Courtney said, sighing, "can't say that I have one."

Behind Sinclair stood two of the five Army MPs assigned by the Provost Marshal to act as Sinclair's bodyguards. After hearing of the attack scenario, they stared at each other. Sergeant First Class Earl Chambers, dressed in civilian dress, cleared his throat and came around to face Sinclair.

"Ma'am, with all due respect, I and Staff Sergeant Wilson, would like to volunteer our services to your attack plan."

"Very well, you're both assigned to my team. Get yourself ready to go in the next thirty minutes."

"Yes, ma'am," Chambers said.

Sinclair watched as the two burly MPs walked out of the conference room and hoped they'd come out of this in one piece.

Moments later, frowning, Sinclair flipped her hair back deep in thought. The plan seemed incomplete. Something wasn't right, or some missing part was not yet identified. Scratching her head, she realized what that was; extra firepower. Just small arms alone may not be sufficient in a running gun battle. She needed a heavy vehicle, something with more firepower and more concealment for the advancing teams.

There was no time to have one assigned to her from the infantry units. So, the closest she had to any riot vehicles were with the German police inventory.

She turned, facing Detective Schneider, and directed her question to him. "Do you have any armored type vehicles we might use?"

"We have two 6x6 APCs, armored personnel vehicles. A Mark A-8 called a TPZ-1 and nicknamed the "Fuchs-1.""

"What type of armaments does it have?" Russell asked. "And how soon can we get one?"

"Well, they have three machine gun placements," Schneider replied, "and a smoke grenade launcher: The body is of steel armor reinforcement. And I could have one ready for us within twenty minutes."

"That should do it," Sinclair said. "Can you please have it ready for our use as soon as we reach the ranch?"

"Will do," Schneider said. Reaching into his pocket, he pulled out his cell phone and placed the call to his superiors.

After a few minutes, Schneider pocketing his phone glanced over at Sinclair. "My superiors have given their approval for the APC and have also placed two helicopters on standby with medical personnel for evaluation and treatment of the wounded. Also, they have set two ambulances on standby."

Sinclair's face lit up. Inhaling a deep breath, she said, "That's a noble gesture on their part. Please thank them for us."

That is another something I didn't include in the planning stage, she told herself. *I need to stay focused.*

"I already did," the detective replied.

"There's something else," Detective Schneider said in a low voice.

"Yes?"

"It concerns your father," Schneider replied in a hushed tone.

Sinclair stiffened at the mention of her father. She stared long and hard at the detective.

Silence once again fell over the room.

Agent Sinclair held her feelings in check, dropped her eyes from him, and asked, "Yes. What about my father?"

He did not immediately answer, as if he didn't want to come out and say it. "We ... I mean, our investigators recovered a video from a bystander of your father's kidnapping."

Sinclair stared at the detective. She took a deep breath before replying, and asked, "Can I have a copy?"

"I'll have one sent to your phone," Schneider replied.

Sinclair sat back in her chair. For a moment she remained silent. At last, she said, "Thank you, Detective."

She knew there was nothing to gain from the video. The only thing it confirmed was that Banks was holding her father prisoner at the ranch. And right now, *that* was her goal: Her father. Everything else was secondary.

She needed to keep things in perspective. The attack plan needed to go forward.

Keep it together, Belle, for Dad's sake, she told herself.

Turning to Russell and Courtney, Sinclair said, "We'll walk behind the APC giving cover fire to Stone's team."

"When do we leave?" Stone asked.

A silence settled in the conference room, waiting for her orders.

"Within thirty-minutes," she said as she glanced at all those around her. "Let's gear up, check our weapons, and be ready to mount up by that time."

"Roger that."

———————— · ———————— · ————————— · —————

With darkness falling and rain clouds threatening overhead, two black Chevy SUVs were being loaded in the underground area beneath the Russian Consulate with enough armaments to start a minor war.

Colonel Borovkov was riding shotgun in one SUV with Captain Kuznetsov driving. Five armed FSB agents, dressed in black military battle dress, sat shoulder to shoulder in the vehicle. The second vehicle already had seven more FSB black-clad agents waiting to drive off.

It was six-thirty in the evening, on a cold dark as sin night, when they abandoned their vehicle on a side street next to the Moscow State Exhibition Hall. With barely any street lighting around the hall, Povarov parked in on the curb.

Then, as a sudden cover of ominous clouds crossed over them, the beginning of some snow flurries fell as they exited the vehicle. One by one they stood on the curb with each holding a suitcase bomb.

From where they stood, they could make out the well lighted Kremlin and other offices in the square.

"We know what to do and where we need to be," Povarov said, extending his hand to his comrades. "Good luck to all."

Abakumov and Tokarev nodded their understanding. They shook hands and then nimbly walked away from each other.

With Abakumov and Tokarev waiting, they watched as Povarov walked around the outside perimeter high wall of the square and disappeared around the corner. Next, it was Tokarev, and after a few minutes, he too disappeared.

Povarov's destination was the FSB headquarters on Lubyanka Square, a walk of maybe fifteen minutes. He was lucky that all he came across was a beggar sitting on the street resting his back against a wall. He didn't see or meet with police officers or soldiers through the darkened streets. It resembled a ghost town. *Did they know what was going to happen?* He asked himself. Maybe, maybe not, but he wouldn't let that chain of thought hinder his mission.

Minutes later he was standing at the back of the FSB headquarters. There were several lights throughout the area. Povarov kept well outside their illumination as he circled the back-high fenced wall, coming close enough to a secluded section devoid of any lights hidden from windows or doors. Then he made out several open containers.

Suitcase in hand, he sped through to the spot and froze upon hearing voices coming from around the outside of the immense building. Unknown to him, he had tripped a silent alarm.

This was his spot, as outlined in his orders. As silent as he could, he crept toward it.

Seconds later, he was between two unlit metal containers. Kneeling, he laid the suitcase on the ground in front of him and opened it. Keying in the phone number given to him by Carl Benz, he found the arming switch and hesitated a moment, sighed, and then flipped it on. With the device armed, as the red light showed, he closed the case, stood and placed the bomb in a container, stuffed with trash, and covered it over.

Pulling out his cell phone, he called the ranch. On the third ring, he said, "Bomb placed and armed."

Getting an affirmative reply, Povarov's part ended.

Stepping away from the containers, Povarov heard at least two sets of footsteps coming his way. He pulled his handgun, keeping it at the ready. The footsteps came closer and just as a cat from out of nowhere, darted in front of him, two armed guards stopped and yelled for him to raise his hands.

Povarov had no intention of being arrested, or questioned, not tonight!

Raising his gun, he fired two successive rounds at the soldiers, then turned and ran. However, both soldiers had already raised their assault rifles at him before he had taken his shots. Only one soldier fired his weapon on automatic, unloading several rounds at the fleeing man, while the other soldier had been shot dead.

Povarov had taken two steps when several shots plowed through into his back. Unable to stand, he slipped to the ground, onto his knees, as blood seeped from his body. Another shot rang out. It entered the back of his head with such force that the body slammed forward onto the concrete.

Within a matter of minutes, as if in quick succession, three nuclear bombs detonated in the city!

As the first bomb detonated, Abakumov and Tokarev were walking away after arming their bombs. Once they heard the detonation, they turned and knew they wouldn't survive the next few seconds. Staring off at the center of the city, they saw a noiseless flash followed by a blinding light and intense pressure, as a tremendous explosion and large ball, resembling a mushroom of yellow and white, shot up into the sky lighting the night as if it was daytime. Seconds later, their bodies were irradiated by the thermal radiation.

The bombs created a destructive force for well over several kilometers, destroying everything in its path. The Kremlin, along with everything in its epicenter, were engulfed and utterly obliterated!

———————————— · ———— · ———— · ————————————

Inside the ranch house study room, Banks sat back in his chair, laced his fingers behind his head, and closed his eyes. A few minutes ago, he'd finished dialing the numbers to one, then the last two Russian suitcase bomb's phone numbers and laid the telephone on the desk beside the other two.

He was alone when he'd received confirmation from his three comrades in Moscow. When he'd dialed the numbers to the bombs, Banks determined the three as expendable; pawns in a game of chess, a means to an end.

Banks thought about it but had no regrets. The same was true for his comrades traveling to the U.S. Whether they could make it was still up in the air.

Now, with that business concluded, he had more pressing worries to attend to. There was Colonel Sinclair. Now that was a strong, stubborn old man, he mused. But he'll weaken and give up the information he needed.

The one thing on his mind was the daughter, Jacqueline. Did she already know of his whereabouts? And was she planning to attack his ranch? No doubt. He assumed that the agent already knew the ranch's location and be visiting soon and were prepared for it; from the very first he'd known about her and was ready. If that was the case, she would in all essence—seal her father's fate.

Things were looking up, he thought. Soon the U.S. would get the same treatment Russia just received and his revenge would be complete. His hopes of a third World War were looking up.

—45—

It was thirty minutes past ten in the morning when the President of the United States, Phillip Anders, wearing a grey two-piece business suit, with a white shirt and red tie, approached the Situation Room.

Fifteen minutes earlier, Anders interrupted in the middle of enjoying breakfast with his family in the President's residence had an urgent request for his presence in the Situation Room. Kissing his wife and three-year-old daughter, he dressed and left the residence, followed by his Secret Service detail.

Now, halting at the threshold, he scanned around the huge oak conference desk. These were a few chosen members of his cabinet.

All the surrounding leather-backed chairs were empty except for six. To the left side of the desk sat the Chairman of the Joint Chiefs of Staff (CJCS), four-star General Earl Fleming. Next to him was the Director of the CIA, Jonathan Fakes, and to his right sat the President's Chief of Staff, Brigadier General Alvin Meadows. On the other side of the desk was the Deputy Director of the CIA, Rear Admiral William Savage. To his left the Secretary of Defense, Richard E. Harper, a former U.S. Army officer and a defense contractor lobbyist. He was a tall, heavyset, middle-aged man. And last was William Conrad, the Deputy NSA Director, having taken over on the death of Steven Summerset.

Anders could have sent for the rest of his cabinet, but now wasn't the time for political guesswork. Those in the room would furnish the information and would recommend action if need be. So, for now, they would be his counsel.

Around both sides of the room sat the advisors and attaché, some in military uniform and others in civilian attire, attached to each of the President's staff members.

Continuing into the room, those in attendance stood and waited for the President to have a seat. Anders took his seat at the far end of the vast desk, leaned back in his chair, and with eyes narrowed, stared at everyone around him.

Acknowledging them, the President said, "Gentlemen, thank you all for coming at such short notice. So, give me the latest update."

A moment of silence as each staff member was waiting for the NSA Director to open the briefing.

"Mr. President," Conrad chimed in. "There's been a massive attack on Moscow. It's believed two nuclear devices went off simultaneously at about 0500 hours, their time."

Anders, although not surprised, had known of the imminent attack on Moscow and had warned President Gadjiyev. The chances of another world war significantly reduced, if not stopped; although the terrorist was an American agent. Had Gadjiyev taken his warning, did he leave Moscow, and warn its citizens of the impending danger? He could only hope so.

Anders leaned back in his chair and rubbed his chin. Any steps the Russian government had taken to stop the attack were not sufficient. "Christ, how bad is it?" he asked.

"Damn bad, sir," General Fleming replied. "Conditions on the ground are still coming in. We have our friends in Israel to thank for the updates. Also, according to British MI-5, they report the Kremlin, along with the FSB headquarters, was destroyed. Those within a radius of several miles were killed. As of this moment, casualty's numbers are unknown, but they may number in the thousands. Fortunately, sir, the center of Moscow isn't a residential neighborhood, so the death toll may not be so high."

The President sighed. Frustrated, he shook his head, "So, our agents in Germany failed to find the bombs in time?"

Without a word, they all nodded and assumed it was just a rhetorical question.

Fakes said, "We know Banks was behind this, but what do we have on the coup attempt by the Russian military, and do we have any Intel on why and who is running the government?"

"According to reports gathered by our agents in the field," the NSA Director replied, "and from the CIA and M1-5, there have been speculations the Russian military has been in discord with their President. Several generals and staff officers are reported missing. Most of what accounts for the military has been, according to the reports, killed. Most of those were officers, and some enlisted personnel, who refused to go along with the way the government was being led. Some favored the old style of government with some going as far as favoring the capitalist free enterprise and trade freedom as we have it in the U.S."

The Director paused. "As far as who is running the government, I would assume it still is the President and his people."

Anders frowned. "Throughout Russian history," he said, "the military, since the days of Lenin, have tried to take over the government from the grasp of the civilian political machine infesting the government. They have also failed in this latest endeavor."

Then behind the NSA Director, his attaché, with a phone in his hand, rose stepped behind the Director and whispered in his ear.

"Mr. President," Conrad said as he rose from his chair. He reached for the TV remote, clicked it on, and seconds later satellite images in real-time came on the screen. "Sir, we have our NROL-32 spy surveillance satellite in geosynchronous orbit around the Russian capital as we speak."

Impressed with the speed and timing of those involved in positioning the satellite, Andes asked, "Tell me about the satellite. And was this one of our newest eye-in-the-sky satellites we sent up?"

"Yes, sir," Conrad replied. "The NROL-32 is American's most advance spy satellite, and besides video, it can provide eavesdropping capabilities."

Seconds later, the images on the screen showed a mass of white and dark clouds surrounding the two blast areas. The area covered by the satellite stretched for miles in all directions. Then, in some locations, they saw complete devastation of buildings toppled over with dust clouds everywhere. As the dust settled, several bodies appeared on the screen, but no signs of life were visible.

To the President, the images on the screen resembled an Armageddon scenario out of a Hollywood movie. Not since bombs fell at the closing of the Second World War, in Japan, had such a cataclysmic event befallen human-kind. Anders forced himself to relax.

God Almighty, is this what is waiting to happen here? He asked himself.

Turning back to his CIA Director Savage, Anders asked, "All right, Admiral, that would explain the coup and Banks. Can you tell me what's being done to find and capture Banks? And I need to know what steps we've taken to stop them from committing the same to us."

Savage thought about his questions for a few seconds and responded, "Since we've known beforehand of the possibility that the bombs may come through into the U.S. Fakes and I have been in touch with our agents in Germany. They've recently exposed several aspects of the investigation, sir." He paused. "For one, we know how the bombs are being transported and we have the tail number of that aircraft. We have photos of the terrorists in the plane and know how many of them there are."

Anders smiled. "That's splendid news."

Savage continued. "Sir, and as we speak, our agents in Germany are about to attack Banks' area of operations."

That was news he'd wanted to hear.

"Also, Mr. President, we've coordinated with NORAD. We have provided them with the description and tail number of the aircraft. The Air Force will keep several F-35s in the air and on ground standby. Homeland security will cover key specific entry points into the U.S."

Savage paused. "Sir, we have the best personnel and equipment ready to capture or destroy their entry into the U.S."

This was precisely what he needed; Anders thought to himself as he closed his eyes for a moment. "Very well," he said. Turning to his Chief of Staff, "Alvin, see if you can patch me through to President Gadjiyev's private cell phone."

Brigadier General Meadows nodded, "Yes, sir."

Once she'd given the word to proceed, things moved swiftly from there.

Six-fifty-five on Sinclair's watch was when they arrived just after nightfall.

Darkness swept the landscape, while in the far distance, they made out several lights and their target—the ranch. They had turned off their headlights just about a quarter of a mile before arriving at the foot-path entrance that led through the wooden fence adjoining the ranch. The small convoy traversed slowly along the earthen track bound on both sides with tall dark oak trees which branched out over the road.

One by one, the vehicles halted behind Detective Andreas Schneider's lead vehicle, followed by the armored vehicle and the rest of the group. They parked on the dirt road just on the outskirts of the ranch. Throughout their drive, dark menacing clouds kept them company, holding the threat of rain.

Exiting from her vehicle, Sinclair, wearing the black (BDU) Army Battle Dress Uniform and black combat boots, ambled over to the back of her vehicle and opened the trunk. Then, as she stood there for a moment, she spoke into her throat-mic: "Everyone, let's get ready, we move out in five minutes."

After receiving the expected affirmative replies, Sinclair reached into the trunk, grasped her black bullet-proof vest, and donned it. Next, she grabbed her Blackhawk load-bearing vest with enough front pockets for six ammo magazines.

Sinclair followed by removing her pistol holster, tying it around her right thigh, and then onto her load vest. She placed her night optical device around her head, flipped it down over her right eye, and checked it. That done, she flipped it back up, and as an afterthought, grabbed two Flash-Bang grenades and hooked them onto her vest. Then slung her M-4 Carbine rifle around her shoulder, slid it back around to the front, and held it at the ready position.

Moments later, with her group by her side, and all in their battle dress equipment similar to her own, they stood with weapons at the ready position. She watched their serious expressions as she drifted back into combat mode. The CID agent was going into battle with only one other person Sinclair knew as a comrade-in-arms; FBI Agent Dan Russell.

She frowned, concerned, and bit her lip as her thoughts turned to her fiancé, Tom Price, who was still in a coma; she prayed for his swift recovery. The image of her father, being kidnapped, remained vivid in her mind's eye. He was somewhere in that ranch house, alive: Sinclair would not let her mind think differently. She drew in a deep breath and collected her thoughts. Turning off the disturbing and distracting chain of thought, she found Schneider glancing her way.

Sinclair stared at Detective Schneider. "Detective, please lead the way."

With a nod, the detective walked away.

"Captain Stone," she said, "your turn. Follow behind the detective with your group. The rest of us will follow suit. Schneider, lead on."

Sinclair looked forward, out over Captain Stone's shoulder and beyond that to the ranch. With no mishap, in the next few minutes, they would be in position.

At that same moment, inside the fence line leading onto the ranch, and less than a third of a mile from Sinclair's position, the twelve-man Russian FSB group led by Colonel Borovkov and Captain Kuznetsov, had finished their preparations for their attack.

A few seconds before, they thought they heard noises coming from their immediate right, but could not discern if they were from guards or worse, from the Americans.

They were ready for both.

Colonel Borovkov glanced at Kuznetsov. "What do you think ... the Americans?"

The Captain glanced away from her and turned to where they had heard the noises. "It's too hard to tell from this distance. It may have come from the roving guards."

"You may be right," she replied and asked, looking around at the men, "Is everyone ready? Good. Lock and load. Let's move out in a straight line."

At the ranch, ex-German Kommando, Captain Hermann Weber, had positioned his men around the house and up in the barn. Anti-personnel landmines placed out several feet away from the fence line stretched for several yards left and right of the open field and set to explode when at least two kilograms of pressure applied or when a person stepped on them.

Several M18A1 claymore mines placed at random were almost center from the house and the wooden fence line and monitored by his men down by the side of the barn. The rest of his men had selected specific sectors of fire while armed with sniper rifles. For the past few days, Banks had warned of a possible armed force coming to attack the ranch. Weber was ready in the event they showed. Those attackers were in for a deadly surprise. They wouldn't know what hit them, he thought.

With him, and one other mercenary wearing night optical devices, they made out movement and identified several black-clad men jumping over the fence line toward his right flank and slowly started approaching the house.

"Sector-One, be ready with the claymores," Weber ordered through his Com-Link. "I'll let them get close to the landmines and then we'll hit them, standby."

"Roger that, sir," Sector-One replied. The man was at the far end of the barn at ground level. He held one electrical firing device which could set off three claymore mines at a time. Two other firing devices were at the ready next to his feet.

"Sector-two," Weber said, activating his Com-Link once again. "Stand by with the machine gun placement." The machine gun was situated just inside the main window of the house and pointing downrange.

Then to make matters worse for the attackers, the thunderclouds arrived, and with it, the rain pelted the landscape as the wind whistled over the battlefield.

<hr>

The attack groups were ready, and in just under five minutes, then Sinclair gave the go-ahead signal. But the rain came down in sheets, almost darkening the night with a thin veil of blackness, and they were just able to catch a simmering ghost-like image of the house. The rain was icy cold, and the wind didn't make matters any easier.

Captain Stone's five-man SEAL team was the first over the fence, and as he came to a stop on the other side, he looked down in both directions and didn't see any guards present.

As they took several steps forward, they dropped to their knees, weapons pointing to their left as a sudden series of explosions rocked the fence line toward their left side. Not sure what was going on, they flipped down their night optical devices and Stone watched as a group of individuals became caught in the middle of the explosions. Three individuals went flying backward as the blast caught them head-on, dead before they hit the ground. Russians were the first thought that popped into his mind.

Stone aimed to get to the house. Back on his feet, he said through his throat mic, "Up on your feet, men, this ain't any time for—"

But he didn't finish his sentence. As they ran forward, two explosions detonated as two of his men fell dead to the ground, cut to pieces by shrapnel. They kept running, not stopping for anything, when a sudden onslaught of small arms fire chewed up the ground on their left side, as bullets whistled over their heads.

Returning fire, they came under machine-gun fire from the house. Two more of his men went down, leaving himself and one other member still alive. Then veering away from making a frontal attack on the house, Stone and James Earl, his fellow SEAL member, ran as fast as their legs could carry them towards the side of the house as bullets whizzed by them in all directions.

It was at that moment that the rest of Sinclair's group climbed the fence and started running forward. With MPs Chambers and Wilson each walking side by side of Sinclair, they heard her cut loose with her weapon on full automatic and followed her example.

With bullets flying left and right, SGT Wilson took a slug to head and dropped to the ground as Chambers kept running alongside Sinclair. Watching her run hard, zigzagging left and right, making herself into as little of a target as she could, Chambers did the same as they both missed a landmine by inches apart from each other. Bullets zinged past them as others struck at the ground in front and to their left side.

Chambers took two rounds, one to the left shoulder and one to the right leg, cutting him off from the person he was detailed to guard.

—47—

Sinclair watched in dismay as they took her two MPs out of the battle.

Click, her weapon went dry. On the fly, ejecting the spent magazine, Sinclair instantly loaded another. Still, on the run, she jacked in a live round aiming the weapon out in front of her and started firing once again, when a sudden force pushed her backward several steps as three bullets plowed into her rib cage and one that went clear through her left shoulder!

"Son of a bitch!" she yelled, dropping to a knee, feeling for signs of blood seepage, when her hand came back with blood. But her vest had saved her life. The agent rose and ran forward into the fray.

The machine gun wreaked havoc on the German police officers and Russians alike, when three German police officers fell, caught in their tracks, dead.

Sinclair stopped and kneeled. She needed cover. "Get that damn armored vehicle in here now!" she screamed into her throat mic.

"Roger that," came the quick reply.

Sinclair rose but reflexively ducked back down just as several bullets swooshed above her head.

Damn!

From inside the woods, she heard the armored vehicle rushing down. From her right side, she saw Russell and Courtney running full speed. Sinclair watched helplessly as they riddled Courtney with a barrage of bullets, as she collapsed to the ground. Rushing to her side, she saw Russell catch a bullet to his left shoulder.

Russell, disregarding the pain in his shoulder, or the blood seeping down his arm, checked for her pulse but didn't find one. Closing her eyes, and still kneeling, he opened with a sustained rate of fire at the house.

This was just fucking crazy, and we fell right into their trap! The thought ran through Sinclair's mind.

"Get up, *God* damn it, Sinclair, move!" she screamed out.

Hearing a loud rumbling noise behind her, Sinclair halted just as the armored vehicle stopped abreast of her and the rear hatch lowered. "Get in," came the voice of the German driver through her earpiece just as two remaining German police officers, along with Schneider, made it to the back of the armored vehicle. Russell, forced to abandon Courtney's body, also clambered aboard, just as small arms firing assaulted the front of the vehicle, pinging off into the darkness.

With the hatch raised just above the ground, the vehicle gradually moved just as it took fire from the machine gun emplacement inside the house. Then two simultaneous explosions from two claymores rocked the vehicle but didn't cause any damage.

"Could use one of you to man the machine gun on top," the driver said again through the Com-Link.

Russell volunteered and started for the hatch. He cut loose with a salvo of fire aimed at the barn and saw two mercenaries go down.

Seconds later, the front right side of the vehicle struck a landmine and came skidding to a resounding halt, crippled.

"End of the line, folks!" the driver yelled.

They were just short of a hundred yards to the front of the house. So, Sinclair and the rest of the group leaped out and set up two groups, one to go left and the other to the right.

But no sooner were they out when a swarm of small arms fire drove them to the ground. None of the rounds came close to them as they sought cover behind the vehicle's armored protection.

Carefully, they moved away from the vehicle onto open ground facing the front of the house, firing their weapons in automatic mode.

Sinclair on the fly loaded a 'HE' high explosive round into the chamber of her launcher and aimed at the machine gun's position. She briefly had to stop to pull the trigger. And just before she let the round fly, a bullet hit her right leg.

Dropping to her good knee, Sinclair pulled the trigger. The explosive round with a resounding *Thump* flew through the window and seconds later exploded with a resounding *Boom!*

The machine gun emplacement went silent.

Back on her feet, with the rain pelting her, she ran once again as fast as her wounded leg could carry her. She kept pressure on the trigger, firing her M4 Rifle, and heard it click on yet another empty magazine. Loading a fresh mag, her group started taking fire from two fronts, one from the left side of the four remaining Russian FSB agents with Colonel Borovkov and Captain Kuznetsov by the Colonel's side, and from the open doors of the barn from three mercenaries led by Captain Weber.

The American agents and German police officers moved as one toward the barn, firing a constant volley of fire that cut down two more mercenaries along with Captain Weber. One, then another, of the German police officers, went down dead as the last of the mercenaries in the barn fell. Then silence met the group from that quarter as they swiftly dashed into the barn.

<hr>

Realizing they were alone when they saw two more FSB agents get killed in front of them, the Colonel and the Captain ran back into the woods and disappeared.

In the thick of things, Captain Stone and James Earl rushed down toward the back of the house and came to a halt at its corner. Taking a peek to determine if any guards were present, and seeing none, they calmly walked around and came to a back door.

Standing against the wall, Stone cracked the door open.

At the threshold, Stone removed a flash-bang grenade and threw it into the room. Once the grenade went off, Stone pushed the door wide and stopped. Leading with their handguns, they entered. Then, as one went to the left and the other to the right of the door, they entered and stopped once again.

Stone heard what he believed were three quick gunshots that came from somewhere in the house and to his left side. They ambled in that direction and stopped again. He listened. No further sounds. He glimpsed a wide-open door down the hallway. Once there, he threw another flashbang down into what he believed was a basement.

Stone and Earl rushed down a short flight of stairs and stopped by the landing. Through the thin smoke of the grenade, they saw a lone figure hanging from a rafter. They ran to its side and Stone checked for a pulse and found a faint heartbeat. Removing his combat knife, they cut the figure loose and laid him flat on the concrete flooring.

Stone knew instantly who he was—Colonel Sinclair!

"Captain, I think there's a door toward the far end," James Earl said. "I'm gonna see where it leads."

Captain Stone heard Sinclair calling from upstairs.

"Sinclair, I'm down in the basement!" Stone yelled back. "Get down here quick."

Running, Sinclair found the open door leading down into the basement. Down the flight of stairs, she flew, taking them two at a time. Soon she stood on the concrete flooring, her gun leading the way into a semi-darkened basement when she came to an abrupt stop as she spied Captain Stone kneeling by a body.

Sinclair let out a high-pitched yelp as she recognized it for who it was; her father.

She didn't run to his side. She felt paralyzed to the spot. Stepping forward was difficult enough. Then she moved. The strain of advancing a step was telling on her. It was like slow motion. She felt dizzy. Her gun hand was shaking. Instinctively, she recoiled; sure her father was lying dead on the concrete ground in front of her eyes

As if from far away, she heard Stone say, "There's a faint pulse."

Shaking her head, and before she knew it, she'd had taken several steps forward.

Captain Stone rose, and holding onto her, he tenderly shook her and she came alive once more. "Dad?" she mumbled, "Dad?"

"He's hardly alive," Stone said. "I guess they didn't have time to finish him, but you can see the torture marks and three bullet holes in his chest."

Sinclair crouched beside her father, and taking his hand, she clasped it around her face and cried as tears of joy effortlessly flowed down her face.

48

With Captain Stone tending to the injured man they had rescued, that he assumed was Agent Sinclair's father, SEAL team member, James Earl steadily weaved his way through the shadowy darkened tunnel under the ranch.

Minutes later he stopped, squinted, and couldn't make out anything ahead for the inky darkness of the tunnel. Flipping down his night optics, he made a minor adjustment and saw that the tunnel veered toward the left just a few feet ahead. Not encountering anyone coming up from the basement earlier, just as they'd heard the three gunshots, he assumed whoever shot Sinclair's father had taken to the tunnel for his or their escape.

Earl crouched low and crept forward. After a step or two, he would stop and stare down on the ground, looking for any likely trip-wired booby traps armed with explosives. He was also alert to an ambush.

Arriving at the turnoff, Earl poked his head around the inner corner, peered down the dark tunnel, and spotted a lone individual pointing his weapon in his direction.

Was he seen? He asked himself. *But they would've taken the shot once he'd seen me.*

Grabbing a small canister from his equipment vest, he armed a flashbang grenade and said, "Fire in the hole!" and tossed it down the tunnel. Just as he expected, a barrage of bullets raked the wall to his right!

Boom!

The grenade exploded as a blinding flash of light was followed by a cloud of white smoke, covering the spot his would-be enemy had occupied. Earl stepped forward, walked faster, finger pressure steady on the trigger, sent a volley of hot lead down the tunnel, and heard someone yelp in pain.

Continuing forward through the almost cleared smoke, Earl made out an unmoving figure lying face down on the ground. Stopping, he aimed his weapon at the man's neck and pulled the trigger once.

Now he was sure it was a corpse.

Stepping over the body, he kept going. Once again he stared at the ground several times, always keeping a careful watch for trip-wires. Then far ahead he saw a flicker of light in the otherwise dark tunnel.

Then his right boot snagged onto something on the ground, and he froze, swallowing hard. Looking down, he saw a trip-wire on his boot. He blanched. His eyes widened at the sight.

Removing his combat rifle from around his shoulder, he let it drop to the ground. Slow as he could, he knelt and reached out and held the wire with his fingertips. Sliding his boot back away from the wire, he breathed a sigh of relief. Following the wire to its source, Earl found the two-inch detonator and pulled it from the device.

Retrieving his rifle, he kept making slow but steady, cautious forward progress.

Minutes later, he arrived at the end of the tunnel and dashed out into the night. Looking around, he saw a parked sedan toward his right with no one in sight. He then suspected the possibility of a second car which may or not was a getaway vehicle.

Once beside the remaining car, he pulled a flashlight from his utility vest and shone it on the ground next to the sedan. It was as he suspected—a second car. He made out the extra set of fresh tire tracks on the broken ground and reckoned that someone had escaped.

Shaking his head, he turned around and went back through the tunnel toward the ranch house.

By the time Earl returned, the rain had stopped. He made out two medical UH-72 Lakota Euro-copters on the ground in front of the ranch house. Two minesweepers, provided by the local German Army, had finished setting off the remainders of the landmines.

They had parked two ambulances head to head, alongside the house, as medics treated the wounded, including Russell, who had suffered a minor shoulder wound. They lined the dead in a row on the ground and wrapped them in body bags. Two medical coroner's wagons parked to the side of the house were loading the dead onto the bed of the vehicles.

———————

As soon as the medics released Russell, he went in search of Courtney. Searching through the dead, he found her and unzipped the bag away from her face. Taken a step back, he stopped and staggered back to the corpse that was once a vibrant, attractive woman any man would love to call his own. Kneeling, he stared at the beautiful, peaceful face of a woman he would never forget. Leaning an elbow on a knee, the FBI agent took shallow breaths.

Russell rose and steadied himself, swallowing hard. He could've easily learned to love her, but there wasn't enough time for them. They had something of a thing between them, but not love in the full sense of the word.

His wounded shoulder ached, but the pain in his heart was far worse. Despite the harsh chill of the night, beads of sweat, mixed with the dust kicked up by the wintry winds, flowed down his expressionless face.

"Thank you, Captain Stone," Sinclair said, "for a job well done."

"No problem," Stone replied, in a soft tone, holding on to her hand, and then releasing his. "I'll help with the cleanup. One thing though, we found no trace of Banks."

A momentary silence followed, broken when James Earl joined them.

Earl said, "I just came from an underground tunnel that led from the basement out past the ranch. One vehicle was present. However, I found fresh tire tracks leading away from the mouth of the tunnel and I believe Banks, and whoever was with him, made a clear getaway in that second vehicle."

Both Sinclair and Stone stared at each other.

"That's not good," she said. "He still has control of the nukes and there's no telling when he'll set them off."

"Yeah," Stone said. "He'll go to ground and we may never find him."

"We'll hunt the son of a bitch down," Sinclair vowed.

Stone bowed his head, nodding.

Seconds passed, then they heard the whirling of the chopper's rotors turning and Sinclair said, "Guess that's my cue to get on board. Thanks again for all the help you and your team have given me."

"My pleasure, ma'am," Stone replied. "It was an honor working with you."

With her father sedated, and on a stretcher secured in the chopper, Sinclair stepped up, sat, and closed the sliding door. A minute later the chopper lifted, heading toward the closest hospital in the area.

49

Hidden deep in the foothills of the Ural Mountains, and far from Moscow, a sprawling complex served as a secret getaway for Russian President Ilya Gadjiyev. He made sure he and his families were transported there soon after the warning of President Anders of a possible nuclear attack on Moscow by domestic dissidents against his regime.

They build the property on land belonging to a longtime friend of the Russian president. The main house, one of two structures, had grass roofs, shielding it from American spy satellites and furnished with affordable looking Scandinavian style furniture.

Reclining on a multi-cushion sofa, he sat watching on a large-screen television; the destruction wrought on his capital by nuclear explosions. The reports were earth shaking. He couldn't believe what had occurred.

If it weren't for the American President's warning of the attack, Russia would be at war with the U.S. launching nuclear weapons in retaliation. However, notwithstanding that, it was an American double agent who set the bombs off. Gadjiyev wasn't totally convinced the double agent wasn't a plant by the CIA to wrest control of the government and place their treacherous puppets in charge. The bad news for him was the attempted takeover of his regime by people he'd trusted for years may have been turned by the Americans.

The written report by his most trusted ally, ex-KGB operative Oleg Grin, was ominous. He was running out of options. However, the only option left to him was the total removal of those on Grin's report. Not just removing them from office, but having them disappear from the face of the earth. Otherwise, he would remain precipitously vulnerable. He had to take swift and dangerous action.

He reached for his private cell phone and punched a single pre-programmed number. "Oleg, you have the green light."

———

Grin made his preparations long before the president called, with the go-ahead, having previously recruited four trusted friends, ex-KGB operatives, with whom he'd conducted several missions together during the cold war. He planned down to the last detail the methods he would use to eliminate those on his list. It was his prime method of assassination.

His pre-planning included day and night surveillance on the President's Chief of Staff, the Ministry of Defense, and the FSB Director; including the head of the FSB in Germany who would be eliminated by the next ranking FSB Agent at the consulate: Captain Alexei Kuznetsov.

Chief of Staff Pyotr Ivanovich, along with his assistant, were both programmed to die in a car bomb already planted under Ivanovich's driver's seat. Followed by the Ministry of Defense, Viktor Mordvinia, in the same manner as Ivanovich, and the FSB Director, Sergei Ulyanovsk, would die by a bomb lodged by the gas stove in his small modest apartment.

There were also six minor high-ranking officers assigned to the FSB headquarters, and three officers from the Naval Headquarters involved in the conspiracy. They'll round up these individuals, arrested them, and die in a firing squad.

———

One KGB agent, assigned by Oleg to keep tabs on the Chief of Staff, watched from his car parked across the opposite side of the street, as his target arrived at his residence. As Ivanovich pulled into his driveway, the agent picked up a small metal remote control box from the passenger's seat, set the remote switch to arm, and depressed a button. Seconds later, an explosion rocked the car as white and dark flames shot up into the sky, leaving the car a piece of molten metal as he saw the engine ejected about 40-50 yards from the explosion. The same was true for the Ministry of Defense and the Director of the FSB.

Two hours later, having rounded up and arrested the nine high-ranking officers in a meadow surrounded by tall trees and snow-covered grass, they were blindfolded, shot and their bodies set on fire.

Once Grin had completed his assignment, he dialed President's Gadjiyev private line and said, "Mission accomplished, sir."

At the Russian Consulate in Stuttgart, as Captain Kuznetsov sat while lounging in his room, he received a phone call from his friend and old KGB Commander, Grin. He also received a long text message describing the role Colonel Elizaveta Borovkov played in the attempted overthrow of President's Gadjiyev's government. He sat up straight and read the entire text message, intrigued and mystified.

Kuznetsov read through the text once again. Finished, he closed his cell phone. He understood that his country had elements that distrusted and hated the government and President Gadjiyev's politics.

But damn, a coup! He shuddered at the implications and all the bloodshed that would follow.

Shaking his head, he found it implausible that anyone would harbor the overthrow of the sitting Russian President and the government. It just seemed to him to be so far-fetched.

Still, he always kept an open mind in politics and the government. Besides that, it was a request tantamount to a direct order that he understood from his old commander and friend. The request was for the immediate elimination of the Colonel. But Grin demanded the act done within the hour.

Kuznetsov poured his second glass of vodka and downed the liquid. Then, he arose from his chair, pulled out his MP-443 Graph 9mm handgun from his holster lying beside him, attached a suppressor, tucked it behind his back, and walked out of his room in search of the Colonel.

He'd always found the direct approach to any problem was always the best course of action.

Walking down the hallway, he climbed a set of stairs to the second floor. At the top landing, he turned right down a short corridor and stopped in front of the closed door leading into the Colonel's office. Reaching for his gun, he clicked off the safety and held it by his side. Turning the knob on the door, he pushed it open and peeked in to make sure she was there. He heard the tune *Zhuravli;* one of the most famous Russian songs about World War II.

"I see you, Captain, please come on in," Colonel Borovkov said in a friendly tone.

The Captain took in a deep breath. Without missing a heartbeat, he raised his weapon and fired a round at the colonel sitting behind her desk. The bullet entered her forehead and exited behind her head as a spatter of blood and brain matter splashed behind her onto the closed window.

He called Grin. "It's all done, my friend."

"Excellent. Wait for further orders."

———————————

They'd been on the road an hour and twenty minutes. The car sped along the A5 autobahn, traveling north, with their last destination just at the outskirts of Frankfurt to the town of Bornheim, just west of the Rhine River. On this clear late September evening, traffic was minimal on both sides of the autobahn. With no snow or rain forecast for the rest of their drive, they would make excellent time arriving before midnight.

That's if no one is on our tail, Banks thought to himself.

Carl Benz, behind the wheel of his silver 2019 BMW, exited and re-entered the autobahn to make sure they weren't being followed. With Banks satisfied they were in the clear, they resumed the long drive.

Banks had narrowly escaped with his life, and if it hadn't been for Benz, yelling at him from the stairs of the basement they've come under attack, they never would have made it to the car and their escape.

However, just before they ran down the tunnel to Benz's car, Banks had pulled his weapon and shot Colonel Sinclair three times in the chest. With Benz pulling Banks down into the tunnel with mercenary, who would stay back in the tunnel to make sure no one would follow; they got into the BMW and sped off. A minute later, they heard a muffled explosion and gunfire coming from the tunnel.

With a briefcase that Benz had stuffed with cell phones and a laptop, Banks was could still receive phone calls from his comrades in the United States.

According to the flight plan Bobrov was following, he should arrive in U.S. airspace in about four hours. Enough time for him and Benz to set up his base in Bornheim.

Soon, he would have his ultimate revenge on the CIA and the Pentagon. In the meantime, he was already making plans to have Sinclair come under his gun sights. With her father dead, she was the last piece of business he had to attend to. It would take careful planning and coordination to see it done.

—50—

The twin-engine G600 Gulfstream business jet rocketed through the night sky at its maximum 0.925 Mach speed, or 666 mph, below the speed of sound.

Bobrov was piloting the jet and making good time.

Although the cabin had seating for nineteen passengers, the jet was rather small. However, it suited the purpose of transporting its four passengers across the Atlantic and into the U.S. mainland. With its long circular body, and a sharp cone-shaped nose with low mounted wings and T-tail, the two Pratt and Whitney engines placed on both sides of the fuselage, wouldn't break the sound barrier, but it was fast enough for the flight to the mainland U.S. without refueling.

Strapped in the luggage compartment were the four nuclear suitcase bombs.

Bobrov had fallen asleep behind the controls of the jet as it flew on automatic pilot. Asleep in the cabin, on the spacious beds, were the two teams assigned to their missions. Team-One's leader was Objedkov with Team-Two's leader, Anton Zemitsov, along with Rybakov.

A beeping noise soon woke Bobrov from his sound sleep. It was the warning indicator he'd programmed to warn him they were approaching U.S. airspace.

Disengaging the autopilot, he took control of the jet, and from his current altitude of twenty-eight thousand feet, he decreased altitude, flying just at NOE (Nap-of-Earth). Reducing his speed to that of cruising level, he hoped to maintain a small configuration and avoid radar detection. With the jet's transponder deactivated, he felt rather confident that he was almost invisible; but for how long? He didn't know.

The moon was full and bright as he piloted the jet without the outside running lights to show his presence. At his cruising speed, he figured to make the U.S. airspace within an hour.

The United States Air Force Boeing E-3 Sentry, normally known as AWACS, Airborne Warning, and Control System, employed mobile long-range radar surveillance. The aircraft, derived from the Boeing 707, known for its distinctive rotating radar dome above the fuselage. Now, a jet out of 552nd Air Control Wing, at Tinker AFB, Oklahoma, with a flight crew of thirteen, it was flying along the eastern seaboard.

Flying at thirty-thousand feet, its current mission was to detect the movements of a specific type of aircraft; a business aircraft called a Gulfstream G-600 before it entered U.S. airspace. If detected, two standby F-35 fighter jets would soon scramble to intercept.

Inside the aircraft, three airmen manned their radar monitoring screens as the radar subsystems permit surveillance from the earth's surface up into the stratosphere, over land and water. Once detected, flashing indicators warn of the presence along with information as to the aircraft's description and transponder location.

The rest of the passengers of the G-600 Gulfstream jet woke. Then, all four donned camouflaged uniforms and sat munching on sandwiches and drinking coffee as they waited for the plane to land. All four had their assault rifles and handguns on the seat beside them, ready at a moment's notice.

Twenty minutes ago, the jet crossed into U.S. airspace as Bobrov banked to the left in a heading that should line them up to the Rhode Island Sound. There he would land just outside the Newport State Airport, and according to his research, it didn't have flights in or out in the middle of the night.

Once the jet landed, he would disembark the two teams and take off for Canada and a new life.

Or so that is my plan, he thought.

About half-an-hour before reaching land, the Gulfstream zoomed through the sky, keeping a tight heading, as it approached ever faster over the Atlantic Ocean to Bobrov's pre-planned choice of the landing site.

Several minutes later, aboard the AWACS aircraft, airmen watching his computer screen, removed his earphones and yelled out to Captain Wiston, "Sir, I have contact with a jet flying NOE about three hundred miles due east from our position. It doesn't show a transponder fix."

Captain Wiston approached his radar man, leaned in over his shoulder, and stared at the screen. "Can you determine if it's the Gulfstream we're searching for?"

"No, sir," the radar man responded. "It's too far, and without a transponder fix, I can't get its identification."

"Commo," Captain Wiston yelled over his shoulder, "Contact Marine Corps Air Station, Beaufort, South Carolina, and have them scramble two F-35 fighter jets!"

"Yes, sir," the commo man responded.

Ten minutes later, two F-35 fighter jets lifted off from the Marine Corps Air Base runway, streaking toward the Atlantic Ocean. Both jets banked toward the left and about two hundred miles up the Atlantic seaboard.

They had flown across the Atlantic and were now about twelve minutes from the point of St. John's as Bobrov adjusted the jet by banking left toward Rhode Island.

He gazed out the windshield, across to the horizon, and could make out the contour of the land. The flight deck of the aircraft, with its ten large touch screens, provided air traffic, environmental data, maps, destinations, and other important information to the pilot.

With less than thirty minutes before making landfall in Rhode Island, Bobrov increased his speed; they were almost there.

Bobrov suddenly saw through the night sky, two twin pinpoint sets of lights fast approaching their position. Passenger jets, he thought. No, they couldn't be ... these were in a left-to-right formation with darkness in between.

Fighter jets!

Oh, shit! He thought. *They got our position.*

There wasn't too much time before the two jets were visible. He had to do something quickly. Touching the map screen for the area, he saw that he could make the land at the Glace Bay north of Sydney before the fighter jets intercepted him.

Losing altitude, Bobrov flew above the ocean waves, just as the fighter jets flew above the Gulfstream. Increasing his speed, he flew the jet closer to the bay.

The two F-35s rapidly circled back and activated their afterburners! Ten miles, the instruments showed. Then, in an instant, it turned to five miles.

Three miles and then he was over land. A moment later, he felt pounding on the top of the jet.

"*Shit, damn,* we're being fired on!" he yelled.

From the cabin, someone was yelling at Bobrov, "Nikolai, what's going on?"

"Get your seatbelts on," Nikolai replied, "this could get bumpy."

Bobrov saw a patch of land long enough where he could land. He lowered the landing wheels, dropped the nose, touched land, and bumped once, twice as the fighter jets streaked across the sky just under ten thousand feet above the G-600! In passing, they fired a barrage of bullets that raked the ground all around the passenger jet.

Breaking hard, he eventually came to a halt in an open pasture. This was as far as they were going to go until the fighter jets departed. If they didn't, he would have to abandon the jet.

Bobrov went back in the cabin, stared up at the jet's ceiling, and noticed three bullet holes. But the engines had functioned well enough for the landing.

Fifteen minutes later, not having heard or seen any signs of the fighter jets, or anyone come to investigate, Bobrov turned the jet around the way they came, and with increasing speed, he had the jet back in the air in minutes. Flying several hundred feet above the ground, he set the course for Rhode Island.

Now that someone knew where they were, he had to stay below radar to Rhode Island and pray they did not detect their location.

Without further mishap, he flew over Cape Cod Bay and Rhode Island. Over the Bay, he found a good landing place south of Nickerson State Park by the Mid-Cape Highway. Coming in for a landing, he didn't see any vehicles, or human life, as he picked a secluded patch of gravel road long enough to land on.

Here, he bade farewell to the two teams as they disembarked from the plane and unloaded their cargo.

Stepping out of the cockpit, he walked out of the plane and stood there for a moment watching the teams getting ready for the walk to the highway.

Objedkov turned to Bobrov and said, "What are your plans now, Nikolai?"

"I'm going to wait here just long enough to check on any damages to the plane, then get back in the air and head for Canada to start a new life."

"Good luck with that," Sergeev said.

Unknown to Bobrov, several police cruisers were fast approaching his location.

It had taken Bobrov close to fifteen minutes to repair the holes. Back in the cockpit, he started the engines and taxied to the secluded patch of gravel road he'd touched land on.

Within several minutes, Bobrov's plane shot across the sky, heading due north for Canada and freedom. Unknown to Bobrov, the F35s fighter jets had locked on his jet. He would not make the coast of Canada.

For several miles, they walked in hoping to see homes from where they could steal a car when off in the distance they came onto a well-maintained farmhouse with two structures; a house and a large barn. They scanned the surrounding area and didn't see any other farmhouses. Fixing their stares on the farm ahead of them, they saw no indications that anyone was awake except for the twin amber porch lights visible on the house.

Objedkov recommended only two of them would search the ranch for the possibility of a vehicle. He and Sergeev would go forward. The other two nodded.

Walking at a fast clip, they made their way forward, and minutes later, they approached the side of the barn. It appeared rundown, with fading red paint and a broken down sliding door.

Objedkov turned to stare at Sergeev. "Stay here and stand guard."

He stepped around the side of the barn and walked toward the sliding door and entered. Removing a penlight from his pocket, he clicked it on and scanned the inside. Objedkov saw a black four-door Chevy Silverado 4x4 pickup truck covered in dust. Opening the door, the cab interior light came on. A good sign the battery still had a charge.

What a stroke of luck, he thought

Climbing behind the steering wheel, he searched for the keys. Not finding any, he grasped several wires from under the dash and pulled them free. Finding the two wires he was looking for, he hot-wired the vehicle and with a loud knocking and rattling sound it started up. After a few seconds, it settled down to a low rumble.

Not waiting around for the owners to wake and investigate, he set the gear in drive, pulled out of the barn, and stopped in front of Yuri who climbed onto the passenger seat. As they pulled away from the farmhouse, they didn't see any lights come on in the main house.

Yuri cranked his head around and stared back at the house. He kept watching but still did not see any lights come on. "There is no one home, Sergei."

"Good for us ... and them," Objedkov said rather ominously

"Yeah, guess you're right."

—51—

They sat in silence as Objedkov drove, each in heavy thought of the devastation they were about to unleash in the next few hours. They could live with the deaths without a blink. This mission meant far more than money!

They were the two factors that seemed to play in their favor, Objedkov thought about their mission. First and the more important of the two, they would conduct their operation in Washington on a Sunday when there shouldn't be that many pedestrians or vehicles in or around the city. Second, they would do it in the early morning hours. At this time of the night, the local police may well change shifts, and leave the city of Washington D.C. less protected.

If everything went according to plan, and if he survived the mission, Objedkov mused with a smile, he'd be sitting pretty enjoying the rest of his life in some secluded cabin in some remote corner of the world. Money was inconsequential; he would have lots of it.

The Chevy Silverado moved easily down the Mid Cape Highway, to Providence, Rhode Island, then onto Interstate 95 South to Washington, D.C.

Objedkov, having purchased a map at a gas station where he'd filled the tank, estimated their travel time was about eight hours; a four-hundred-ninety-mile drive. Each of them would take turns driving. They stayed within the speed limit hoping to avoid a police traffic stop which would end badly for the police officer.

Minutes later, Objedkov was the first to see a phalanx of police cars on the opposite side of the highway. Their sirens were wailing with blue lights flashing. He knew where they were heading, but they were a little too late and going in the wrong direction.

Sergeev, sleeping in the passenger seat across from Objedkov, woke with a start roused by the sirens. Pivoting his head left and right, he made out the police cruisers on the opposite side of the road as they drove, as if the devil himself was behind them.

Yuri said, "They are a little too late."

"Funny, I was thinking the same thing," Sergei said with a grin.

A half-hour had passed when the FBI agents and the local police couldn't find any evidence of the suspected terrorists reported having landed on the secluded gravel road. With the assistance of the local law enforcement, the FBI set up check-points in a twenty-mile radius especially, on the Mid Cape Highway. However, unknown to the authorities, the terrorists had already slipped through their fingers.

"According to skid marks, the plane landed here all right," Bruce Adams, the FBI agent in charge, said to the other officers. "It would appear we need to contact the FAA about that plane. But now they're in the wind."

They pulled over in the small town of College Park outside of Baltimore.

"Drive to the University of Maryland parking lot," Anton said. "Let's see if we can find a better vehicle and ditch this one."

Zemitsov just nodded.

With the others still fast asleep, they drove slowly around the almost empty University lot when they spotted an old dark-blue Ford SUV. "Pull alongside the SUV on your left, Anton. I think we found our next vehicle."

With rain falling, and lightning crackling in the sky, it took ten minutes of breaking into the car, getting it hot-wired and back on Highway-One heading to Washington.

Fourteen miles, and twenty minutes later, they left Highway-One and turned onto Interstate 395 South, past North Capitol Street, G Street. And then after several more blocks, a right onto 17th Street NW, which led them to the CIA Headquarters building on the right side of the road.

It was Team-Two, Zemitsov, and Rybakov, who were the first to disembark.

Zemitsov drove past the barricaded entrance to the underground parking lot and then passed the building for half a block more. The street was one-way with large American Sycamore trees planted on the brown-colored sidewalk. There was no traffic and no one on the streets. He stopped and pulled over to the curb. They each grabbed their suitcase bombs and trotted away from the SUV.

Zemitsov felt they were too close to the building, out in the open, and easily spotted. But with no one on the street and no passing vehicles, he and Rybakov kept walking, trying to find their spot to place the bombs.

In the meantime, Team-One, Objedkov, and Sergeev pulled away from the curb on their way to the Pentagon.

Unknown to Team-Two, the moment their SUV came onto the street, video cameras had been tracking them. The SUV's license plates were recorded and passed on to the local police department. Facial recognition software was up and running.

With photographs of the alleged terrorists, they compared the images coming through the software. Then, as the two individuals made their way slow and careful to the building, they got a hit on two of the four photographs supplied to Homeland Security by the FBI.

An RDT rapid deployment team, consisting of twenty agents from the FBI and the Department of Homeland Security, encamped within the CIA building, were placed on alert status. It would take them a few minutes to assemble in the underground garage.

Minutes passed just as Rybakov, with the help of Zemitsov, were about to open one of their suitcase bombs. Zemitsov, who was watching from up ahead of the building, thought he heard a slight commotion, and then suddenly, he could see several men armed with assault weapons streaming out onto the street and sidewalk turning in their direction!

With no warning, an unexpected volley of bullets raked their position around the sidewalk with rounds kicking up asphalt and coming close to them.

With rain falling hard around them, and just as Rybakov rose, with Zemitsov already taking a bead on the shooters, Rybakov's head exploded in front of him. But not before two agents went down by the accurate shooting of Zemitsov's assault weapon.

They left Zemitsov little time for thinking. Instinctively, he calmly backed up, still firing his weapon, when it locked on an empty magazine. However, just as he turned to run, a barrage of bullets impacted his back. He struck the sidewalk hard, but still alive. Taking haggard breaths, he stared and then taking one last breath, he died, never knowing what had gone wrong just as the gun smoke cleared.

———————————

Sergei Objedkov heard what he thought could be weapons fire coming from behind them. He stopped and pulled off to the curb. However, just as suddenly as it started, it stopped. A moment of eerie silence followed. *Could they have spotted the other team?* It was a thought. *Should he continue his mission?*

Ah, hell, Sergei thought, *they have already paid me to fulfill the mission. And by God, I will!*

"You heard it too, didn't you, Sergei?" Yuri asked.

"Oh, yeah, I sure did."

For the first time, Sergei felt a twinge of fear.

"What do you think, turn and cut tail, or ...?"

"We continue."

"Fine by me," Yuri said, staring straight ahead.

Soon thereafter, they entered the bridge over the Potomac River. Halfway through, their eyes lit up as they glared at police flashing lights at the exit of the highway off the bridge. Objedkov came to a stop, set the gear for reverse, and backed up slowly. But then they saw more police vehicles coming to a stop and forming a barricade at the bridge entrance. Coming to a stop, he set the gear in park and stared straight ahead.

They had them blocked in!

They couldn't go forward nor back! Caught red-handed, and with nowhere to go, they both came to the same conclusion as a voice thundered on a bullhorn, "You're surrounded! Give up and you'll live!"

"We can't outshoot them," Objedkov said almost matter-of-fact.

"But we can blow them to hell!" Yuri said in defiance.

"First, let's see if we can negotiate. We have bombs."

"Can we trust them? They could have snipers ready to shoot."

"Yes, true. But shouldn't we at least try?"

"What! Are they going to give us a ride to the airport? And a prison cell with a window?"

Objedkov calmly thought for a second. "I think you're right. Okay, I'll wave a white flag. But you have the suitcases open and ready for detonation if they shoot me. Agreed?"

"Yes, sir, I agree."

Objedkov extended his hand to Yuri, who shook hands with his old KGB comrade.

"It's been an honor working with you."

"We had a great time together."

"Yes, yes, we did."

Objedkov pursed his lips. "We'll go in a blaze of glory, my friend." He took a white handkerchief from his pocket and opened the car door. Before he could take a step onto the concrete, a single bullet crashed into his skull and he slumped over, half in the car and half out.

Yuri was frozen for an instant as he saw three masked men racing toward the car brandishing automatic weapons. His fingers trembled to open a suitcase when a sudden barrage of gunfire ripped through the windows and windshield from three directions as he died in a hail of bullets.

—EPILOGUE—

The Beginning of the End

Seven Months Later

Lieutenant General Bradford S. Roland, the EUCOM commander, staff officers, and enlisted personnel from various bases in Germany, were standing in formation as the EUCOM Army band in a corner played, *The March of Glory* tune attesting to the grandeur of the pomp and circumstances of those in attendance for the promotion ceremony of Colonel Sinclair.

On this cloudy overcast Monday morning in March, at the parade field outside the EUCOM Headquarters, they stood at parade rest and waited for the appointed officer to open the ceremony. The three MP companies also stood at parade rest, as three of their staff and their company commanders stood beside their unit Guidon's and waited.

Colonel Richard Longstreet Sinclair, the Provost Marshal for the European Command, stood in the center of the group. He was a tall man with a six-foot frame and broad shoulders. To his right was his daughter, Chief Warrant Officer Jacqueline Sinclair, the Agent in charge of the Stuttgart-based (CID) Criminal Investigation Division.

In the bleachers off to the other side of the field, were the visitors, wives, officers, and enlisted members of those attending military police companies.

"Welcome to Patch Barracks, the United States European Command general staff promotion ceremony," a Lieutenant Colonel addressed the crowd. "I'll be your narrator for today's ceremony."

After announcing those distinguished guests in attendance and their families, the narrator read of the accomplishments of Colonel Sinclair since becoming a valued member of the command. Once finished, he said, "Attention to Orders."

All in the parade field snapped to attention. He continued. "Order Number 45-11 reads: The President of the United States has reposed special trust and confidence in the patriotism, valor and fidelity, and abilities of Colonel Richard Longstreet Sinclair. In view of these qualities and his demonstrated potential for increased responsibility, he is therefore promoted in the United States Army to the rank of Brigadier General by order of the Secretary of the Army."

General Roland turned smartly and faced Colonel Sinclair's left shoulder. He produced a silver star, depicting the rank of Brigadier General, reached and lifted the shoulder loop and pinned the star to it, and again, he turned back.

On Colonel Sinclair's right, his daughter Chief Warrant Officer-CW3 Jacqueline Sinclair made a left turn and faced her father's right side. Also producing a silver star, she pinned it on his shoulder loop and returned to the front.

Then the band played *The Washington Post* marching tune, and the military police companies marched in front of the officers offering their salutes to the two staff generals and the American flag in passing.

After the ceremony, a lone individual, standing with the support of a pair of crutches, gradually made his way across the parade field. Dressed in a two-piece dark single-breasted suit, white shirt, and navy-blue tie, he stopped a few feet from General Sinclair and his daughter, Jacqueline.

"General Sinclair, my congratulations on your promotion, sir."

The General and Jacqueline turned, and their faces flamed into immediate astonishment.

"It's me," Tom Price said with an ironic smile, "Well, most of me, at least."

For a moment, Jacqueline became motionless, unable to pull her eyes away from her fiancé who she thought was still recovering in a U.S. hospital.

Still staring, she practically jumped into his arms.

"Easy, love," Price said, as they hugged and kissed. "I have damaged goods." But the kiss lingered. Seconds later, they separated, and staring at her beautiful eyes he said, "I've got a lot to tell you."

"And so do I, so let's not waste any time getting to it." She gave him the sexiest smile of her life as she squeezed his arm. "Will you excuse us, Dad?"

General Sinclair nodded. He grinned as the pair, now united, marched off arm in arm.

Keep reading for a special sneak peek of
Victor Alvarez's new *CID Agent Jacqueline Sinclair Novel*:

THE PRICE ON HER HEAD

—PROLOGUE—

Matthew Banks was preparing to enjoy his favorite drink, Bombay gin on the rocks with a twist of lime—relaxing while waiting for his friend to arrive. After his second drink, a knock sounded at the front door of his quite luxurious alpine home.

Built in 2010, it was a four-bedroom, three-bathroom property on a half-acre, landscaped lot with unobstructed mountain views, an enormous living room with two overstuffed sofas—wall mounted large screen TV—and two glass walls of windows, let in the warm afternoon glow of the sun.

Another knock sounded.

As he set down his glass of gin, he glanced at his watch. Half-past one: His friend Carl Benz was early. However, the next two visitors would arrive within the hour. The last visitor should arrive two hours later. He was the head of a mercenary group operating in Europe.

The first two were by special invitation; assured the amount of twenty-five thousand dollars each to offer their pitch for a sensitive operation. But only one would win. They were the go-between of two effective international bounty hunting unions.

Thinking back, Banks had been fortunate his good friend, Benz, had arrived in the basement of his hideaway ranch, just as he killed Colonel Sinclair. But that had been several months ago. Today, he hoped would bring a means to the death of American CID Agent named Jacqueline Sinclair, who played a crucial role in his defeat, and her close associates, FBI Agent Daniel Russell working out of the Frankfurt, American embassy, and DIA Special Agent Tom Price, Sinclair's fiancé, assigned to the Stuttgart, American Consulate.

With his laptop opened on the coffee table in front of him, he clicked on the video feed from his outside CCTV camera. Zooming in on the individual, he recognized his friend, and then shut off the computer.

Seconds later, he rose and walked across the luxury European cobblestone floor to answer it.

Carl Benz was a tall, dark, clean shaven-man, and for his age of seventy-two, he was athletic, with five-feet-nine, broad shoulders, and narrow hips. His black hair close- cropped showed signs of graying alongside the temples. His eyes were a steel gray that stared back at his close friend Matthew Banks.

Banks sipped his drink and then set his glass on the coffee table and waited to hear what his friend had to report.

Having preferred coffee to hard liquor, Benz had set the warm cup of coffee on the table and sat back on the sofa. "I've set everything in motion, my friend. The first of our visitors will arrive by helicopter, and also the last visitor."

"I would like you to meet them out at the helo-pad and escort them in, Carl."

"No problem, Matthew."

"How deep was your vetting on the two bounty hunter unions, Carl?"

A slight pause as he caught his breath.

"Extensive," he replied. "These were the two unions that seemed to honor contracts and can carry out what you have planned." He paused a second and then continued. "They seemed to accept your offer with a sense of curiosity. They always made it a point that bounties of men or women had enormous price's on their heads and always above the law, in dealings with their legitimate business. The two unions comprised the world's elite—German KSK forces, or Kommando Spezialkrafte. Currently disbanded, several had offered the unions their professional service. There are several freelance assassins also offering their services. Some are AWOL personnel from the U.S. Army and other branches of service from around the world."

He continued. "They operate like the forebears of the American Wild West when they collected their bounties—dead or alive; however, in your plan, you're asking that they collect them alive! However, the complicated art of bounty hunting today has left a sour taste in the leaders of most countries. Some who don't mind their occupation has given them a sort of sanctuary in their countries; for a price. They have no boundaries and roamed from one country to another collecting their bounty unhampered by the law."

"Excellent, my friend, you never disappoint." Banks said, once again with his drink in hand, and then downed it.

Benz bowed his head. "One point comes to mind, though, Matthew."

Banks searched his friend's eyes. Did he see dissent there? Questioning his actions? However, all he found was a mild curiosity in his eyes. "Go on," he said.

"May I suggest a different price on the bounties?"

A long pause, as Banks seemed to take on his suggestion. "What do you have in mind?"

Benz looked up with a slight frown. "Well, instead of the one million American dollars for each of the bounties," he paused for a second as he ran his fingers through his thick hair. "May I recommend reducing it down to a hundred thousand?" Benz was the accountant of Matthew's estate that transferred over to him on the death of his father. The Banks' estate tied to many multi-use buildings around the world and its estimates were worth over eight billion dollars in assets. However, Matthew's last operation set him back a quarter of a billion dollars. So, he was both the friend and the astute accountant, always monitoring the monies.

Banks cleared his throat. "Carl, one thing I have learned about men, such as these, is that they won't commit for less than one million per head," Banks replied. "That's why I committed to one million dollars on Sinclair. Now, with the other two, I agree that the hundred-thousand would be sufficient: Not chump change by any means, but enough to have them commit. Plus, it gives them an incentive to carrying out what I have planned."

A little later, they heard the thumping of two helicopters landing in front of the home.

The first two visitors were right on schedule.

They sat facing Benz and Banks in one of the empty rooms designated as the conference room. It was devoid of any typical furnishings associated with a bedroom or hanging paintings or photos. The single piece of furniture positioned center of the room was a large cherry Racetrack conference table with four armchairs.

Both of the visitors were over 50 years of age, black-skinned, of medium height, and slender build. The one, with a patch over his left eye, named Lev Murati, and the other with a three-inch scar to the side of the right eye introduced himself as Varya Berisha.

These two were no doctors, lawyers, or accountants. They were the eldest sons of their respective leaders of the two international bounty hunters unions who stood in line of succession to claim the title *Boss* upon the death of their fathers. The Go-Betweens who answered to their leaders, and they alone, could accept or decline a job on the spot.

The two, Murati and Berisha, had since childhood become good friends when they trained blood, sweat, and tears with their father and members of the union. Once they turned twelve, they both took part in live operations. However, it wasn't until they became young adults that the elder Murati determined to own a bank and sent his son to college. With young Murati off to college, Berisha also sent his son Lev to attend the same college as his friend, as he, too, desired ownership of a bank.

Now, they were respected legal owners of two separate banks. One was in Switzerland and the other in France. They operated independently of each other. However, the banks were fronts as they dealt in large amounts of currency. They made enormous sums from the family business. Money laundered for the process of making *dirty* money appear legitimate instead of ill-gotten; a highly profitable business enterprise.

"Gentlemen, thank you for being here on such short notice," Banks said, opening the meeting. "I know you're very busy men, so

I'll get to the point. First, would you supply my associate, Mr. Benz, with an account number and name of the bank to where we will transfer the sum quoted for your appearance? And for your trouble, you'll both receive the same sum."

Once they provided bank account numbers to Benz, Banks leaned forward and continued. "So, only one of your organizations will take on the job outlined to both of you beforehand. The other group will be placed on standby in the event the other cannot live up to the contract. Is that clear?"

Murati sat forward on his chair, reached into his jacket pocket, and pulled out a cigar. "Would you mind if I light it? He asked Banks."

"By all means, please do."

Grasping his lighter from out of his pants pocket, Murati lit the cigar, puffed on it twice, and leaned back. "As to your question, Mr. Banks, it's crystal clear."

Berisha just nodded and smiled.

"Excellent, then we agree," Banks said. "Would you like to start Mr. Murati?"

"Thank you, sir," Murati said. "I have forty-five hunters at my disposal. They're all seasoned, well-trained soldiers. They have prior service experiences from different branches of their countries' military service. We will provide transportation to and from the job site. We will also provide equipment, however, you must provide the ammunition, and possibly other weapons, as we see fit."

Berisha stood and pushed his chair back, lighting a cigarette, he said, "I too can provide, thirty-seven personnel. All seasoned professionals. We can also provide transportation to and from the job site. We carry international credentials in the event the local police agencies get in the way. But one thing, Mr. Banks, we will provide all weapons and the ammunition."

The meeting went back and forth for half an hour, each side explaining what the job may entail. When it ended, it left Banks to decide who would win the contract.

"Gentlemen, on the table are dossiers of your targets. But foremost is your primary target; a formidable female American Federal Agent named Sinclair. Also enclosed is a plan that needs careful attention before the actual hunts will take place. Read it and adhere to the instructions or you will not get paid another cent."

Banks waited for a reply.

Murati and Berisha both nodded while reaching over to grab a folder. They both read the contents to themselves.

A few minutes passed.

"It reads," Berisha said, lifting his head from the folder, "that you require the targets kept under surveillance, their habits learned, and a suitable location be chosen before making the grab."

Murati and Berisha stared at each other and nodded.

"Yes, you have in a few words dictated how we should run our operation," Murati said almost with a growl. "And that we need to transmit to you the time and place we will make the grab before we can commit."

"Yes, I need assurances you'll not screw up this operation." Banks replied, "A lot hangs in the balance. You'll answer directly to me and keep in contact regarding every step of your operation."

"There is a lot you require," Murati said in a low voice.

Without hesitation, Banks said, "Take it or leave it. And do remember you'll be working for me."

After a brief pause, Murati puffed on his cigar and rolled it between his teeth, thinking. "When would you expect the hunt to start?"

"The date will be on the 30th of November."

The two bankers agreed.

"Good, I've already decided which one of your groups will go and which one will be on standby," Banks said as he rose. "I accept the contract placed by Mr. Berisha."

With the arrival of the Swiss mercenaries, Banks and Benz required them to guard the home. The price was right and all parties agreed. Twenty mercenaries would control and defend the grounds until Banks ended their contract.

—1—

Six Months Later

Tom Price woke and turned over on the bed expecting to have her warm body in which to curl up, but she wasn't there.

It was a little unusual because he always seemed to be the first to wake. Every once in a while, he would wake as a nagging thought crept into his consciousness ... *he didn't belong with this woman*. However, hearing her say she loved him every day dispelled his Machiavellian notion.

A light drizzle of rain fell from the early morning sky. Their bedroom was chilly, moist, and shrouded in darkness with only the morning rays of the dying moon filtering through the half-opened curtains that threw dappled shadows onto the wooden floor. Soon the rain would clear and morning rays of the sun would light and warm the bedroom.

For Price, it's been a year since being wounded while participating in a mission with a group of U.S. Army Green Berets in Afghanistan. An agent with the Defense Intelligence Agency (DIA) Price, after his operation, was told he wouldn't be able to walk again.

He proved them wrong.

Price was at *her* on-post quarters at Patch Barracks, Stuttgart, Germany. It was a Monday; the start of the new day in mid-November and months had passed since he came back into her life, wrapped his arms around her, and confessed his undying love. It was the day he would never forget: the day at her father's promotion ceremony to the rank of Brigadier General when he at last felt her body next to him. It had taken months of convalescing and physical therapy to once more walk unfettered.

Turning around and facing the plate-glass door leading onto the balcony, he rose and draped a robe over his naked body and sauntered to the door.

Leaning up against the edge of the glass door, he saw her then—Jacqueline Belle Sinclair; his beautiful fiancé. She was standing with her back to him, up against the rails of the balcony, legs crossed, as a gentle breeze and cool rain played with her hair. The dying light of the moon cast her shadow on the wooden floor balcony.

Almost soundlessly, Price slid open the door not wanting to frighten her. However, she heard for she half turned her face to the side, tilting her head somewhat in his direction.

"Belle," he whispered, calling out to her. "Belle, honey ... we're going to be late for work." *Yeah, right?* He was the one that was going to be late. He'd be lucky to have breakfast started. Price was due in his office early this morning on an important conference call with his boss.

If he wasn't there, there'd be hell to pay.

For weeks now, they would trade over from her home to his apartment in Stuttgart, and only on weekends, if their workload and schedule permitted and dinner out on a weekday.

It wasn't the best of arrangements, but it would do until they married. And when would that be? That was still up in the air; both were a little afraid to commit to a date. Was he or Sinclair having second thoughts? He, for one, didn't think so. And he strongly believed she wasn't either.

Wordlessly, she didn't turn to face him and stared straight ahead.

Sliding the door further open, he entered the balcony, strolled up to her, and wrapped his arms around her in a loving embrace. Sinclair turned in his arms, facing him. Their lips met as they kissed softly for a second and then they let go of each other.

With a smile, she placed her hand in his and said, "Let's go into the bedroom; we have plenty of time." She then hurried him toward the bedroom, eager to have one last quick romp before they left for work.

And then suddenly, halfway there, a loud knock sounded at her front door.

They paused, she with a frown and he with a disappointed tilt to his head.

Another knock resounded from the main door to her military quarters, this time louder than the first.

"Guess I should answer that," she said.

Not expecting a reply from Tom, and while straightening out her robe, Sinclair walked down the hallway, stopped at the front door, and peeked through the fisheye lens. She made out a female uniformed MP silhouetted against the porch lights and then heard a third knock. Unlocking the bolt and turning the doorknob, she eased open the door.

Backing up a step, the MP, a first lieutenant dressed in full military police uniform and standing about five-feet-nine, blond-haired and slender figure, stared at the agent.

"Agent Sinclair," the MP said her voice low and composed. "Sorry to have troubled you so early in the morning, but you and Agent Tom Price have been ordered immediately to the office of the Provost Marshal."

For just a moment Sinclair just stood facing the MP, concern and worry written on her face. If it was so important to send an MP to her quarters, then why her father hadn't called her was a complete mystery.

"Do you have any idea why the PM insists on seeing Agent Price and me so early in the morning, Lieutenant?"

"No ma'am, I'm not able to speculate, only that you should be there ASAP."

Speculate. Damn, she must be a West Point Officer, Sinclair thought.

Sinclair took a deep breath and rolled her eyes. "Very well, Lieutenant, let them know I'll be there soon."

"Yes ma'am, I'll be waiting in my car."

Sinclair did a double-take and wearing a frown asked, "And why will you be waiting?"

Not missing a beat, the MP replied, "They have instructed me to escort you and Agent Price to the PM shop."

After twice attempting to call her father without success, they prepared to leave. Later, behind the wheel of their vehicles, the lieutenant pulled her MP sedan out in front of them. Seconds later, the three vehicles slowly moved away from the housing area and would soon arrive at the Provost Marshal's office.

Agent Sinclair and Price had no idea their lives would be turned upside down in the next several days. They would become the subjects of international bounty hunters, each with a price on their heads—but Sinclair was the number one on their hit list, to be taken alive at all costs! The others would be inconsequential pawns.

Sinclair and Price both began climbing the stone steps which led to the second floor of the Provost Marshal's office. As they did so, uniformed personnel, and some in civilian attire, passed them by without a glance. Although still fairly early in the morning, the building already was in full swing.

They walked shoulder to shoulder without uttering a word. Both lost as to the reason they'd been summoned. Price kept thinking of his boss in Washington. The man was going to have a fit he did not show up for the conference call. *"Shit happens,"* he told himself.

This had better be good!

Sinclair thought about her father. Was there something wrong with her old man? She didn't think so. Hell, just last Saturday, they had spent a quiet dinner at his quarters so that couldn't be the reason. This was huge. But why didn't he let her know in the first place of the upcoming meeting? Something didn't click. However, it was no use thinking anymore about it; she'd know soon enough.

She glanced over at Tom and smiled. Just as he turned his head in her direction, he showed her one of his *It'll be all right* grins.

The CID Agent returned his grin with a wink.

The PM shop, as most of the military police preferred to call it, was a converted Nazi-era two-story headquarters that housed the Nazi Army Panzer Regiment's 7 and 8 and the Panzer Brigade in the Panzer Kaserne (literally meaning "Tank Barracks") from 1936 to 1938.

A moment later, they entered the elegant lobby which led into the offices of the PM, Brigadier General Richard Longstreet Sinclair; Agent Sinclair's father. The General had spared no expense in decorating it with wood paneling throughout and pictures of past Provost Marshals hanging side by side on the side walls.

The PM, with a six-foot-three broad-shouldered frame, had only been a one-star general for several months. A West Point graduate, and a veteran of over thirty-six years' service to his country, with a goal to become the next Provost Marshal General of the U.S. Army. A lofty goal, but one he knew he could surmount.

Mary Elders the General's secretary, an attractive fortyish blond woman, stared up at them as they stepped into the lobby. "Go right in you two, he's expecting you."

With a nod and a smile at Elders, Sinclair passed by on her way to her father's office. At the set of double doors, she stopped and knocked lightly as Price stood off to one side of her while they awaited a reply.

They waited, but there was no immediate reply.

Then the double doors opened and there stood the General, tall, handsome, and smiling at his daughter. "Come on in you two, get some coffee, and let's sit. I have some pressing information to tell the both of you."

Five minutes later, they sat around the general's oak desk. Agent Sinclair and Price were sitting side by side as they faced the general with warm mugs of coffee, waiting for him to start the show.

General Sinclair sat back in his chair, with his elbows on the armrests and fists clasped in front of him, stared at his daughter then onto Price. "I won't keep you two any longer than I have to. You're going to be very busy for the next couple of days and you must prepare for it."

Sinclair frowned, concerned as she quickly glanced over at Price, who sat forward on his chair, inclined his head, and then stared straight at the General without saying a word. Her father's tone worried her; seriousness she had not heard in quite some time.

"Sorry for all the melodrama," the PM remarked, making eye contact with his daughter. "This was the only way I knew to get you here. I didn't want to call you, Belle, because I knew you'd throw endless questions at me. I wasn't about to answer them on the phone. I've been keeping something of an eye on you. I've had the patrol supervisor check up on the two of you. You'll know in a few minutes why I took such precautions."

A momentary pause passed between them.

General Sinclair leaned forward and placed his elbows on his desk. "You're both in mortal danger!"

Price shrugged and nodded as his eyes widened ever so slightly. With a frown, he leaned back in his chair and waited with a sense of curiosity as his thoughts turned to Belle...

It was over two years ago, when assigned to assist her on their first mission together, that he'd been in and out of danger with her. Was this going to be any different? He stuck with Belle as if her very life depended on it. And the way this conference was going, he believed it would. Nothing had changed; they always worked better together, no matter the dangers thrown at them.

Sinclair's expression remained blank. "Go on, Dad. We're listening."

She let her mind wander some...

It was after her first combat experience when an RPG exploded near her and a four-inch piece of shrapnel tore through the side of her stomach and left a permanent five-inch scar, that she'd felt a semblance of fear. Because of the wound, she could not bear children. Something she'd kept from Price and her father. Yet the fear factor had not emerged to keep her from her duties. Several times, in the past two years, she'd come face-to-face with death, which made her indifferent to it. So now she smiled in the face of it. Someday, she wouldn't be able to escape death. But for now, she just took it one day at a time.

After another brief pause, the PM plowed ahead. "Last night, I received a Top Secret memorandum from the FBI in Washington; routed from the White House through channels. Only a handful of people have seen it. It pertains to both of you." Now he looked at them both as they looked over at each other. He continued. "The FBI has arrested a person of interest in one of their cases. I won't go into the details, only to say, that their suspect had information that would prove invaluable..."

General Sinclair leaned back in his chair. "During their interrogation, the suspect talked about a plan hatched by an unknown party and presented to a so-called freelance bounty hunter he'd met overseas. It would seem, according to the suspect, they had set a large bounty on a Government agent working out of Stuttgart and on a few others. After accepting his plea deal, he summed it up to his interrogators; a million dollars was the price on her head, which belongs to you, Belle, and a hundred thousand each to two others. One to our FBI friend, Dan Russell, and the other," here he stared directly at Price, "Tom it's you. However, how, when, and where are unknown. Speculation by the FBI led them to believe these guys are a notorious band of international bounty hunters."

General Sinclair stopped and gazed at the two in front of him. But he locked eyes with his daughter. His blood ran cold at the mere thought of his daughter and Price, along with FBI agent Russell, being hunted by international bounty hunters.

Price ... *Holy shit, bounty hunters ... Mother Fu...*

Price knew his strengths and his weaknesses and how far fear can drive any man. But, with Belle, he could never imagine getting into a physical brawl with her—he'd lose. And besides, he'd seen her in action and she was tougher than a pine knot!

A hush fell over the office; you could hear a pin drop.

"Mother of God," Belle breathed as she stared at her father. *Fucking bounty hunters are after us!*

Blinking away the strangeness of it all, Agent Sinclair blanched as her mind raced. Not in a million years had she'd ever expected something like this. They were being targeted. This seemed like a personal vendetta by someone she'd worked a case on before, her analytical mind pondered. But only one person was bold enough, and with that kind of capital, to pull this off—a CIA double agent!

Agent Sinclair launched out of the chair. "Damn it!" she said, surprised at her outburst. "Guess what? The fucking asshole may be back!"

"Who?" Both the PM and Price spoke as one.

Belle growled. "Matthew Banks!"

—ABOUT THE AUTHOR—

Victor M. Alvarez was born in Puerto Rico, and at nine his family moved to New York City and was later drafted into the US Army. He received airborne training, ranger, military police schools and later jungle warfare training. His military awards range from Jump Wings, Vietnam Cross of Gallantry, awards of the Purple Heart, Air Medal, and Army Commendation Medal, among other many awards. He makes his home in New Smyrna Beach, Florida.

—NOTE FROM THE AUTHOR—

Word-of-mouth is crucial for any author to succeed. If you enjoyed
The Theseus Conspiracy, please leave a review online—anywhere you
are able. Even if it's just a sentence or two. It would make all the
difference and would be very much appreciated.

Thanks!
Victor M. Alvarez

Thank you so much for reading one of
Victor M. Alvarez's novels.
If you enjoyed the experience, please check out
our recommended title for your next great read!

Requiem for the Dead

"An electrifying military thriller reminiscent
of Mark Greaney and Brad Thor."
–BEST THRILLERS

View other Black Rose Writing titles at
www.blackrosewriting.com/books and use promo code
PRINT to receive a **20% discount** when purchasing.

www.ingramcontent.com/pod-product-compliance
Lightning Source LLC
Chambersburg PA
CBHW010727100726

47899CB00009B/2954